Sherwood Untold: The Journey

by **Ekaterina Crawford**

Second Edition

The Ninth Gate Publishing

Books That Take You Places

Published by The Ninth Gate Publishing, 2018
Copyright © 2018 Ekaterina Crawford
Proofreading and editing – Lucy Furlong
Artwork and Cover design – Yennifer Ice

This book is a work of fiction. All characters, except real historical figures, all incidents, organizations and dialogue in this story is the product of the author's imagination and should be considered as such.

A CIP catalogue record for this book is available from British Library.

ISBNs:

Paperback: 978-1-912696-01-7
Kindle: 978-1-912696-02-4
EPUB: 978-1-912696-03-1

The Ninth Gate Publishing
120 Baker St.,
London, W1U 6TU

www.ninthgatepublishing.co.uk

Acknowledgment & Dedication:

I dedicate this book to my husband, I know some may say it's a cliché but without him none of this would have happened.

If it wasn't for his decision 12 years ago, to pack our bags and leave the country we were living in, I'm almost certain that I wouldn't have had the chance to explore my creativity and see my writing flourish. Every step that we have taken has led us to this moment and I wouldn't have made this particular journey if it hadn't been for that leap of faith we made together all those years ago.

Thank you very much for all the love and inspiration, for being with me, for being there for me. Thank you for believing in me. Thank you for being my first and most rigorous critic. Your participation and opinion mean a great deal to me.

Thank you to my lovely sons for their endless love.

Thank you to my first readers. I don't need to name you, you know perfectly well who you are. You have been with me during that long year I spent creating this story, during which you patiently waited for the birth of each new chapter. Thank you very much for dedicating your valuable time to this cause. Thank you for your critique and comments, without them, this book wouldn't have been as it is now.

And last, but not least, special thanks to English actor, Richard Armitage for his detailed interpretation of the character of Guy of Gisborne, which made me look at the medieval villain in a new light.

Thank you.

Author's Note:

Many stories have been written about the forest outlaw – Robin Hood. Tales of his adventures fit so nicely into our history and everyday lives that we will never know if he was, in fact, a real person or a fictional character.

As in the case of King Arthur, in legends, Robin Hood is surrounded by factual historical figures. The stories of his adventures are handed down from one generation to the next. Storytellers come up with new, unbelievable adventures and it seems we will never know if Robin Hood ever existed, or if he was the product of someone's imagination; a tale, created to help children unwind at bedtime.

A few years ago, I came across a TV series produced by the BBC – Robin Hood. From the very first episode, I was hooked. I liked the series so much that I watched all 3 seasons (and for those who do not know, it is over 30 episodes) in the space of one week. Yes, there were many sleepless nights! But it was not the character of Robin Hood who caught my attention, it was his rival – Sir Guy of Gisborne.

Those of you who have watched the series may, perhaps, suggest that I developed tender feelings for this character because the actor who played Gisborne made a remarkably handsome baddie. That probably did play a part, but, to tell the truth, I was more interested in seeing how the actor interpreted and delivered the complex personality of his character to the audience.

I guess, I couldn't always agree with the fact that the anti-hero of the story should be destroyed – get what he deserves, so to speak, – dramatically killed in the final battle, put to jail and executed for the whole world to see, or sent to exile till the end of his days. Don't get me wrong, I'm not talking about the main villains of these stories. They deserve all the punishment they get. I am talking about their "right-hands", their "commanders-in-chief", those anti-heroes who, despite being a background to the main villain, play a very important role in the telling and development of the story. Who, while being their "hands" and "swords", perhaps, against their better judgement and own will, are doing all the dirty work for their masters.

This is exactly how I saw Gisborne. Watching how, in over thirty episodes, the actor developed his character; I came to realise that he might not be as bad as he seemed to be at first sight. To me he looked more like a lost soul, a person who was trying to find his place in society, working his way up by any means possible (and here I do mean ANY means), looking for happiness and compassion, everything that he was denied in life.

While watching season 1, I was intrigued by the story line that developed between him and the lead female character. However, at the beginning of season 2 of the series, it became obvious that nothing good would ever come out of Guy's "relationship" with Lady Marian. Witnessing the development of their "love" story, it was quite clear, that for them, there could be no other end but a sad one.

When I finished watching the series, something strange happened. It felt as if someone waved a magic wand and said "cook, little pot, cook", and my imagination began to fire pictures, descriptions and dialogues at me. My head flooded with ideas, I was afraid it was going to explode. So, I decided – why not? Why not try to put all my thoughts on paper, who knows what would come out of it, and so, it began.

The characters of my story – Robin Hood, The Sheriff of Nottingham, Guy of Gisborne and other historical figures of mediaeval England – have already been featured in lots of books and movies. Try as we might to come up with something original there is not really much room – either Robin is trying to steal something from the Sheriff, or the Sherriff is trying to catch Robin, and so on. To re-phrase that, when writing a story, following the original, classic, version of events, the plot would not be interesting, and, I guess, it would be quite boring, actually. So, I decided to create something simple but at the same time new, a new story with surprising and unexpected twists. Something that would interest any audience, not just the fans and admirers of the series. Something that in years to come I could show to my children and proudly say: "You know, your mum wrote that!"

Speaking of children, one day I was watching my younger son (he was not even three at the time) playing with his toys – Batman, Robin, Cat-Woman and Bayne. He put them all into a big toy car and took them on a trip to the beach, and then to the adventure park. I was surprised to see this company getting along together so well and asked him, shouldn't Robin and Batman chase and fight Bayne. What he said touched me very deeply: "Mummy, you do not understand, Bayne is a good guy now. I made him good!"

Perhaps, this is exactly what I have tried to do. To some extent I have tried to make Guy of Gisborne good, to show his better side, his human emotions. I guess I've always had a soft spot for bad boys, those who are lost and in need of saving. Don't they say that light is always drawn to the dark?

It is important to mention that the character of Guy of Gisborne isn't always featured in the traditional Robin Hood stories, like for example, Prince John or the Sheriff of Nottingham. So it is still a big question if he is a real historical figure or, as Robin himself, is a product of someone's imagination.

Initially this book was planned and, indeed, was written as an independent, complete story. However, as I started editing the original version, more ideas of how to make it even better, to make it even more interesting and thrilling started to pop into my head. I put myself in the "reader's shoes" and then I wrote and re-wrote the ending of the story, until I myself was convinced and became very interested to know what would happen next. And so, I got the idea to create a trilogy – Sherwood Untold.

I hope that this book will be interesting to not only those who watched and loved the BBC series Robin Hood, or those who follow and admire the works of Richard Armitage. I hope that my stories will go beyond ordinary fanfic, will find their audience and conquer the hearts of those who love romantic adventures.

It is very likely that the story will have some discrepancies and be inconsistent with real historical events and, quite possibly, metaphysical processes, but let's not be pragmatists and sceptics. Life is hard enough as it is, and always comes up with new challenges for us to deal with. Let us be romantics, and believe in miracles, in happy endings and that true love can conquer everything.

This story is about who we are, and about the decisions that we make in our lives. This story is about life: life and loss, life and death, but most importantly, this story is about love. Love that changes us, love that overcomes all obstacles, love that crushes us into pieces, throwing us to the very bottom of existence. Love that gives us wings and lifts us to new heights – love that makes us better human beings.

I hope you will enjoy reading this story as much as I enjoyed writing it.

Ekaterina

"Everyone sees what you appear to be, few experience what you really are."
(Niccolò Machiavelli, The Prince)

Chapter 1:
Awakening – Part 1

It was dark.

The light had gone, and the darkness took her into its loving embrace. She could not see anything around her as she began to move forward, barely knowing where to go. A fresh breeze came from the darkness and wrapped around her like a cold blanket, sending shivers through her body. She glanced back hoping to see something, anything, but there was nothing there. She was surrounded by pitch-black darkness.

"Where is that magical light, pulsating and shimmering like a living being, hypnotising me, drawing me in? Where is it? Where am I? What is this place?"

One question after another flashed through her mind, but she didn't have the answers. She was enveloped in blackness.

She walked carefully and slowly, with her arms outstretched, taking one step at a time. The floor was uneven and slippery; water squelched beneath her feet.

Step – halt, another – halt. She moved her hands around, blinking helplessly, trying to focus her eyes, hoping to see at least something. Nothing.

Step, another step, and then a third one. She lost her footing and, clutching empty air, she tumbled down. She did not fall far and, in just a fraction of a second hit the ground. A dull moan escaped her.

*****

It was dark.

She lay on the cold ground, not knowing where she was or what had happened to her. She drifted in and out of consciousness, struggling to surface, only to sink back again.

In this state of half dream half reality, she tried to wrench her head off the ground, all in vain. Her body resisted, sending spasms of excruciating pain to every limb with each new attempt.

*****

11

When she regained consciousness, Christine Hawk, one of the best practicing barristers of the legal firm "Laferi and Partners", found herself in an unusual state. Her body ached as if she had taken part in a sparring session in her martial arts class the day before, but she knew that this was not the case.

Yesterday was a very important day in her life. She was to be engaged to a successful doctor – Mark Laferi – son of the owner and main partner of the legal firm she has been working at for the past ten years. Barely able to understand where she was and, most importantly, what had happened to her, Christine knew one thing for sure – she was not engaged!

Wherever she was at this very moment, she was thrilled that the shagging bastard was nowhere near her. She cursed herself for being such a naive and stupid fool, for trusting his pretty words and sweet promises. She knew perfectly well what kind of man Mark Laferi was. They had known each other for almost fifteen years and over that time, Christine had been able to study his character, down to the very last detail.

Mark was a very talented doctor, a gift from God, some said. Saving people's lives was his daily routine. His precision and concentration in the operation theatre garnered him respect and recognition among the medical elite of England. However, that was only behind the closed doors of the theatre. In his day-to-day life, he was the exact opposite. He was a slug with one hideous trait – the inability to take responsibility for his own actions.

He was a weasel, who got himself out of trouble – needless to say, troubles he himself created – by shifting the blame onto everyone and everything else. Careless and carefree, before reaching thirty, he succeeded in seducing and breaking hearts of hundreds of young ladies and women. His wildness had cost his father, a well-known lawyer and highly respected person, a lot of nerves and money.

When Mark was 25, after another scandal, Philip Laferi, who had grown very tired of his son's behaviour, gave him one last warning. Mark had to grow up, and complete his studies at the medical faculty of Harvard, where he had already been expelled from a year earlier. His father, who had always been honest with Christine about his recalcitrant son, had told her then about the letter he had received from the Dean, the letter, which referred to Mark's behaviour, as "not compatible with his chosen profession...". Christine knew, for Mark it was a choice of either going back to Harvard or to being cut out of the inheritance. In conversations she witnessed between Philip and his son, Mr. Laferi Sr. had not sugar-coated his son's prospects. "I'll cut you out and you'd have to piss off!" as he eloquently put then. Mark had taken the sensible option and disappeared, off to conquer America.

When, some eight years later, he returned home, London would not have recognised the former playboy. Mark had not only managed to finish his degree but, as part of his postgraduate practice, he had gained work experience, and for a few years had worked in a large clinic. Returning home after his long absence, he brought back souvenirs and cards with views of the White House and Brooklyn Bridge for his father, as well as references and high recommendations that helped him to find a good job. In a few years' time, he had become one of the best surgeons in the country.

Tall, blond, blue-eyed, Mark had become an outstanding professional, but neither within the time of his studies nor later, at the postgraduate practice, could he overcome his weakness for the fairer sex. Yet, even so, he could not resist the exceptional character and personality Christine possessed.

Before Mark left for the USA, he tried but could not win Christine's affections. She was only eighteen, and had just lost her mum to cancer, and was still trying to come to terms with her loss and her new life. Her mind was preoccupied with too many other thoughts and problems to pay attention to the advances of the blue-eyed Casanova.

On his return to the UK, she knew that Mark had set himself a goal to win his 'goddess', as he often referred to her, and, without wasting any time, proceeded with the task. Christine did not deny that she considered this tall, blond man, very attractive, and openly enjoyed his company. His time at Harvard had played its part in making of a man out of him. Mark was interesting in conversation, charming and gentleman-like, and he knew how to treat a woman. Yet despite all of that, Christine had not had any deep feelings for him. Knowing his previous reputation, she tried to keep a distance, hoping not to fall under his spell, but she knew he never lost hope. Christine tried to resist his charms for as long as she could. They had known each other many years and she, to some extent, saw him as an older brother, not a lover; however, after many persistent advances, she gave up and now, three years later, Christine Hawk and Mark Laferi were going to announce their engagement.

On that ordinary summer day of the twentieth of June two thousand and fourteen, there was expected to be a completion of some long and exhausting court proceedings. On behalf of her firm, Laferi and Partners, she was arguing in court to defend the interests of the firm's largest client. Christine and Philip, as well as their opponents, knew perfectly well that the defendant did not have any substantial grounds to build the case. They had to wait for the technical completion of the process – the decision of the presiding judge. Anticipating a successful completion to the process, the legal office of Mr. Laferi Sr. had planned a dinner reception. On that evening, her and Mark were due to make their engagement official.

*****

Christine walked into the building of the High Court and, as always, having exchanged a few words with the young girl at the reception desk, she went straight to the second floor where her client's representative was already waiting for her.

"Good morning, Miss Hawk," said a court clerk and bowed his head in admiration. "Despite this early hour, you look lovely, as always!" he added with a light blush.

"Hey, Peter! Thank you, as always," Christine answered with a smile.

She made herself comfortable in a chair, placed the court papers on the desk before her and asked the clerk to bring coffee.

"Black! No sugar! Please!" she called after the young man as he exited the room.

He smiled but did not answer. He knew her preferences quite well. He returned a few moments later and placed a small cup on the table before her.

"Cedric was here," he said smiling, mischievously. "Been here a few times already this morning, actually. He was looking for you. He's acting strange today, you know."

"It's alright, nothing to worry about. I expect that speaking with me is the only wise thing he can do now," Christine smiled. "I'm sure he wants to make a deal and offer a settlement."

She winked at the clerk and relaxed in her chair.

"If his client wants to walk away with his head held high, they don't have another choice," she took a sip of her coffee and carried on. "Our speech yesterday has already damaged their reputation and they don't have arguments to build a defence," she bent down to her bag and picked up a pen, "and, if Cedric will carry on with his nonsense, the judge will have the case struck out for wasting his valuable time and award us additional compensation. So," she lifted her pen up and waved it in the air as though she was a teacher, "he doesn't have any other option but to try and settle with us before the hearing."

She picked up her coffee, toasted with the cup and emptied it in one big gulp, and as she did so, someone knocked on the door. The clerk exited the room but walked back in immediately.

"It's him again!" he said unable to contain a grin. "Please be kind to him," he added almost laughing.

Cedric, a man in his early fifties, looked young and boyish for his age. He, like Christine, was a successful barrister with many years of experience. They had worked together many times before, but this was the first time they had met on different sides of the argument. Like a schoolboy before an important exam, he was very anxious, getting ready to discuss his client's offer with her.

Christine opened the door and paused for a moment. Cedric was waiting for her at the far end of the hall. She left the room and, having given him a long look, slowly walked in his direction. A triumphant smile decorated her face, her left brow was lifted slightly – she held all the aces and they both knew it. A man could not have any other option but to surrender any hope of negotiating a bearable settlement on behalf of his client.

Their conversation was short. Christine had all the instructions from Philip and her client to finalise the details of the settlement, as well as to negotiate fair compensation for the legal costs of her office. They quickly drafted preliminary paperwork and notified the judge that both parties had agreed to settle the case. Having finished with that, she returned to her office to notify her future father-in-law about the successful completion of the case, and to check if everything was ready for that evening's celebration.

*****

That was all yesterday... but today... today, she didn't know where she was or what had happened to her. She couldn't feel her left arm and her left leg was twisted and painful. Her head ached and every new sound resonated inside it with a strong impulse of pain. She didn't know how long she had been unconscious, but slowly she began to regain her senses.

It was damp and dark, and somewhere close by she could hear water. Water seemed to be flowing somewhere above her head and then, after overcoming obstacles, falling down as a cascade, creating a small waterfall, which, under other circumstances, she was sure she would probably enjoy.

Not being able to see anything in the dark, she only had her hearing to depend on. She could hear the cheerful chime of drops of water. Water was so close that from time to time she felt splashes on her face. It was helping to keep her awake. As soon as her body and mind were about to give up and drift off into oblivion, new droplets of water fell on her face, helping her to regain her senses.

She was trying to stay awake, trying to reconstruct the events of the previous day in her mind. Everything was a blur.

She had to make a considerable effort before her mind ceased to resist and her memory began to reproduce small fragments and individual images. Like slides from a projector, they started to appear in her mind.

There she was leaving the high court building... There was the car, picking her up from the coffee shop and taking her back to Gray's Inn... There she was walking into the office building and slowly climbing up the stairs... Why did she put on new shoes? Her feet were burning...

Like a wild mountain stream, her memories rapidly descended on her.

Chapter 2:
How Long?

June 20th, 2014
London

The offices of the law firm Laferi and Partners were situated at Gray's Inn, one of the four Inns of Court in London, located at the junction of the City, Westminster, and Holborn – a calm and quiet place in the historic heart of London, with old architecture, although much of it had been destroyed in the Second World War.

Built in the fourteenth century, the Inn saw its heyday in the era of Queen Elizabeth I. It was the place where her advisers and lawyers had worked. Now, this area, as well as three other Inns of Court, was a sort of legal community, and every self-respecting lawyer, who wished to argue in court, had to become a member of this reputable institution. The Chambers of Gray's Inn housed the offices of the company Christine worked for.

The car continued past the main square and stopped at the entrance of the Chambers. Despite the early start, and the pressure of the trial, and the fact that she was wearing terribly uncomfortable shoes, Christine jumped out of the car with ease. She was in an excellent mood.

Even at this early hour, the sun had already started to heat up the air. She took the few steps that separated her from the entrance and plunged inside to the coolness of the old building. The hands of the old-fashioned clock in its heavy carved wooden frame hanging by the entrance, told her it was only half past ten. The hearing was done with and she had plenty of time before the reception dinner.

Christine winked at the girl at the reception desk, made a gesture asking her not to notify Mr. Laferi of her early arrival, and proceeded straight to his office.

"Oh heavens!" she muttered. "Why did I put on these shoes?"

Christine had excellent taste and was always very elegant in her choice of clothing. In her day-to-day routine office work, she adhered to comfortable clothes, preferring jeans and bright, eye-catching blouses above everything. For meetings, jeans would be swapped for business suits, but in the courtroom, her outfit was always official and conservative.

Despite being almost six feet tall, at any hearing and official court meetings, she complimented her suit and a strict one-tone blouse with high-heeled shoes. She dominated in a courtroom, and that, to some extent, inspired awe in her opponents. Today, as always, her dress was very simple but elegant.

Cursing her shoes, she climbed up the stairs. She quietly knocked on the door and, not waiting for an answer, entered the room.

The owner of the firm, Philip Laferi, stood facing a huge window that covered two-thirds of the wall opposite the entrance to his office. Amused by something that was happening outside the window, he stood there, smoking his pipe, filling the room with the pleasant, slightly intoxicating scent of Virginia with a dash of vanilla and prunes.

He turned around. Gracefully, with the gait of a black panther, Christine entered the room and walked towards him. Philip's eyebrows flew up in surprise; Christine smiled but did not say a word. In a childlike manner, she rolled her eyes and made an innocent face.

She kept this soft, slightly cheeky smile for special occasions like this. They both knew the meaning of this expression too well. Philip grinned back at her and then laughed out loud. His hearty laughter echoed through the empty corridors of Gray's Inn. The girl at reception smiled unwittingly.

"I did not doubt you for a second, my girl!" he said, still laughing.

He moved closer and gave Christine a tight bear-like hug, practically squeezing out all of the coffee she had drunk since morning.

"Well, sit down, tell me everything!" he said, pointing to a double sofa in the corner of his office.

"May I?" she asked, glancing at her shoes. She could not wait to be rid of those instruments of torture.

"Of course!" Philip laughed again. "I don't even understand how you walk in them!"

She sighed in relief as her burning feet touched the cool surface of the office carpet.

"Mm... That's better!" she purred and plopped onto the soft leather sofa.

Not wasting time on small talk, she quickly conveyed to Philip the details of her conversation with Cedric and arrangements for the settlement.

"So," she said, "now, we just need to finalise the documents, which I'll do right away," she attempted to stand up, but Philip stopped her. His big hand touched her shoulder.

"It was a long, difficult process. You worked so hard, you need some rest. My secretary will draft all the paperwork. She too, you know, needs to do a little work. Sits there all day reading her gossip," he winked at Christine.

Philip returned to the window and lit his pipe. For some time, he stood there, quietly puffing rings of smoke towards the ceiling. He was thinking. Christine knew this habit of his to smoke in silence, going through the thoughts that troubled him. Not wanting to distract him with unnecessary chatter, she closed her eyes and made herself comfortable on the sofa.

For a while, it was quiet in the room; nothing disturbed them but the occasional sound of the water cooler as it released air bubbles into the bottle.

She opened her eyes again when the sofa cushion suddenly bent underneath – Philip had sat next to her.

"Are you certain you are making the right decision, my dear?" he asked.

"What do you mean?" replied Christine.

"You know what I mean," he took her hand in his. "You know perfectly well what I mean..." he repeated. There was sadness in his voice.

"What? Do you mean to say you no longer want to have me as your daughter-in-law?" she asked in genuine surprise.

"Of course, I want to!" he smiled widely.

He moved closer and hugged her very tightly. She rested her head on his broad chest.

"You know I love you like my own daughter! It's you that I am worried about. I do not want you to marry Mark because it is your duty or because you feel obliged to me. I want you to be happy. And, may I be forgiven, I don't think my son is the best candidate."

"He's changed, Philip. I'm sure of it. Please, give him a chance," Christine smiled in return. "I am sure it's going to work out for us, and besides, I will always stay with you," she winked at him and they both laughed.

Philip patted her hand, lifted his heavy body off the sofa and walked back to the window. With a little sadness, Christine watched as he slowly moved away, remembering the first day they met. She was but sixteen back then. Now she was no longer a girl but a beautiful young woman who, by her thirties, had already had her fair share of hardship and grief.

"I just want you to be happy," Philip said wistfully. "I will ask my chauffeur to take you home," he added, placing a fatherly kiss on her forehead, and left the room.

Fifteen minutes later she was sitting in Philip's luxurious car. Before leaving the office, she had removed her lacy pull-ups and stashed them in her handbag. She made herself comfortable in the back seat of the car, stretching her legs to their full length. Her shoes and briefcase full of papers were tucked under the seat.

"Philip is right," she thought. *"I need to get some rest."*

Later that day she would attend the reception dinner celebrating the end of the trial, in addition to her engagement. Tomorrow she and Mark were to fly to Spain, where they would spend two whole weeks together; away from work and their busy London life. Christine smiled, thinking of him, her, the sea, the villa and two weeks of undisturbed sex...

"Shall I take you home, Miss Hawk?" asked the chauffeur. "Mister Laferi did not give me any instructions."

"Yes," she said at first, but then she looked at her watch. The small hand was slowly creeping towards half past eleven. "No," she added after a short pause, "take me to Park Lane, please."

The car moved. Christine rolled her jacket into a small pillow, tucked it under her head, and closed her eyes.

*****

After circling for a little while around the busy London streets of an early afternoon, the car stopped near one of the mansions in Park Lane.

Two blocks of flats in this four-storey building belonged to Mark Laferi. The flats on the basement and ground floor levels were converted into a two-storey apartment. The upper part of the house had been converted into a consulting room and medical office, where Mark saw his patients. Although both parts of the building were connected through the small hall and a staircase, each could also be accessed through separate entrances.

Mark had asked Christine to move in with him but she did not like living in central London – all the hustle and bustle of busy London life was not for her. Her work schedule did not help either – early mornings and late meetings required flexibility. Of course, she quite often stayed overnight at his place but always came back to Kingston where, eight months ago, she had bought a semi-detached house. There was nothing she liked more, than taking a break from busy London life in that quiet little house of hers. Going there for the weekend, meant peace and quiet, space and fresh air. Sometimes she would just sit in the garden for long hours, recharging herself with the energy provided by nature. Techniques of relaxation and meditation also played an important role in her day-to-day routine. And, if time allowed, she tried to practice the Chinese art of Tai Chi.

Richmond Park, the epitome of the peace and space she sought, was only a fifteen-minute walk from where she lived. There was a riding school in the grounds of the park, at which, twice a month, Christine went riding. The society, in which she revolved, had its rules and long-established foundations and required a specific set of skills. Riding was one of them.

All the parking spaces in front of Mark's block of flats were occupied. The car drove past the entrance and stopped at the end of the street. Christine got out, threw her jacket over one shoulder, took the briefcase in one hand, grabbed her shoes by the heels with the other, and headed towards Mark's door.

It was a warm summer day, just gone midday and the sun was shining brightly in the blue sky. Christine walked slowly, softly stepping on the hot pavement with her bare feet. She was humming a tune she had just heard in the car and could not quite get rid of. Her moves were smooth and silent; she felt great.

As she walked past his windows, she saw Mark in the basement level of the house, which contained the kitchen and dining area. Pedestrians had a perfect view of what was happening inside the flat if the blinds weren't closed, while the occupants could only see the legs of people passing by. Practically naked, with only a bath towel wrapped around his hips, Mark was carefully studying the contents of his fridge.

"Still undressed?" she thought, surprised. *"Oh, what a sleepyhead... Although, it might be for the best."*

The pressure of the trial had weighed heavily on her. Although she tried to deny it, she knew she was stressed and tired. And what was the best way to relax?

There was only one thing she could think of at that very moment.

Mark knew how to give a woman real pleasure, like no other. She smiled to herself as she felt tension beginning to build in her abdomen – a wave of desire sweeping through her body. She took a deep breath, filling her lungs and then exhaled slowly. In a few moments, she would be in his strong, experienced hands. Christine slowly climbed the stairs leading to the entrance; she opened the door with her key and silently entered the house.

She paused at the door for a moment and picked up the morning mail. She left her jacket and envelopes on top of a small cabinet in the hallway, placed her heels in a shoe-stand by the door, and walked on.

The aroma of freshly brewed coffee and toasted bread filled the house. She could hear the kettle begin to boil in the kitchen.

"Honey, I'm home," she cried softly.

"I'm in the kitchen, sugar. Come here, I can't hear you," she heard in response.

"Sugar?!" she made a confused face, briefly looked around, and turned to the mirror that hung in the hallway. "Am I in the right house?" she asked her own reflection and laughed quietly.

Christine walked down the stairs and entered the kitchen. Mark was standing facing in the opposite direction, pouring coffee into cups. He heard the footsteps but did not turn and carried on with his task.

"What did you say, pumpkin? I didn't hear you. Do you need sugar?"

"Nope," she purred quietly and, moving close, playfully bit his neck. Still not turning around, Mark lifted his hand to embrace the woman behind him. "You know, I don't take sugar with my coffee, dear," Christine whispered right into his ear.

"Jesus Christ!" Mark shouted out in surprise and jumped a good half metre to the side. There was horror in his eyes. "You... you..." stammering, he repeated over and over again. "Christine?!" It took him a good fifteen seconds to finally manage her name.

"I believe I am..." she said, smiling cunningly. "Were you expecting someone else?" she looked around and tried to make a serious face, yet could not help but smile. His terrified look amused her.

"What... What are you doing here? Why... When did you come?" He bombarded her with questions, frantically looking around. "What time is it now?" he looked at the wall in search of a clock. "What are you doing here?!" he asked again, this time almost screaming.

He took another step back and stopped as his back pressed against the kitchen counter. There was nowhere to retreat now.

"Friday... play date! Remember?" Christine answered with a serious face, and, with a cat-like gait, walked towards him. "Your mummy just left..." she said, moving closer still. Her long slender fingers touched his broad chest, slid to his stomach, and traced further down. "We have a couple of hours until she comes back, and I have a few ideas how we can spend the time," she added with a sly smile.

With an innocent face, in a flick of a movement, her fingers untied the knot of the towel that covered his hips and thighs. Mark gasped and stumbled to the side; clutching the towel firmly to him, not letting it drop to the floor, he tried to cover his naked bits.

A moment later, they heard a noise from the upper floors. Christine raised her brows in inquiry.

"Is there someone upstairs?" she asked calmly.

Mark didn't answer and rolled his eyes to the ceiling. Silently, Christine moved away from him, sat down on one of the four high kitchen stools and crossed her legs. They didn't have to wait long. A few seconds later, they heard steps quickly walking down the stairs.

"Ma-aa-rk," called a female voice.

Christine looked at Mark. Her eyebrow arched, demanding an answer. Her facial expression had not changed, but her playful mood had disappeared.

"Mark, what happened? I heard you scre..."

Whoever was attached to the voice had obviously seen Christine in the kitchen, and stopped mid-sentence, with a gasp.

Being a very calm person by nature, Christine never engaged in quarrels or provoked the same. In every situation, she remained a proper lady. Her work, on a daily basis, helped her practice self-control. In the courtroom, her expression almost never changed; remaining strict and restrained at all times. Her reaction to whatever was happening could be seen only in her eyes. They either smiled, gleaming mysteriously and playfully, if everything went as she planned, or flashed with cold fire. Those who knew and met her in the court preferred the first option because there was no escape from the fury of the latter.

And now, her face seemed the same as before – soft and calm. Christine pushed off from the kitchen counter and turned the stool to face the young woman.

Wrapped in a large bath towel, with her hair still wet from the shower, Helen, Mark's assistant nurse, stood there staring at her, with her hand over her mouth, clearly shocked. Young, cute, not very tall, bleached blonde, and in her twenties.

"Even better than I expected!" she said, and, piercing Helen with her eyes, added with an ironic smile. "The whole medical team is in the house! Getting ready for an examination, my dear? I can see the lady is already undressed and waiting," she smiled coldly and turned to Mark.

Christine looked straight into his blue eyes, burning through them. Mark just stood there not daring to move, still holding the towel with both hands. By the look on his face, it was obvious he was trying to think of some sort of excuse. But no matter what lies he could have come up with, he would not be able to get out of this situation.

"Don't bother, darling," said Christine. Whatever he wanted to say, she didn't want to hear it. "And as for you, my dear," she threw over her shoulder, not even turning to face Helen. "I'd suggest you gather your things and get out of here. Now."

The woman tried to speak.

"Out!" said Christine through clenched teeth.

She turned her head halfway, so Helen would understand that the offer to pack up and get out was indeed addressed to her.

It had been no more than fifteen minutes since Christine entered the house, but it seemed like she had been sitting on the kitchen stool forever. Time moved slowly. Her back stiffened but she was still sitting dead straight, looking right at Mark. Though she was still looking at him, her gaze had changed. Her eyes were directed at him, but she looked straight through him, as if not seeing him at all.

"How long?" breaking the silence, she asked coldly.

Mark swallowed.

"Do not lie to me!" she snapped. "How long?!"

"We... Hm..." a voice spoke behind her.

With mixed feelings of irritation and bewilderment, Christine shook her head, she then sharply turned her stool and faced Helen.

"Are you still here, my dear?" she asked with a tone of genuine surprise. "I thought I had made myself clear. You have exactly five seconds to get out of here unless, of course, you want me to kick you out naked!"

It seemed that, only now, the nurse had realised that the threat of being sent out into the street naked was real. She swiftly turned and hurried upstairs.

Christine got up from her seat and took a few steps towards Mark.

"How long?!" she asked again losing her patience.

"Four months," he breathed out.

Christine laughed. She got the answer she was waiting for; without saying another word, she turned around, and went to the stairs.

"Christine... Wait!" he called after her. "I can..."

"No, you can't..." she snapped.

But after just a few steps she stopped. She turned around and slowly walked back in Mark's direction. Her face and eyes seemed softer.

"Christy..." he said as his lips stretched into a wide grin. "Darling..."

Still holding the towel with one hand, he stretched out the other as if welcoming her into his embrace. Christine smiled softly in return but in the same instant, her facial expression changed. Her blue eyes scalded him with cold fire. The corner of her lips twisted into a slight smirk, the fingers of her right hand rolled up and clenched into a fist and, with all her strength, Christine punched Mark on the nose.

"What the f...!!!" was the only thing he managed.

Mark clutched his nose with both hands. The towel dropped to the floor leaving him standing in the middle of the kitchen completely naked. Blood ran from his nose down his fingers, a few drops fell onto the floor beside him.

"You... you... you broke my nose!" stammering, he bent to pick up the towel and pressed it to his face.

"I thought you were a doctor," she laughed coldly. "I am sure you can handle that."

As she headed for the door, Christine noticed his phone lying on top of the kitchen table. She entered the passcode and dialled a number. When she heard the voice on the other side, she pressed the loudspeaker button and handed the phone to Mark.

Mark stood silently, holding the towel to his face with one hand and the phone to his ear with the other.

"Mark, I know it is you, why aren't you saying anything?" Philip asked, worried.

"Hey, Dad," Mark began, still holding the towel to his nose. "I wanted to tell you..." he continued slowly.

"Mark, what's wrong? What has happened to your voice?"

"Christine and I..." he said hesitantly, "we..." Mark paused again but Christine waved her hand, inviting him to continue. "Well," he stopped again. "The engagement is off," he managed at last.

"Cancelled? What?! What are you talking about? What happened! Where are you? Is she with you?! And for heaven's sake, what happened to your voice?"

"She broke my nose," Mark said quietly removing the towel from the swollen part of his face.

On the other side of the phone, Philip burst out laughing.

"Well, knowing my girl, I can assume it was not over nothing... Who did she catch you with?" he asked, still laughing.

Mark had no intention of continuing the conversation and ended the call.

Christine left Mark in the kitchen in the company of his broken nose, collected her things in the hallway and walked out. It had been no more than half an hour since the car had dropped her off, to the moment her life had turned upside down. She could no longer imagine her life with this person. The past four months he had been fooling around with her, making plans for the future together, but all the time screwing his assistant behind her back.

"It seems people really never change..."

She felt dizzy from the fresh air. Swallowing the lump that began to build in her throat, she fought back the tears that were trying to escape. Christine walked down the stairs and slowly wandered off, down the street, toward the tube station. But after just a few steps, she felt as though she was riding on a huge carousel and the world had begun to spin around her. She couldn't breathe. She was suffocating.

She dropped to her knees in the middle of the street, gasping for air but still couldn't breathe. The feelings that she was trying so hard to keep inside gushed out. Tears flowed from her eyes, and she did nothing to stop them. She felt used and betrayed, she felt humiliated and trampled on. Her quiet tears turned into loud sobs, she could no longer contain herself. Behind the facade of a strong woman, was a lonely human soul, longing for a simple happiness, a heart that had now shattered into pieces.

She shuddered as someone touched her shoulder.

"Are you all right, love?" a male voice asked.

Christine looked up. A man of sixty was standing next to her. Still sobbing she shook her head.

"Are you ok? Do you want me to call anyone?" he asked, concerned, and reached for the phone in his pocket.

Swallowing her tears, she shook her head again. In this world, there was no one... no one who could comfort her now.

"Come on, love, let me help you up," said the man. "A pretty lady like you shouldn't be sitting on the ground," he added and held out his hand.

Only now did Christine realise that she was sitting in the middle of the road. A London black cab was parked right behind her. Carefully holding her elbow, the man led her to the car.

"Jump in, I'll take you home. Where do you live?" he smiled.

"Kingston," she replied, as if her mind was still floating far away. "But it's too far away..."

"There, there, love," replied the taxi driver, helping her into the cab. "Don't worry about that," he said, returned to his seat and started the engine.

Chapter 3:
The Rainbow

After spending an hour in endless London traffic, the taxi stopped in a quiet area of south west London. Tudor Drive was hidden among the idyllic and peaceful streets of the suburbs, on the border between Kingston-Upon-Thames and Richmond – one of those streets that you walk past as you go on with your day and never remember its name. Situated in a quiet and cosy neighbourhood of closely built Victorian houses and densely planted with trees, the street had a rustic look; a green oasis in the midst of noisy and smoky London.

For most of the journey, Christine was silent, staring at the built-in TV screen. One after another, Travel Channel commercials changed before her eyes. Not that she noticed anything. She was transfixed, blankly gazing ahead, into the emptiness before her. From time to time, she looked at the grey carpet that covered the floor and picked at it with the heel of her shoe.

Like a hive of disturbed bees, thoughts circled in her head in complete disarray. They swarmed, swamping her mind, provoking a terrible headache. The weather was not helping either. It was almost two o'clock, and the sun was still beating down, high in the cloudless sky.

Christine unlocked her phone and opened a weather app – it showed twenty-nine degrees and clear skies. She was not surprised. Outside it felt like the inside of a hot pizza oven. The air-con in the taxi did not work so she opened both windows. It took the edge off a little. Occasional gusts of wind blew into the car, bringing a little relief from the relentless heat.

Buried in her thoughts, she occasionally glanced out of the window to determine her whereabouts and the time remaining until this trip was over. The heat became unbearable. She wiped her face with a paper tissue and continued to stare at her phone, sliding her finger across the screen, swapping the weather app between Kingston and Santa Cruz de Tenerife – the place where she and Mark were supposed to fly to tomorrow night.

Consumed by the monotonous motion, flipping through the pictures with the names of cities back and forth, she suddenly realised that the weather forecast for the rest of the day in Kingston had changed. A large black cloud, pierced by a lightning bolt now looked at her from the screen. The new forecast predicted thunderstorms ahead.

"Strange..." she muttered softly, staring at the blue sky. For as far as she could see, there was not a single cloud.

The cab stopped by a small two-storey cottage. The taxi driver helped Christine out of the car and patted her in a friendly manner on the shoulder.

"All will be well, love," he smiled, trying to catch her eyes. "No matter how bad things may seem right now, believe me, tomorrow will be another day and you can think of it all as a bad dream."

Christine smiled in return and reached into her bag for money, but he stopped her.

"Don't worry about that," he smiled again. "And promise to keep your spirits up!"

He winked and returned to the car. The taxi made a U-turn and soon disappeared into the distance.

Slowly, Christine took the last few steps that separated her from the front door. She hesitated for a moment, as if afraid that another surprise might be waiting for her behind the closed door. After a brief pause, she turned the key and entered.

She crossed the threshold of the house and sighed in relief. Everything was as she had left it in the morning, except, probably, for a few envelopes of fresh mail that now lay on the floor. In the corner, by the door, stood the suitcase that she had packed for the trip; her passport and boarding pass were on a small shelf by the mirror.

"Don't even dream about it!" she smiled and patted the pot-bellied suitcase. "You, mister, are gonna stay home! And so am I..." she breathed out.

She drank a glass of water and brewed a fresh pot of coffee. Climbing the stairs to her bedroom, she freed herself from the jacket and pencil skirt she had been wearing, leaving them on the floor where they landed. She unbuttoned her blouse and crossed the room to a large, old-fashioned mirror in a heavy wooden frame that stood next to her dressing table. Silk slip, lace underwear, tall, toned body, high firm breasts; she considered her reflection. Her long brown hair was pinned up high on her head; a small lock curling around her neck.

"What else did he need?" she asked her reflection in a bitter voice.

The heat continued to torment. Christine went into the bathroom and washed her face with ice-cold water. The droplets dried instantly as they touched her burning skin. This, although not for long, brought some relief. She headed back to the bedroom where her phone produced a light buzzing noise. A familiar number appeared on the screen. She sat down on the bed and pressed the green button.

"Are you all right, my dear?" at the other end, she heard Philip's voice. He spoke first and sounded very worried.

"As good as one can be," she answered, hesitating for a moment, "considering the situation."

"I'm so sorry, my dear," he continued. "I should have known. If there is anything I can do for you..." she could hear from the tone of his voice that he was very upset.

"Oh, Philip!" she said softly. "Don't blame yourself. You had nothing to do with it! Well, almost nothing," she smiled to herself. "Besides, it's my fault. At my age, one should be able to see into people," she added with notable sarcasm.

"Would it be foolish of me to expect you at the reception dinner tonight?" Philip asked cautiously. He knew of course that she would refuse, but deep inside he hoped she would reconsider. "You've worked so hard on this case and..."

"With all due respect," Christine did not let him finish, "I'm not in the best mood for social events. I need some time alone to clear my head."

"Of course, of course! Rest up, dear," answered Philip. "Hey, what would you say," he continued after a pause, "if I sent you on a vacation, eh?!" it was obvious he himself was thrilled with the thought.

"I do not..." she began at first, but immediately changed her mind. The idea of spending some time alone, away from everyone, seemed like a perfect solution. "With pleasure!" she replied cheerfully. "Do not want to lose the tickets... Then again, the Villa is booked for 2 weeks. It would give me enough time to recover. But I just want to ask you for a favour."

"Anything you want!" Philip laughed.

"Can you, please, make sure that Mark does not show up there? I have a feeling that in a few days, as soon as everything calms down a little, he may decide to pay me a visit," her voice was cold now. "I beg you to talk him out of this idea."

"Agreed! I will take care of Mark. I give you my word, he won't bother you," he said.

"I'll call when I'm back," said Christine, making it clear the time had come to finish their conversation.

"Yes, of course, honey. Rest well, and do not forget the old man, call me!" said Philip.

Talking to her had calmed his mind, and he sounded now like he was in a much better mood, than at the start of the call.

Christine said nothing and dropped the call. When she hung up, the phone rang again – there was no caller ID on the display. She hesitated. As she stared at the screen, the call dropped.

"It's probably for the best," she thought.

She did not want to talk to anyone, but the phone rang again, breaking the silence of the room with its low buzz.

"The same unknown."

She pressed the answer button, realising too late that she was making a mistake.

"Christy... darling," spoke a familiar voice.

"You have some nerve calling me right now," she snapped.

"Christy, my love!"

"What do you want?" her voice was cold, and a little rough.

"It's not what you think, my dear," Mark began to wriggle.

"Really?! Oh, please, enlighten me then... But, on second thoughts – NO! I've already seen and heard more than enough today," she snapped again but continued. 'Tell me, was she the only one?"

"What do you mean?" he asked.

"Oh, come on, Mark, you know exactly what I mean."

"Christy, how can you think such a thing? It was only a momentary fling... nothing serious." He sounded as though he was trying to convince himself of that in the first place.

"Oh, that's enough, Mark! At least once, admit it! At least once in your life be honest!" she exploded.

His silence was the answer she dreaded. Like a sharp knife, it sunk deeper into her heart.

"Goodbye, Mark," she said dryly.

She disconnected the call and put the phone back on the nightstand. For some time, she sat there in silence looking straight ahead. The phone rang again. Christine muted the sound and cancelled the calls several times, but the person on the other end had no intention of giving up. The phone kept ringing, breaking off only for a few seconds between the calls.

"Stop calling me!" she said angrily.

As if the phone obeyed, the calls stopped.

Christine looked at her watch. The time was twenty to three. She looked out of the window – the sun was still shining brightly, but the heat had gradually begun to subside.

She took off her silk blouse and pulled light riding slacks and her favourite sky-blue top from her closet. Pausing for a moment at the dressing table, she looked at the small black velvet box. Christine opened it and took out a ring, which, as planned from this evening on, she would be wearing after being officially engaged to Mark Laferi. The stones glittered and sparkled in the sunlight. She smiled and put the ring back into the box. She placed her watch beside the box, and from her jewellery box took out a silver bracelet made in the shape of two intertwined snakes with small emerald eyes. The bracelet was a gift from Christine's mother for her sixteenth birthday. It was not very trendy, but one of the few things from her that remained. Now more than ever Christine wanted to feel her close. She put it on.

She grabbed a light jacket, her riding boots, and her car keys and walked outside.

*****

The riding school was just a fifteen-minute walk from her house, but there was no way she would walk in that heat, under the merciless rays of the summer sun. Christine got into the car and switched on the air con. The stream of cool fresh air blew in from all directions.

"That's better!"

The journey took less than five minutes, and at three o'clock sharp, Christine parked her Mini in the car park, in front of a small building at the riding school.

"Christine!" exclaimed the owner of the school – Monica, a woman with a lively face and deep brown eyes. "What brings you here? I didn't expect to see you so soon."

"I know I said I wasn't going to come back this month, but I'm going on a vacation for two weeks and I was hoping I could see Richie."

"Yes, of course," Monica replied. Then, an odd look came to her face. "I should warn you – he's been acting rather strangely since the morning."

"Strange? What do you mean? Has anything happened? Maybe it's the heat that's taking a toll on him?"

"I don't know, really, but I've never seen him like this before."

Christine changed her ballerina pumps for her high black riding boots with spurs, locked her bag and keys in a small locker, and, together with Monica, went in the direction of the stables. They walked in silence.

"Is everything ok?" asked the instructor. "You look very... lost or something," she could not find the words to describe it. It was not in her nature to poke her nose into someone else's business, but for all the time they had known each other, she had never seen Christine like this. Always cheerful, happy and chatty, today she was quiet and consumed in her own thoughts.

"Yes. Everything is fine. Just a long week," lied Christine, trying to put a convincing smile on her face.

A strong smell hit her nose as soon as they entered the stables.

"Uffff!" Christine moaned, covering her nose. "I love Richie, I do, but I don't think I will ever get used to this..."

"Stink?" laughed Monica. "You, obviously, do not understand! Smells like roses!" she added and took a long deep breath of hay, horse sweat and manure.

"Yuck!" Christine shuddered in disgust, and they both laughed.

As they came closer, they heard a loud neigh and shouting from the far end of the stables. Cursing as he walked, a man with a bucket and brush walked out of Richie's stall and slammed a small door behind him. The expression on his face said it all. The horse had given him some unpleasant moments.

"I don't know what's wrong with him today," he muttered, walking past the women.

Richie was a tall, dark, three-year-old bay stallion. In the dim light of the pen, he seemed almost black, but outside, in the broad daylight, his sides cast different shades of rich chocolate and dark honey. As he saw his rider, the horse made a loud noise, reared and menacingly stamped his hooves on the wooden floor.

Christine tried to put her hand on his back, but the stallion moved away from her, snorting angrily.

"Do you mind if I take him for a ride?" she asked.

"Yes, no problem," replied Monica, and added as she left, "He is yours for an hour, as usual."

Christine stayed in the stall. The stallion calmed down a little but still was visibly nervous, shifting restlessly.

"It's all right, my boy," she said quietly and made a small step towards him.

Ritchie continued to move from side to side making angry noises, rearing a few more times. She spoke to him again, gently.

"It's all right... Shh, it's ok."

This time she managed to put her hand on his back. Feeling her gentle touch, the horse calmed down but snorted again and buried his snout into her chest.

"Oh, you just missed me!" she finally realised. "I'm sorry, I'm sorry. I know, I was busy," she patted his muzzle. "How about we saddle you up and go for a ride, hm?" she lifted his snout and looked into his eyes. "Just you and me!"

Richie snorted happily in response and ten minutes later, she was in the saddle.

"Well, you know the route," she said to him, clicking her tongue and gently pressed her legs against Richie's sides.

Slowly the stallion went out of the gate and headed towards a familiar path.

*****

Richie knew the route well; from the school to the small path, to the gate, across the road, till the car park, past the café, bear left and then the same route back. Usually, the entire ride took them just under an hour. So today, as with any other day, walking out of the school gates, Richie went on his usual trail.

The heat subsided. They rode slowly. Christine gently swayed in the saddle, and from time to time, picked up the reins and guided the horse when it was necessary to overtake other riders. She looked around, regarding the familiar scenery. Mothers with prams and small children enjoyed the warmth of the summer day; dog owners walked their pets. Far from everyone, on the border of the forest, she could see the big antlers of deer that lived in the park. With their offspring, they grazed at the edge of the forest, not yet taking the risk to come any closer.

From time to time the sun hid behind the clouds and then came out into the blue skies again. Christine closed her eyes and lifted her face up to the sun. Its warmth gently caressed her skin.

They rode on for some time. She opened her eyes again when, riding past the café, her stomach produced a characteristic sound in response to the smell of toasted bread and fresh baking wafting from the shop. She realised that besides a few cups of coffee, her stomach had not seen any real food today. Not risking falling off the horse in a hungry faint, she decided to stop for a little refreshment. Christine tied Richie to the fence surrounding the café and went in.

She picked up a panini with tuna and cheese, a bottle of water and a couple of apples for Richie, handed the sandwich to a young man behind the counter and sat down at the nearest table. It seemed that the timer on the press grill was deliberately trying to starve her to death. Every time Christine lifted her eyes up to the digital monitor, the time had decreased by only ten seconds. When the bell finally rang, she happily jumped up from the table.

"Oh, someone is hungry!" the young man said cheerfully.

Christine didn't have a chance to reply, her stomach, speaking on her behalf, issued another loud rumble. She smiled shyly.

"Ok, ok! I'm hurrying!" the young man laughed. "Five forty-five, please," he said, handing her a paper bag containing the sandwich, apples and water.

Christine gave him ten pounds and while the young man counted the change, her stomach growled loudly twice more.

"Are you starving yourself, dear?" he smiled, handing her the change and a big chocolate chip cookie. "This is on the house! And no more diets!" he narrowed his eyes, trying to sound as strict as possible.

Despite this confusion, Christine felt much better. As she walked out of the café, she found Richie engaged in his favourite pastime – digging a hole in the ground with his hoof. As she approached, he happily shook his head.

"Look what I've got," Christine showed him the apples. "One now and one when we get back. Which one do you want, green or red?"

The horse stared at her with its big brown eyes, framed by long lashes.

"What is there to decide…" she could read in his eyes. *"I want both and I want them now!"*

"Well, let's choose right or left," she said, moving her hands behind her back.

Richie snorted impatiently and stamped his foot, insisting that there be no compromise. He wanted both apples and he wanted them now! Christine gave up. She smiled and patted his mane. She put the red apple back into the paper bag, bit into the green one, broke it in half and gave them to the horse. He greedily stuffed both pieces into his mouth and chewed loudly. As soon as he finished with the first apple, he stretched his snout trying to get into the bag for the second fruit.

While Richie munched on apples, loudly chewing, smacking his lips and bending his ears with pleasure, Christine ate the cookie. She then untied the horse, climbed into the saddle, and they continued their ride. While Richie slowly walked along the road, she chewed on her panini, holding it in one hand and the reins in the other. The stallion, having received his treat, behaved and carefully walked down the path.

Time flew by and soon they had to return to school. Christine did not want to go home just as yet.

"Monica," she asked the owner of the school, as soon as the woman came out of the office, "do you mind if I take him for a little longer?"

"Darling, I'm sorry," she began, "his next session is in half an hour. You can…" the loud ringing of the phone did not let her finish.

She made a sign to Christine not to leave and retired to a small office to answer the call. A few minutes later, she came back. Smiling broadly, she hurried to announce some good news.

"Looks like today is your lucky day!" she exclaimed.

"I very much doubt that," Christine muttered quietly.

"You can take Richie for another hour," said Monica.

"What?! Why? You said…"

"His next session just got cancelled," said Monica. "He is all yours for another hour."

"Oh, thank you!" Christine hugged her.

"It's alright," answered Monica, slightly embarrassed, as she tried to free herself from the tight embrace.

*****

Richie whinnied happily when he once again felt his rider in the saddle and went off on the familiar route towards the school gates. As soon as they came out of the gate, Christine pulled the reins. The horse stopped in surprise, he knew the route and could not understand why he was being so rudely interrupted. Christine lowered herself to his ear and hugged his neck.

"What would you say, if we go that way?" she said softly.

She tugged the reins slightly to the left, ordering the horse to turn. This side of the road also had a small path but, after a few hundred yards, they entered a nearby grove and got lost in the forest.

The horse snorted and tried to turn back – he didn't like the place. Christine insisted. She pulled the reins harder and patted his croup. After resisting for a while, the animal gave up and turned in the direction he did not want to go. Christine clicked her tongue and gently pressed his sides. The horse slowly walked along the trodden path leading into the depth of the park.

After some time, they were surrounded by tall trees, their branches entwined in strange patterns high above her head. The path, with tall maples and chestnuts on both sides, wasn't wide but was sufficient for one rider.

The further they rode into the park, the less she could hear the noises of the city. The noises of cars and people in the park gradually dissolved and the space around them was now filled with the sounds of nature – rustling leaves and the twittering of birds. It seemed they were discussing this unexpected visitor who had disturbed their peace.

The leisurely pace of the stallion and monotonous rocking of the saddle did its job. Very soon, Christine was no longer looking around. Her eyes were open, but her head was disconnected from what was happening in the here and now and had moved her to the events of this morning, into her childhood, her youth...

Thoughts swirled in her head, quickly jumping from one episode of her life to another. Like slides reproduced by her memory, they did not linger for long and changed fast. Memories, one after another, like sea waves, rolled on, consuming her completely, and then retreated slowly to make way for the next one.

She was thinking about her life. She was almost thirty; she had a career, a house, a job that she enjoyed. She had a comfortable living, but her life was empty. She was alone, with no family, no friends. She had many acquaintances, but they all had families, children, and lives of their own. In this large city of millions, she was lonely. And now, her hopes for love and happiness had been snatched away from her.

A sharp gust of wind returned her to reality. It wrapped her in its cold veil, sending goose bumps all over her body. She shivered and looked around, not knowing where they were or how they had got here. Richie stopped and calmly munched the grass, occasionally waving his tail about.

They were on a huge meadow, tightly framed by tall trees. From where they stood, it looked as though the meadow was shaped in a perfect circle, and in its centre grew a tree of incredible size with a huge trunk and large branches spreading wide and rising high into the sky. She was used to seeing big old trees in parks, but this one was several times bigger than anything she'd ever seen before – a fantastic giant, mesmerising in its grandeur.

Christine ran her eyes up, trying to trace the height of the tree from its roots up to the crown. The bright sun, which shone right above it, as if resting on the top branches of this magnificent giant, blinded her for a moment. She blinked helplessly a few times in vain, trying to regain focus. It seemed there was a glowing light coming from the base of the tree, but she didn't pay much attention to it at first, as the whole meadow was flooded with sunlight.

A new gust of cold wind distracted her from her peaceful contemplation of nature. Huge black clouds crawled towards them from the north. The sun was still shining through the clouds but she could no longer feel its heat. A strong wind started to blow. It ruffled her hair, blowing from all different directions at the same time. Richie made a distressed sound; the sudden change in the weather unsettled him.

Christine looked around, trying to figure out which side they had entered the meadow, but wherever she looked, over and over again, her eyes were drawn back to the giant tree in the middle of the clearing. Gathering clouds brought darkness but a faint, slightly visible light continued to shine from the base of the oak.

Rolls of thunder came in from behind the forest. The stallion made an angry sound, expressing his concerns about the shift in atmosphere. Another moment and thunder rumbled right over their heads. Richie reared in fright and almost threw her from the saddle. Christine dismounted and took him by the bridle, trying somehow to calm and reassure him. The next moment the heavens opened. A flood of cold water came down from the sky, emptying the contents of black clouds, which, by this time, had completely covered the sky.

Rain lashed her face, and the wind harshly blew in from all sides, throwing wet hair over her eyes. Fighting nature, Christine was trying to lead the horse out of the open meadow. Richie reared with every new rumble of thunder. It took great effort to hold on to the reins and stay out from under the hooves of the terrified animal.

When they finally got under the cover of the trees, they no longer felt the rain. Not that it mattered. In those few minutes, Christine was soaked down to the last thread. Richie calmed down a little, yet still breathed anxiously and trembled with each, already retreating, rumble of thunder. Trying to reassure the frightened animal, Christine hugged his neck. She spoke to him in a soft voice, trying to explain that it was just the rain, and soon it would be over, but it had little effect, if any at all.

Little by little, the rain subsided. It was time for them to go back but Christine still could not figure out where they were.

"What could be more foolish than to get lost in a public park? I have to warn Monica that we will be late," she thought, patting her pockets in search of her phone.

It was not a Sherlock Holmes kind of deduction when, not finding the phone in her pocket, she realised that she had left it back home. She swore quietly, trying not to disturb an already frightened stallion. She continued to stroke his muzzle, promising him a tasty treat, as soon as they were back at the school.

"You do remember how we got here, don't you?" she was trying to catch his eyes. "Richie is very smart, Richie can find his way back, can't he?" she stroked his neck. "And when we get back, I'll buy you a pack of delicious and juicy apples," she promised.

This promise clearly excited the horse, and he began to march on the spot, turning from one side to another, looking around as if trying to figure out where they had come from.

By this time, the rain had already stopped, and in the distance, above the trees, the bright sunlight began to break through the clouds. And then, the animal, which by that time had calmed down, made a strange noise, reared again and tried to break free. Richie whinnied loudly; his eyes expressed incomprehension and fear. Christine had never seen him like this before. She traced his gaze and turned in the same direction.

She immediately understood the reason for his behaviour. The sky had almost cleared, the sun was shining high above the trees, and the entire meadow was filled with bright light, but the light was not coming from the sun.

*****

That something behind her was shining bright, shimmering in shades of gold and silver. The light came from the trunk of a tree, consuming it as if the tree was shining from the inside. Rays of light and their reflections were dancing around on the leaves of the bushes and trees that surrounded the clearing. Spellbound, Christine looked at this miracle, which had appeared from nowhere and now was before her eyes in its full splendour. She had never seen the Northern

Lights and was sure that this stunning beauty, this breath-taking manifestation of light that appeared before her, was exactly that.

Everything was suddenly quiet. The birds stopped singing. The silence around her was occasionally broken by odd sounds, produced by Richie – the agitated animal was making angry snorts and crushed bushes behind him every time he tried to back off. He wanted to get away from this place as far and as soon as possible. Unlike Christine who, unable to take her eyes off this magic light, was still staring at the shining tree.

Curiosity overtook the fear, and very cautiously she took a step forward; then a second and then a third. After the fourth step, she came into the clearing. The reins tightened in her hand. Not allowing her to go any further, the horse dug all four limbs into the ground, refusing to move. Why was she dragging him there? What was happening in the clearing was seriously disturbing him.

"Oh, come on! Don't be a coward," Christine encouraged him.

Not paying attention to his behaviour, she tried to take a few more steps forward, but Richie stood still, rooted to the spot.

While they were fighting this silent argument, the shining in the meadow came alive, it was pulsating, flowing, creating a magical illusion of rotation. Apart from white and gold colours, it now shone with all the colours of the spectrum. Appearing, and disappearing again, they were then replaced by gold and white splashes and sparkles of blue, pink and purple. Christine never thought that such colours could exist, but there they were, in front of her eyes, in all their splendour. She couldn't take her eyes off them. She was utterly mesmerized, as if bound by a magical spell. She was afraid that if she turned away, even for a fraction of a second, this beauty would disappear.

Richie whinnied again and pulled her to the side, away from the danger that he thought was hiding in that glow.

"All right, all right! We'll go back," Christine shook her head and came back to reality from the hypnotic trance of the magical light that was still shining brightly in her eyes. "But you have to remember how we got here."

Richie made a happy sound and swayed his head. Stamping his feet heavily on the ground, he once again began to look around, he wanted to get out of this strange place as soon as possible.

Christine mounted the saddle. Her clothes were still wet and very uncomfortable, but she did not feel the cold; her excitement was too great.

At first slowly, making his way through the thicket of shrubs and trees, and then gradually picking up speed, the horse walked on to a barely noticeable path and broke into a canter. The promise of his so loved juicy treats gave him additional speed.

After a while, they were riding through thinning woods. From time to time, Christine was looking back to make sure that the magical glow was still there, but it seemed it had no intention of disappearing. The light was still gleaming through the foliage.

Soon she began to notice familiar places. There was that funny tree with a forked crown, which reminded her of the hump of a camel; there was the low shrub with beautiful white flowers, whose fragrance filled this part of the park. They were on the right track.

Very soon, they rode out of the forest and galloped towards the school. The black clouds that had covered the sky, were now slowly making their way towards the horizon, giving way to the sun. Against the high background of the blue heavens shone two broad arcs of bright colours. They decorated the boundless sky, becoming an integral part of its blueness.

Christine had often seen a rainbow, but this time it was different. This time there were two of them. As a magic giant yoke, they hung over the forest; mirroring one another, reflecting each other's colours in the reverse order. Old people said that seeing a double rainbow was meant to bring good luck. As she rode underneath the coloured bow, Christine closed her eyes for a moment and made a wish.

Back at the school, she took Richie to his stall and gave him the promised apples, borrowing two from the stall worker. She was still trembling. She had to get back to the clearing, so the bag of apples, promised to the stallion, swiftly moved down on her list of priorities. Not that Richie minded, he was happy to accept what was given to him and loudly chewed his treats. She patted his mane and gently kissed him goodbye.

As she ran out of the stables, she collided with Monica and nearly knocked her down.

"Thank God!" Monica exclaimed. "What happened? Where have you been? We started to worry."

"Everything's fine! We just got a little lost... then rain..." Christine was uttering disjointedly. Hoping to end this conversation as soon as possible, she now and then lifted her eyes to the sky. "Have you seen that beauty?" she could not help but mention it at last.

Monica looked up but could not see anything extraordinary.

"Like I've never seen a rainbow before," she said, still not being able to understand what in this ordinary phenomenon of nature, so very much excited her friend.

Christine could not and did not want to wait any longer; she had to go back right this moment. Since she saw that light she, as though still under its spell, felt drawn to it.

"I'll leave the car here for a while," she said, and not waiting for an answer, hurried out of the gate, leaving the school mistress to stand in the middle of the yard, barely understanding what was going on.

On the riding school grounds, Christine still somehow restrained herself, trying to look as calm as possible, though it was a great effort. As soon as she was out of the gates, she ran.

She remembered the way well and now was running through the forest, back to the clearing. Bushes, trees, everything flashed before her eyes. Her feet stumbled; she tripped a few times and was out of breath but did not stop.

Soon the forest thickened around her and she changed to a brisk walk. Her legs tangled in the roots and fallen branches; tired but determined, she continued to make her way through the trees. There in the distance, through the green of the forest, she could now see the glimmer of the familiar light. With a few more steps she finally reached the place she so desperately wanted to get to.

Reaching the clearing, she stopped and rested her hands on her knees trying to catch her breath. Her heart was pounding in her chest, ready to jump out.

Christine looked at the centre of the clearing. The light continued to pour out of the old tree. She still could not believe her eyes. Colours shone and sparkled, filling all the space around her, but it seemed that while she was gone, they had become deeper, more vivid. As a magical magnet of enormous power, the light was drawing her in. Spellbound, she stepped into the clearing.

Slowly, carefully taking each step, trying not to scare off this beauty, she began to move towards the tree. At first, it seemed that the light began to fade, but taking just a few steps forward, she realised that it was nothing like that. The light did not fade but somehow retreated. It was retreating to the centre of the clearing, back to the tree, calling her in. Step by step she was closing in...

As she approached the tree, she realised that it was much bigger than she had originally thought. It was a giant oak of immense size, which, judging by its circumference could have been a thousand years old. Its crown rising high above the clearing; its shadow covering a good twenty meters in diameter. The light was coming from the opposite side of the tree. She walked around.

Like an ancient cave, a huge cleft appeared before her eyes. The light was coming from there and now retreating, like a giant octopus, drawing its huge tentacles in. Following the light, Christine did not notice that she had walked into the tree.

The light was glowing, whirling and dancing before her, forming the shape of a sphere. It wasn't bright at first – barely visible to the eye. Then it became more distinct, growing in size, getting bigger and brighter with every passing moment. Soon it had doubled in size, and in the next instant it rose above her head. Christine could not take her eyes off this magic.

The sphere of light released an outer perimeter, which now occupied most of the space inside the tree. Christine took a timid step forward. Now she was standing inside the outer perimeter, in front of a bright pulsating sphere.

A chill ran down her spine. It seemed that something moved inside the sphere. Her palms were wet, her throat dry. Afraid to take her eyes off this stunning beauty even for a fraction of a second, straining her eyes, she was looking at the bright light.

"Another shadow and another movement?!"

Startled, Christine pulled back. She could not believe what she saw and rubbed her eyes. Maybe she was just imagining things, maybe it was just the reflection of light playing with her imagination. Not realising what she was doing, she reached forward. Inviting, the sphere of light moved towards her.

Christine took a long deep breath, she accepted the invitation, and walked into the light.

Chapter 4:
Awakening – Part 2

The splashes of water that fell on her face helped her once again regain consciousness.

Christine lifted her head slightly and tried to look around, but every move – even something as simple as raising her head off the ground – demanded an incredible effort. It felt as though she had spent many long hours in this place, although how many exactly she didn't know. Her sense of time was long lost. The left side of her body was completely numb. She could hardly move. Wincing in pain and accompanying every movement with a low groan, she somehow managed to move her foot to a normal position, but any attempt to free her left arm from underneath her body resulted in excruciating pain, the apotheosis of which was the feeling of a thousand needles piercing her simultaneously.

She gathered all the strength she could find in her exhausted body, gently lifted her head off the ground again and opened her eyes. But this effort was in vain as she was unable to determine her location. The pitch-black darkness surrounded her. She blinked a few times and, straining her eyes, stared into the blackness – there was nothing. A great void looked back at her.

Feeling weak, she lowered her head back to the ground and shut her eyes. Tight, tighter, very tight – until they hurt. She saw the stars; bright flashes and sparks of light that, when she was a little girl, her mum used to call "the stars". As a child, she had learned to use this trick. Waking up at night from a bad dream or when trying to fight a night monster that crawled into her room, she would close her eyes very tight and use these bright flashes to light up her mind and scare off the fears and night terrors.

Memories of youth and childhood came over her...

When she was a little girl, she loved to look at these imaginary stars. In the evenings, just before bedtime, her and her mother would sit in an armchair in her room or lie together on her mother's large bed; they would shut their eyes and tell each other what images their imaginations had crafted.

Christine thought of her mother – her kind eyes, and warm, soft hands – how much she wanted to feel her loving embrace, again to become that little girl who woke up in the dark from a bad dream and called for her.

"Mum..." she called softly into the darkness, but there was no one to answer.

Over the years since her mother's death, there wasn't a single day when Christine didn't think of her. She had never known her father. A military man, he had been killed in action when Christine was still a little girl. That was, of course, what her mother had told her. In their house, they had a few photographs of her father, or, to be more precise, photos of a man in a uniform standing against the Union Jack.

When she was little, she had often spoken with the photo, sang songs to it, and talked to it about her achievements at school. But, as time passed, she had come to realise that this image had nothing to do with her family. It was just a picture of an officer – one that her mother placed in the house to create a fatherly presence in her life. This feeling grew stronger day by day. And then, when no one from his family came to her mum's funeral, or after, when nobody came for her, offered help or support, she knew it for sure.

Philip Laferi was the man, who to a certain extent, became like a father to her. He was the one who took over the important role of mentor in her life. Philip and Christine met when she was not yet seventeen. By that time, her mother was already very ill and rarely left the house. The young girl had to forget about her education, take charge of the family finances, and care for a sick mother. She was torn between multiple jobs, looking after her mother and failing attempts to prepare for her A levels.

The catering company, which had employed Christine, had provided freshly prepared lunches for the entire staff of "Laferi & Partners" and six times per week, Christine visited Gray's Inn. Philip liked this sweet, well-read and chatty young girl. Every day, while distributing the food, she told interesting pieces of news or stories. She always seemed happy, but her eyes never smiled; they reflected all the hardships and problems that had fallen on her frail shoulders.

Philip loved talking to her. From their very first meeting, he had noticed her interest in the law and especially case studies. For her fairly young age she was very inquisitive and well-read, witty and funny, and happy to hold a conversation on a variety of topics. In spite of his tight schedule and workload, Philip always tried to spare a moment or two to exchange a few words with her.

Christine had felt uneasy about this. She was unable to understand the cause for such behaviour and thus, receiving obvious interest and attention from this grey-haired lawyer, she started avoiding him. At one point, she even asked her manager to move her to another part of London so they would cease contact altogether. With her already significant problems, she didn't want to encourage courtship from this grand gentleman. Noticing her sudden change in demeanour, Mr. Laferi Sr. set out to clarify the matter without further delay.

That day, shortly after lunch, Philip made his way to the office library, where, to his great surprise, he found Christine looking through the pages of the civil act law. He didn't expect to find her in the office at this time, as she had never stayed for longer than her job required, but he was delighted just the same. This would be the perfect opportunity to make things straight between them. He knew that in this part of the building, they were unlikely to be disturbed.

He had quietly entered the room, closed the door behind him, and, to ensure they would not be disturbed, moved the sign above the entrance to the "busy" position. He had taken a few steps towards her and coughed slightly to indicate that she was no longer alone in the room. Christine had been so consumed by her fascinating read that she had jumped in surprise and dropped the book. All fifteen hundred pages of the code of laws had dropped loudly to the floor.

When she had realised who had disturbed her peace, she had been very quick to draw her own conclusions about his intentions.

"This old man and I," (at the time Philip was only fifty,) *"alone... at the rear of the building... there is nobody around... soundproof door. Calling for help is useless..."* her face froze in horror.

She took a few steps back, trying to evaluate her chances of escape – there weren't many. Her back touched the old fireplace, and she immediately reached for the first thing she could grab. Christine prepared to defend her honour.

Seeing this before him – her eyes wide open in horror, face as pale as chalk, and to top it off a poker in her hand – Philip had looked at her in confusion. When he had finally realised what conclusion she had drawn about his intentions toward her, he had burst out laughing, flinging his head back in whole-hearted enjoyment. His loud laugh was heard on the street outside.

"Why is he laughing? What's so funny?" she was taken aback.

Not understanding what was going on, she couldn't take her astonished eyes off him. She had expected anything but this, but with his whole being Philip shook with laughter and the room shook with him. His loud hearty laugh echoed through the corridors of the old building. It was as if he had turned into a laughing bag, like the ones that you touch once and they laugh hysterically for minutes. He couldn't stop – it was as though someone invisible was poking his sides.

Christine stared at him blankly, still clutching her improvised weapon. When she finally realised the absurdity of the situation, which she herself had created, she had dropped the poker on the floor and giggled, and a few seconds later, she had burst into laughter. It was the first time Philip had ever seen her eyes smiling.

They'd laughed, standing in different corners of the library until their bellies hurt and their faces turned red. When they'd finally stopped, exhausted, they had sat in the big comfortable chairs that stood in the room and had a long conversation.

"Never judge a person and his actions, without knowing the true cause that provoked him to act one way or another," Philip had told her then and Christine remembered his words forever.

Thus, began their friendship. Over the years that passed since that day, they still remembered this incident and laughed every time it was mentioned.

After that day in the library, Christine, on several occasions, had witnessed the brief but fiery encounters between Philip and his son Mark. It soon became obvious to her that Mr. Laferi Sr. simply wanted a close family: understanding, comfort and companionship; everything that was denied to him by his own son and that he found in the company of the young girl.

They continued their meetings and conversations when she delivered meals to his office, and once a month, Philip was invited to her mum's for a Sunday lunch that Christine, with great pleasure, cooked for the three of them. She had never had a father and was sincerely happy for Philip's company. He told her about interesting cases and changes to the law. They discussed news and books, and if she asked for his advice, he never refused and was always glad to help and share his expertise and experience with her.

Their sympathy and affections were mutual and, while Mark got himself into new scrapes, disgracing his father – a famous lawyer – with his wild adventures, Philip sought refuge and peace of mind in Christine's company.

It had been almost a year since they first met when Christine's mum died. She knew that her mother's end was inevitable, and tried to prepare herself for that moment, but as ready as she could be, it hit her very hard. For a while, she was in some kind of limbo. Hours stretched into days, days mixed up with nights. When she returned home from the funeral, she spent days crying. She was alone. In the whole world, she was alone, and there was no one there for her – not anymore, not a single soul.

Having fatherly affections towards Christine, Philip had decided to take over her guardianship. She had gladly accepted his help and support. He helped her sort through the routine and admin paperwork after the funeral. He had organised the sale of the apartment that Christine inherited from her mother, and personally supervised the preparation and execution of the contract. Even so, most of the money she made from the sale went to pay off the bills for hospital care, medicines, nurses and debt for the funeral.

Noting Christine's eager interest in legal work, Philip had taken her on as an apprentice and personally took charge of her education. He helped her to get into a law school and paid her tuition fees. He was a strict but fair teacher, insisting that she receive a good education, which later would help her to get on well in life and society. All that she knew, all that she was, and what she had achieved by her thirties, she owed to him.

Christine was very grateful for his help and support, yet she refused to accept payment for her education as a gift. She called it a loan, and, after graduation and post-graduate work in the legal office Laferi & Partners, and, subsequently, in her own practice, she repaid it in full. Despite Philip's objections, she added a generous amount of interest to the repayment. Being left without parents and on her own at a young age, she had quickly learned to be strong, and deal with her fears and problems.

But right now, at this very moment, when she neither knew nor understood where she was, or what had happened to her, more than anything, she wished her mother was close. Yet she knew that was impossible. A lone tear rolled from her eye, trickled down her right cheek, and fell silently to the ground.

"No! This is neither the time nor the place to get soft!" Christine tried to pull herself together.

After a brief struggle, she somehow managed to pull the numb limb from underneath her body. Her bracelet had pressed hard into her skin, creating an impression of snakes' heads on her wrist. Moaning in pain, and with extra effort, Christine rolled over onto her back. Lying motionless for a while, she slowly began to massage her left shoulder, forearm, wrist and fingers. She knew that wherever she was and whatever she needed to do to get out of this place, she would require all of her limbs to be functioning.

She slowly rolled her fingers into a fist, returning the flow of blood that had been cut off for an unknown period of time. At first, she could barely move. Her hand, feeling like a stuffed papier-mâché toy, lay motionless beside her; her fingers wouldn't obey. Christine could not even manage the simple act of wiggling her fingers. She couldn't feel her hand at all, let alone move it.

It took some time before her hand began to acquire feeling. So lying on her back in a semi-conscious state and not having enough strength to bring her body upright, she continued to stare into the darkness over her head and around her, trying to see anything. There was nothing.

Soon her eyes become used to the dark. At some point, she thought that she could distinguish some shadows and images, although it was impossible to give them any definite shape. To her great regret, except for dripping water, there was no other sound.

She tried to listen harder, but other than a metronome of uniform droplets and quiet splashing of water somewhere near, there was no other sound. It was quiet. Quiet and damp. She felt it in the air and on the ground around her. While lying face down, she got wet, and now her back was taking the brunt of it.

"Am I near the pond or perhaps on the riverbank? But why it is so dark and quiet? Where are all the people, why can't I hear anything?" she was puzzled.

Gradually, the cold began to sneak into her clothes. She shivered at first but soon her whole body was shaking. After a moment, a loud sneeze escaped her. It echoed a long time into the depths of this strange place.

Immediately the darkness filled with a new sound. At first, it was quiet, she could barely hear it, but as it moved closer with every second, the sound grew stronger and louder. It seemed that in a moment it would consume her and all the space around.

Raising her body slightly, she rested an elbow on the ground and tried to peer into the darkness. In vain, she strained her eyes; she could not see much, but the sound was moving closer. Advancing from the depths of the darkness, it grew, filling the entire space. From the blackness, the dark mass separated and with great speed, making screeching-chirping sounds moved towards her. Her heart bumped loudly under her ribs and froze – bats!

"A sewer?! A grotto?! A cave?" thoughts raced in her head.

Christine barely had time to duck to the ground; she buried her head in her arms and covered her ears. The creatures above her flew so low that they touched her hair and scratched her hands with their sharp claws.

Everything happened very quickly. The vile screeching swooped past her and slowly dissolved in the distance. Not daring to open her eyes, Christine held her breath, trying to calm her pounding heart. She was listening to the receding sound, trying to determine its direction. In another moment, she could hear, like the pop of the cork from a champagne bottle, the creatures break free from this place of darkness. Their squeaks mingled with the sound of the wind and rustling leaves. Christine could now clearly hear much farther than she could see with her eyes.

Lifting herself from the ground, she sat, and then slowly stood up. Limping hard on her left leg, her right hand on something that she identified as a wall, she moved slowly towards the sounds. Stepping carefully in the darkness, she moved forward, with the tips of her fingers barely touching the wet stone of the wall. She limped slowly and carefully along the bumpy surface, afraid to disturb other local inhabitants. She tried not to think about what might be crawling under her feet, but as luck would have it, her imagination drew the most disgusting pictures.

Either her eyes had become accustomed to the dark, or she was moving closer to the light, for she began to distinguish some shapes and forms in front of her. Surrounded by stone walls on all the sides, she was in a cave. As she moved forward, she could see a glimmer of daylight ahead. A fresh breeze was coming from the distance. Forgetting all the pain and lameness, she quickened her pace, as fast as the slippery surface under her feet allowed. Step, another step, and finally she was free.

Bright sunlight hit her directly in her eyes. After the pitch-black darkness of the cave, it blinded her. Images, transmitted by her brain, blurred and swam in front of her. A gentle, light breeze ruffled through the young leaves and played with her hair. After the damp mustiness of the cave, the fresh air intoxicated her. Panting heavily, Christine gasped for its freshness. She looked around. Ahead, to her left, to her right, and under her feet – from all sides, she was surrounded by greenery. Green bushes, green trees, green grass, and high above them, the blue heavens with the merciless scorching, sizzling ball of the sun.

"But, of course! I am in the park, where else could I be?"

Now she remembered everything. She went to the park with Richie, they were caught in the rain and then she desperately wanted to come back to the clearing, but it seemed she had got lost.

"No, wait... I got to the clearing, I saw the light... but what then..."

She knitted her brows, trying so hard to remember. Her mind refused to collaborate, locking up the memories of what had happened to her before she woke up in the cave with the black veil of emptiness.

Christine turned around and was now facing the entrance of the cave. She thought she saw something glimmering above it and went up on her tiptoes to see better. That didn't help. She took a few steps back and tiptoed once again – still nothing. She was moving backwards in tiny little steps.

"I must look where I step!" flashed through her mind as she lost her footing.

Unable to regain her balance, Christine tumbled down the earthen hill. Trees, leaves, sky, sun, ground; trees, more leaves, blue sky all flashed before her eyes. The sound of branches cracking mixed with a scream and the thud of her body hitting the ground resonated loudly in her ears as she fell. Her descent put each and every part of her body into contact with the bumpy and uneven surface of the hill. It didn't last long. At the bottom of the hill, her head met with the trunk of a tree. It all happened very fast; the impact, a dull moan.

Then the horror of the fall was replaced by the peaceful quiet of darkness.

Chapter 5:
Twenty-Four Is Too Many, Take One

June 21st, 1192
Nottingham Castle

That morning, John Wesley, the Sheriff of Nottingham, woke up earlier than usual. The bright colours of the dawn had just begun to take over the morning sky, and the Sheriff was already blissfully stretching his limbs.

He was a stocky man, aged just over fifty, height slightly below average, his physique was strong enough, but matched his age. His silver hair was cropped short not to attract unnecessary attention to an already receding hairline.

The Sheriff was lying in a giant bed that occupied a good third of his room. The remaining part of his room was also set with particular grandeur. A wide oak desk covered with various papers, a carved chair with velvet cushions, and a high chest of drawers were all decorated with elaborate patterns of the same style. On the side of the room, opposite the bed, there was a large fireplace, closed with a heavy fireguard, which occupied half the wall. Above it and all over the perimeter of the room, the walls were decorated with hunting spoils. These included the head of a deer, with huge branching antlers, and a wild boar with long, sharp teeth. The wild pig was a masterpiece, with an expression so fierce that, even stuffed and hung on the wall, the animal terrified those who visited the room. Animal skins covered the stone floor of his bedroom. The Sheriff was very proud of his trophies.

If there was nothing important planned for the morning, like the collection of taxes, or a meeting with the local nobility or an execution, Wesley preferred to luxuriate in his bed until noon, leaving the affairs of county to his most trusted person, right-hand man and commander-in-chief – Sir Guy of Gisborne.

But today, despite the early hour, the Sheriff lay in bed, straining his wide-set, slightly bulging eyes, at the curtain canopy stretched over the top of his bed. He lay wrapped in a warm duvet, stuffed with goose feathers, with only his head peeking out of this cosy cocoon.

Today was the day he had waited so long for. A few days ago, the Sheriff had received important news from London. Prince John and his associates, one of whom was, of course, the Sheriff of Nottingham, had finally put into action a new plan they had developed, to rid England of the Prince's brother – King Richard I.

The task ahead was not an easy one. Due to the constant attempts to take Richard's life, he was well-guarded. His men, spies, and supporters were scattered all over the country, so the scheme demanded comprehensive work and had been planned to the last detail. A letter that was delivered to the Sheriff via secure channels, said that some days ago, an assassin – specially trained in a distant country in the ancient arts of combat, alchemy, poisons, and others unknown in England – was making his way to Nottingham. The last lines of the letter, which according to long-established tradition was burned and scattered to the wind as soon as it was read, said that precisely today this person would arrive in Nottingham.

The Sheriff and his people were assigned an important role – to meet the assassin in Sherwood, supply him with food, fresh transport and anything else he may require, and to ensure his safe passage to Portsmouth, where he would board a ship sailing to Normandy. From there the assassin would make his way to the Holy Land. After that, the next link of this traitorous chain would come into action, but, unfortunately, the Sheriff was not aware of its role in the scheme. The Prince had planned everything so that the parties involved in the conspiracy only knew the specifics related to their part in his plan.

The Sheriff of Nottingham was a prudent and calculating man and would not have missed the opportunity to use this advantageous situation for his own selfish interests.

"Why not kill two birds with one stone?" he thought.

He was sure that no one would notice if the assassin extended his stay in Nottingham for an extra couple of days, and as a way of payment for the Sheriff's hospitality, would help him to get rid of that rather annoying forest outlaw – Robin Hood.

Driven by a desire to start this wonderful day as soon as possible, Wesley got out from under the covers, sat on the edge of the bed and lowered his muscular legs to the floor. But as soon as his toes touched the icy stone, he immediately jerked back, shivered all over, retreated back to his warm nest and curled up under the duvet.

The fire had died long ago, the room was cold and damp, and although duty called, the prospect of him getting out of the bed did not inspire great optimism. The Sheriff decided to delay that unpleasant moment a little longer. He made himself comfortable under the duvet and closed his eyes slightly. Drowsiness immediately overtook him.

"But how can I, on such an important day!" he flinched.

However, the early hours of the morning did their job and slowly the Sheriff began to sink back into a deep sleep.

"No, no, no! I cannot sleep!" trying to persuade himself, he sat up.

He leaned back against a pile of pillows and lowered his blanket down to the waist. The freshness and coolness of the morning did not give him much comfort, but at least, did not allow him to fall back to sleep.

"Gisborne should be in the castle by now," he thought.

He had urged his deputy, nay warned, his faithful servant to arrive at the castle as soon as the sun was up. The time had come for him to learn the details of the plan and about the important role assigned to him.

"Gisborne!" he shouted, stretching the word in his usual manner. A long echo rolled through the sleepy corridors of the castle, but to his great surprise, there was no answer. "Gisborne!" he repeated again, this time tersely, adding more volume to his already loud, and slightly hoarse voice. Patience had never been one of the Sheriff's virtues.

This time the door creaked softly, but the person who appeared on the threshold was not the one the Sheriff had expected to see. Yawning widely, the sleepy guard entered his bedchamber.

"Good morning, Your Grace," he said quietly. The guard bowed deeply to his master, who now with the face of a dissatisfied, capricious child sat on the bed. "Is anything the matter, Milord? You called."

He closed the door behind him and leaned against it. The poor man was barely awake and to stand straight without additional support was a rather difficult task for him.

"I did not call for you!" slammed the Sheriff as soon as the guard closed the door. "Where is Gisborne, huh?! Why is he not here yet?" he demanded, lounging on soft cushions.

The Sheriff could not understand why the castle was still a sleepy hollow when His Grace was already up and shining.

"My Lord, Sheriff, Sir Guy is yet to arrive," said the guard timidly. "But I'm sure he will be here soon. The sun is just beginning to rise, your grace," he added, not knowing how else to calm his raging master.

The Sheriff sat in silence for a while, drumming his fingers on the back of his hand. Noting that the guard at the door had begun to doze off, Wesley quietly cleared his throat, attracting the attention of the sleepy servant.

"Is there anything I can do?" the man started.

"Yes!" said the Sheriff, not even trying to conceal his annoyance. "Send people to Locksley, order them to bring that sleepyhead, Gisborne, here immediately," he commanded and then added in a soft and polite tone of voice uncommon to him. "There are some urgent matters that require his attention."

"Yes, your grace," the guard bowed and turned to leave.

"NOW!" the Sheriff had shouted so loudly that the man jumped in fright and barely maintained his balance, tripping over the threshold of the room.

The Sheriff threw off the blanket, sat up and swung his legs – he had to repeat his failed attempt to get out of bed. He picked up the hem of his nightdress, and, like a hare in a spring meadow, carefully jumped from one animal skin to another, trying not to step on the cold floor with his bare feet. He got to the window, where the picture that presented itself before his eyes would have taken any normal person's breath away; any normal person – but not the Sheriff of Nottingham.

The sun began to rise from behind the forest, illuminating the sky with the golden shades of dawn. It covered the tops of the trees, embracing Sherwood with its bright gleam.

But the Sheriff did not see this beauty. He was consumed by his dark thoughts, anticipating the success of the conceived plan.

"A plan so carefully developed will certainly deliver the desired results, I am sure of it. In a couple of months, Richard will be dealt with and then I will wallow in wealth, surrounded by gorgeous women."

The cool morning breeze swayed the tops of the trees and blew into his face. He could hear the castle gates open and horses gallop towards the city gates. Riders set off for Locksley.

"It's going to be a fine day!" the Sheriff muttered softly, with a crooked smile.

*****

As fast as the narrow forest paths allowed, four horsemen rushed, at high speed, through Sherwood towards the city of Nottingham. A man on a tall black stallion with heavy, freshly shod hooves, rode ahead of the group. The steed's long mane flew with the wind, occasionally whipping his rider in the face.

A match to his stallion, the horseman was dressed all in black: black leather pants, a jacket laced high at the neck, a long black coat and gloves; his feet were clad in high black riding boots with sharp, shiny spurs. If it was not for the fair skin that contrasted all that blackness, one might have thought that Death itself was riding through Sherwood.

Dark and slightly curly hair framed his tense face. The man galloped his stallion, mercilessly pushing sharp spurs into the sides of his raven horse – Sir Guy of Gisborne was not in a good mood!

During his years of service to the Sheriff, he had seen it all. He had suffered much humiliation and was used to the relatively careless and neglectful treatment he had received from his master. To some extent, he had developed immunity to it, but today the Sheriff had crossed the line.

Guy of Gisborne occupied several important posts among Nottingham's nobility. He was the Sheriff's deputy, his right-hand man, his chief-in-command and now the Earl of Huntingdon. How dare the Sheriff treat him like a page! How dare he send for him like this at the break of dawn and drag him out of bed? Gisborne knew perfectly well that he was supposed to arrive in Nottingham early in the morning and was already mounting his stallion when the castle guards arrived at Locksley with a message that, despite the early hour, his lordship, the Sheriff, was furious, for the simple reason that his deputy had not even tried to make an effort to comply with his order and arrive at the castle in time.

Left without parents at the age of sixteen, without a home and any means of existence, and with the burden of a younger sister, Guy had tried to make his way in life by any means possible. When he was twenty, he arranged his sister's marriage, yet to put it correctly, he practically sold her to a rich man twice her age. Now, at thirty-five, he knew he had acted wrongly, but at the time it had seemed the only choice.

Looking for a better life here and there, at the age of twenty-three, he ended up in the services of John Wesley, long before he became the Sheriff of Nottingham. Understanding the hopelessness of the lad's situation, Wesley had gladly taken Guy under his wing. But it was not only feelings of pity and fatherly love that induced him to do that. Wesley had placed great hopes on this young man and never forgot to remind him of that.

A few years later, Gisborne had gone from being a simple servant, engaged in all kinds of work, to being his confidant. Having spent some time on his education and training, Wesley had begun to entrust him with far more complex duties. Assignments of a 'private nature', as his patron used to refer to them. Assignments that needed to be kept in complete secrecy and executed with precision. Of course, Guy's services were generously rewarded. The young man could not even imagine that after all the vicissitudes and difficulties he had had to endure, that his life would finally take a more promising turn.

At first, Guy thought of Wesley as a noble and honest man and was immensely grateful to him for his guardianship, but just when the tasks assigned to him became more sensitive, Gisborne finally realised the essence of the man. Unfortunately, for him, this revelation had happened too late. Guy was tangled up in Wesley's intrigues, and, needless to say, he had had nowhere to retreat. He had no family, no real friends; no one to whom a young man could turn to for help or advice. Wesley, like a serpent, the tempter, continued to play him as a pawn in his game of chess, twirling him at his own pleasure, whispering his new plans into Guy's ears along with sweet promises of wealth and a title, in return for his valuable and faithful services.

Before reaching thirty, Gisborne had not only become Wesley's confident, but also his right-hand man and deputy, and also a man who sorted out all his problems. It was Gisborne who cleaned up after Wesley's messes and did all of his dirty work. He had become his sword, his undertaker. So, five years ago, with the faithful support of his faithful deputy, John Wesley was able to concoct a plot and, without spilling a drop of blood, as he proudly later said, became the Sheriff of Nottingham.

Having received the majority of votes at the Council of Nobility, Wesley was able to take his post and solemnly enter the Castle of Nottingham as the new head of the region. Such an outcome of the election, of course, would not have been possible if three of Wesley's main opponents had not met their ancestors a few days before the voting took place. Nobody knew of this, apart, of course, from Wesley and Gisborne, who did his best to assist them with their untimely passing.

Once he became the Sheriff of Nottingham, Wesley kept his promise and thanked Guy for his faithful services by transferring the village of Locksley to his ownership. Yet, for Gisborne it was just the beginning. At the time, he did not know about the Sheriff's association with Prince John and their ambitious plan to kill the King of England.

*****

The men rode out of the woods and galloped their horses towards the city gates by a wide road that split a barley field into two halves.

"Open up!" ordered Gisborne from afar.

The horses slowed their pace but did not stop. Seeing the approaching procession, the guards on the battlements hurried down to lower the drawbridge and open the heavy gates. With a soft creaking noise, the portcullis rose just high enough to allow the riders in and thundered to the ground as soon as the four crossed the city border.

Through the narrow, deserted streets of Nottingham, the horses galloped in the direction of the castle. As they rode into the castle square, Gisborne reined Raven slightly, threw his leg over the horse's head and swung himself off the saddle. Not saying a word, he handed the reins to one of the guards at the square and hurried up the steps leading to the castle. His cloak, like black wings, blew behind him. His servant, Allan A'Dale, tangling in his own feet, followed his master, trying to keep up.

The corridor. The stairs. Another corridor and another staircase.

"Why such a hurry?" pleaded Allan, having difficulty keeping up with his master. "We've come already. One minute will not make much of a difference," running after Gisborne, he jumped up several steps at a time.

"We were summoned," Gisborne said through clenched teeth. "Hurry up!"

When they finally reached the entrance to the Sheriff's bedchamber, Guy ordered his servant to wait, softly knocked on the door and, not waiting for an answer, entered the room.

"Good morning, Your Grace," he attempted his most calm and respectful tone. "You... demanded me to come immediately," Gisborne bowed his head.

He walked to the bed and leaned against one of the posters.

"Demanded?! Me?" the Sheriff looked genuinely surprised. "Not in the very least!"

Wesley was already fully dressed and in a good mood. Coming close to his servant, he looked at his grim face.

"Did you sleep well, my boy?" he asked nicely, looking up at Gisborne.

"I hope you did not drag me all the way here only to ask how I slept?" Guy replied, not even trying to hide his irritation.

"Manners, Gisborne, where are your manners?" he shook his head in disapproval, mocking his deputy, turned around and slowly danced toward the table.

"Sheriff!" snapped Gisborne.

"There-there, Gizzy, relax!" his playful mood vanished in a moment; the smile disappeared from his face.

Guy hated when the Sheriff addressed him in such a disrespectful way but said nothing, and clenched his teeth, trying not to show his anger.

"Come," the Sheriff said shortly and waved his head, inviting Gisborne to come closer to the table. "I have an important assignment for you," he began in a conspiratorial voice.

Guy moved closer to the table and stopped in his favourite pose – feet at shoulder width apart, tall, straight back, hands crossed on his chest. Dark, almost black locks curled around his tense face.

Trying to speak as quietly as possible, the Sheriff carefully and in full detail delivered to his deputy particulars of the plan developed by the Prince. A plan that, according to the letter that the Sheriff received, had been brought into action a week ago. A plan in which he, Gisborne, was assigned an important role.

The silence in the room was occasionally broken by the low rattling of Gisborne's metal spurs hitting the stone floor. Listening to the Sheriff, he shifted from one leg to another and the leather of his outer garment made a slight creaking sound.

Listening to his master, he shook his head several times and released a few tense sighs. Guy could not believe what he had just heard. Now it was clear why within the past few months the Sheriff so frequently absented himself from Nottingham and visited London. But why it was all kept from him in such a secret, he could not understand.

"Why did you not tell me about this before, my Lord?" His voice sounded a mixture of anger and hurt. "Do you not trust me? I thought that over the years I was able to prove to you my loyalty!"

"There, there, Gizzy, do not be like that," the Sheriff patted him on the shoulder. "Are you a young lady to be making scenes? I will have to limit your contact with Lady Marian, you're now becoming more like her!" said the Sheriff with sarcasm.

Identifying yet another sarcastic joke, Gisborne made an effort to stretch his lips in an attempt to smile. He did not find the Sheriff's banter in any way amusing.

"You know, if a lot of people are privy to a secret, it ceases to be a secret and we..." the Sheriff made himself comfortable in the chair by his desk, "and we, in our situation, do not need any leaks. Besides," he paused, leaning over a map that was spread out across his table, "if I had even the slightest doubt about your loyalty, trust me, you would have been hung already," he finished, not even lifting his eyes to Gisborne.

The last phrase sounded so calm and indifferent as if the Sheriff spoke of some routine business. An uneasy chill ran down Gisborne's back – he had his own reasons not to doubt the Sheriff's words. He shook off the thoughts and tried to focus on what his master was saying.

Well, to help to smuggle an assassin to Acre is fine, but the Sheriff's desire to use him to kill Robin Hood was a massive blow to Gisborne's ego.

"I can deal with Hood myself," he snapped angrily. "I do not need..."

"Blah-de-blah-de-blah..." the Sheriff interrupted him in his usual sarcastic manner. "If you are so capable," this time Wesley looked straight at Gisborne, the expression of his face changed. "If you are so capable, then why on earth is this outlaw not yet dangling with a rope around his neck, hm?! You are incompetent!" he hissed like a swamp viper. Having let off steam, he continued as if nothing had happened. "Now, how many people do you have?"

"Twenty-four," answered Gisborne, swallowing another insult.

"Twenty-four is too many," muttered the Sheriff.

"I can take..." Guy tried to continue, but was once again interrupted.

"Mmm..." the Sheriff drawled. "Still too many. Take one," he was now looking at the map, measuring out the distance. "Take that one... your boy... what's his name... John!" Wesley finally managed to remember.

"Allan," Guy corrected.

"... or him... you know better," the Sheriff answered, still consumed by his own thoughts, but then blurted out in his usual manner, "What the bloody difference does his name make? Take him and ride by the South Road to Sherwood's border," he ran his finger over the map, pointing out the direction. "There you will meet the assassin, and bring him here. I hope that is not so very difficult!?" he looked at Guy.

"As you wish, my lord," Guy bowed his head. "What does he look like?"

That, in the present moment, seemed like an appropriate question but nonetheless, the Sheriff was thunderstruck. Only now, Wesley realised the difficulty of the situation. He had been so consumed by the spy games and the conspiracy that he had forgotten to ask Prince John this tiny significant detail – a description of the assassin.

The Sheriff was silent.

"Sheriff?" amused, Guy raised his eyebrows.

"Erm... I do not know," he breathed out quietly, his bulging eyes darted from side to side.

"I beg your pardon?" Gisborne could not conceal his astonishment. "Whatever do you mean?"

"I don't know!" blurted out the Sheriff. "You ask me? As if there would be a crowd of people wandering around that part of the forest!" he said and then for a moment he was silent, picking at his short beard. "I'm sure you will figure that out, my boy. You have never let me down!" he added in a more amiable tone.

Guy silently turned to leave but stopped when a creaking voice spoke again.

"I do not doubt you for a moment, but! If you fail this..."

As Guy turned, he saw a malicious smile on his master's face, his fingers crossed together, forming prison bars, symbolising the fate that awaited Gisborne if he failed. Guy did not say anything; he simply bowed again and silently exited the room.

Allan was dozing quietly, just outside the door, leaning against the wall.

"Get up!" Gisborne kicked his servant lightly.

Startled, Allan jumped up to his feet.

"Agh! Is everything ok?" he looked around slightly concerned. "Are we still in favour? I got a little nervous when we were summoned like this. I wasn't sure, you know, if we would go from here straight into the dungeon," he chuckled.

"Watch your tongue!" Guy said roughly. "We have a job to do. Saddle the horses, we set off immediately," he headed towards the stairs.

"Immediately? What about breakfast?" protested Allan. "What work can there be done on an empty stomach?! And besides, I do not do hor…"

At these words, Gisborne turned sharply on his heel and in one giant leap was standing in front of his servant, like a huge mountain blocking the dim light of the corridor.

"Saddle my horse!" he snapped, scalding his servant with a fiery gaze.

Guy turned around and hurried down the stairs. His heavy footsteps echoed loudly in the morning silence of the castle.

*****

Gisborne waited for his servant to finally prepare their horses. Without fail, his dark figure attracted much attention. A tall handsome man, dressed, as always, all in black, standing in the middle of the castle's square. He proudly towered over all the guards and sentries, not to mention the ordinary peasants and servants, hurrying about their usual business, scurrying back and forth at this early hour. A new day had come to Nottingham.

Guy stood leaning against the scaffold, which was built in the centre of the square, right in front of the entrance to the castle. He held gloves in his right hand; the long, slender fingers of his left hand rested on the hilt of a large carved sword that hung on his side. From afar, one might have thought this figure was the epitome of peace and tranquility, but the reality was far from it. Clenched teeth, sharp cheekbones, and nostrils that flared widely with each breath, indicated the contrary. A wild storm raged inside him. The day had just begun and the Sheriff had already humiliated him twice.

"Oh, my time will come…" Gisborne tried to keep visibly calm. "Where the devil have you been?" he could not contain his temper any longer and shouted at Allan when the servant finally walked their horses out of the stables. "We should have left long ago."

"I picked up a bit of food," Allan patted the travel bag, attached to the saddle. "How can we travel without breakfast?" he asked once again with a tone of genuine surprise in his voice.

Guy rolled his eyes; he had had enough!

"We're not going for a picnic," he snapped and got up from his lounging position.

He took the reins from his servant, patted Raven's mane and led him to the gates.

"By the way," hurrying after his master, Allan asked suddenly, "where are we going?" he still did not know the purpose of their trip, which for him was very unusual.

"We are going," Gisborne quickly mounted into the saddle, "to the South Gates," he said, adjusting his cloak and making himself comfortable.

"South Gates?" Allan repeated after him. "But that's on the other side of Sherwood! It is at least..." he paused for some time, trying to calculate the distance, "two hours... or more?" he added, doubting his own words.

"Exactly!" barely restraining himself, Gisborne said and added, mimicking a respectful tone. "So, how about we get going? Shall we..." he made a gesture with his hand.

"Alright, alright," the servant said, climbing onto the saddle. "But I still can't understand why we're going there?"

"Will you shut up!" barked Gisborne and, abruptly turning his horse, rode off from the castle square and through the streets away from the castle, towards the city gates.

Allan, still not able to understand what exactly he had said to displease his master so much, obediently followed behind.

Chapter 6:
The South Gates

Leaving the city behind, the men galloped their horses into the forest. The light morning fog wrapped the field in its thin veil; everything was in a transparent haze. Having entered the woods, the riders slowed down a little but continued to spur the horses. They had a long journey ahead.

At the Big Stone, the forest trail split in two. The northern part went towards Locksley then, bypassing Nedelstoun village, stretched through the forest, and joined with the Portsmouth Road, which led to the southeast coast of England. Unlike it, the South Road led straight into the forest, skirting the village of Clun, and then a large forest lake. Its long, twisting ribbon ran deep into Sherwood and came out on the opposite side in a large clearing, which among the locals was known as the South Gates.

Most residents of Nottinghamshire preferred to use the northern route, due to its better placement and links with other roads and, of course, its security. The southern part of the forest was rough, hard to access and navigate; locals did not dare venture in further than the village of Clun or the forest lake. People also spoke of evil spirits that lived in those parts of Sherwood and often witnessed strange and unexplainable things. Even Robin and his men tried to avoid the South Gates and didn't visit the area without good reason to do so. According to the Sheriff's plan – it was a perfect place for a rendezvous! An assassin sent by Prince John would, without much difficulty, be able to get into Sherwood unnoticed. From there it would be up to Gisborne and his servant to ensure the assassin's safe passage to Nottingham.

*****

Neither of the riders uttered a single word on the journey. Much to the Sheriff's deputy's surprise and, perhaps, relief, his servant was silent and focused. The young man rode quietly, constantly looking around, hoping not to stumble upon a gang of forest outlaws. And, although he knew that Robin Hood rarely visited these parts, meeting with him today was the last thing he wanted.

After an hour and three-quarters of hard riding the men arrived at the South Gates – a large clearing, surrounded on all sides by tall trees. The sun had slowly risen above the forest, and was shining shyly through the young leaves.

Entrusting Allan with the difficult task of hiding the horses in the closest undergrowth, so that they were not seen from the clearing and the road, and the even more complex task of remaining quiet, Guy carefully walked around the perimeter of the clearing, looking for the best observation post. Finishing the rounds, he returned to his servant and sat on the trunk of a fallen tree, almost on the border of the forest.

He chose the perfect spot. As though on a huge throne, he made himself comfortable at the junction of two thick branches. He wasn't visible among the leaves but had a great view of the clearing and the only road that ran into it from the northeast side of his vantage point. Now, it was only a waiting game.

Allan finished tying up the horses to a young maple, he then sat at their feet and began to unpack his supplies. After a quick nibble, he gave water to the horses from a large leather flask and sat down again, leaning against the tree. The tension of the morning's adventures began to take a toll on him and in less than five minutes he was fast asleep.

He woke up to the sound of a soft rustle and immediately jumped to his feet. A twig snapped somewhere very close by. Blinking nervously, Allan looked around. There was no one near. Gisborne was also nowhere to be seen.

"Sir Guy?!" he called for his master quietly, but there was no answer.

Straining his eyes through the greenery of the forest, he called again, this time a little louder.

"Gu..." he only just managed before someone grabbed him firmly from behind. A large, strong palm covered his mouth.

A cold sweat broke out on his forehead; he could feel the sharp steel of a dagger poking into his ribs.

"Why the devil are you shouting?" a familiar voice whispered in his ear.

"Oh, Sir Guy! Thank God!" Allan freed himself from his master's hold. "You scared me to death!"

"I've told you, we're not here on a picnic," Gisborne managed through tightly clenched teeth. "Do you want the whole of Sherwood to know that we are here? You were told to keep quiet!"

"Well... I..." this hadn't often occurred, but Allan was lost for words. "Excuse me, Sir," he said at last. "By the way, you have not told me what we are doing here?"

"The Sheriff is expecting a guest," Guy said, trying to sound as calm as possible. "We are here to meet and escort him to Nottingham – very simple."

"Here? But no one is ever here!" Allan briefly paused then carried on cautiously. "Well, except for the wild animals and the evil spirits, of course," he added, and once again looked around. "Could they not find a better place for a meeting?"

"Above all people, they have forgotten to ask your opinion!" said Gisborne, cuttingly. "Go, take my place, I want to rest a while," Guy pushed him in the direction of the tree.

Muttering something under his breath, Allan turned towards the improvised observation post, but did not go far. A strange noise echoed through the forest. He stopped and shot a horrified glance at his master. In the silent peace of the morning forest, every sound was more pronounced and intense.

With hideous squeaks and screeching, a flock of bats, breaking through the forest, rushed in their direction. Gisborne barely managed to duck, and Allan, covering his head with his hands dropped to the ground like a sack of flour. With heart-rending cries, the creatures flew over their heads and headed towards the clearing.

"Wow! That is a bit extreme for so early in the morning!" as soon as things quieted down Allan rose up to his feet, still shaking and panting heavily.

"Quiet!" hissed Gisborne and pressed a finger to his lips. "There's someone here. Bats do not fly during the day; they sit in their caves and shelters. Someone has disturbed them. It may well be our guest," he said, looking around and very slowly, his fingers curled around the hilt of his heavy sword, gripping it tightly.

"Yeah? Well, you would know better," said the servant, with real fear in his eyes.

"Let's split up," ordered Gisborne and slowly began to move forward.

Somewhere to their left, not very far off, they heard a muffled sound, as if something heavy had rolled down a hill. Birds broke out from their seats and anxiously started to flounce about among the trees. Then there was a loud scream and a cry, the sound of something crashing through the branches and twigs, then another cry. Then some moments later, all went quiet.

For a while, the men stood in silence. Peering through the foliage, they tried to see anything through the green, but in vain. Anxious birds were still circling above their heads.

"Let's split up," quietly repeated Gisborne and made a sign to his servant.

The men drew their swords and, moving as quietly as possible, advanced in the direction where, a few moments ago, they heard the cry.

"Sir Guy," Allan whispered, moving the branch of a tree out of the way, "I think I see something."

Gisborne squinted but shook his head.

"No, over there, near the tree," the servant pointed in the opposite direction.

Guy turned his head and then finally understood what Allan was talking about. Under the tree, he saw a body.

"Go and check," he said almost inaudibly.

"Me?" Allan tried to protest but, meeting the stern gaze of his master, he obeyed.

Stepping very carefully, he went over to the body which lay on the ground. Gisborne watched intently; his gaze focused, the sword was out of its sheath – he was ready for any surprise. Allan circled around the person for a moment then glanced back at Gisborne and shook his head.

"Master! It's a woman!" he whispered as he came closer.

"A woman?" Gisborne repeated after him, surprised.

He looked through the foliage, trying to see the person lying under the tree, but could not see anything except their back.

"I think she's dead," Allan said cautiously.

"Are you sure?"

"Well, I didn't examine her too closely," stammered the servant. "But she's not moving, and I don't think she is breathing."

"Then go and check again," Guy pushed him towards the tree.

"Master, please!" begged Allan. "You know what people say about these parts of Sherwood... Let's go back to the clearing, meet who we need to meet and return to Nottingham. I do not like this place!"

"Enough of these tales and superstitions," Gisborne rolled his eyes.

He pushed his servant aside, and, without lowering his sword, cautiously moved forward. To his surprise, Allan was right. On the ground, by the base of the tree, a woman lay before him.

He walked closer very quietly and gently touched her with the tip of his sword; she did not move. Guy leaned forward in an attempt to see her face but it was hidden under her long dark locks; the woman was lying on her stomach. He knelt down beside her, then slowly and very carefully he turned her onto her back to face him.

Using his teeth, he pulled off his gloves and gently, barely touching her, brushed the hair from her face. For a while, he stared at her, studying her features. The woman's face was calm and still. In any other circumstances, he might have thought her quite beautiful, but right now, it was not possible to judge. Leaves and small twigs were sticking out from her long, tangled hair; her face was covered in scratches and dirt; a huge bump and bruise decorated her forehead.

"My God! She is alive!" Guy pulled back as he noticed a slight movement.

With every new breath, her chest was rising and falling slowly and imperceptibly. He reached out and caressed her cheek. In response to his touch, the woman slowly opened her eyes.

"Can you hear me?" he asked, looking at her face, but she didn't answer.

A pair of expressionless blue eyes looked back at him. Her gaze was empty.

*****

"Can you hear me?" he repeated.

The woman didn't answer but sighed heavily and closed her eyes. While his master was studying the woman, Allan cautiously crept closer.

"It's very strange," Gisborne looked around. "What is she doing here? The nearest village is far, and this..." he touched her forehead.

The woman shuddered at his touch and with a groan, turned her head away.

"I will move her there," Gisborne nodded his head in the direction of a fallen tree. "We cannot leave her here. Go to the nearest village and bring a cart. We'll wait here for the Sheriff's guest and then take both to Nottingham. The Sheriff will decide what to do with her," he said.

He carefully took the woman in his arms, she moaned softly as he picked her up. Every touch gave her much pain. He walked slowly, gently holding her. Allan helped as best as he could, clearing the way and pushing the branches of densely growing trees out of the way. Having reached the big tree, Gisborne laid the woman down on the grass.

"Now, quickly, to the village and back," he ordered, "and not a word to a single soul! Just keep your mouth shut altogether, do you understand me?" he added sternly.

"But, Milord, I never talk," Allan protested at first, but, realising it was not the best time to engage in long arguments, he untied the horse and quickly departed in the direction of the nearest village.

Guy returned to his post. He sat quietly, listening to every sound, mindfully watching the woodland, the meadow and occasionally throwing a quick glance at the woman that lay next to him. She hadn't regained consciousness, and only the slow rise and fall of her chest indicated that she was alive. The silence of the forest was occasionally broken by the cry of a lonely bird. Minute after minute slowly dragged by, it seemed as though time had stopped.

*****

He didn't know exactly how much time had passed since Allan departed. Only the sun that had risen above the forest and was now slowly sinking behind the tops of the trees on the other side of the clearing had served as an indication.

Finally, the silence around him was broken by the rustling sound of leaves and crackling noise of broken twigs and branches. Soon the cause of the noise appeared before him. Allan was moving fast through the trees, clearing the way as he walked with his sword.

"I... phew..." pausing after each word he said trying to catch his breath, "I... brought... a cart..."

Gisborne raised an eyebrow and opened his mouth to ask a question, but Allan was ahead of him.

"Do not worry, Sir. I was very careful!" still trying to steady his breath, Allan bent over, resting the palms of his hands against his knees. "Nobody saw me; there is no one in the woods! Robin and his gang are in Clun and will be there until the late evening. Today they are sharing their spoils with the villagers. All the people have gathered at the church. It was no problem for me to sneak in and out right under their noses," he finished feeling satisfied with his achievement.

"Well done!" Gisborne approvingly patted him on the shoulder.

"What about you, Sir? Have you met the person you were waiting for?" Allan looked around with interest. "I cannot see anyone..."

"No," Guy said, with noticeable disappointment. "No one except..." his gaze stopped at the sight of the woman lying on the grass. He paused. "No..." he muttered, "it cannot be..."

He refused to believe the thought that suddenly flashed through his mind, but the more he resisted, the stronger it grew inside him. His throat dried, his heart started beating rapidly and was now loudly pounding in his temples.

"No, no..." he staggered, not daring to tear his eyes from her.

In dismay, his face froze like a wax mask. If this woman was indeed the one they were sent to meet, the Sheriff would never forgive him if anything happened to her. Gisborne rubbed his sweaty neck, remembering the Sheriff's promise to send him to the dungeon if he failed. He tried his best to keep calm and brush away his dark thoughts.

"Master," Allan called softly, still not being able to understand what was happening. He had never seen Gisborne in such a state. "Master, what has happened? You look like you have seen a ghost," Gisborne was silent, still looking at the woman. Allan followed his gaze. "Do you think..." he paused and came closer. "Sir Guy, who was it that we were sent to meet here?" he asked bluntly.

Guy quickly repeated his morning conversation with the Sheriff, omitting, of course, the real reason for the assassin's arrival in Nottingham.

"Oh, dear Mother!" breathed out Allan. "The Prince... the assassination of Robin." He regretted asking the question in the first place.

He moved closer and leaned over the woman, and for a moment, he studied her face with interest.

"She looks," he trailed off, not being able to find the right word to describe her, "different, in a way, if you know what I mean..." he added after a short pause. "Definitely not one of the locals," he forced out of himself. "Just look at her clothes!"

Only now, did Guy understand what Allan was saying. He'd spent several hours with this woman and had not paid the slightest attention to what she was wearing. He was so focused on the purpose of their trip and the task assigned to him by the Sheriff that he had missed this important detail.

For a local person, the stranger would have been dressed very unusually. Trousers of an undetectable colour, that were too short and had been stained with dirt; a dark jacket which was torn at the shoulder. The shirt, cut tight to her body, was soaked through and covered with dirt to the point that it was impossible to determine its original colour. She was wearing high black riding boots.

"Yes..." he mumbled quietly.

He still could not believe this was happening to him. He knew that Prince John and the Sheriff were willing to resort to any tricks to get their way, but for Gisborne this, first and foremost, was another blow to his ego.

Two years ago, in the Holy Land, Robin Hood prevented him from killing King Richard. The attack had been planned down to the smallest detail. For a few months, under the pretext of severe illness, Gisborne had not left his house. The residents of Locksley village were strictly forbidden from visiting him or approaching the house, in order to avoid the spread of the disease. To add more credibility to the story, the Sheriff's personal physician had visited the "patient" every day. While this performance was played out in Nottingham, the master of Locksley had travelled to the Holy Land where, on the orders of Prince John and the Sheriff of Nottingham, he had made an attempt to assassinate Richard the First. Gisborne got so close to the successful completion of the task that, for the briefest of moments, he had allowed the success to overshadow his mind. His vigilance slipped and that was enough for Robin, who at the time was serving as the King's personal guard, to disrupt his plans. The Sheriff had been furious and only a miracle had saved Guy from his reprisal. But now, everything was different...

"How could the Prince employ a woman for such an important task!? Unbelievable!" he thought and added after a long pause, his mind still refusing to believe. "Maybe you're right... We need to get her back to the castle as soon as possible. I'm guessing you left the cart on the road?" he added in a slightly rude, but very familiar tone.

"Yes, Sir! You have seen yourself, the road through to the forest is very rough, I wouldn't have managed to get the cart anywhere near here," answered Allan.

"Alright. Take my horse," Gisborne ordered.

He carefully picked the woman up in his arms. She sighed loudly but made no other sound.

"Lead the way," he said through clenched teeth.

*****

A light, smooth, monotonous rocking had a soothing effect on Christine's completely confused consciousness. Her mind refused to register what was happening with her and to provide some, or at least any, reasonable explanation. She felt as if she was drifting on the high seas, recovering for a moment and then again losing her sense of reality.

She was making tremendous efforts, trying to swim up to the surface, only to, once again, plunge into the darkness of oblivion. After a while, she gave up her struggle and sunk back into the darkness.

*****

For the first time that day, Guy did not have to hurry anywhere. Sitting tall on his trusted stallion, he rode him slowly along the right side of the cart, shooting occasional glances at the woman that lay there, covered with his cloak. She neither moved nor regained consciousness. She occasionally shuddered and her eyes moved restlessly under the tight curtains of her eyelids.

"Did you say something, Sir?" Allan startled and nearly dropped the reins.

Sitting at the front of the cart, he had begun to doze off under the swaying movement of the wagon.

"I don't think we will get to Nottingham before dark," he continued without waiting for a response from his master.

"It is most important that we DO get there," said Guy. "Hold on tight to the reins and watch the road!"

*****

"... watch the road..." said a stern male voice.

Christine had surfaced back to reality. The fresh breeze caressed her face, bringing with it new smells of musty hay and wet wood, of fresh grass and fir-needle.

"Umm," wrinkling her nose Christine breathed out noisily, trying in vain to escape the smell of horse manure that sharply hit her nose. *"This smell could raise the dead..."* flashed through her mind. *"Richie... Why is he here? I took him back to the school..."*

She opened her eyes. The bright light blinded her for a moment. It hurt her eyes and she immediately closed them, but soon repeated the attempt, this time more slowly, carefully allowing the flow of bright light in. The first thing she saw as she opened her eyes was the high blue sky framed by the tops of tall young greens. Sparse fluffy clouds like huge pieces of cotton wool, floated above her.

Despite her confused state, and mesmerised by this beauty, she looked at the sky above her, not daring to take her eyes off it. Soon the sky to her right began to acquire a slight yellow-pinkish hue – the golden sun was going down behind the forest. It played in the leaves, releasing its bright sunbeams to run freely among the green trees.

"But of course, I'm in the park," a soft sigh of relief escaped her. *"But why am I rocking back and forth, and what is that strange sound?"*

Christine tried to raise herself up on one elbow, but her body hurt from the top of her head to the tips of her toes, even the slightest movement resulted in a sharp spasms of pain. She abandoned this idea and rolled her eyes around, looking around, yet trying to move as little as possible.

She was lying on a small wooden cart lined with straw; a heavy black cloak had been thrown over her. The strong strange smell that came from it reminded her of something, but what exactly she could not remember. Tall trees were slowly drifting past on her left-hand side. At the level of her eyes and ankles, large wooden wheels were squeaking softly as they span.

A man dressed in a leather vest worn over a light shirt with wide sleeves drove the cart. He sat at the edge facing the road. Christine couldn't see his face, only the back of his head with curly brown hair and ears, slightly sticking out in opposite directions.

On the right-hand side of the cart, she saw another man riding on a tall black stallion. He seemed young, but the tense, strained expression on his face spoke of the troubles and hardship he had seen in his life. Dressed in trousers and a jacket made of black leather, the rider sat proud in the saddle, keeping his high chest and broad shoulders in perfect posture. Dark hair framed his profile – strong, pronounced cheekbones, a defined chin, thin, as if a little tense, lips, a straight nose that seemed a little long, but gave its owner's profile a certain charm. The man was handsome and, judging by his proud posture, he was well aware of it!

Not able to control her mind, and not realising what she was doing, Christine was still staring at the rider, unable to take her eyes off him. The man rode in silence, consumed by his own thoughts, but then as if he felt he was being watched, he suddenly lowered his gaze. A pair of blue eyes met with hers. For a moment, they stared at one another.

"Mark also has beautiful bright eyes," thought Christine, *"but these...these are like bottomless lakes...and, oh those long, dark eyelashes."*

Alertness, curiosity, and surprise were in his eyes, as was tension and concern. His expression was cold, but there was something in his eyes, something different. Christine saw a small hint of sadness and tenderness that flashed deep within the eyes of the black rider.

Gisborne looked straight at her. Highlighted by the light of the setting sun, her big eyes changed in colour from blue to green. She was about to say something and opened her mouth when the cart's wheel bumped over a large rock. Allan had fallen asleep. The cart was thrown up onto a mound and shook Christine. Excruciating pain spread throughout her body – fear and a plea for help reflected in her eyes when the cart lifted off the ground. Then there was only pain.

She moaned softly and, descending back into oblivion, closed her eyes.

Having received a good slap from his master, for his carelessness, Allan decided it would be wise of him not to comment on the subject. He gripped the reins tighter and focused on the road ahead. It was still a long journey to Nottingham.

The sun slowly began to sink below the horizon.

*****

John Wesley spent all day in anticipation.

Since Gisborne and his servant had left the castle, he could not find any peace. To the great surprise of his servants, he refused breakfast. Quickly sorting out all the morning routines, he retired to his bedchamber where he stayed until lunch, pacing back and forth in anxious expectation.

"What if they meet someone? What if someone was eavesdropping?" his thoughts did not give him any rest.

In cases like this, one cannot be too careful and let down their guard even for a second. Oh, there was too much at stake.

"What if! What if? What if..." flashed through his mind. "Oh! What I am going to do with Gisborne if he fails me!" he muttered quietly, continuing to pace the room.

Excessive stress caused a terrible headache. His good mood from the morning was gone. Around two o'clock the Sheriff had moved to the dining room. He picked at a little piece of roast partridge, drank a glass of wine, and again retreated to his bedchamber.

Wesley was trying to sleep, read, sort out the maps and papers on his desk, but nothing could tear him away from thoughts of the two men who, early in the morning, had left Nottingham. He circled around his room from one end to the other about two hundred times, changing the length and speed of his steps as well as their direction – from right to left, then from left to right, diagonally, around the furniture and so on. Unable to find peace, he was like a wild animal, locked in a cage. Even the execution of one of the prisoners performed at sunset did not lighten his mood. With a completely indifferent face, he watched as the poor man was jerked up on the gallows, and then he retired again to his chambers. The Sheriff could not understand what was happening to him. Executions were the best sport and remedy and always worked for him. This caused serious impact on his, as it was, unpleasant mood, plunging him into an even greater gloom.

The sun went down. The evening began to settle over Nottingham, but the Sheriff continued to wait, standing by the window, anxiously peering into the darkness. The life of the castle slowly began to subside, so it could start again tomorrow.

Wesley startled. In the evening stillness, he heard the sound of approaching horses. Not wasting another second, he rushed out of his room. He couldn't wait to meet his guest of honour – the Prince's envoy. He came down the stairs and waited again but now it did not bother him much, today he had spent all day waiting, so a few more minutes wouldn't make much of a difference. Gleefully, he rubbed his hands in anticipation. His mood had begun to improve.

The guards had long closed and locked the gates and were peacefully talking, sitting on the empty barrels near the entrance. They had lit a flame in one of the barrels and were gathered around it to keep warm.

Finally, the sound of the horses could be heard behind the gates.

"Open up!" Gisborne's harsh tone boomed in the quiet of the night.

The guards began to move, fulfilling the order. With a squeaking sound, the cart, followed by the horseman, slowly entered the castle yard, the horse and his rider looked exhausted. As soon as the procession crossed the border of the castle square, the grille fell down behind them with a loud gnash.

Lightly and easily, like a summer butterfly, the Sheriff descended the stairs.

"What's with the transport?" he asked Gisborne, nodding his head toward the cart.

He no longer could, and did not really want to, conceal his excitement. Not waiting for his deputy's answer, he continued his interrogation.

"Well, Gisborne, where's my guest?" he asked. "Have you met him, hm? Where is he?"

"She..." said Guy. He paused after the first word and then continued. "She is in the cart."

"SHE?!" What did not seem an important designation in the first place, made the Sheriff jump up in surprise as soon as Guy repeated the word. "What do you mean "she"?!"

The castle square was lit by a dozen torches that hung on the walls around the perimeter. Snatching one of them, the Sheriff hurried back to the cart. Shedding light on the person inside the cart, he recoiled. A flood of swearing crashed down on Gisborne.

"What the bloody hell is going on here! Who the hell did you bring me?!" shouted the Sheriff. "Who I ask you...? Who, have I asked you to bring me, huh?!"

The silence in the square was broken only by the occasional snort of the horses and the ringing clatter of the Sheriff's boots caused by his hectic movements. In the darkness of the night, the light of his torch followed him, shifting from side to side.

"My Lord..." began Gisborne.

"To hell with my lord!" the Sheriff shouted, mocking him. He almost blurted out "Where's my assa..." before, gathering his senses. He covered his mouth with his hand and dragged Gisborne aside. "Where is my assassin?!" he hissed. "Why have you brought me this woman? Does she look like an assassin? A clue – NO! Who is she?! Where did you get her?" He would not calm down.

Guy quickly conveyed to the Sheriff what had happened to them in the forest near the South Gates.

"We stayed there for the whole day, my lord, but there was no one else except for her," he said. "I..." he tried to continue, but Wesley did not let him finish. He raised his hand, cutting off his deputy mid-sentence.

The Sheriff of Nottingham was silent. He was thinking, pulling on his short beard. His gaze was wandering aimlessly, his face tense. He was running the complex scheme through his head.

"Could Gisborne be right? Could she be the one we have been waiting for?" he thought. *"It is very unlikely, although I can't forget what happened last year..."*

The year before, Salah-ad-Din had sent a squad of deadly female mercenaries to kill his visiting nephew.

"...ugh... *that caused me too many troubles!* Very well, we will deal with her in the morning," he said at last.

The Sheriff walked to the cart and once again looked at the woman. She was as pale as snow and breathed heavily. Sweat had broken out on her forehead.

"Allan, here quickly!" ordered Wesley.

"I am here, your grace," said Allan jumping up to his feet. He had hoped that everyone had forgotten about him, and was sitting quietly on the ground behind the rear wheel of the cart, munching on some dry bread.

"Prepare the room, move her to the castle and get my personal physician here, quickly!" the Sheriff commanded. "Today you will stay in the castle," he turned to Gisborne, "tomorrow morning we will discuss everything and write to the Prince."

"As you wish, Milord," said Guy and bowed.

"Go rest, my boy. Tomorrow I will need you fresh and rested," the Sheriff patted him on the shoulder.

Gisborne did not have to be asked twice. The day had exhausted him. He bowed to his master once again and retired. However, he was not able to get to the room allocated to him in the castle as soon as he had wished to. His plans were not destined to be fulfilled just yet.

"Sir Guy," a familiar female voice called out as he was about to enter his room.

A young girl of no more than twenty, with large brown eyes, came into the light from the shadows of the doorway.

"Lady Marian?" he was genuinely surprised. "What are you doing here?"

On any other day, and in any other circumstances, Guy would have been very glad of her company, but now all that he wanted was to get to bed as soon as possible.

"It's late, why are you still up?" he asked.

"How can I sleep," she cooed in a tone as sweet as a dove. "The Sheriff is acting very strange today, you..." she moved close to him, "you and Allan have been absent since early morning. There is obviously something happening in the castle. What is going on, Sir Guy?" she put her hand on his shoulder and tried to peer into his eyes.

"Nothing," he said wearily in an unfriendly voice, with his whole being trying to resist her charms.

"Guy..." she said, trying again to catch his eyes.

"Nothing," he said more softly. "Nothing, that should concern your pretty head," he added, removing her hand from his shoulder. "You should not be here, go to your room."

"I've been to the dungeon to see my father," she said suddenly changing the subject. "The Sheriff is refusing to feed him, again. Sir Guy..."

"Marian, it's late," he interrupted her. "Tomorrow, I will speak with him, tomorrow," Gisborne clearly didn't have any intention of continuing this conversation. "Good night," he added, and entered his room.

The bolt on the door squeaked loudly as he locked it. His belt and sword crashed to the floor with a loud bang, his gloves and jacket landing next to them. He was too tired to remove his boots. Gisborne collapsed on the bed and fell asleep as soon as his head touched the pillow.

*****

With a loud, sharp gasp, Guy broke away from his nightmare. Breathing heavily, he sat on the bed, arms tightly wrapped around his sweaty head. The same dream had been haunting him for a long time now.

There were people, lots of them. They were all dead. He knew them all, every single one of them. He remembered their faces; faces of those he killed – men, women, children and elderly. He remembered the expression in their eyes, begging for mercy. Almost every night they came to him in his dreams. They stretched their dirty, cold hands towards him, trying to drag him with them into the darkness.

It had been almost a year since they first came to him in the night. Since then, he had learned how to deal with them, to turn off his feelings. But, despite the fact that in his rational mind he knew that it was only a dream, almost every night he revisited this nightmare and almost every night Guy of Gisborne woke up in a cold sweat.

This night was no exception, but tonight it was another dream.

He dreamed he was chasing after someone, rushing through Sherwood Forest on his raven stallion, and the ghosts following him, hovering, floating above the ground. They pursued him, stretching their cold hands towards him. The horse stumbled and Gisborne tumbled down. The next moment he was on the ground, unable to move. A man stood above him. Guy had never seen his face before, the man had a sword in his hands, the same sword that just moments ago, had been hanging on Guy's belt. With a heart-breaking cry, the man lowered his sword, piercing through Guy.

He was sitting on his bed still panting heavily. The blood throbbed in his temples; large drops of sweat covered his forehead. The summer night was stifling, and only occasionally a faint night wind blew in through the window. He washed his face with cold water. It took the edge off and made breathing easier. He pulled off his wet shirt, wiped his sweaty chest and back, and threw it on the floor.

He was tired and wanted to sleep, but was afraid that if he closed his eyes, the nightmare would come back again. He took off his boots, pulled the heavy blanket off the bed and lay down not covering himself, allowing the light breeze to cool his hot body. For some time, his tired eyes studied the pattern on the ceiling above his head. His mind wouldn't switch off, again and again reflecting on the day's events. His mind projected the face of the woman he had found today in the woods, her blue, almost transparent, bottomless eyes...

His body was still trying to fight off the tiredness and slumber, but with every breath, his eyelids grew heavier and heavier... He soon gave up and, not being able to open his eyes again, surrendered into the caring embrace of a deep sleep.

Chapter 7:
The Wait

Trying to remain unseen, Lady Marian Norton was making her way through the dark corridors of the castle in the direction of the stables. She couldn't be at peace until she knew what was going on. It was obvious that the Sheriff and his deputy, Guy of Gisborne, were once again up to something, but what exactly, she did not know and that frustrated her terribly.

Gisborne and his servant had been absent from the castle since early morning. They weren't seen in the training camp, or at his home in Locksley. To top it off, at this late hour the Sheriff's personal physician was summoned to the castle, although Wesley himself did not look unwell. This was all very strange indeed and didn't give her any peace of mind.

She did not succeed in her attempt to get any information out of Gisborne. He made it perfectly clear that he wouldn't discuss anything with her and, to say that he had looked terribly tired would have been an understatement. The man was shattered. Now there was only one way.

Moving silently along the walls of the dark, stony corridors, Marian got to the stairs and quickly went out into the courtyard. The guards were preoccupied with their gossip and paid no attention to the little shadow that briskly moved along the wall.

"Allan…" she called out quietly.

He had just finished undoing the horses' saddles and was getting ready to leave.

"Allan!" she called again, this time a little louder.

"Marian? What are you doing here?" he asked, surprised, and looked around. "They may see you! You know you are under house arrest here, not a guest. You shouldn't be here! The Sheriff…"

"No one will see me," she interrupted, "but if you are going to shout so loudly…" in her pleasant voice he could hear a tone of irritation. "We need to talk!" she said and moved to the far end of the stables, away from the castle guards, and made a sign beckoning Allan to come closer.

"Well, what is it, Marian?" said Allan, he wanted to protest but knew it was no use to argue with this stubborn young lady.

"Allan, there is something happening in the castle! I'm sure the Sheriff is plotting again. Where have you been all day? I tried to talk to Guy, but..." she chattered on. Her face looked worried.

"Marian, please calm down. My head hurts as it is!"

"Where were you all day?" her voice was now a demanding loud whisper. "I need to know! I'm sure it's about..."

"Oh, Marian, please, enough already. Stop looking for conspiracy and plots everywhere," prayed Allan. "The Sheriff sent Gisborne and me to meet someone, that's all. We went, we met, and we are back. And now..." he wanted to continue, but she didn't let him finish, interrupting him again mid-sentence.

"Meet? Who?" She refused to give up.

"I don't know all the specifics," Allan said quietly, still nervously looking around. "The Sheriff called us in this morning, then he sent us to the South Gates. There was..." Allan yawned loudly.

"What was there?" demanded Marian. "Allan, what was there?" she shook his shoulder.

"Mmm? What was I saying?" he was ready to doze off. "Oh, yes," he remembered finally, "we went to the South Gates. There was a woman."

"What?! A woman? What woman?" Marian's eyes widened. "Who is she?"

"Marian, how on earth should I know who she is?" Allan sighed. "The Sheriff sent us to meet someone, besides her there was no one else, so we brought her here."

"Allan, it's all very strange and suspicious..." she thought for a moment. "And then, what happened after? Why is the doctor here?" She gave him no rest.

"I do not know," Allan shrugged, "she was probably attacked or something. You know yourself what people say about those parts. When we found her, she was already that way. I mean, unconscious."

"Apparently, she must be very important for the Sheriff, if he sent for his physician at this late hour..." Marian trailed off; the lack of understanding frustrated her even more. "Allan, we must warn Robin!" she said after a short pause. "I am sure there is something going on! You should..."

"Uhh-uh," Allan interrupted her, "I, should do nothing!"

"How can you say that?" she was indignant. "You know the Sheriff! What if it's about the King? You should send a message to Robin!" she ordered, and added with a cute smile, "Please."

"The only thing I should do right now, Marian," Allan yawned again, "is to go to bed! And I suggest you do the same," he could hardly stand up straight. "Still neither the Sheriff nor Robin will be able to do anything until tomorrow," he finished, and walked away, leaving a bewildered Marian to stand in the middle of the stables.

*****

"I did everything I could, your grace," a man spoke behind Wesley.

The time was long past midnight, but the Sheriff did not have the slightest intention of going to bed. He stood by the window of his bedchamber, looking at the dark night sky. The stuffiness of the day had finally retreated, and he enjoyed the fresh coolness of the night breeze.

"Pray, do not tell me that she is dead," said Wesley not moving an inch, there was sarcasm in his tone.

"Oh, no, your grace, I did not mean it that way."

The Sheriff slowly turned to face his servant. He was a short man in his early fifties, who wore a long dark robe and a low velvet cap, and looked more like a priest than a doctor. He was still standing at the door, not daring and, perhaps not wanting, to come any closer.

"She's alive," he said and added after a brief pause, "at least for now. I think the next few days will be crucial."

"What do you mean few days?" the Sheriff's eyes flashed. "I need her tomorrow, conscious and with explanations!" he snapped.

"I understand your concern, your grace," said the doctor, "but there are things in this world that are beyond our control," he added philosophically. "I have treated her wounds," he continued slowly, giving the Sheriff an opportunity to digest the information. "With the exception of a large injury and a bruise on her forehead, the rest are just small scratches and cuts. I would not worry about them too much," he paused again and was silent for some time. "The left leg might be broken... there is a large bruise and swelling around the ankle, but it might also be just a bad sprain," he finished his report.

"Alright, alright," said the Sheriff a little calmer and, making a sign to the doctor that he could leave, returned to the window.

"There is something else, your grace," the physician said in a low voice.

The Sheriff said nothing, only tilted his head to one side and raised his eyebrows questioningly. The physician poked around in the folds of his gown, pulled out a piece of cold metal and handed it to the Sheriff.

"Here! It was on her arm," he said quietly.

"Nothing special," the Sheriff smiled back at him, briefly examining the object that was given to him, "an ordinary bracelet. What is the reason for such mystery over some trinket?" he was about to put it on his desk.

"No, you are wrong, your grace," this time the man spoke even more quietly. "This is drip silver! I understand a little in alloys and metal works, but I have never seen the melt and the finish like this, only heard about it. I believe this to be the work of masters from the East. You will not find anything like this in our parts."

"Hmm?" the Sheriff looked at the bracelet shaped into two intertwined snakes. "So, what does it tell us?"

"Well, I am not sure, however, on her back, there's also…"

"What's on her back?" this time the Sheriff could not conceal his interest. He walked closer. "What's on her back?" he asked again.

"A drawing!" the doctor whispered finally.

This Wesley had certainly not expected. Looking straight into his eyes, he softly echoed his words.

"The same snakes, your grace!"

Wesley paused, trying to comprehend what he had just heard.

"Perhaps, Gisborne was right to have decided to bring her to the castle," he thought. "I must see it!" he said at last.

*****

"This is getting rather interesting," Wesley finally said, after a long silence.

Mesmerised by the details of the drawing, his bulging eyes intensively studied the smooth bare skin of the woman's back. A little above the waist, under the base of the rib cage, two snakes connected by their tails formed a circle. Their bodies entwined in a twisted pattern, heads looking towards one another. The creatures' mouths were open, baring their yellow teeth; red tongues were sticking out in a warning. Each scale and crease of the snakeskin was carefully drawn. It seemed that a few seconds more and the drawing would come to life, and in the silence of the room, they would hear the threatening hisses of the snakes.

"Speak of this to no one!" the Sheriff mused, stroking his beard.

The physician gently lowered the woman back to the bed and adjusted the covers. Wesley walked slowly around the bed and peered into the woman's face. She was breathing heavily. Her face was pale; sweat broke on her forehead.

"I gave her some herbs to relieve the fever," said the servant, "and to help her to sleep."

"Yes, yes. Very well," mumbled the Sheriff quietly as he continued to pull his beard. *"Is she really… Unbelievable! I must immediately write to the Prince,"* the thought suddenly flashed through his mind. After a long pause the Sheriff turned to the doctor, "How long do you need to bring her to her senses?"

"With luck," he pointedly waved his hands, "I think three or four days. As I said, the next few days will be crucial."

"You have two days!" ordered the Sheriff. "And about this," he swung the bracelet on his finger and dropped it into the pocket of his robe, "and that," he nodded his head in the direction of the woman, "you speak to no one. Do you hear me, not a single word!"

"Rest assured, your grace," the man bowed respectfully.

"You answer to me with your head," said the Sheriff and went towards the exit. "Two days!" he said without turning his head.

He walked out of the door and went straight to his room. He should write to Prince John immediately!

*****

Morning greeted John Wesley, the Sheriff of Nottingham, at his desk in the company of a bottle of ink, a quill and the remnants of burnt candles.

He, once again, quickly re-read what he had written on a piece of paper. A short and, as it seemed to him, very clear letter, containing only a few lines. It thanked the Prince for sending a gift that, to the Sheriff's regrets, was slightly damaged on the way. However, he, the Sheriff, assured His Highness that it would be no trouble at all for him and his servants to repair the gift, bring it back to its full functioning order and to forward it on to its final recipient in the Holy Land. Proud of his ingenuity, Wesley folded the paper and was about to seal it, when someone knocked on the door.

"Who's there?" the Sheriff asked, hiding the letter among other papers scattered over his desk.

"It's me, your grace," Gisborne's voice came from behind the door.

The Sheriff got up and, leaping across the room with the ease of a forest deer, unlocked the door and let him in.

"Oh, you're just in time!" said the Sheriff, locking the door behind him. "Here, take a look," he handed the piece of folded paper to his deputy.

Guy read the contents several times. If he did not know what was going on in the first place, this message would have made absolutely no sense.

"Milord, are you certain that the Prince would understand what you intended to say?" he returned the piece of paper to the Sheriff.

"And what do you propose?" protested Wesley. "Do you want me to write openly? My dear Prince..." mocking his deputy, the Sheriff began to recite the alleged text, "the person you have sent to kill the King... You either are an idiot or have not slept well today!" he blurted out.

Melted wax slowly dripped onto the paper. Gisborne gritted his teeth. He knew how the Sheriff loved to tease and mock him, but these constant insults were now beyond any decency, not that decency was one of the Sheriff's virtues.

"Bring my messenger," Wesley said dryly when the wax that sealed the edges of the paper had finally cooled.

Gisborne did not answer; he bowed and walked out. After some time, he returned in the company of a puny young man dressed in leather pants, a heavy fabric jacket, and high boots; a small leather bag hung at his side.

"This," began the Sheriff giving him the sealed envelope, "you will take to London and deliver directly to His Highness – Prince John," he made a significant pause. "Do you understand? Directly to him!"

"Yes, your grace! Deliver it personally into his hands!" repeated the young man reassuringly.

"You ask the Prince to immediately write a response, and immediately, do you hear me, immediately return here. Do you understand? Immediately! You have one week," he handed a purse with coins to the messenger. "This is for the journey," said Wesley. The young man was about to open his mouth, but the Sheriff predicted his question. "You will get another when you are back with an answer."

The man put the letter in his bag, hid the money in his pocket and was gone.

"Come with me," said the Sheriff as soon as the messenger disappeared behind the door and his footsteps stopped echoing in the hallway.

After walking down a long corridor and making sure that no one was following or eavesdropping on their conversation, the Sheriff gently knocked on one of the doors located at the very end of the hallway. The sleepy physician opened the door.

"Good morning, your grace," he said, twisting his mouth in an attempt to overcome a yawn.

"Have you spent the night here?" the Sheriff asked in surprise and strolled inside the room.

"Yes, Sir, I did not want to leave her alone. Just in case," he replied.

"Well done! That's our man! Eh, Gisborne?" the Sheriff winked at his deputy and shook the physician's shoulder so hard that the poor fellow almost collapsed to the floor. "Well, how is our patient?" Wesley strode to the bed, impatiently rubbing his hands.

"I am afraid, not very good, your grace," said the physician. "She developed a fever several times during the night; I gave her some herbs and once again treated the wounds, to prevent any infection. For now, we can only wait."

"Okay, okay, you do your magic! You have another day to revive her," the Sheriff waved his hand, giving a sign to the man, that he was no longer needed and could return to his duties, but then changed his mind and called him back.

"Tell me, my boy, what do you think about this," Wesley called Gisborne closer and asked the physician to lift the woman off the bed.

Guy swallowed hard. He tried not to show his reaction, but the feelings were too strong for him to conceal. The blood rushed to his temples.

"Can she really be..."

The physician laid the woman back. Like a ghost, she was pale but even with this unnatural skin colour she looked very beautiful. The doctor had washed her face and hair. The scratches and cuts that yesterday were bright red, had paled and become almost invisible. She was beautiful, but her beauty was different – different from what he was used to seeing in the women and girls of nobility that often gathered at the receptions arranged by the Sheriff of Nottingham. It was as if some magical aura surrounded her. Something about her was different. She was different, but why and how he could not understand. Here she was lying in front of him – beautiful, quiet and peaceful – unlike the mercenaries whom he had met in the Holy Land.

"Hmm" Gisborne managed after a long pause.

"That's exactly what I say "Hmm"!" the Sheriff repeated after him. "You'd better tell me what you really think about it. Maybe," he shot a quick glance at the bed, "well, you know..."

The Sheriff knew that although his physician had never betrayed him, discussing questions like these openly in his presence was still a very dangerous affair.

"I do not know, Milord," said Guy, still lost for words, "to tell the truth, I have not met a woman with a tattoo before. Except for..."

"Exactly!" the Sheriff nearly jumped with excitement. "I have also thought about them," he added, meaning, of course, the Salah-ad-Din's mercenaries who visited them a year before. "So, maybe, you were right, my boy," he patted him on the shoulder, "maybe you were right."

Guy stretched his lips in the likeness of a smile. It was not very often Wesley indulged him with praise or a kind word.

"In any case, we will soon find out whether or not we are right," the Sheriff and his deputy headed for the door. "The letter to London is sent and now we cannot do anything but wait," he finished, walking into the corridor.

*****

As the men exited the room, a quick shadow rushed through the passage towards the dark aisle but even so, it had not escaped the Sheriff's sharp eyes. Not saying a single word, merely with small movements of his eyes, he gestured for Gisborne to check. What Wesley liked about his deputy most, was that after all the years of his service, Guy could understand him without words.

Stepping silently, Gisborne moved down the corridor toward the aisle. The shadow froze as if it was not there. Coming closer, the man slowly drew out his sword. A soft rattle of metal echoed through the quiet hallway. Guy ducked into the passage, deftly grabbing the person hiding there by the collar, not allowing the poor soul any chance for escape. But as quickly as he did this, just as quickly he jerked back. He unclenched his fist, his face expressed confusion mixed with horror.

"Lady Marian!" taking a few steps back, he lowered his sword.

"Oh God, your leper girlfriend is here again!" the Sheriff said behind him. "I'll leave you to it then. Find me when you're done," he was about to leave, but added, now turning to face the young girl. "And you, my dear, do not forget that you are not here on a sightseeing tour, but under house arrest! I urge you to restrict your movement around the castle unless you want to accompany your dear papa," his fingers clasped together representing prison cells. "My patience is not limitless!"

"What are you doing here?" asked Guy as soon as the Sheriff disappeared around the corner. "I could have killed you."

He sheathed his sword and, taking her hand in his, gently kissed her fingers.

"I... I..." she tried to come up with an explanation for her being in this part of the castle. "I got lost," she made an innocent face and tried to free her hand.

"Marian," he smiled.

Gisborne tilted his head to the side and looked at her. His face stretched into the triumphant smile of a cat that had been given a large bowl of cream.

"Do you think me a fool to believe this? What are you doing here?" he said, in a stricter voice.

"I, I was worried about you," she finally said, lowering her eyes.

It was an extreme measure that Marian resorted to only on rare occasions and in very important circumstances. Now, it seemed to her, was one of those times. She knew of Guy's feelings towards her, and, to some extent, she hated herself for playing with him, but there was no other way to extract from him the important information she was seeking.

"Last night you looked so upset and tired, I was worried," she looked at him with her big brown eyes and smiled sweetly.

Guy listened carefully, still holding her hand. It was obvious he enjoyed this very brief moment of closeness and had no intention of letting her go.

"And then as I passed by this door, I heard your voice and decided to wait for you here," innocence herself, she blinked a few times, flashing those long black lashes to add more value to her words.

The lie was played perfectly, the result was immediate, and Guy let down his guard. He stepped closer and placed another gentle kiss on her hand.

"I can't believe it is true... I've waited. I've believed that one day," he said softly, "my patience would be rewarded."

He slowly ran his fingers through her soft hair. Not realising it herself, Marian was trapped – caught in between the wall and a tall, strong man. His lips, longing for a kiss, moved closer to her face. Marian swallowed hard.

"Sir Guy!" his servant's voice called behind him.

Gisborne breathed out heavily – once again they were interrupted. His nostrils flared like those of a raging bull.

"What?! What do you want?" he said angrily. "Can't you see I'm a little busy?" It seemed to his master that Allan possessed the uncanny ability of arriving at the most inopportune moments!

"Uh, I think the Sheriff was looking for you, Sir," he replied, finally finding the words. "He is in the Great Hall."

Gisborne groaned and pressed his forehead against the wall.

That short moment of confusion was just enough for Lady Marian to get out of the awkward situation she had got herself into.

"We will continue our conversation," Guy said with a slight, respectful bow and, placing another kiss on her hand, turned sharply on his heel and walked away.

"He almost got you!" Allan chuckled softly when his master disappeared around the corner.

"Phew!" the girl could barely utter. "That was close! Thank you for coming to my rescue, Allan. But you know he will be very angry with you when he finds out that you have lied to him."

"Nah, it's fine, I am sure the Sheriff would have wanted him anyway. But next time you should be more careful, only if, of course, you do not want to find yourself at the altar in a wedding dress," the young man laughed louder.

"But I've learned something!" Marian said proudly, ignoring his comment. "The Sheriff wrote a letter to the Prince. We must warn Robin, and intercept..."

"Oh no! Here we go again," Allan said disappointedly. "Stop playing these games, Marian, or, I'm telling you, it will be the end of you."

Allan shook his head and went to find his master. Marian had no other choice but to return to her room and spend the rest of the morning there.

*****

Will Scarlet rushed through the forest from his observation point back to the outlaws' forest hideout, skilfully jumping over stumps and fallen trees. At twenty years of age, he was the youngest of the gang and often was entrusted with the task of monitoring the forest roads. His sharp eye and sensitive ears had never failed him. And so, this time – as in many others – noticing a lonely rider on a hill, Will raced back to camp to warn the others.

"Robin! Little John, Friar!" he called as soon as he ran into a grotto hidden amongst the forest green.

The outlaws' residence consisted of several makeshift rooms. Kitchen, bedroom and the lounge that occupied a large part of the cave; in the depths of the cave was arranged a small storage room that stored food supplies, quivers with arrows and heavier weapons.

Friar Tuck was busy preparing breakfast; Robin and John were working out a plan to rob a food wagon that was set to arrive in Nottingham in a few days' time. The men were so engaged with their tasks that they did not hear Will the first time he called.

"Robin!" Will called again. "There is a rider on the northern side of the trail, he is coming our way," he said. Robin got up from his seat. "I think that in ten minutes or so he will be at the Big Stone. We can easily check what's in his pockets," he suggested.

"Alone?" Robin asked surprised.

"Yes! No guards, no convoy," said Will, still trying to catch his breath.

"Good!" said Robin. "John, you come with me. Friar, you stay here and look after the camp... and our breakfast!" Robin winked at him.

Little John took his favourite weapon – a huge cudgel, Robin took a quiver of arrows and attached a small dagger to his belt.

"Lead the way!" he said when the three men came out of the grotto.

The half-asleep messenger rode slowly, cursing himself for not being able to negotiate with the Sheriff for more time for his trip. Now he'd have to ride day and night, making only small stops in order to get to London and back in time.

And so, he rode, absorbed in his thoughts, when out of nowhere, a man wearing a dark green jacket appeared before him. A large hood was covering a good part of his face. Next to him were two more men. One – a hairy manly figure, in his forties, who in appearance more resembled a bear than a man; the second – much younger, tall and thin as a reed in the swamp, and it seemed that if the wind blew a little stronger, the young man would break in half.

Without a doubt, the messenger knew who was standing before him.

"Greetings to you, my good man!" said the man in the hood cheerfully. "I am Robin Hood, and these are my friends!" he nodded towards the people accompanying him. "On this wonderful day, I would like to tempt you with an interesting offer."

The rider sighed heavily; he did not want to listen to any offers, but to continue his journey as soon as possible.

"So!" continued Robin. "Because it's a lovely day and I am in a very good mood," he said, smiling broadly, "I will give you a choice. Option one – you now will give us a third of what you have and we let you go in peace. Option two – you resist, and we will take everything! The choice is yours!"

"Go to hell!" cursed the horseman.

He tried to spur the horse, but the animal was not able to move – the big man gripped the reins tightly with his huge hand.

"As you wish, my good man," Robin mimicked a bow. "Let that be all!"

He made a sign to his friends, and in a fraction of a second, the rider was knocked to the ground and held there by Little John. Will quickly worked his way through his pockets.

"Let me go, you bastards!" fumed the man. "You will pay for this! You will be hanged!"

"I think I've heard it before!" laughed Little John, carrying on with the task.

As they finished examining his pockets, Will handed Robin a small purse.

"Just this," he said slightly confused.

"Yeah, not much," uttered Robin and added, speaking to the man, who was spitting angry curses at them. "Why are you, my dear Sir, traveling light?" he bounced the purse of coins in his palm. "Let's see if he is hiding anything in his boots. Or pants."

"Seems to me, there is not much in his pants either!" Little John looked at the bottom of the man's body and winking to his friends burst out laughing.

"Let me go! How dare you!" protested the man struggling with futile attempts to free himself. "I'm just a messenger, I'm going to London!" he shouted, but as soon as the words had flown out of his mouth, he immediately regretted them.

"Messenger?" repeated Robin. "Well, why did you not say so before, my dear friend!" he grinned. "And pray by whom, and why, have you been sent to London?"

Robin went to the horse that was now tied to a nearby tree. It was not too much trouble for him to find the sealed letter, hidden in the folds of the messenger's leather saddle.

"You can't open it!" cried the messenger, desperately. "You, you... you'll be hung!" the man whispered as the red seal cracked and crumbled.

"Me? No. You – yes!" Robin winked at him and unfolded the letter.

*****

"I do not understand," Robin ran his eyes over the text of the letter several times. "It doesn't make any sense," he held the sheet of paper out to John, but he only shrugged, the big man could not read.

"What does it mean? Who are you taking it to?" demanded Robin, knowing perfectly that this message could only have one recipient.

"To Prince John," the man whispered.

There was no point in denying it any further, the letter was opened and read. The messenger ceased his struggles and, with a heavy sigh, exhausted, he sprawled on the ground.

"What instructions do you have from the Sheriff?" Robin asked after a brief pause.

"I have to deliver it personally to the Prince, wait for an answer, and return to Nottingham," said the messenger.

"Very well! You do exactly that," said Robin, not paying the slightest attention to the paling, fearful face of the messenger.

"How..." he mumbled. "How exactly do you expect me to do that? The letter is opened! I will be hung!" he knew too well what fate awaited him now.

"Do not worry about that," said Robin, helping the man to his feet. "We can fix it! But..." he looked into his eyes. "On one condition! I want to see the answer before the Sheriff," he held out his hand to the man.

The remaining blood drained from the messenger's face, as if not a living person, but a ghost, stood before Robin. He looked at him horrified but his shaking hand instinctively reached forward and answered the handshake.

Two hours later, the letter was sealed and returned to the messenger. The man, still barely comprehending what had happened, climbed on his horse and rode off.

The countdown had begun. Before him lay the most uneasy task of getting to London and back in seven days – there was not a minute to lose.

*****

Having discussed the content of the letter with the other members of the gang, Robin had decided it would be wise to speak with Marian as well. Although she was in the castle under house arrest, she was still a very valuable asset and might have important information.

It was not difficult for him to get into Nottingham unnoticed and quietly slip into the castle. Wasting no time, Robin went straight to Marian's room and was very surprised not to find the girl there. With nothing else to do, he sat on a chair at the back of the room and waited.

He didn't have to wait long. Very soon, he heard light footsteps in the hall – someone hurriedly approached the room. A moment after he could hear louder and much heavier footsteps. Just outside the door, he heard two voices.

"Lady Marian, this morning we could not finish our conversation," said a male voice. "I would like to..."

"Again he is trying it on with Marian!" inside the room Robin made a displeased face.

"Sir Guy, please, do not continue," the girl answered. "I... I'm a little tired and need rest."

Robin tensed as the door began to open. If Gisborne came in along with Marian, which was very unlikely, although anything could be expected from that bastard, he would be noticed immediately. In a single heartbeat he crossed the room, and hid behind the door; where he would be harder to see, and, if need be, he would have more chances for escape.

"Sir Guy, please," the door opened and Marian quickly slipped inside the room, shutting the door right in Gisborne's face.

On the other side of the door, there was a sigh of disappointed irritation, followed by the sound of retreating footsteps. Marian sighed with relief. This time she was able to escape, but Gisborne would not stop in his attempts.

"What, been flirting with Gisborne again?" very close to her ear she heard a familiar whisper. "You are going to make me jealous!"

"Robin!" she threw herself on him. "You have no idea how glad I am to see you!" she kissed his cheek. "We need to talk!"

"Hmm," he stepped back and made a stern face, but his eyes still smiled cheerfully. "Judging by how you greet me," he rubbed the cheek just visited by her lips, "you have not missed me much."

Marian came closer, gently threw one arm around his neck and caressed his stubbled cheek with another.

"Is that any better?" she asked, barely touching his lips with hers.

"Not sure I understood," he purred in response. "I think we will need to try again, just to be sure."

He wrapped his arm around her waist pulling her closer to him. Their lips met again.

"Mmm, that is so much better, my love," he whispered, enjoying the kiss. He sat her on his lap as soon as their lips parted. "You have no idea, how much I want this all to end as soon as possible, so we can finally be married. I cannot think of you being here alone when you could be with me. And especially with that one!" Robin nodded towards the door. "Crowing over you."

"The Sheriff does not talk to me much," she responded as if she had not understood what he was talking about. "And then, you know..."

"I'm not talking about the Sheriff," Robin interrupted, suddenly his face was serious. "I hate to think that you are flirting with Gisborne. Him living in my estate is bad enough, I could not bear it if he gets my girl too!"

"Oh, Robin of Locksley!" she hugged him again. "Do I, once again, detect notes of jealousy in your voice? You know that Sir Guy does not mean anything to me. Although, if you get to know him a little better, he is not as bad as he seems. And again," Marian made a dreamy face, "I cannot deny that he is very good looking and knows how to please a girl," she added, teasing Robin.

Robin gritted his teeth in anger. He knew that Marian was playing with him, but he could not contain himself all the same.

"I did not come here to discuss the virtues of your boyfriend!" he said through clenched teeth, resentment in his voice. "I need to know what's going on in the castle."

He guided her to the window, away from the door, and trying to speak as quietly as possible, repeated the content of the letter that he and his men had intercepted earlier. Marian's face became anxious.

"Yes, you are right; the letter doesn't really make any sense. If only..."

Robin listened to what she was able to find out from Allan about his and Gisborne's trip to the forest, and the woman that they had brought to the castle.

"Allan said that she was unconscious when they found her. Apparently, someone attacked her. Do you know anything about that?" she asked, and then continued. "The Sheriff's doctor is here and since yesterday evening has not left the room where she is kept. And this morning I overheard the Sheriff and Gisborne talking about this letter. The rest you know already."

Robin didn't answer. The young man was thinking, trying to process the information he had just received.

"What if?" he said quietly and then exclaimed. "Well, of course! Now everything has fallen into place. We make a good team, you and I!" he patted her on the shoulder, but she looked at him blankly.

"Can you, please, explain, I don't understand."

"The letter mentioned the gift that was damaged, right? You said that Gisborne had brought a woman from the forest, and she is still unconscious?"

Marian continued to stare at him helplessly.

"The Sheriff promises to send the package to the Holy Land, to the final recipient," Robin continued.

At first, Marian just shrugged her shoulders, but then she slowly began to understand what he was referring to.

"You think they mean to send her to the Holy Land?" asked Marian. "But why? What will she do there?"

"Well, certainly not to sing him a happy birthday song," Robin quipped in response.

"Who to, Robin? Who is he? I'm completely lost now!" she pleaded and paused, but then it finally occurred to her. "Do you think they want her to kill Richard?" not daring to believe her own thoughts, Marian asked fearfully. "Uh, the Sheriff is a snake! And Guy!" she sighed with disappointment.

"That's right, your dear, good man," teased Robin.

"We must stop them!" she jumped up, ready to rush into battle that very instant.

"Not so fast, my love," Robin stopped her, "for now it's only speculation; we don't have any evidence."

"I'll get the evidence!" she said, not a hint of doubt in her voice.

"No, you must not interfere. If what we assume is right and they are actually planning to murder the King, it could be very dangerous," Robin looked worried. "I think that you shouldn't stay here, let alone get involved with this business. Today or tomorrow you must leave the castle."

"And where would I go, Robin? With you, to the forest?" she said with a sad smile. "You know, I cannot do that. And then," the tears sparkled in her eyes, "do not forget that my father is in prison. The Sheriff..." she paused. "I do not even want to think what he would do to him if I run away," she buried her face in his shoulder and cried softly.

"Don't worry, my love," Robin soothed her.

It hurt him to see her like this, but there was little he could do. Marian was right, she could not leave the castle while her father was in the dungeon.

"I'm sure we'll figure something out. We will stop the Sheriff and Gisborne, and help Richard get back to England. And then," he wiped her tears and took her face in his hands, "and then we will get married! And you will become the Lady of Locksley," he kissed her.

"Unless, of course, you carry on flirting with Gisborne! In that case, you have a very good chance of becoming the lady of the manor well before Richard returns from the Holy Land," he chuckled and winked at her.

"Oh, I love you, Robin of Locksley," she sniffed and hugged him, laughing softly. "I will keep an eye on what's happening at the castle and try to give you news, if there is anything important."

"No, you stay out of it, it's not safe," Robin quietly opened the door and looked out, assessing the situation. "Just watch and listen. I'll see you in a couple of days," he gently kissed her nose and disappeared into the darkness of the corridor.

*****

Gisborne silently stood by the bed. The woman, who four days ago he had brought from Sherwood Forest, was still lying motionless. Despite all the reassurances and promises of the Sheriff's physician, nothing had changed. As on that morning when Wesley had shown him her tattoo, she breathed slowly and evenly, without showing any signs of improvement.

Sometimes he saw her eyelids twitching, sometimes her body shook and trembled all over, but she hadn't once regained consciousness. The huge bump on her forehead was healing and now it was just a big bruise that had begun to fade.

Four days had passed since he had brought her from the woods, four long days and even longer nights. That night, when they returned from the South Gates with this unusual cargo, was the first time that he dreamt of his death. He felt these events were somehow connected. His nightmare returned again and again. Every night Guy died, pierced by his own sword, just so that in the morning he would come to this room and wait... wait for when she would finally open her eyes. He did not know who she was and where she came from, but he was convinced that she would have answers.

Gisborne startled when the door creaked loudly behind him.

"Ah! You're here again!" said the Sheriff's croaking and nasty voice. "If I didn't know of your *"passion tendre"* for our dear Lady Marian," he added, mimicking a strong French accent, "I would have thought you'd fallen in love, Gizzy."

Guy tried not to react to this insulting comment, only his nostrils unwillingly flared out. There was so much he wanted to say to the Sheriff but he swallowed his words calmly. And now, as always, he simply stretched his lips into a faint smile and walked away gracefully. He stood by the wall, leaning heavily against it, his arms crossed on his chest.

"Well, how is our patient?"

The Sheriff leaned over the bed. He was hoping to see some progress but over the past four days, nothing had changed. At that moment, the doctor entered the room.

"Aha! Just the man I need!" the Sheriff rubbed his hands. "What news do you have for me?"

"I'm afraid there is nothing new," the man replied.

An unpleasant silence fell in the room, the tension that was building up over the past few days, was now creeping towards its climax. The Sheriff's patience was wearing thin and today it had reached its limit. Wesley exploded.

"For the past four days, this is all I've heard!" he shouted.

"She is getting better. I just need a little more time," said the physician, in an apologetic tone. "You can see for yourself, my lord…"

"I see nothing!" stormed the Sheriff. "You promised me two days, it's been four now and you keep telling me…"

"Your Grace," a soft voice behind interrupted him in mid-sentence.

"What?!" the Sheriff shouted, hysterically turning to face his distraction.

The startled guard jumped in surprise and dropped his axe. The room immediately filled with the loud crash of metal hitting the bare stone. Despite the clatter of metal, Gisborne had not taken his eyes off of the woman and thought that – for a fraction of a second – she had opened her eyes.

"Did she really…" he thought startled but another hysterical cry from the Sheriff distracted him from these thoughts.

"What?!" Wesley shouted again.

"There… there…" stammering, the man tried to answer.

"Fire?! Flood?! What is there?!" he demanded. "Stop mumbling!"

"It's Lady Marian, m-m-Milord. She says she urgently needs to speak with you," he finally managed to squeeze the words out of himself.

"Oh, for the love of God!" the Sheriff threw up his hands. "It is worse than any fire or a flood! Gizzy, deal with her!" he ordered.

Gisborne bowed and silently exited the room.

Despite his tender feelings for Marian, her timing now could not be any worse. He could not and did not really want to speak with her right at this instant. Longing to get back into the room, he quickly explained to her that His Grace, the Sheriff, was very busy and would not be able to deal with the improvement of the quality of her father's stay in the castle's prison at the moment. Guy then returned to the room and closed the door right in Lady Marian's curious face. She had tried to peek inside, but except for the Sheriff's angry face, she could not see anything.

Locking the door behind him, Gisborne returned to his previous spot and, not saying a single word, rested his back against the wall, calmly watching what was happening before him, trying to ignore the ear-piercing cries of the Sheriff.

Chapter 8:
You Almost Fooled Me!

Her confused mind continued to play games.

Christine was regaining consciousness and then once again, sinking deep into oblivion. When the misty veil in her mind gradually faded, she thought she could hear sounds and voices, but then all was silent yet again.

A dim light flickered through her eyelids, but some seconds later, everything plunged back into darkness. Shadows and images like wild sea waves crashed towards her, consuming her entire being, then slowly retreating. A huge, giant, dragon-like monster crept closer and closer from the depths of her consciousness. His eyes burned with cold fire, his jaws with sharp crooked teeth spewed a horrible stench.

She ran through the dark and endless corridors to the light, not knowing where she was or where she was running to. The passages were lined with doors on both sides, and she pushed them as she ran, trying to find a place to hide away from the monster, but the doors wouldn't open. She ran towards the light but no matter how long and how fast she ran, she couldn't reach it. The darkness around her, like a living being, thickened and grew stronger. The beast chased her; another second and it would catch up with her and tear her apart.

Finally, one of the doors opened, Christine slipped inside and slammed it right on the monster's muzzle. She leaned against the salutary metal barrier that separated her and the bloodthirsty creature.

Bang! She was knocked to the floor but quickly jumped to her feet and ran back to the door. Blow, another blow. She clung tightly to the door, realising deep inside that she didn't have the strength to withstand this monster. She was too tired. She could hear the rattle of its claws, tearing the door from the other side. The room around her filled with the sound of the metal pieces clattering across the stone floor. With a wild roar that echoed like thunder, the creature burst into the room.

Christine flung her eyes open. The bright light blinded her instantly, forcing her to immediately close them again. She was breathing heavily.

"It was a dream! It was just a bad dream."

Now, she could clearly hear voices around her, she was no longer alone. Not daring to open her eyes just yet, she listened cautiously.

"… stop mumbling!" said a gruff male voice.

Another voice, a very quiet one, spoke back but she could not make out the words.

"… deal with her!" the same voice spoke again.

Then she heard footsteps, some rattle, and clatter, and then there was silence; but it did not last long. Christine could hear the same rough voice talking again, but talking much more quietly now in a low whisper, and then it was joined by another voice. They spoke too quietly for her to understand what they were talking about. She, once again, heard the soft creak, then heavy footsteps, and then all was quiet.

She tried to open her eyes but it was easier said than done. Having been closed for several days, they hurt from the bright daylight. Trying not to move and not to attract unnecessary attention, she peeked through her slightly opened eyelids.

She was lying on a bed in an unfamiliar room. Right in front of her, with his back to the wall, stood a tall man dressed in black. His tense face seemed familiar, but she couldn't remember where she had seen him before. He stood calm and motionless, arms folded on his chest, as though he were at the theatre, watching an action scene playing out before him.

The available view didn't give her the full picture of the room, but she could see and hear the two other men who were wearing strange, or better to say, old-fashioned clothes. A short-haired, slightly chubby man of medium height, with an expression of great annoyance, was swiftly moving around the room. Muttering something, the man was restlessly shifting about the perimeter, occasionally addressing the others present, in a harsh tone.

Several times he ran up to the bed, staring at Christine's face and listening to her breathing. Each time he did so, she froze and almost stopped breathing.

"Well, when is she going to wake up, huh?!" he once again asked loudly, looking straight into her face.

It was so unexpected that Christine almost jumped up but quickly managed to pull herself together; she was determined not to "wake up" until she understood what on earth was going on. The man continued to measure the room with quick steps. The others present didn't really pay much attention to his obvious struggle, which apparently annoyed him even more.

"Why? I am asking you, why does she not wake up, hm?!" he asked again and this time it seemed the question was addressed to himself.

He ran to the tall man, a question in his eyes. The man in black neither moved, nor changed his position, his eyebrow rose slightly. He heard the question but, unfortunately for his interrogator, he didn't have the answer.

"Both of you, come with me!" said the little man, hardly restraining his anger and irritation. "I have a burning desire to chop someone's head off!" he added passionately.

The face of the second small man in strange clothes changed instantly. The blood drained from him, the man became as white as chalk, but the one who was pacing the room reassured him.

"No, not to you, don't be afraid! I can still find some use for you," the rude man patted him on the shoulder. "Who do we have next?" he said, rubbing his hands impatiently as he turned to the man in black, who still stood motionless, leaning against the wall.

Soon the trio exited the room and closed the door firmly behind them. The room fell silent. When the noise of their steps faded in the corridor, Christine opened her eyes, lifted herself up on one elbow and looked around.

"Where am I? Who are these people? What the hell is going on here?!"

*****

With a quiet groan, she sat up and looked around.

Pain swept through her body – arms and legs ached, the merciless drums clattered in her head like hammers in a forge. She ran her fingers over her body, checking every limb, and to her surprise, except the slight bump on the forehead and tons of bruises that covered her legs and arms, there was no greater damage; but her body ached like hell. She didn't know where she was, how much time she'd spent here, and most importantly how she had got here; the room was unfamiliar and looked very strange.

It wasn't big but was spacious enough. There was no wallpaper or paint or any other décor, stone walls and a ceiling surrounded her. Except for the few candlesticks and torches that hung around the perimeter of the room, she was surrounded by bare grey stone; smoothly hewn, polished, grey stone. A table, a few chairs, one of which was covered with a pile of rugs, a large fireplace with a dying fire – that was the setting. The fireplace had a familiar smell that brought back memories of her childhood, memories of cold winters when her mother would light the fire with wooden logs, those long gone, distant memories.

A big window was to her right. It looked, however, more like a hole in the wall that someone had forgotten to lay with stone. There were no frames, no glass, no curtains, but a big wooden shutter-like panel lay on the floor next to it. Expecting that the window would be able to offer her some sort of clue as to her whereabouts, she headed towards it.

Her first attempt to get up on her feet failed. She felt dizzy and, losing her balance, plopped back onto the bed. Luckily, a fluffy mattress softened her landing. She repeated the attempt, this time trying to control every movement.

The sun was shining brightly through the window, warming the stone floor. Taking slow and cautious steps, she went to the hole in the wall and looked out. A wide, vast, endless green ocean greeted her – on all sides a solid wall of forest surrounded her. Christine moved closer to the window and leaned over the windowsill. Her room was about ten metres above the ground. There was a green lawn at the bottom and stone walls on both sides. On each side at a distance of about two to three metres away from her own window, she could see the same emptiness, but there was no way she could get to them.

She returned and sat on the bed, trying to recover from her memory the series of events that led her to where she was now. She struggled in vain. The last picture that came to her mind was a ride in the park, then – nothing.

Christine got up again and walked around the room. On the table stood a mortar, cones, and a number of small jars and pouches with various herbs and roots. From all this sorcery, the smell of lavender and valerian were the most familiar to her and probably the strongest. Other pouches smelled disgusting to the point of making her feel sick.

She had been so pre-occupied by the inspection of the room, that she only now realised the clothes she remembered herself in had been changed for a long, light robe similar to a nightgown, and what she had thought was a pile of rugs on the chair were, in fact, clothes. Christine looked through the pile, but the outfits were nothing like what she was used to seeing or wearing. She opted for a long dress with wide sleeves, trimmed with intricate embroidery, and tried it on; it was too big by at least a size, but what choice did she have? It was not in her style to wander around an unfamiliar place in her underwear.

She pulled the dress on, on top of her robe. The dress had laces, which were meant to fit it tighter to the body, but she had difficulty figuring them out. Somehow she managed to lace herself up, and as she did so she listened to the sounds outside the door. Then, making sure there was no one around, she quietly exited her room.

She walked down a long, dark, damp corridor and found herself at a crossroads. One of the hallways went further into the depths of the place and then disappeared into darkness; the second went to stairs leading down into a larger hall. Having already spent god knows how much time in darkness, Christine took the stairs.

The hall was airy, spacious and consisted of minimal items of furniture. In the centre of the room was a large, carved throne-like chair with several pillows of dark velvet and gold embroidery laying on the seat. Nearby was a table, decorated in the same style. On the table stood a decanter, a goblet and a metal plate with scraps of some food. Around the perimeter of the room, were placed several benches and long wide tables. On the walls hung heavy curtains of dark-red and burgundy tapestry, some of which were tied up by thick garters with tassels of gold thread. The parts of the walls that were not covered with curtains were decorated with stuffed animal heads and their furs.

On one wall, in a place of distinction, there was a portrait of a middle-aged man in knightly armour. The painting was partially covered by a heavy drape as though the subject was not in favour, despite being a person of significance. The knight portrayed seemed to be furtively peeking into the room; watching events unfold from his hiding place.

"What is this strange place... How did I get here?" she could not help but wonder.

At the far end of the room, she saw another, barely visible door that was covered by a heavy curtain. There were no other entrances or exits from the hall, and, because she couldn't go back yet, she decided to continue by that route.

Making sure that there was no one in the room, she carefully stepped onto the steep wooden stairs leading down into the hall. Reaching the bottom, Christine quickly walked across the cold stone floor towards the only door – she was desperate to find answers. The floor was smooth, slippery and extremely cold as if she was walking over thin ice, not polished stone.

"Heating would certainly benefit this charming little place," she mumbled in a low voice.

She walked fast but, as she reached the door, she hesitated. There she stood staring at the dark surface, yet not seeing anything before her, as if her brain had blacked out. She did not know how long she stood there, maybe seconds, maybe minutes, maybe half an hour had passed since she came into the hall. She held her breath for a moment and pulled the little metal handle. The door did not budge.

"Perhaps it's for the best. Perhaps I do not need to go there? Maybe I should go back and wait for those three to come for me? But who are they and what do they want from me?"

Anxiety, doubt, fear – all the feelings mixed inside her. Her hand hung undecided but a small, shy inner voice said that she was on the right track. Prompted by the invisible force, she took another step towards the door and stopped. She took a deep breath and pulled the handle, this time with extra effort. The door moved and Christine, tripping over the threshold, stumbled into another corridor.

It was not as large as the one she had just come from and looked more like a secret passage. There were no pictures; the walls were decorated with neither curtains nor tapestry. In contrast to the previous room, the walls here were bare grey stone, which made her feel even colder. Rubbing her freezing shoulders and trying to wrap herself tighter in the scanty attire she had on, she moved forward.

At the end of the passage, she saw another door, and not hesitating for a second, walked towards it, but a few steps later she stopped as she sensed movement on another side. Her heartbeat quickened. Taking a few deep breaths, trying to calm down, she took a few small steps and walked forward until the door swung open. Startled, she recoiled and pressed her back against the wall. Her heart skipped a few beats.

Two young girls, in aprons and caps, wearing the same old-fashioned dresses, walked into the passage. One of them was carrying a large wicker basket filled with apples; the other a tray with a roasted piglet and a few bunches of grapes.

Not paying the slightest attention to Christine, the girls walked along the hall cheerfully chatting away. Coming alongside her, they curtsied and then one of them, the girl with rosy chubby cheeks, looked at Christine, whispered something into her companion's ear and they both giggled softly. Reaching the door, the girls glanced back at her once more and disappeared into the hall.

For a while, Christine stood in the corridor, not daring to move. She had forgotten she was walking barefoot on the stony floor and got terribly cold, but then she couldn't feel the cold anymore as heat flushed through her body. Her cheeks burned. It was some time before her heart calmed down and took its previous measured rhythm.

A new door brought her to a new hallway – much larger and lighter than the previous one, with tall windows on both sides. It was also very lively.

People in strange clothes moved swiftly along the hall, into various rooms and back again; everyone was busy with their chores and didn't pay much attention to a woman who seemed to have appeared out of nowhere. Those who passed by her greeted her with a curtsy or slight bow of the head, and some occasionally whispered and pointed in her direction.

Christine cautiously moved down the hallway, watching, with great interest, what was happening around her. At some point, she thought, she must have wandered onto the set of a historical drama or a "day in medieval England" project; otherwise, none of it made any sense.

She turned a corner and came out into the gallery. What she saw there did not clarify anything, but only confused her even more.

The balcony overlooked a square, surrounded on all sides by high walls. Huge gates with heavy bars were guarded by several soldiers in weighty armour; the square was packed with people.

In the centre of the square on a large wooden platform, she saw a huge hewn stump. One would not need to be a genius to guess its purpose, nearby stood a well-built man with a mask on his face and a large heavy axe in his sturdy hands. Near the entrance to the platform, Christine noticed two miserable looking, dirty and exhausted people. Somewhere in the crowd, she heard a familiar voice; it was not difficult to determine where it was coming from.

The owner of the nasty squeaky voice was sitting on an elevated, high-backed chair; his hand with a large ring on one finger was resting on the armrest. A tall man in black stood to his right, – his face was tense and unfriendly, and his hands were crossed across his chest.

"For the crimes committed against the state," the hoarse voice spoke again, "by the power vested in me... Blah-de-blah-de-blah... you can proceed!"

The hand with the ring rose up and fell down again into its original position, giving a command to the executioner.

One of the wretches was dragged to the scaffold. With a terrible heartfelt cry, he broke free and tried to run, but did not get far. In one giant leap, the man in black got to him and pinned the man the ground with his huge sword.

Eyes wide-open Christine watched the scene. She pulled back and hid behind a pillar, not daring to take her eyes off what was happening in the square.

The second man was dragged onto the platform. He pushed, kicked and screamed, trying to save his life but it was no use. A deep punch to the stomach from one of the guards cooled his ardour. A few moments later, he was on his knees, hands tied tight behind his back, his head on the stump.

A swing and the whistling of an axe as it moved through the thin air, then the sound of crunching bones... It took two hard blows for the executioner to separate the head from the body. The blood flowed like a river. Someone shouted, someone cried, but Christine did not hear any of that. Not daring to move, she froze in terror.

"There must be some reasonable explanation. There must be!" she assured herself.

She closed her eyes and listened, straining her ears. More than anything in the world, she now wanted to hear "and cut! Thank you, everyone!" but it was not happening. Soon after, the crowd had faded as people left the courtyard. The bodies were dragged to a far corner of the square and piled up under the wall, the executioner wiped and packed his weapon and began to wash the blood from the platform. As if nothing had happened, the owner of the husky voice and the tall man had not moved, and were continuing their peaceful conversation.

Slowly it began to sink in – this was not a movie, neither was it a result of her vivid imagination, nor a dream, but brutal reality. Her head began to spin. Her heart rose in her chest, and she felt as though her stomach had turned inside her. Her pulse thumped in her temples. She vomited bile.

Gathering all the strength that she had left, she rushed back to where she came from, bumping into people and furnishings as she ran. As in her dream, she ran down the hallway from the terrible monster that was chasing after her. She ran into the room, slammed the door behind her, and leaned against it, as if trying to shield herself from reality. Powerless, she sunk to the floor by the door. The horror of what she had just seen was still alive before her eyes.

"What has happened to me!? Where am I?" pounded in her head. *"Who are these people?! No, these are not people! Barbarians! A group of religious fanatics or a secret brotherhood or...?!"*

She did not even want to think about that "or".

Thoughts raced through her head at high speed. They followed one after another creating complete chaos in her already confused mind. It hurt so much, she thought her head was about to explode. Christine clasped her hands around her head and pulled her knees up to her chest, tears flowing from her eyes.

"I have to calm down, I have to pull myself together," she told herself, swallowing the tears, but it was easier said than done. The buzz of the circling thoughts made it impossible to relax even for a second.

*****

Sensing that he was being watched, Gisborne, without interrupting his conversation with the Sheriff, glanced up. The woman, who less than an hour ago, lay in bed unconscious, was now standing on the balcony of the upper gallery with a terrified look on her face.

"Your Grace," he said quietly.

At that instant, the woman rushed away. One moment she was standing there motionless; a second later, she disappeared inside the castle.

The Sheriff questioningly raised an eyebrow.

"Your grace," Gisborne began again but held his tongue, "with your permission, I would like to absent myself for a little while," he said. It was his intention to meet with the woman first and speak with her without unnecessary witnesses.

"Secrets, secrets," the Sheriff teased him. "Give my sincere regards to the Lady of your heart," he winked. "Then find me, once you are done with your amorous affairs."

Gisborne bestowed upon the Sheriff his favourite smile, and, barely concealing his impatience, retired. Traversing the stairs two at a time, he soon got to the room, where in the past few days he had spent most of his time. Now he would get some answers!

Making sure that everything was quiet behind the door, he opened it and entered the room. The woman was sitting on the bed and turned her head to the sound; her eyes were red from tears.

*****

"It's him!" flashed through her mind. *"He's come to kill me! Just as he killed that unarmed man."*

She jumped to her feet and opened her mouth to scream, but in one giant stride, the man was beside her. Gisborne grabbed her firmly, not allowing her to move. A black glove covered her mouth.

The horror froze in her eyes.

"I will not hurt you," he said quietly. "I'll remove my hand if you promise not to scream," he looked straight into her eyes.

Christine nodded her head slightly. Guy lowered his hand.

"Who you are?" he asked. "What are you doing here?"

Seizing the moment, Christine made a failing attempt to break free, but the man held her even tighter.

"Let go of me... You're crushing me!" she whispered.

"Who are you? What are you doing here? Who sent you?" demanded Gisborne, giving her a little shake. She could hear a threat in his voice.

"I don't know what you're talking about. Let me go, you're hurting me."

Christine struggled to free herself from his hold but could barely move the upper part of her body – her opponent was much bigger and stronger. She could only see one way and, swinging her leg back with all the strength she could gather, kicked the man in the groin.

His face twisted in agony, excruciating pain spread through his body. He let go of Christine, grabbed his injured part and with a deep long groan sunk to his knees, however, a moment later, he was back on his feet. His ice-cold blue eyes scalded Christine. The pain and anger from insult of the inflicted assault clouded his mind.

"Don't come any closer!" warned Christine.

Gisborne did not hear her. Bloodthirsty, with the facial expression of a raging, wild animal, he moved towards her, but just a few seconds after, he was on the floor, his face down, his arm twisted behind his back.

"I told you not to come any closer!" Christine said twisting his arm even more.

As Gisborne growled in pain, the door opened and the Sheriff appeared on the threshold.

"Ah! I can see you are feeling much better, my dear," he said happily, and, as if nothing was happening, strolled into the room.

Christine released the man's arm and took a few steps back. Groaning heavily, Gisborne rose to his feet, unsuccessfully trying to ignore the pain between his legs.

"What's going on in here, Gizzy?" asked the Sheriff, amused; it was not often that he saw his deputy lying on the floor defeated, especially by a woman.

"What's going on here?!" Christine repeated after him. "That is exactly what I'm asking, what the hell is going on here! Who are you people? What do you want from me?"

"She... She tried to escape," breathed out Gisborne.

"What?!" protested Christine. "He attacked me! You have five minutes to explain who you are, and where I am, or..."

"Or what!?" cut off Gisborne.

"Oh, trust me, you haven't seen anything yet!" she took another step back, preparing to defend herself. At this point, the money and time spent on self-defence training and martial arts classes seemed like a good investment. "Who are you and what do you want from me?" Christine asked, once again, but this time more calmly. "If you have kidnapped me and are looking for ransom money, you are unlikely to succeed in your venture."

"A ransom? How interesting..." mused the Sheriff. To his credit, even with such a strange turn in events, he maintained a cold-blooded calm. "You've come to us, my dear," he took one-step towards Christine. "You just don't remember. You hit your head and spent four days unconscious," he came closer and seeing a completely lost expression on her face, gently took her hand in his. "You are in Nottingham."

"Excuse me?" Christine's eyes widened in surprise. "What am I doing in Nottingham?"

"What's your name, my dear?" asked the Sheriff, ignoring her question.

"Christine. Christine Hawk," she muttered softly. "But what am I doing here?"

"Hawk!?" Gisborne issued a sarcastic laugh. "Hawk, like a bird?"

Christine shot him an angry glare.

"Gisborne!" the Sheriff snapped and continued in a soft voice. "I do not think it is time to make fun of our guest, can't you see, she's a little confused..."

Still confused and disoriented, Christine looked at the people standing in front of her.

"Gisborne?!" she repeated softly with an expression of genuine surprise on her face. "Sir Guy of Gisborne?" she chuckled. "And he is laughing at my name!" she added as if to herself, although it was obvious to the people present, to whom this sarcastic comment was directed.

"How dare she!" Guy gritted his teeth even tighter; he was barely able contain his anger.

"And you?" Christine looked at the second man who was still holding her hand. "Oh, no-no, pray do not tell me. Let me guess!" she made a thoughtful face. "The Sheriff of Nottingham?" she could no longer hold back her smile. "But, of course!" she sighed with relief. "I'm in Nottingham Castle!"

This time, the two men exchange confused glances. Christine gently pulled her hand out of the Sheriff's hold, playfully narrowed her eyes and quickly looked under the bed.

"Where's Robin?" she asked, then took a turn around the bed and looked underneath it from another side. "Well, you've made quite a show!" her expression changed instantly, she gently pushed Gisborne in the shoulder as if they were old friends. "You almost fooled me! I have been to the jousting tournaments in Leeds Castle and heard that Warwick Castle also does this kind of performance but I didn't know that you guys had joined in as well. I always thought that Nottingham Castle was just a museum. Bravo!" she clapped her hands several times. "Congratulations! Very good performance and so realistic!"

Christine stretched out her hand to the Sheriff, but he wasn't moving. A mixture of surprise, shock and bewilderment showed on his puzzled face.

"Thank you very much indeed for the wonderful entertainment, but I'd appreciate it if you could now direct me to the nearest phone. I'll call a taxi and sort myself back to London."

There was an uncomfortable silence in the room.

"A phone? A taxi? I'm afraid I do not understand you, my dear," the Sheriff spoke first, breaking a moment of awkward silence.

The look on his face spoke for itself – he had never heard these words before.

"I... I'm in Nottingham, right?" quietly uttered Christine, still thinking she was in the middle of a theatrical show in one of the medieval castles, supported by one of the heritage trusts, however with each passing second, her confidence evaporated.

Her legs weakened and she slowly sunk onto the bed. The realisation of what was actually happening poured over her like a cold waterfall. She shut her eyes tightly, wishing it was a dream, even if it was a nightmareish one... She wanted to wake up on the morning of the twentieth of June – the final day of the court hearing, the one that she had spent so much time on, the one that over the last few months had occupied her thoughts. But deep inside she knew it wasn't a dream.

"What day is it today?" she asked quietly, not knowing if she really wanted to hear the answer.

"It is the twenty-fifth of June," said the Sheriff smiling. "You've been here for four days."

"The twenty-fifth of June, one thousand..." she paused.

"The Year of our Lord eleven ninety-two," Wesley finished for her.

Suddenly, her heart sank; adrenaline rushed through her veins and hit her in the temples. She closed her eyes, took a deep breath and let the air out slowly.

"Eleven ninety-two..." she echoed quietly.

*****

Christine sat on the bed in silence. Her empty gaze was directed ahead.

A kaleidoscope of emotions overwhelmed her at that very moment: fear, confusion, panic – everything mixed up, everything and nothing at the same time. Like an artist who stares at a blank canvas before starting work, she tried to look into her mind, but cold emptiness looked back at her. What was happening to her now was beyond any reasonable explanation, and made absolutely no sense, but at the same time, there she was, right there at the dawn of the thirteenth century.

"Are you all right, my dear?" the Sheriff spoke first. "You look like you have seen a ghost. I understand that four days is a long time, but once you are, for a change, feeling a lot better, how about we get on with the business. Shall we?"

"The business?" she repeated and raised her eyes to him. *"What business can I have here? Who do they take me for?"* she wanted to protest, but couldn't utter a word and just stared silently at the man in front of her.

"Business, business, my dear! I do hope you remember the purpose of your trip?" the Sheriff leaned forward and studied her face. From the way his bulging eyes burned through Christine, she knew he didn't trust her.

"No, I don't remember," she said, still a bit hesitant, trying to pull herself together.

If these people were mistaking her for someone else, the best she could think of was to play along, until she could work out what they wanted with her, how she happened to be here and, most importantly, if and how she could get back.

"To tell the truth," Christine lowered her voice a little, "I'm still very confused. Everything is mixed up in my head."

"Well, I am not surprised! You have hit your head so marvellously!" said the Sheriff and touched the bump on her forehead.

Christine shuddered, whether from the cold touch of his fingers, or the pain that instantly resonated in her head, she wasn't sure.

"Gisborne, do you not have some important business to attend to?" said the Sheriff, making it clear to his deputy that his presence in the room was no longer required.

Gisborne was about to say something and had already opened his mouth but the Sheriff was not inclined to hear it.

"Leave us," Wesley snapped not even looking at him, but Gisborne didn't move.

"Well, you've heard your boss!" said Christine, not realising where this bravery and impudence came from, and waved her hand towards the door.

Whatever was happening to her, and whatever these people expected from her, she was certain it would be prudent of her to spend time with the noble gentleman Sheriff. It would be easier to gain information only having to fool one person at a time rather than two.

Gisborne didn't reply to her sarcastic comment, but every word that he did want to say was clearly written on his face. First, the Sheriff treated him like a pageboy and now this!

"What does she think of herself!" he thought but swallowed the words that hung dangling from his tongue and bowed respectfully before exiting the room.

"You must forgive my deputy," said the Sheriff, "he's young, chivalry and manners are not his forte".

He held out his hand, helping Christine up from the bed.

"Perfect, perfect!" he murmured, walking around her. Christine stood before him, tall, straight back, chin slightly raised. "Stunning, I'd rather say! What grace!" he continued to admire. "I would have never guessed that the Prince would have entrusted this role to a woman, although, I have to admit, a great choice!" Christine smiled shyly at the Sheriff, hastily trying to work out how to act from this moment forward. "Richard, let's not forget, as many of us are," his face stretched into a pleased smile, "is a true admirer of female beauty, and for you, my dear, I am sure, it would not be difficult to get close to him," he rubbed his hands impatiently. He already saw himself basking in gold and glory. "Well, sit down, sit down," he finally helped her to the chair.

"I'm very glad you approve of the Prince's choice," said Christine. "But, if I may, I would like to learn a little more as to the final destination and the purpose of my journey," she added, making herself comfortable on a chair.

"Did he not tell you, my dear?" asked the Sheriff, surprised.

"Unfortunately, the Prince didn't go into too much detail," said Christine. "He told me that when I get to Nottingham, you, the Sheriff, would relate all the details to me."

"Something is not right," thought the Sheriff.

Wesley raised an eyebrow. It was not what they had discussed with the Prince. The assassin, leaving for Nottingham, should have received all the necessary instructions, and the Sheriff and other members of the plot were meant only to assist him to get to the Holy Land.

Christine felt it instantly. The last eight years that she had spent in the courtroom served her well, making her a wonderful psychologist. She had learned to feel the mood of her opponents and anticipate their next step. The gut feeling had never failed her. In that curve of his brow and slightly inquisitive look, Christine immediately felt a threat.

"Frankly speaking," she began softly, "it's very sad to admit," she paused, watching the reaction of her opponent, "you've noticed quite rightly that I have so marvellously bumped my head so, to tell the truth, I can hardly recollect the events of recent days." In that she was not lying, she really couldn't remember anything that had happened to her. "I remember leaving London. I remember riding through the woods. I woke up in the castle, and then him," she nodded her head towards the door, "attacking me! So, I beg for your assistance."

She smiled slightly, playfully narrowed her eyes and looked at the Sheriff. It worked! The man relaxed a little.

"I really hope that the blow has not affected your main skills, hmm?" he asked in his usual sarcastic manner.

"You may rest assured," assuming her new role, she repeated a slight bow of the head, as she had seen from Gisborne. "Needless to say, I believe you have just had a small demonstration of my abilities," she bared her teeth in a wide smile.

The Sheriff stretched his lips, in a pathetic attempt to copy her broad open smile but his gaze was still wary.

"Please," he said, inviting Christine to follow him, and walked out of the room. "Guards!" he shouted loudly causing Christine to jump up. "Just a precaution, my dear," he added when two armed men appeared in front of them as if from out of nowhere.

*****

Back in her room, Christine sat in silence for a long time, trying to process what she just heard, praising her own ability for self-control. She barely lifted her brow but her heart stopped for a moment and everything inside her froze in horror when she heard the Sheriff's words "to travel to the Holy Land and assassinate the King of England – Richard the First".

She could not kill the King! or to go to the Holy Land for that matter. She needed to get out of this horrible place; a place where heads were chopped off on a daily basis – sometimes even for no reason – and where anyone who objected to the regime was thrown into prison.

She had to get out of this place as soon as possible but that was easier said than done. Her conversation with the Sheriff had shone some light on how she had ended up in Nottingham Castle. But the questions remained – how had she come to be in medieval England, and most pressingly – how could she return back to her own time?

She went to the window and stared at the forest that spread out around the castle like a vast ocean. Somewhere out there, in the depths of Sherwood was the answer.

At dusk, the sun began to sink behind the horizon.

She was far away from home, too far away. It seemed that no one had ever made such a journey. The discovery of America by Columbus, or the first trip around the world by Magellan, seemed insignificant, a trifle, compared to the distance she had managed to cover – it wasn't only the kilometres that separated her from her home but more than eight hundred years of English history.

However, she had, somehow, managed to step into history, – at the time of Richard the Lion Heart – and was expected to save England from this, as the Sheriff precisely put it, "worthless" king. With all that, there was one thing of which she was certain, before her deception was revealed, and while the Sheriff and his allies were convinced that she was the one who they thought her to be, she had to get out of there. But where should she go? That was the most important question she still couldn't find the answer to.

Someone knocked on the door. Christine didn't have a chance to say anything, before the door opened and the man in black appeared in the doorway. This time, Guy of Gisborne wasn't alone. Allan followed behind his master, carrying a small tray of food and a decanter of wine.

"The Sheriff has ordered me to arrange some food for you," Gisborne said roughly and pointed to the table where his servant was to put the tray.

Leaving the tray on the table, Allan didn't hurry to leave the room and studied the woman. Even in these clothes, she didn't look like anyone he had seen before. Her posture, turn of the head and direct, open gaze were quite unusual for the women he had seen in Nottingham. Even Lady Marian, who was of noble blood, was nothing like this stranger. As he continued his observation, the woman didn't pay him the slightest attention, not taking her eyes off Gisborne.

"Seems we've begun our acquaintance on the wrong foot," she said finally, trying to relieve the tension.

"Precisely, on the foot! I do fear what fate could have awaited me, had we begun our acquaintance on the right one," he quipped. The wound from the insult was still fresh and very deep.

"Oh!" exclaimed Christine with a chuckle. "Just look at him! Obviously, you have never been kicked in the nuts, Milord?" she raised an eyebrow and mimicked a bow.

"You've insulted me!" he spat out and took a step forward, looming over her like a black cloud.

Although Christine was quite tall, the man before her was by far her superior – he was significantly taller and looked terrifying.

"I'll leave you to it," said Allan quietly, realising that the situation in the room had begun to heat up. "If you need me, I'll be outside," he said and slipped out into the corridor.

Christine and Gisborne didn't seem to pay him any attention, still looking at one another, drilling each other with their eyes.

"Excuse me! But if you wouldn't have..." Christine began but stopped.

She took a deep breath and closed her eyes for a moment. No matter how irritated she was, she knew that in her position, she needed to win over as many people as possible. If she wanted to get out of this place alive and unharmed, she needed to gain trust, especially of this one... Guy of Gisborne, who, in her opinion was a complete arsehole, obviously held an important post in the Sheriff's office and could prove to be very useful.

She exhaled slowly and opened her eyes.

"I'm sorry," she said calmly and without a hint of irony. "I shouldn't have done it. But you yourself..." she paused, knowing that she might be heading in the wrong direction again. "I'm sorry," she repeated. "Let's start over again, shall we? My name is Christine Hawk. Hawk – like a bird," she repeated his own words, smiled, and held out a hand to him. "Truce?"

Guy didn't say anything, he just grinned at her gesture, abruptly turned and exited the room. Leaving Christine standing with her hand outstretched.

"Ough! What a proud, stubborn arse! It will be harder than I thought..."

Wandering around the room, her eyes stopped on the tray of food. She came closer. Despite the fact that she had spent four days without any food, consuming only herbal teas, force-fed to her by the Sheriff's physician, the sight of food didn't appeal to her. From what was proposed to her by the Sheriff she shuddered and felt sick again. She smelled the contents of the decanter, the strong scent of the fermented grapes hit her nose, her head began to spin.

"Do they want to poison me? Then why go to all the trouble of saving my life in the first place? Oh, the Sheriff was telling me a very eloquent story of my rescue and revival. All the effort, just so they can poison me later with the local cuisine?"

She went to the door and peeped into the corridor only to come, once again, face to face with the rude twerp, who no more than five minutes ago, had left her room. In the middle of the hallway, Gisborne and his assistant were having a passionate conversation.

"Excuse me, what's your name?" completely ignoring the master, Christine spoke to his servant.

"Allan A'Dale, ma'am," he bowed in reply.

"It's very nice to meet you, Allan. Can you do me a favour?" she smiled at the slightly confused young man. "Would you be so kind to take that," she pointed to the tray, "back where it came from. And instead bring me back freshly boiled hot water and maybe some dry bread."

"Yes, of course," he replied and hesitating a little went off to carry out her order.

Christine retreated to her room, leaving Gisborne to stand alone in the dark corridor. Yet, less than a minute later, the door swung open and he leisurely strode in. Christine didn't say anything but raised her eyebrow questionably.

"What? You are going to starve yourself?" he asked, grinning impertinently.

"What's wrong with him? Does he have any manners?" Christine thought, and added out loud, with an expression of sincere amazement on her face. "You're so worried about the state of my health that you've decided to condescend to a conversation with me, Milord?"

Gisborne rolled his eyes.

"Anyway, I'm also concerned with my well-being," she said calmly. "According to the Sheriff, I've been here what, four days? So precisely in order to avoid any potential health problems, I would prefer to stay off any heavy food for a day or two. Water and some bread will do just fine for now and then, we will see."

"Are you, in addition to your main skills, also possessed of the gift of healing?" he added with an obvious tone of sarcasm.

"I possess the gift of common sense, my dear Sir," ignoring his sarcastic remark, she retorted. "If, after so many days spent without food, I should stuff myself like a hippo, trust me, it wouldn't end well," she patted him on the shoulder.

"What is a hippo?" his expression suddenly changed and became childlike, genuinely puzzled.

"A hippo?" she repeated after him, her eyes widening. "It is an animal that lives in Africa, why..." not truly comprehending the question she attempted to explain, but stopped, seeing a complete lack of understanding in his eyes. "Never mind."

An awkward silence fell in the room. Gisborne went to the window and stood there with his back to Christine, arms folded across his chest. He stood for a long time not saying a word, staring into the evening sky. The questions that he came into the room with were still in his head, but to his own surprise, he couldn't find the strength to voice them.

"I need to get to know her a little better."

Guy turned his head a little and looked at her over his shoulder. Christine sat on the bed motionless, and seemed to be looking straight at him, but at the same time looking right through him, into the void... He was ready to speak, but as soon as he opened his mouth, the silence of the room was broken by a soft knock on the door. Allan returned with the water and bread.

"Thank you," Christine shook her head as if waking from a dream. She smiled and took the tray. The young man blushed.

"You're welcome, ma'am, if there is anything else you need, just let me know," he said, still a little embarrassed.

"Absolutely, you'll be the first to know," she winked at him and gave a long look to Gisborne. "Now, if you gentlemen wouldn't mind, I would ask you to leave. Good night," she gently nodded her head towards the door, making it clear to the men they had to go.

"Goodnight, ma'am," Allan bowed and walked out first.

Gisborne followed him in silence.

"Good night, Milord," he heard her voice but was too proud, too stubborn, and too angry to reply.

Finally, she was alone. Christine breathed out heavily; fatigue mixed with irritation. She touched the pitcher, it was still hot, and poured some water into a goblet. She drank the first cup and the second followed immediately after. The hot water wrapped her insides in a warm blanket. She broke off a piece of bread, rolled it between her fingers and held it to her nose. It didn't smell bad. Christine put a ball into her mouth and chewed slowly but she couldn't swallow it. On the first attempt to send the piece down, her stomach reacted with a strong gag reflex. The food would have to wait for a while.

She finished the remnants of water and, with a deep sigh, lay down on the bed.

She was very tired. On this one day, she had endured more than in all her thirty years, yet deep inside she knew it was just the beginning. The tears rolled down her cheeks. She pulled her knees up to her chest and curled into a ball. Sobbing softly, she cried herself to sleep.

Chapter 9:
The Nottingham Castle

The night was airless and stifling.

Christine dreamed of her home, the time when her mother was still alive, the time when she was still a little girl. Some pictures from her childhood followed by episodes of her youth. She dreamed of Philip and their Sunday lunches, the feeling of home, warmth, and security when he was around. She was once again running towards the light. Someone was following her through dark corridors. She saw the Sheriff's face, his shifty bulging eyes, and a disgusting smirk. Then blackness thickened around her.

Then from the darkness of the night came those sky-blue eyes – his eyes – Guy of Gisborne's eyes. His gaze was anxious but at the same time full of tenderness, and there was a voice; a quiet, soft, deep, velvety voice.

"It's okay... I've got you... You're safe now..."

Christine thought she could feel his strong arms around her, holding her tight, protecting her from the night's horror. A moment later, it was all gone, and she was surrounded again by pitch-black darkness.

She opened her eyes.

"What a strange dream," she thought still panting heavily. *"What does it all mean?"*

Did it mean anything at all, or was it simply in her head? Was it just a trick of her confused mind that filled her sleep with events of the past? Christine aimlessly stared into the blackness in front of her. The shadows on the ceiling played with her imagination. She sat up. She didn't know how long she had slept but it was dark outside, only the moonlight shone through the window, leaving a bright streak of light across the floor.

She went to the window and breathed in the coolness of the night air. A huge moon stood over Sherwood. The black sky, covered with millions of stars, seemed vast and boundless. Not a single sound broke the silence of the night.

Christine went back to bed, took off her dress, and crawled under a heavy blanket. For a long time she lay on her side, watching the reflection of the moonlight pouring onto the stony floor.

When she opened her eyes again, there was bright light outside the window, and where in the night there had been a path of moonlight, the sun now made its way instead. Her dress was neatly folded on a chair; the smell of freshly baked bread filled the room. Someone must have come in while she slept and she hadn't even noticed.

"Someone was in here? Someone was watching me while I slept!" she thought. *"Allan? Gisborne? The Sheriff?!"* at the thought of the latter she shuddered. She had only known him for one day but had formed a strong opinion that never in her life had she met a more disgusting person.

This morning, Christine felt much better, and despite the inner emotional strain, her body felt rested and a great deal stronger than the day before. Her head didn't hurt as much as yesterday, but she felt tension in her limbs and the consequences of her fall were still vividly perceptible in every muscle of her body.

She reached up, stretching her stiff muscles. Her hands stretched to the ceiling, she tilted to the left, then to the right and back. She leaned forward, bent her knees and dropped her head down; she moved her shoulders and swayed her head back and forth, releasing the tension. She straightened her knees and felt the blood rushed through her veins. Christine stood up, took a deep breath and let it out slowly.

"Much better."

She walked to the table. The pitcher was full of fresh hot water. Next to it stood a medium sized bowl also filled with water and a piece of white cloth. She rinsed her face with warm water, dried it with the improvised towel and then dressed. She drank a little and then soaked a small piece of bread in water and put it in her mouth. She chewed it slowly and then swallowed very carefully. This time it slipped straight to her stomach not causing any discomfort. She smiled. Things had begun to improve.

She spent the next two days in her room, leaving it only briefly to stretch her legs in the nearby corridors, and she didn't venture any further. The Sheriff and his deputy came in several times to enquire about her health, even though they all knew that Wesley's primary interest was to know how quickly Christine would return to a normal state and would be able to proceed with her duties. She continued to play along with this performance, assuring His Grace that only a few more days would be required for her complete recovery. She tried to disguise it, but cringed in disgust every time the Sheriff of Nottingham appeared in her room. His voice was rough and gravelly. Christine thought she had never heard anything more horrid in her life. His deputy was not extremely welcoming either. Over the course of the two days Christine had not seen anything else from him except that arrogant, smug smirk he would affect each time he spoke to her.

On the third day, she felt well enough to explore the castle. Early in the morning, after some exercise and a light breakfast, she threw a small, knitted shawl, brought to her the day before by Allan, over her shoulders and exited her room. She followed the only route known to her: down the corridor, through the reception hall, down the small passage to the large hallway and on to the gallery overlooking the castle courtyard.

*****

Life in Nottingham went on with its usual routine; people were busy with their daily chores.

With a loud screech, the castle gates opened for a large cart loaded with food and other supplies. After a careful examination, it was allowed on the grounds of the courtyard. The man, who drove the cart got down from his seat and taking the horse by the bridle, went by his usual route, somewhere further down the courtyard in the direction of the smell of freshly cooked food.

Guards carried out their morning routine and allocation of the posts. Half of them were wearing metal armour, with helmets that completely covered their faces. The men were armed with heavy swords; some had bows and quivers with arrows on their shoulders. Having received all necessary instructions, four heavily armed guards, accompanied by two soldiers in lighter armour, made their way out of the castle gates and soon disappeared from sight.

Another four heavy armoured guards remained in the square, in the company of a dozen soldiers dressed in high boots, tight pants, and loose-fitting linen shirts. All of the guards and soldiers were tall and strongly built, but one of them stood out from the rest.

The "Black Knight" – it not for the first time that Christine had referred to Guy of Gisborne by such a name. He was standing in the middle of the square with his back to her, but even so, he was hard to miss among all the people around him; and it wasn't because he wasn't dressed differently to the others – still in the same black leather breeches and black leather jacket with metal buckles; not because he, by at least half a head, was taller than any of the guards – his stately figure and mop of dark slightly curly hair could have been seen from afar. Tall and handsome, he was well built, with big, strong hands that were accustomed to wielding a heavy sword. His broad chest and shoulders had seen many battles, his sturdy legs walked many miles but were also used to holding tight to the sides of Raven. It was discernible by his demeanour and scornful way of speaking that he had a touch of noble blood.

Giving instructions to his soldiers, he didn't see her until one of the guards moved closer and whispered something into his ear, nodding towards the upper gallery.

Gracefully, as if enjoying every moment of his unspoken triumph, Gisborne slowly turned his head to face her, one eyebrow slightly arched, the corners of his lips curled up. Over the past few days, Christine had often met this haughty expression.

She smiled faintly and raised her hand to greet him. Gisborne bowed his head in a welcoming gesture but turned away from her and carried on with his business. He seemed neither bothered nor interested in her presence. A few moments later, however, he changed his position; turning slightly to the left and, without breaking his conversation with the castle guards, now had a perfect view of the upper gallery. From time to time he shot quick glances towards her.

With great interest, Christine watched what was happening in the square, but no matter how hard she tried, her gaze involuntary returned to Guy of Gisborne – the man clearly dominated those present.

Holding the huge raven stallion by the bridle, Allan appeared from the stables and led the stallion to his master. In one swift motion, Gisborne flung the hem of his cloak out of the way and, with incredible ease for a man of his physique, mounted the horse. At the sight of his muscular thighs and buttocks tightly wrapped in black leather, Christine sighed softly.

Fascinated, she forgot herself and couldn't take her eyes off his figure. A lustful smile appeared on her face, and her pulse quickened. During their brief acquaintance, she had already concluded that Gisborne was an egregious arsehole, but without a doubt, he was a pretty damned good-looking one. Christine smiled at her thoughts.

"Enjoying the view, hm?" the Sheriff's husky voice spoke behind her.

"Oh yeah!" she uttered softly but her cheeks flushed deep red immediately as the realisation of what she had just said came to her. "I didn't mean it like that."

"Of course, you didn't, my dear," said the Sheriff with a cat-like smile on his face. "But you cannot deny that my boy is very handsome," he added still smiling.

"Yes, I have to admit, there is something about him," said Christine trying to steady her heartbeat. "He's your son?" she asked suddenly – it wasn't the first time that the Sheriff referred to him as such.

"Oh, no-no, I do not have any children. At least, not that I know of," he let out a disgusting laugh.

Christine tried to smile but couldn't appreciate the humour. The Sheriff, although not an old man, looked repulsive, and from what she could remember from the ballads and Robin Hood stories, was a cruel, calculating, insolent and abominable man. The idea of him having a family and an heir seemed unimaginable.

"But I have known him for a long time," continued the Sheriff, "and taught him a lot. I gave him a decent life. He is not my son, but rather my creation. I've made him who he is today," he added proudly.

"An arrogant arse and a ruthless killer?" the words slipped from her mouth. "You should be very proud of yourself, Your Grace," she bowed respectfully.

They exchanged strained smiles. The Sheriff didn't say anything, but it was obvious her comment wasn't to his liking.

They stood in silence for a while, watching the action developing in the square. Gisborne, Allan and two soldiers mounted the horses and were ready to go on their daily tour of the local villages.

"Leaving this pleasant topic aside," the Sheriff finally said, when Gisborne, accompanied by his servant and several soldiers, had left the courtyard and the sound of their horses had faded beyond the castle gates. "I was told that you are refusing to eat. I assumed that after such a long journey you, on the contrary, would be quite famished. Or, perhaps, my dear, our humble food is not to your liking?"

"Please, don't get me wrong, your grace," said Christine. "I don't, in any way, mean to be ungrateful. I appreciate your concern, but as you know, I have travelled from afar and, after spending a few days without food, I'm not sure how my body would react to an unfamiliar cuisine. I wouldn't want to take the risk. However, if you don't mind, I would like to ask your cook to do something for me."

"Name it and it will be done," promised the Sheriff. "In the end, it's in my best interest to get you fit and proper as soon as possible, as the prompt execution of my plan depends on that," he added with a thoughtful smile.

"Perfect! Then, with your permission, I'll make arrangements. And one more thing, please, if you do not mind. I've wanted to wash and refresh myself, and, if possible, to find a quiet corner where I can stretch my muscles and start training to prepare myself for the execution of your plan. After all, four days spent lying in bed without movement could have affected my abilities," she smiled widely.

Christine knew what effect that direct gaze and smile of hers had on others, and especially on men. She didn't flirt or give false promises, she disarmed her opponent with her directness and vim and had often used it in her work.

"I am sure it can be arranged," said the Sheriff and tried to copy her smile. "I'll have one of my servants take you to the kitchen, and then we will find you a suitable place for training."

She thanked him for his concern and was about to leave when he spoke again.

"Oh, yes, I almost forgot! I believe this belongs to you," he handed her a small pouch made of black velvet.

Christine opened it and pulled out a bracelet of two intertwined snakes. A sigh of surprise and relief escaped her.

"I didn't expect to ever see it again," she said softly.

Her voice was barely recognizable; a hint of joy mixed with sadness was in it. In this distant land a small piece of home, a piece of her life, something that wouldn't let her forget who she was and where she came from. It was something that would serve as an incentive for her speedy return home. Christine put the bracelet on. Silver droplets sparkled in the summer sun.

"Beautiful little thing is it not. It was on you when my men found you in the forest," said the Sheriff. "But, to tell you the truth, I prefer the interpretation you have on your..." he paused meaningfully.

Christine's eyes widened and her hand instinctively moved to her lower back.

"No, you did not..." she blushed. "You mean, I was... Who else has seen it?" she almost pleaded for an answer.

"The Doctor," said the Sheriff. "Well and Gisborne, of course," he added, after a pause. Christine really hoped to not hear that name. "But do not worry, they'll keep your secret," he assured her.

"It's no secret that I'm worried about," replied Christine, "but the fact that my b..." she paused, struggling with indignation, "my private parts became public."

"You do not have to worry, my dear," he said playfully, "and besides your "private parts", as you call them, are very attractive, you do not need to trouble yourself that you have offended us in any way," he laughed out loud.

Christine shuddered at his hideous laughter.

*****

After a long debate, Christine managed to convince the Sheriff's cook that she didn't want any exotic dishes, neither roast suckling pig, nor a quail. The woman looked surprised and a little disappointed when out of all the proposed delicacies, Christine chose one of the big chickens and simply asked it to be cleaned of feathers and entrails and cooked into a broth. She was certain this would be the best solution for the food problem over the next few days.

While in the kitchen, Christine couldn't escape the feeling that she was being watched, but no matter how hard she tried, she didn't see the voyeur until the very last moment. Just when she was about to leave, Christine turned around and their eyes met. The cute face of a young woman was lurking in a dark corner of the kitchen but as soon as she realised she was seen the girl retreated into the dark and didn't reappear.

Having given orders regarding her food, Christine went back to the room allocated to her in the castle, but she did not get far before she, once again, felt the same inquisitive look. Quietly looking back over her shoulder as she walked, Christine saw that the same girl was following her, hiding in the shadows of the doorways. This person piqued her interest. Couldn't the Sheriff find another candidate? This spy seemed very inexperienced.

After making several wrong turns and walking a few extra laps around the dark corridors, Christine finally got to her room. The day wasn't as hot as yesterday, and standing by the window, she enjoyed the cool breeze that broke into the room, softly playing with her hair.

Her head was full of thoughts, which cramped inside in complete disarray, and made very little sense. She tried to pull herself together and look at things reasonably, but how was that even possible? How could she look reasonably at something that had no reasonable explanation and made absolutely no sense? Her pulse quickened and her head began to hurt again.

She closed her eyes, took a deep breath and then exhaled slowly. It seemed to help a bit... She sat on the bed.

Her mind was restless; she aimlessly looked at the things that surrounded her, the setting that had now become so familiar. She looked before her but didn't see anything. Her gaze was directed inwards, deep inside; her fingers slid back and forth over the silver snakes that encircled her wrist.

"To attempt an escape through the main castle gates is impossible, it's very well guarded, but even if I succeed, where would I go? Even if, by some hypothetical turn of events I was able to slip through the guards and get outside the gates, what then? There's no doubt that the Sheriff doesn't trust me; that is why I am being watched all the time. Still, I cannot understand why this task was assigned to a young girl. Is there really no one more experienced?

If I try to escape now, it will jeopardise my position, the deception will be discovered and I will certainly be dead. No, it would be a hasty and premature decision. Before doing anything sudden or stupid that potentially could cost me my life, I have to weigh all the possibilities and investigate what is outside the gates. But even with all of that, an important question still remains – how did I end up here...?"

In her head, in the place that should have stored the memories of what happened to her in the park after the storm, there was still emptiness. Only two people might have had the answer – the Sheriff of Nottingham and Guy of Gisborne.

She was still drifting far away in the sea of her thoughts, sliding her fingers across the cold silhouettes of silver snakes for comfort, when the door opened and the Sheriff of Nottingham, this time accompanied by Allan, appeared in the doorway.

"Your lunch, my dear," said Wesley and, waved his hand, pointing to where the servant was to put the tray, "as well as your dinner, and, one may presume, tomorrow's breakfast", he said with undisguised sarcasm. "I just hope you're not going to starve yourself. I repeat: I have great plans for you!" he said thoughtfully as they exited the room.

It was quiet outside for some time, and then she heard a low conversation and the sound of retreating footsteps. Christine peeked out of the door and bumped nose to nose into Allan. She looked at him questioningly.

"The Sheriff has asked me to watch after you..." he trailed off. "To make sure that you are not disturbed, ma'am, until Sir Guy organises your protection."

"In other words, he asked you to watch me, so I don't go wandering around the castle unsupervised?" she muttered.

"If there's anything you need, ma'am, let me know. I'll be here."

Christine didn't answer and went back into her room.

"If things continue this way, I won't have much chance of escape."

She sat down at the table and drank the broth. To her surprise, it tasted quite nice. She broke off a small piece of chicken and sipping the rich broth, chewed it slowly. Only now, did she realise how hungry she was. The first piece was followed by a second, and the second by a third. She tried to persuade herself not to rush but the hunger was stronger than she was. She soaked the morning bread in the broth, and one by one swallowed the chunks. Now, she was unable to stop. Common sense began to break through to her mind only when her hungry stomach was full. When both chicken legs and thighs had been munched away, she stopped, and polishing it all off with another gulp of broth, she lay down on the bed and immediately fell asleep.

Christine didn't know how long she slept for, but woke up feeling considerably better. She stretched and got out of bed, then went to the door and listened. It was quiet. She looked outside and found that, to her great surprise, there was no one there. Not giving it a second thought, she left the room.

The cold grey walls of the seemingly endless corridors contributed to her already gloomy mood. She turned a corner and walked to the next staircase when, once again, she felt that inquisitive look she had experienced before. The same young woman was following her yet again. Christine felt very annoyed by this obvious presence, but being unable to get rid herself of her tail in this unknown place, she wandered around the dark corridors for about half an hour, before returning to her room where she spent the rest of the day.

*****

The sun began to sink behind the horizon. Christine stood by the window, not daring to take her eyes off the bright golden splendour of the sunset. Immersed in her own thoughts she watched the slow movement of the clouds. She turned away from the window when the sun finally sank behind the forest. The dark figure of the Sheriff stood before her. Startled, Christine jumped to the side.

"Jesus Christ!" she exclaimed.

"Oh no, just me," the Sheriff said with a wide grin.

"Is it a habit of yours, to walk in wherever you want without knocking, your grace?" she asked with obvious irritation in her voice.

"This is my castle," responded the Sheriff in a lazy tone, while he showed a lively interest in examining the remains of her lunch, which still stood on the table. "I go where I want, when I want and how I want, my dear," he bared his teeth in a smile and continued after a short pause. "I have not yet had the opportunity to evaluate your abilities to their full, but I have to admit, I like you better when you are unconscious... There is too much noise from you... um, what do you say, Gisborne?"

Only now did Christine notice a second person in the room. He stood in the shadows leaning against the doorframe; one hand rested on the hilt of his sword, the other lay on the belt of his breeches.

Gisborne made no sound, not that it was necessary, his smug, arrogant smirk spoke louder than any words he could ever voice. Not being able to resist the urge, Christine narrowed her eyes and made a face at him. It was completely out of her character, but she couldn't help it. His vain, cocky looks and self-righteous smile was getting on her nerves.

"What does this arrogant arse think of himself?"

"Well, that's not why we are here. Come," said the Sheriff inviting Christine to follow him.

She followed the Sheriff down the hallway and staircase, down another corridor and another staircase; dark and repetitious, they succeeded one after another. Christine soon realised that she hadn't been in this part of the castle before. Trying to keep up, she quickly walked after the Sheriff, with Gisborne following after her. The next staircase appeared to go further down, underground. At the end of another corridor, they found themselves in a spacious hallway. The air here was humid and hot.

As the Sheriff opened one of the doors, the hot steam broke through.

"After you, my dear," he stepped aside making way for Christine.

Carefully she walked in but couldn't see a thing – everything was covered with hot mist. The heavy door slammed behind her. In panic, she rushed back, helplessly groping over the wooden surface looking for the door handle yet not being able to find it.

"What the hell is going on? What do you mean by this? Let me out!" she pounded on the door as hard as she could.

To her surprise the door opened and, tripping over the threshold, Christine stumbled back into the hallway. She felt the heat and the dampness of the hot air, droplets of sweat covered her face, and her long locks hung heavily on her shoulders.

"What the hell!" she repeated angrily and took a determined step towards the Sheriff. She was halted by Gisborne stepping forward and barricading his master with his tall strong frame.

"Too much noise! Too much noise..." from behind Gisborne's broad shoulders she could hear Wesley's hoarse voice.

"You wanted to clean yourself up, my dear?" he asked.

"What?" Christine stared blankly at the men.

The Sheriff walked towards the door, once again inviting her inside.

"No, thank you. You first, your grace," she said hesitantly.

Wesley went in, Christine followed. The hot mist had lifted and everything now made sense. A large wooden structure stood in the centre of the room – a barrel of enormous size was lined with a light-coloured cloth and filled with hot water.

"Well, I didn't expect that," she said a little overwhelmed and added turning to the Sheriff. "Thank you!"

"We'll leave you to it," he said, preparing to leave, "unless, of course, you need help," he added smiling disgustingly.

"Excuse me?" breathed out Christine.

"Why, of course, I would be delighted to offer you my help," murmured the Sheriff. His fingers ran through the lacing of her dress, and he touched her hand gently. "But, you see, I'm a little old for such exercises. He, however," the Sheriff nodded in Guy's direction, "would be delighted to rub your back, eh, Gizzy?"

Gisborne bared his teeth in a wide smile, and took a few steps towards Christine as he undid the rivets of his jacket and reached for the laces on his shirt. His facial expression declared his eager willingness to take advantage of the Sheriff's proposal.

"Another time, perhaps," Christine tried to laugh it off. She lifted her hand and stopped Gisborne just a few steps away from her.

Echoes of the loud laughter of the Sheriff and his deputy rolled through the corridors, as the men headed for the door, leaving Christine alone in the room.

*****

A relaxing and rejuvenating hot bath was the cure her exhausted body and mind so longed for.

She quickly pulled off the dress, threw it onto a chair and went in. The water was so hot that it almost scalded her but gradually her body got used to the temperature. She held her breath for a moment and then plunged herself into the hot water.

It had been a long time since she had experienced such bliss. She sank into the scalding liquid so that only her head remained on the surface, but soon she dipped her head under as well, so that only her eyes, nose and lips remained above the water. Letting go of her body weight, she closed her eyes and relaxed, allowing the water to gently keep her afloat.

The air smelled of roses; on the side of the bath, she saw two small bottles with lavender and rose oils. Christine washed her body and hair, and then for a long time lay in the bath. She closed her eyes and gave herself over to the gentle, silky embrace of the water that softly splashed over the sides with her every move. The scent of burning firewood and candles soothed her exhausted mind better than any aroma spa.

When the water cooled down, she opened her eyes again, got out of the bath and put a large piece of fabric cloth, which served as a towel, around her body. She dried herself and, while remaining completely naked, wrapped her hair in the same piece of fabric, erecting an exotic turban on her head. She felt hot, and every cell of her body was relaxed. Slowly, not missing an inch, she generously rubbed rose oil into her skin.

*****

"Goddess..." the Sheriff whispered softly.

All this time, in a neighbouring room, he had been watching Christine bathing, his eye glued to a small hole in the wall.

"Don't waste your chance, my boy," with a malicious smile, he turned to Gisborne. "She is not a peasant! Such a body, I have not seen, and you can trust me when I say that I've seen a lot of them, in my lifetime. I am sure that your leper friend would not be even close to competing with her," he retreated from the hole and, making way for Gisborne, patted him on the shoulder. "Come on! Why deny yourself a pleasure?"

"I do not spy on women," Guy replied sharply, the good mood he had been in until now vanished.

"Really?! Since when? Are you unwell?" the Sheriff reached out, trying to touch his forehead. Gisborne clenched his teeth and dodged the touch. "Oh, just look at us, how soft and tender we've become..." the Sheriff clicked his tongue. "I wonder what our dear Lady Marian would say, should she find out about your little adventures with the castle maids. You moon after her as a calf after its tit, and then let off steam on the servants. Do you think I don't know about the security chief's daughter?" The Sheriff gave his deputy a long look.

"It's been a while; I did have feelings for her," replied Gisborne quietly.

"Of course, you had, who says you hadn't! Spoiled the girl, made a child, and then sent both to an early grave," portraying mock sympathy, the Sheriff shook his head. "Feelings he had... You think it is so easy to find a good chief of security when everyone, including you, is incompetent... But, come, let's not talk about it," he went back to the hole. "Come, better look at a real woman, while you still have the chance. Who knows what fate awaits her. After all, we are yet to receive an answer from London," he finished and settled comfortably for a better view.

"And if the answer is not in her favour?" Gisborne raised an eyebrow.

"It will be a terrible loss," the Sheriff looked up, for a second he folded his hands in prayer yet immediately returned to his previous engagement.

The door slammed open, startling both men. Christine stood in the doorway.

"How dare you!"

The wet waves of her dark hair lay on her shoulders; her eyes flashed with anger and in the gloom of the room they looked almost black. She was overwhelmed with rage.

"Oh... you... have already finished... and here we are with Gizzy..." only managed the Sheriff.

"Take me to my room," she said, trying to speak as calmly as possible, and turned to leave.

"Of course!" uttered the Sheriff, still bewildered. "Gisborne, please, escort our guest."

Guy came out first, Christine followed behind.

"I hope this little misunderstanding," said the Sheriff a little fawningly, "will not affect..."

He didn't finish; Christine turned abruptly and in two short strides was next to him. He felt as though fire had scalded his cheek, the light noise from a slap rang in his ears for some time.

"Now it won't, your grace," Christine bowed and walked out into the hallway, where Gisborne awaited her.

Still in shock, the Sheriff said nothing, only moved his jaw from side to side and rubbed his burning cheek.

Christine walked quiet. Her footsteps echoed through the silence of the corridors. Guy followed her. As they walked, neither of them said a word; at the crossing of the hallways, she stopped and waited for him to show her the way. Christine spoke only when they reached her room. She turned to face him and looked him straight in the eye. He became uneasy under her demanding gaze.

"I can understand the Sheriff – he's is an old pervert, but you!" she shook her head, frustration in her voice. "I understand that our acquaintance didn't exactly begin in the best way, but," she gasped, "have you never seen a naked woman before?"

She turned away. Her fingers lay on the cold metal of the door handle.

"I wasn't looking," he said softly, as if apologising. The words jumped from his lips, he couldn't understand why but he wanted her to hear it.

"Of course, as you say, Milord."

She turned and their eyes met again. Her face was calm and cold, eyes emotionless. He wanted to say something but couldn't find the right words. For a while, they just stood there in silence, looking at each other. After a long pause, Christine broke the silence.

"Good night, Milord," she said cold and indifferent.

"Goodnight, ma'am," he said and bowed his head, as Christine turned away.

The door creaked closed and she hid inside her room. She sat on the bed and looked out of the window. The moon was creeping up high above the forest.

*****

The hot bath had done its job. That night Christine slept without dreams. In the morning, she awakened to the melodic singing of the birds, and despite yesterday's incident, felt well-rested and was in a good mood.

Clean clothes were laid out for her on the chair and freshly baked bread and broth awaited her on the table. She dressed and after breakfast went to wander around the castle. In the grand reception hall, Christine met the same familiar faces – the Sheriff and his deputy were busy discussing the affairs of the county. She entered and greeted them as if nothing had happened, yet her expression was cold.

"Good morning, my dear!" the Sheriff got up from his seat and went to meet her.

"Miss Hawk," Gisborne bowed his head in a polite greeting.

Her eyebrow arched in surprise, during their short encounter, it was the first time that he addressed her by name.

"Good morning," she said, trying to speak calmly and respectfully.

"How did you sleep, my dear, I hope you had a good night's rest?" the Sheriff took her hand and walked her to his chair.

"Yes, thank you," she answered shortly, still not quite understanding the reason behind this sudden change.

"You must understand," he continued, "what happened yesterday was just a misunderstanding," he rubbed his bristly cheek. "We still have no evidence that you are who you say you are. We had to take precautions and make sure that you were not hiding anything."

"Naked? In the bath?!" she exclaimed. "I guess the person you have sent to spy on me hasn't provided you with all the details?"

"Ough, na-na-na..." said the Sheriff stretching the words. "I have sent to spy on you? I did not send anyone," he seemed genuinely surprised.

"Well, then, perhaps, you have very self-motivated servants, your grace," Christine laughed.

She quickly described the young girl, who like a shadow, had followed her the previous day.

"Remind you of anyone? I don't think she has a lot of experience, though, otherwise it wouldn't have been that easy for me to notice her," she added.

The Sheriff sighed in exasperation and shot a quick glance at Gisborne. One eye movement was enough for his deputy to immediately leave the room.

"So, if you didn't send her," Christine repeated, "who is she and why was she following me?"

"It is Lady Marian Norton," said the Sheriff with a tone of clear irritation in his voice.

"Lady Marian?" Christine knew this name from books. "But why was she following me?"

"Ahh, do not pay any attention, my dear," the Sheriff waved his hand, "although she is here under house arrest, she loves to poke her little nose into other people's business."

"What did she do to deserve house arrest?" Christine asked in surprise.

"It's not her, it's her father!" said the Sheriff. "He was the Sheriff before me, then, how can I put it... was removed. He obviously got very upset and decided to plot against me," Wesley made an unhappy face and was about to burst into tears. Christine couldn't help but smile, the devil looked very convincing.

"But let's not talk about them. You said that you wanted a quiet place to exercise, and I've found you the perfect spot," he said, inviting Christine to follow him.

*****

After the darkness of the corridors, her eyes hurt in the bright daylight. Christine was in a small courtyard surrounded by high castle walls on all sides. There was only one way in and one way out, and on the upper floor was a small gallery and a balcony, along with four perimeter battlements overlooking the outside of the castle.

"I hope this place is suitable for you? No one will bother you here," assured the Sheriff.

"Great! This place is perfect. If only..." she stopped.

"What? Another request?" the Sheriff raised his brows.

"No, your grace, just a favour," Christine smiled sweetly. "You know, these are not the best clothes," she added, straightening the hems of her long dress.

"Oh, of course! What was I thinking? We will find you something more suitable. I'll get it delivered to your room right away," said the Sheriff and left.

An hour later Christine, in soft linen breeches and a light shirt, stood in the middle of the courtyard. Next to her lay a narrow-braided rug that she, with Allan's help, had managed to secure from the stables; a jug of water stood in the shade, near the entrance.

The Sheriff was no fool and didn't trust her, and while there was no substantial evidence that she was who they thought she was, she knew he wouldn't let down his guard. In order to lessen his vigilance, now, it was up to her to show him what he wanted to see!

She took off her boots, rolled up her breeches, and put the boots in the shade, stepping barefoot onto the hot ground. The heat poured through her soles, filling her feet with its soft warmth. She enjoyed this rare moment, her body began to relax, but for what she had planned, she would require not only a relaxed body but also a relaxed mind.

Christine tied her shirt up at the waist and stood on the mat. Then she closed her eyes and, taking deep breaths, slowly raised her hands up and then moved them slowly down again. Forward bend to flat back, plank pose, knees, chest, and chin – Chaturanga Dandasana, upward facing dog, downward facing dog, step to a forward bend, then back to the initial position. The salutation of the sun – she always began her yoga session with this exercise.

A cat. A warrior. A boat. A half tortoise. A tree. A dove and the release of the wind. Christine finished her first stretches. She felt the blood rush through her body, reviving the tired and tense muscles. She drank some water and sat down to relax.

She had hoped for an audience, she hoped that the Sheriff would send someone to watch her, but there was no one in the top gallery.

"I'll be patient. Sooner or later someone will show up. There is no way the Sheriff would leave me unsupervised."

She didn't have to wait long; very soon in the gallery of the upper floor, she noticed the already familiar feminine silhouette of Lady Marian Norton. Trying to remain unnoticed, she was hiding behind the pillars.

Spy or no spy it didn't matter, Marian was exactly the audience Christine had hoped for. She drank some more water, removed the mat, and walked to the middle of the courtyard.

She stood sideways to the balcony, with a perfect view of what was happening on the upper floor. She closed her eyes a little; from the gallery, it would seem that they were completely closed but Christine had an excellent view. She was about to carry on with her workout when a second person appeared.

Cautiously looking around, Allan A'Dale entered the gallery. Even through her half-open eyes, Christine could see how the expression on his face changed from alarm to concern as soon as he saw the girl who was hiding behind the pillars.

Christine didn't want to make the audience wait any longer. She bent her knees, took half-squat position and began her strange dance.

Chapter 10:
You Two Will Make A Wonderful Team!

"Marian! What are you doing here? Guy is looking for you all over the castle!" hissed Allan. "What have you done this time?"

"Shh, quiet, she will see us," ignoring his questions, Marian grabbed his arm and pulled him down with such force that Allan almost fell off his feet. "You'd better look at that!" she pointed to the courtyard.

At first, Allan couldn't understand what she was on about, but as soon as he peeked out from behind the pillar, he immediately understood. Making strange movements with her hands and feet, Christine was moving slowly about the yard. Her hands slowly rose, then fell, then she seemed to stir the water underneath her or spread the clouds high up in the sky. She seemed to be conjuring around an imaginary cauldron in a mystical dance to music that only she could hear.

Fascinated by this unusual sight, Allan didn't realise that he had risen to his feet, and with his mouth wide open, was watching the scene. He had seen something like that before, but where, he couldn't, at first, remember, but, in a moment, it came to him. Of course, he had seen it before!

About a year ago, in Sherwood, he and Robin had run into a group of women accompanying a cargo bound for Nottingham from the Holy Land. These women were doing similar movements just before they slaughtered the entire convoy the Sheriff had sent to meet them. If this was what he thought it was, this woman might be very dangerous.

Consumed by his own thoughts, he didn't notice that another person had walked into the gallery.

"Allan!" a familiar voice called from very close by and startled him.

"Master, I did not hear you coming," he said, still at a loss.

"Have you seen Marian?" Gisborne asked, a look of displeasure on his face. "I can't find her anywhere, she has as good as vanished!"

"No, Sir, I have not seen her," lied Allan, as he turned slightly, trying to block from view the girl who was hiding behind him.

Marian pressed herself against the pillar and held her breath. Gisborne growled.

"Oh, don't you worry, Sir, we will find her. You'd better come and look at this," Allan pointed down.

Christine had been waiting for Guy so she could begin the last part of her workout. She once again stretched her limbs and, making a stern face, began to perform a single kata that she remembered from her martial arts course.

To create the necessary mood, and to make the right impression, she tried to be as dramatic as possible. Breathing loudly and speaking in a language that the others present didn't understand, she moved across the courtyard, simulating punches and kicks, turns and sweeps. She was trying too hard and almost fell over twice, but carried on. There was nowhere to retreat to.

She finished her performance with yet another battle cry, returned to the starting position and bowed to an imaginary enemy. Out of the corner of her eye, she could see that the desired effect had been achieved – two men stood in the gallery with their mouths wide open, not daring to move.

Leaving the courtyard, Christine looked up and, as she walked, gifted Gisborne with a long look. The corner of her mouth curled up into a defiant smile, the very same she had seen from him so many times before. Her job was done, she was satisfied.

Even when Christine was out of sight, Guy stood motionless for a long time. His eyes were wide open, but his gaze was empty. If, up to this point, he still hoped that their guest only pretended to be an assassin, what he had witnessed just now removed any remaining doubt, and yet he still could not believe that such an important task was entrusted to a woman.

Still thinking about what he had just seen, he silently walked back and forth past Allan, oblivious to his servant's presence. Seizing the moment of confusion, the young man gave Marian a signal to leave, but coming out of her hiding place, she collided with Gisborne.

"Lady Marian," he said, more stating the fact of her presence, rather than questioning it.

"Marian! Here you are!" exclaimed Allan imitating a look of genuine surprise on his face.

"Marian! What are you doing here? I have been looking for you all through the castle," said Gisborne, recovering his senses from Christine's display, his voice cold.

"Yes, Marian, where have you been hiding? We were looking for you all over the place." Allan echoed his master's words, deep inside thanking the heavens, that his deception had not been revealed.

"Allan!" Gisborne interrupted rudely. "Do you not have any chores to attend to?" he said, not in the least trying to hide his intention of getting rid of his servant as soon as possible. "Go and check my horse," he said finally and nodded his head toward the door.

"What? Are we going somewhere?" Allan shrugged. "The Sheriff did not say anything," he said naively.

"Get out," said Guy quietly, not turning towards him.

"Out? Why out? What for?" he still struggled to understand.

"OUT!" barked Gisborne. The servant and Marian jumped up in surprise and horror.

Still not able to understand what he had done to cause such displeasure from his master, Allan slowly walked towards the exit.

"Marian, what are you doing here?" asked Gisborne, sternly, when Allan finally disappeared in the hallway. "The Sheriff is very unhappy that you pester his guest. What are you up to?"

"I, um..." she didn't know what to say. "Sir Guy," she carefully put a hand on his shoulder. "please understand, all this secrecy in the castle... It looks like everyone knows what is going on," she paused.

"You mean to say, everyone except you?" he smiled. "Marian, I've told you, it should not concern you. I warned you not to stick your pretty little nose into other people's business," he touched her chin and lifted her face up to his.

"But, Sir Guy," she tried to argue.

"Marian, you will incur the fate of your father if you continue to annoy the Sheriff, and then even I will not be able to protect you," his expression changed, his voice becoming soft and gentle as if he was begging her to show him some affection. "Let me protect you. Let me take care of you," he took her hand and gently kissed her fingers. "Be mine, and I'll protect you!"

"Oh yes! Lady Marian!" a hoarse voice cried from behind. "Please, already, be his and relieve the boy of his misery."

The Sheriff's nasty loud laugh broke the peace and quiet of the gallery. Christine, who was standing next to him, arched an eyebrow, the corner of her lips drew up, she was hardly able to contain a smile. Gisborne gritted his teeth.

"One day, the Sheriff will answer for all the humiliation," thought Guy, as he was still holding Marian's hand. The girl's face flushed with a delicate blush.

"As I can see, you have found her," the Sheriff directed his gaze to Marian. "Have you told her? Did he tell you, my dear?" the Sheriff was no longer laughing. "This is your last warning," he came closer, his eyes gleaming with anger. "One more time! I repeat, one more time, I catch you sticking your nose into my affairs, you will join your father in the dungeon and even he," the Sheriff nodded in Guy's direction, "will not be able to save you! You two, follow me!"

He turned sharply on his heel, and left the gallery. Christine and Gisborne followed after.

*****

Three days later Christine felt much better and stronger. She didn't expect such a quick result, but her exercises had a positive effect not only on her physical but also her emotional state. She was no longer limping, the wound and bruise on her forehead had long gone. She slept much better and in the morning felt well-rested. Little by little, she adjusted her diet, but still didn't overindulge herself with the local culinary delights. As for the rest, it was all the same.

She spent most of the time in her room, practicing yoga and Tai-Chi in the morning and at sunset. In her spare time, she continued to roam around the castle. Still not giving up her hope of escape, she was making notes about the stairways and corridors; the location of the guards and their routines.

Wesley, of course, couldn't help but notice her interest. Christine had to lie that she was developing a new, better functioning system of security and defence for the castle, and, indeed, for His Grace himself, and to achieve that required a clear understanding of how things were organized. The Sheriff was thrilled with the idea and, to his own great joy, and his commander-in-chief's greatest annoyance, had not forgotten to praise her for her efforts in Gisborne's presence.

"Such a strange duo," Christine thought, looking at the two men.

However, despite all this, the Sheriff continued to monitor her very closely, and every day impatiently waited for the news from London. Christine knew that sooner rather than later she would have to come up with something new to maintain the Sheriff's belief in the purpose of her presence in Nottingham.

Every day, she didn't give up the hope of getting outside the castle, but couldn't think of a way to achieve it.

On the fourth day, luck smiled upon her. When, after a workout and some breakfast, she returned to her room, the Sheriff and Gisborne already awaited her there.

"My dear, I have been watching you, and I cannot help but notice that your health has improved greatly. We have already seen a lot of this," he moved his hands, imitating Christine's exercises. "I think it's time to see what you can really do. Today we go to the training camp and you will have the opportunity to show us your skills.

"Get out of the castle?! What great news!" her eyes lit up, she couldn't hide her joy.

"Are you so happy at the prospective of beating someone to a pulp?" the Sheriff chuckled. "She is an interesting woman, isn't she, Gisborne?" he poked his deputy.

Guy grinned in his usual manner, giving Christine a meaningful look.

*****

Not more than an hour later, a company consisting of the Sheriff, Christine, and about a dozen soldiers were in their saddles ready to leave. Everyone was ready, everyone for one person. Raven stood alone in the middle of the castle square, nervously stomping his hoof on the ground. He was not happy with the fact that everyone had already gathered, and his rider was nowhere to be seen.

No, wait, there he was; the sound of his heavy stride could be heard from afar. Gisborne appeared on the stairs but, after a few steps, he stopped and turned back, his broad shoulders obscured the view of the doorway. The Sheriff rolled his eyes and sighed impatiently. Christine got off her horse. Intrigued, she wanted to see what was happening.

A familiar female face was peering from behind Gisborne's large frame. Guy gently held Marian's hand and apparently was telling her something in a soft voice, but the girl seemed more interested in what was happening in the square, rather than the words of her admirer.

Every now and then, her gaze slipped in the direction of Christine and the Sheriff, as if she was trying to memorise everything to the smallest detail. She smiled absently and several times looked up at her companion, but seemed unable to hear a word he was saying. Her attention was elsewhere.

Gisborne kissed her hand and walked away to join the rest of the company, who, by that time, were already tired of the prolonged anticipation. Marian, with a puzzled face, remained on the stairs.

"Finally!" said the Sheriff, annoyed. "I was afraid that we would have to wait here till lunchtime for you finish your love affairs!"

Mounting his horse, Guy swallowed yet another of the Sheriff's comments.

"Open the gates!" he barked, exasperatedly.

He abruptly turned Raven and galloped out of the gates, the others following after.

As they left the castle behind, Christine tried to store in her memory every detail of the route, however, what lay beyond the castle gates, made a strong and very unpleasant impression.

The streets were narrow and dirty. The residents of Nottingham were a match for their city – dirty and ragged. Even seeing the company from afar, many of the townspeople tried to hide, rushing in all directions. Those who didn't escape were bowing down to the ground, the horror frozen in their eyes, giving way to relief when the squad passed by them and proceeded further on its route.

Christine memorised the road, but wasn't sure if she would be able to make this journey on her own, especially if it was under the cover of night. To attempt an escape by the light of day would have been apparent suicide.

As they reached the city limits, Gisborne shouted loudly once again, giving the order to the guards to lift the heavy grille.

Outside the city, vastness awaited them. For the first time during her stay in Nottingham Christine felt free. A soft wind that came from the woods blew in her face and ruffled her hair. She rode a tall bay stallion with a white star on its forehead. Firmly holding the reins, she galloped the horse, trying to keep up with the rest of the company.

They rode into the forest. Gisborne and six soldiers were riding ahead of the procession, with Christine and the Sheriff in the middle. Four other riders were behind them. They slowed the pace as they reached the crossroad. Guy gave orders to the guards that rode with him; four broke away and headed, by a small path, into the depths of the forest.

The fifth guard, a young and not very experienced rider, was almost tossed from his saddle when, being sluggish on the road, his horse was sideswiped by Raven. Unable to contain his irritation, the black knight kicked the guard's horse in the side, causing the animal to rear and almost, once again, lose his rider.

"What's wrong with him?" Christine asked the Sheriff when the company carried on their way. "He seems too agitated, too annoyed and irritated..."

"Agh, do not pay any attention," shrugged the Sheriff, "problems with the girlfriend."

"Do you mean to say that he and Lady Marian?" Christine laughed softly. "But she's..."

"Tell me about it!" said the Sheriff, anticipating her next words. "Like I do not know. Can't understand the whole family, really. Daddy is a traitor, the daughter is following in his footsteps... sticking her nose everywhere, annoying me so much!"

Christine watched as the man in black rode ahead of them. He said nothing, and seemed to be concentrating on the road, not paying attention to either her or the Sheriff, and yet there was something in his posture and the tilt of his head which suggested otherwise.

"Do you think he can hear us?" Christine asked loudly enough for Guy to hear. "He acts like he doesn't notice us, but looks very tense."

"Of course I can hear you!" snapped Guy, not moving a muscle. "One has to be deaf not to hear your prattle."

"Prattle?" Christine smiled, feigning a surprised face.

She touched her stallion's sides with her heels and, leaving the Sheriff behind, caught up with the rider ahead.

"The fact is, my dear Sir, I find your choice of lady," she began.

"My choice of a lady, as well as anything else, is none of your concern!" he interrupted.

"Absolutely! No arguing with that, Milord, but don't you think she is a bit young for you?" Christine continued, ignoring his attempt to end the conversation. "She is about what? Sixteen, eighteen max? You? About forty?" she suggested.

"I am thirty-five, and she is perfect for me," he grinned proudly.

"Well, even if you are thirty-five, you are close to twice her age, and could easily be her father. And, from what I could observe over the past few days, I don't think you love her."

Gisborne gave her a cold look, which Christine completely ignored and continued as though nothing had happened.

"This is not love, Milord, it's – lust. She is young, naive and inexperienced. You want her, because you can't get her. You will taste this forbidden fruit and what then? You will no longer be interested. I'm right aren't I?" she said, looking before her, occasionally glancing in his direction. "For a man of your position, and your ambitions," she looked at him, as if trying to size and measure him up, "you need a woman. A woman who will be able to help you to achieve what you really want."

She raised her eyebrow slightly and looked him in the eye. He felt uncomfortable under her direct and persistent gaze. No matter how hard he tried to deny it, he knew she was right and felt uneasy. For someone who had known him for such a short period of time, she read him perfectly.

"Are you trying to offer me your services, ma'am?" he retorted, trying to laugh it off. "If you'd be a little more persistent, I could seriously consider your proposal," Gisborne laughed, pleased with his joke and gave her a long look.

"In your dreams, Milord!" said Christine with a sweet smile, as she galloped her stallion forward.

Gisborne snorted.

Surprising even himself, the Sheriff did not utter a word, this time refraining from making any comments. These two were a perfect match!

*****

The training camp was nothing like what Christine had imagined, or what she could have expected in the first place. Everything there was beyond her rational understanding.

The compound was surrounded by a high fence on one side, and by dense forest on the others. The camp itself included a stable, a tent, a large wooden structure resembling a shed or barn, and two training grounds. One of the rings was used to train horses, and in the other, soldiers practiced target shooting and techniques of melee combat.

As soon as the company entered the camp, Gisborne swung himself out of the saddle and went straight into the training area, where a dozen young men were practicing attack moves on their straw opponents. Not wasting a moment, he immediately began to give instructions and guide the inexperienced soldiers.

It was a pleasure to watch him; he knew his craft well. His movements, honed by numerous battles, were sharp and precise. Two soldiers attacked him and he worked his sword with such ease that in his hands it seemed as light as a feather. Two more joined the opposition, but it clearly had not bothered him. With the grace of a black panther, he moved around the perimeter of the ring. His moves were quick and accurate. One such thrust would have been enough to kill an enemy outright.

Having dealt with all of his opponents, he came out of the ring. With a loud rattle, the big, heavy sword was tucked back into its sheath.

Sparkling on his forehead, droplets of sweat glistened in the sun; a pair of dark curls fell over his eyes. His broad chest, covered in tight black leather rose and fell, his nostrils flared with each deep breath. With a triumphant smile, he glanced at Christine, then scooped water from a huge barrel and washed his face.

Rivulets of water ran down his face, framing his high cheekbones, running past his lips, and finally, disappearing under the leather collar of his jacket. Guy undid the buckles on the jacket, revealing a strong neck, which he wiped with his large hand. Christine could still see the droplets of water racing one after another down under his shirt. She found herself shamelessly staring at the man once again.

With his whole being, he dominated everyone present. Her heart skipped a few beats, butterflies fluttered in her stomach. What was happening to her? She felt drawn to him. The power and male strength that came from him at this very moment made her head spin. Baring his white even teeth, Guy sunk them into the finger of his gloves and pulled them off slowly, first one and then the other, and tucked them under his belt. Christine stared at him, savouring the movements of his every muscle. She found herself wanting to feel his strong hands, the same hands that only a few moments ago, had so skillfully wielded a sword. She wanted to feel them on her body. She swallowed hard.

"Bravo, my boy!" the Sheriff's voice brought her back to reality. She gently shook her head, trying to rid herself of these disturbing thoughts.

Guy grinned broadly, brushed his hand through his untidy hair, then walked over to the Sherriff and stood next to him.

"Bravo, bravo!" Wesley clapped his hands. "That's more like it!" his complacent face spoke a thousand words. "It's not yours..." he once again moved his hands in the air, mimicking Christine's exercise.

Gisborne said nothing but his lips curled into a cocky smirk.

"Show off!" mumbled Christine, but loud enough to make sure her words reached the intended recipient.

Not saying a word, Gisborne turned to face her and lowered his head in a respectful bow. The insolent grin still had not left his face.

"Well, I guess it's time for you to showcase your skills," said the Sheriff, turning to Christine.

"What, now?"

"Well, when if not now?! I did not bring you all the way here to admire the views. I know what he can do, erm, Gisborne!" he poked his deputy's shoulder.

Guy chuckled softly and bowed to his master once again.

"Alright..." said Christine, trying to sound as calm and cheerful as possible. There was nowhere to retreat.

All three of them entered the ring. The Sheriff clapped his hands, demanding the attention of the crowd. The soldiers stopped their exercise and formed a large semicircle; Christine, the Sheriff, and Gisborne were in the middle.

"Our honoured guest, Miss Hawk, here," began Wesley, "possesses a knowledge hitherto unseen in our region," he made a thoughtful face and held up his finger. "We hope that she will share some of her skills with her humble servants," he gestured toward the crowd and walked away, leaving Christine to stand in the middle of the ring.

While the Sheriff spoke, Christine was trying to figure out as quickly as possible how and, most importantly, what exactly she would be demonstrating to the audience.

"Greetings, brave warriors!" the words themselves flew out of her mouth. "I have the knowledge of single combat that comes from a distant part of the world, called "the land of the rising sun"," she carefully scanned the people that surrounded her. With great interest, the young soldiers listened to her every word. "The style, which I have been taught by the ancient masters, is called Kyokushin and means "Society of the ultimate truth". This style was created many years ago and is considered one of the toughest in martial arts," word for word she repeated what she once had heard from her trainer.

She slowly moved around the ring, carefully surveying the crowd. Like a snake hypnotising its prey, her speech had had a similar effect. As in the courtroom, her audience was there, in front of her.

"Each warrior who begins to master this style," she carried on, "must make vows, and is to be bound by these vows, come what may. Hitotsu, vare vare va, sinsin o remmasi, kakko fubatsu no singi o kivameru koto," she spoke in Japanese. "We will train our hearts and bodies to achieve a strong and a resolute spirit."

She looked at Gisborne; he stood motionless, staring at her with surprise and keen interest. Their eyes met.

"Hitotsu, vare vare va bu no sindzui o kivame, ki ni hassi, kan ni bin naru koto," she said, looking right into his eyes. "We will pursue the true meaning of the way of the warrior so that our feelings are always ready."

Christine looked at the soldiers around her; they stood with their mouths wide open.

"The first, of what my master had taught me, always be ready, always expect the unexpected, and never underestimate your opponent."

"Blah-de-blah-de-blah!" said the Sheriff. "This is all really fascinating, but is it possible to move on from talking to some action?" he nodded his head and a young man of a medium height appeared before Christine.

"Alright..." she breathed out slowly.

The first opponent was too easy for her to deal with. He was heavy and clumsy. Managing to escape his punches, Christine maneuvered, causing him to trip. With a loud sigh, the man fell to the ground.

Her second opponent was more agile, but even so, he couldn't hold on for long. At the second attack, Christine was able to knock him down. Imitating the punch, she stopped her hand millimetres from his face and then helped the man to his feet.

"Impressive, impressive," said the Sheriff, clapping his hands. "But how about a real test?" his mouth stretched into a wide sinister smile. "Gisborne!"

"With pleasure!" his deputy's lips curled upwards as he stepped into the ring.

*****

Guy's leather jacket flew to the ground. He untied the lacing of his shirt so that it would not choke him or restrain his movements.

The deep collar swung open, revealing a muscular neck, shoulders, and a broad chest. Christine knew this wasn't the time to admire his male beauty. She had to fight a man who was far more superior to her in strength and experience.

She took an arrow from one of the soldiers, broke it in half and, using it as a hair clip, pinned her hair up high at the back of her head.

Grinning haughtily, Gisborne brushed back his untidy curls, slowly pulled out his heavy sword and took a stand, ready to attack.

"But I have no weapon," Christine raised her empty hands, alluding to her opponent, so he would lower his.

"It looks like the odds are not in your favour," still grinning widely, he replied.

"It does seem a pity!" said the Sheriff, and folded his hands sympathetically. "Attack!"

Wielding his huge sword, Gisborne moved in her direction.

"God, give me strength," she uttered quietly and prepared to defend herself.

Her opponent was certainly more experienced but he was also much heavier, which, in the given situation, played to her advantage. Although Christine was almost as tall as Gisborne, she was much smaller in her physique and a lot quicker. Several times, she managed to jump aside briskly. In this fight, she couldn't do much but defend herself. She had no weapon, but even if she had, it would be no use – she wouldn't know what to do with it.

Her opponent continued his unabated onslaught, several times the heavy sword whizzed right next to her. Only now, did Christine realise that Gisborne did not intend to play games.

"Are you seriously trying to kill me?" panting heavily, she blurted out, having barely escaped yet another attack.

Guy didn't say anything but bared his teeth in a wide grin. He had no plans or intentions of killing her, not just yet. He was simply playing with her, as a cat plays with a mouse, taking great pleasure from the process.

Trapped like a caged animal, Christine tried to think quickly.

"What if? No, that's stupid! But what if I still try to disarm him."

If she could only do that, she would be able to use speed to her advantage and, combined with a few moves unknown to her opponent, she would be able to knock him to the ground. There was not a moment to lose, but distracted by her thoughts, Christine stumbled and fell. The crowd roared, cheering for their own. Guy victoriously raised his hands up in the air but it was far from the end. To her surprise, he didn't attack and gave her the opportunity to get back to her feet.

"Careful, my dear," laughed the Sheriff, hoarsely. "You need to watch where you're going!"

He was eminently enjoying this entertainment.

Once Christine was on her feet, Gisborne proceeded with another attack. The heavy sword flew and fell. Christine barely managed to duck. It was time to act, otherwise she risked staying in this ring forever.

After a couple of deep lunges, Guy slowed down to catch his breath and that was exactly the moment Christine had waited for. Immediately, she was behind him and not really understanding how, she managed to twist his hand. With a groan, Gisborne dropped his sword and Christine pushed it aside. Now they were on equal terms.

Cheered by the loud cries of the crowd, they faced off against each other, with each of them landing on the ground several times. But it seemed that the spectators no longer cared who was going to win. They were consumed by the fight. Guy knocked Christine down, but, to her surprise, offered her his hand and helped her up. This fight amused him more than anyone else. For the first time in many years, he had met his match – although she was a woman, in spirit, she was a warrior – just like him. She moved deftly and quickly, making moves and using techniques that he had never seen before.

Soon Christine began to tire. Although her morning exercises were good preparation, her opponent, hardened in many battles, was much stronger and sturdier than she was. When she was about to lose hope, fortune smiled upon her. Stumbling, Gisborne tripped and was about to crash into her. Moving quickly, Christine managed to jump aside just before the impact, and pushed him away, giving him some extra speed.

By inertia, Gisborne flew into the crowd and as he landed, collided with one of the wooden pillars that surrounded the ring.

He got to his feet, a familiar salty taste filled his mouth, and blood trickled over his lip. The crowd fell silent. He spat the blood and ran his blazing gaze over the crowd. A second later his fiery gaze stopped on her. Guy brushed his hand over his chin, leaving it red and sticky. He touched his lip; it swelled and ached. It was nothing that had not happened to him before, only this time it was different.

He slowly began to move towards his opponent. His hand slid along the side of his leg and stopped at the edge of his boot. In one swift movement, his long, nimble fingers pulled out a thin curved blade.

"Enough with the games!"

His mood had suddenly changed: he was ready to take revenge for the insult. In two large hasty strides, he was next to her. Christine didn't have time to do anything as she found herself pressed to the ground. Gisborne was on top of her, the cold, sharp edge of the blade rested against her throat. Helpless, she looked at him, fear froze in her eyes.

"Enough!" ordered the Sheriff, anticipating the possible end.

Gisborne ignored his words and pressed the blade harder against her throat.

"That's enough!" the Sheriff repeated. The deathly silence was only broken by the heavy breathing of the two people in the ring.

"Never underestimate your opponent? Is that what your ancient masters taught you?" said Gisborne, echoing her words.

His blue eyes flashed with cold fire. Christine felt a thin hot trickle slowly run down her neck.

"Blood in, blood out," he spat bloody saliva.

Realising the hopelessness of her situation, Christine froze in horror. Did he really want to kill her? Her sense of self-preservation prevailed.

"I'm sorry," she whispered quietly. The metal edge pressing against her throat hurt so much.

"It's too late to beg for mercy," spat Gisborne, through tightly gritted teeth, his voice full of hatred.

"No, I'm sorry for this," she said quietly.

Christine knew that what she was about to do would anger her opponent even more and was likely to add more oil to the already blazing fire of anger, but she had no choice. Gathering all her strength, she, as on the first day of their encounter, kicked him in the groin.

It wasn't hard but enough for Guy to loosen his grip. She pushed him away and rolled over to the side. She tried to stand up, but her shaky legs didn't listen. For a while, she sat panting, not moving, hand pressed against her throat. Guy accepted what was due to him and, in spite of the pain, proudly got to his feet, picked up his jacket and went off in the direction of a large tent.

"Bravo, bravo!" the Sheriff applauded loudly, trying to defuse the situation.

The soldiers were silently watching the scene.

"That's what I call entertainment, quite a spectacle! Help her!" Wesley ordered.

Two men ran immediately to Christine and helped her up. They sat her on the bench and gave her some water. She drank it and, having calmed her breath, moved her hand away from her throat. The blood had already clotted, leaving behind a small wound, which was already covered by a thin scab. She sat for a while, letting her anger cool and then went after Gisborne.

*****

She found him alone. Buckling up his jacket, he stood looking away from the entrance. Hearing someone enter the tent, he shot a quick look back.

"What do you want?" he said roughly, acknowledging the person who had disturbed his peace, and turned away from her.

"I've come to apologise," Christine replied calmly.

"I don't need your apology," he said, turning his head slightly toward her, with a tone of mixed irritation and anger.

"Need or not, it's your business," she said, trying to remain calm, "I'm sorry for what I did. I shouldn't have, but I had no choice."

"There's always a choice!" he barked, turning to face her.

"Really?! What choice did I have, if you don't mind me asking? You were going to kill me!" she said losing her patience.

"You, you..." Gisborne couldn't find the words, anger still clouded his thinking. "You have insulted me!" he said at last. "Again! And this time in the presence of my soldiers!"

"I told you, I had no choice," she said angrily. "Oh you stubborn... I said I'm sorry!"

Guy took a few steps towards her, his face mere millimetres from hers. With each word he said, she could feel his hot breath on her face.

"One more time, one more time you allow yourself something of the sort," he said through his teeth, looking straight into her eyes, struggling to control his anger.

"What then!?" she raised her eyebrows, returning his glare, "You will kill me? You have problems with your temper, Milord. Grow up! And act like the man, that you..."

Christine trailed off, trying to swallow the words that wanted to break free. She had already said more than would have been permitted should she have lived at this time. They looked at each other, a storm of feelings was raging inside each of them. Her words touched him deeply.

With a loud curse, the Sheriff burst into the tent.

"God, I almost killed myself stumbling over the threshold..." stepping inside, he continued to swear. "Who on earth ordered this to be built here?" he asked, looking around.

"You, your grace," Guy replied automatically. He had calmed down slightly and now looked his usual self.

"Hmm?! Strange, I do not remember," Wesley once again looked around, "but it does not matter!"

Unexpectedly, the Sheriff grabbed them both and hugged them so tightly that Guy and Christine almost bumped each other's heads.

"My children!" he exclaimed happily. "What a wonderful performance! I have never seen anything like that. You two will make a wonderful team!" he added, finally releasing them and taking a step back. "We must celebrate! Miss Hawk, would you care to join us today for dinner? We need to discuss some business matters," he rubbed his hands in anticipation.

"As you wish, your grace," she said, unable to understand what was exciting him so much.

"Gizzy?" the Sheriff glanced at his deputy.

Guy bowed his head, but he didn't look happy at the prospect, not that the Sheriff cared.

"Perfect! We will go back to Nottingham, you will make yourself presentable," he clicked his tongue and reached for Gisborne's swollen lip, but Guy avoided his touch, "I will send a servant for you when all is ready for dinner. It is settled then," he added and walked out of the tent.

Before following him, Gisborne gave Christine a long look. He didn't relish the prospect of spending an evening in her company, but if so ordered by the Sheriff, he had no choice but to obey.

Preoccupied with their own thoughts Guy and Christine rode back to the castle in silence, while the Sheriff was in a very good mood and chatted incessantly all the way back.

*****

All evening the Sheriff could not hide his excitement. After dinner, the trio retired to his bedchamber, taking with them a couple of carafes of wine.

Making sure that they wouldn't be watched, the Sheriff closed the door and walked to the table. Guy and Christine obediently followed him.

He poured some wine for Christine, sat her in his chair and stood next to her. Guy was standing by the bed, leaning against one of the posts, arms folded across his chest. His body language shouted how uncomfortable he felt in this awkward situation. To say that he was upset would have been a great understatement. He couldn't believe that the Sheriff had decided to discuss important business affairs in her presence. He was his first deputy, his undertaker, his commander-in-chief, a man who the Sheriff entrusted with the most sensitive tasks and information. Jealousy and resentment burned slowly, deep inside his soul.

Despite his high spirits and a significant amount of wine, the Sheriff, as always, was wary of his surroundings. Hearing noise and footsteps in the hall, he quickly crossed his bedchamber and peered outside the room. Two guards saluted him.

"Ah, very well," he said thoughtfully, "just the people I need. Stay here and make sure that we are not disturbed. You know what I mean," he looked at them.

"Yes, your grace, you will not be disturbed," said one of them, and both men took their positions on both sides of the entrance.

Satisfied, the Sheriff closed the door tightly and returned to the table.

"Are we expecting someone else?" asked Christine. "You keep looking out for someone."

"His leper girlfriend," the Sheriff pulled a face and shook his head in Guy's direction. "But let's not get distracted. Gizzy, come closer," he ordered.

With obvious reluctance Gisborne honoured the gathered company and moved closer to the table. His facial expression, however, didn't change.

"Well, watching you two this afternoon, I've come up with a wonderful idea!" Wesley began in a low whisper. "Miss Hawk, as we can see, feels considerably better, and we can now proceed with the execution of our plan!"

At these words, Christine's throat became as dry as a desert. She had hoped the Sheriff had forgotten about it, but it was clear that not for one day, not for a single moment, had he stopped thinking about how to bring his plan into action. Trying to maintain her outward calm, Christine took a long sip of wine. Pleasant warmth spread inside her.

"I'm not sure I'm ready to go to the Holy Land just yet!" she said softly.

"You don't have to go anywhere, my dear. Well, at least for now," the Sheriff reassured her. "Let's start with the first part," he smiled disgustingly.

"The first part?" Christine repeated after him.

"Well, my dear, you would not argue that I was very hospitable," he began, "and, of course, one would have to pay for that hospitality."

"And who is the unwanted person in question?" Christine understood perfectly what the Sheriff was hinting at.

"Oh, how I would like to say Lady Marian," he laughed in his disgusting manner. "I'm sure, that as a woman, you would easily gain her trust, especially taking into account how eager she is to meet you. And then, bang!" he clapped his hands loudly and added in a loud whisper. "She annoys me so much!"

Christine laughed softly.

"But I am just afraid that someone would not appreciate my efforts. Uh, Gizzy?"

Gisborne stood silently gritting his teeth tighter and tighter.

"Alright, alright," Wesley patted him on the shoulder, "we will keep her alive for a little longer," he winked at Christine.

"You are very generous, your grace," Christine tried to hide a smile.

The next moment, the Sheriff's light mood disappeared as if it had not been there in the first place. He spoke again calmly and prudently.

"Jokes aside. Robin. Rooobin Hooooood. That's who bothers me. That's who is constantly sneaking around, and upsetting my plans." Even now, just speaking about this person, the Sheriff could barely hold back his anger. "You'll kill him! You will do this for me," he said looking at Christine. He bent over the map and circled part of the forest. "Here, the bloody outlaw and his gang hide in this part of Sherwood. You will find him and kill him. Gisborne, you will provide any required assistance."

The Sheriff turned to the window; Guy walked up to him and spoke in a quiet whisper.

"Your grace, I myself can deal with Hood. Her involvement is not..."

"Here we go again!" the Sheriff rolled his eyes. "You two will go to Locksley and together will develop a plan and rid me of this outlaw."

"What?!" exchanging glances, Guy and Christine asked in unison. The prospect of staying in the same house held no allure for either of them.

"She cannot go with me to Locksley! My lord, Sheriff, with all due respect," began Gisborne.

"I'm not asking for your opinion!" Wesley cut him off abruptly. "That's an order! You will spend the night in the castle. Tomorrow morning I will need you, but in the evening, you may return to Locksley. After tomorrow, Miss Hawk will ride on, and together, do you understand me, together, you will do everything possible to free me of that man. Forever! I do not care how you do it. I need the result. I have been waiting too long for this!" the Sheriff finished. A moment later he added hissing like a swamp viper, "I want to see Robin Hood dead!"

He slammed his fist on the table.

*****

Marian raced through the dark corridors of the castle. She didn't care if anyone saw her now, she could hardly restrain her overwhelming feelings. What she heard just now could not be true! Impossible!

Reaching her room, she slipped inside, quickly closed the door and firmly pressed her back against it. An endless rain of tears flowed from her eyes. She covered her mouth with her hands, trying to muffle the sobs, not that it helped much. Her whole body was shaking as she sank onto the bed.

"No, this is not possible. Perhaps I misheard it. I probably missed something and misunderstood the meaning," in vain she tried to calm herself. "Oh, Robin! My love," she whispered through the tears.

She flinched in surprise when she heard someone knock on the door.

"Who's there?" she said softly wiping the tears from her face.

"It's me," she heard a familiar voice speaking behind the door.

"Oh God! What do you want from me now!" she muttered and added loudly. "Go away, Sir Guy, I am very tired and do not want to see anyone."

"Marian, what happened?" by the tone of her voice he sensed something was wrong. "Open the door, I need to speak with you." After today's events he wanted to see her sweet, friendly face.

"What do you want, Sir Guy?" she opened the door a little; her face was unfriendly.

"What happened, my dear?" Guy was taken aback when he saw her tear-stained eyes. He pushed the door with his shoulder and slid one foot into her bedroom. "Are you alright? Is it your father, perhaps? Tell me, what happened?"

"I'm... all right," she managed, trying to keep a calm face.

"If you say so, Milady," he bowed.

Whatever happened, she didn't want to share her worries with him. The tone of his voice changed.

"I wanted to see you, as I'm going to leave the castle for a while. The Sheriff has charged me with an important task. I will spend a few days in Locksley. I bid you adieu," he once again bowed his head and turned to leave.

At these words, Marian, who could no longer restrain herself, buried her face in her hands and started to sob loudly again.

"Oh, my dear!" Gisborne gently took her hands. "Is that why you are upset? You probably overheard our conversation with the Sheriff," he paused. *Could it be possible that she had heard too much?"* flashed thought his mind. "What exactly did you hear?" he looked sternly at her.

"Just that you are going to leave," she lied, still sobbing, "you know how pleased I am with your company and you are the only one who cares for my father," she said in the hope that Gisborne would decide to stay in the castle, although knowing too well that he would not dare to disobey the Sheriff.

"One word from you," he placed a gentle kiss on her hand. "You know that just one word would be enough..."

He trailed off, sensing that someone was standing behind him, Gisborne turned around.

"I'm sorry to interrupt," said Christine, trying to hide a smile.

Guy glared at her, lightning flying from his eyes.

"The Sheriff wants you, he needs to clarify a few details," she added.

"I will come in a moment," muttered Guy with no intention of moving or letting go of Marian's hand.

"I'm afraid the Sheriff wants to see you immediately, Milord," said Christine, and turned to leave.

"We will continue our conversation," Guy once again kissed Marian's hand and left.

It was not difficult for Gisborne to catch up with Christine. Despite the time she had spent in the castle, she was still confused by all the corridors and hallways.

"Who are you laughing at?" he asked roughly, noticing a smile on her face.

"Oh, relax, not at you," she said quietly, and added, noting his surprise. "I'm laughing at myself! I have spent two weeks in this damn place and still can't get used to all these stairs, turns, and corridors."

At the next corner she, once again, took a wrong turn. She laughed acerbically, her frustration erupting as tears glistened in her eyes. Her tension prevailed and she added, seriously, "You have no idea how much I want to leave this damned place!"

*****

The next morning greeted Christine as usual.

When she woke up, the welcoming, soft rays of the sun had warmed her room. Fresh bread, cheese, and cold meats were waiting on her table. Over the last few days, her routine hadn't changed: wake up, warm-up, breakfast, walk through the corridors of the castle, lunch. As for the rest, she didn't know what else to entertain herself with. The Sheriff didn't take his eyes off her; neither had he allowed her to go outside the castle unattended.

That morning, the head of the region himself, and his deputy, were nowhere to be seen. Rising at dawn, the men, accompanied by a dozen soldiers, had left the castle. Christine was alone. Even Lady Marian, who had been haunting her for the past few days, had disappeared. Not knowing what else to do, Christine, with little debate, persuaded Allan to accompany her on a horse ride.

A few laps around the field were the tonic she required. A fresh breeze, the warmth of the summer sun and green grass – being so close to nature had nurtured her vitality and improved her mood, yet it was not to last. Her head cleared, Christine returned to the cold grey stone of Nottingham Castle.

It was almost dinnertime when she again heard the nasty, husky voice of Sheriff Wesley. Together with Gisborne, His Grace was sipping wine in the Grand Hall, lounging on the cushions of his curved chair. Noticing Christine, he cheerfully jumped up from his seat and went to greet her. He offered her his hand and helped her down the stairs, then led her to the table and poured her a goblet full of wine. Loudly banging her goblet with his, he emptied the contents with one large gulp. Christine saluted him back and took a small sip.

The Sheriff was cheerful, kind, and chatted incessantly. He praised how great their day had been and the great success of their journey to a distant village. In contrast, Gisborne was reserved and taciturn and, to her great surprise, not even once over the course of the evening, had he bestowed upon her his arrogant smirk. He looked very tired and barely touched his wine.

"I thought you were to go to Locksley, to prepare for my arrival tomorrow," Christine said.

"I thought so too," he said indifferently. "The Sheriff ordered me to stay for dinner, he wanted to celebrate."

"Celebrate?" asked Christine, surprised. "Is there a reason for celebration?"

"Depends on how you look at it," he smiled wearily. "In one of the villages, the residents began to express their dissatisfaction with the Sheriff. I had to explain to them that they are wrong," he paused. "Now they know what happens to those who disobey authority," he added and walked to the window.

In the shadows of the window, he stood in silence, looking at his right hand. She couldn't see his eyes, yet his face reflected a thousand words and feelings.

"Contempt?" it seemed to her. *"Contempt with himself?"* with great interest Christine studied his face. Guy was still looking at his right hand. Several times, he rolled his fingers, clenching and unclenching his fist. Soon Christine understood the reason – his hand was shaking. Sensing her look, Guy lowered his hand.

"Gizzy, why are you hiding there?" croaked Wesley. "Come, come here, my boy" he called but Gisborne didn't move. The Sheriff filled his goblet and walked up to him. "You showed them today!" he said enthusiastically, patting Guy's shoulder.

To her surprise, Gisborne shook off the Sheriff's hand.

"I'm returning to Locksley!" he said dryly and quickly left the room.

Christine was about to open her mouth to ask the Sheriff what was going on, but he was ahead of her.

"Don't mind him, he's a bit tired," he sipped the wine. "Now that we're alone, shall we continue this conversation in my bedchamber?" his short fingers touched the collar of her shirt, a greasy smile appeared on his face.

"No! No, thank you, your grace," Christine removed his hand and took a step towards the stairs. "Good night," she said shortly, making sure Wesley understood that she had no intention of keeping him company any longer.

She took a jug of wine with her and retreated to her room. She locked the door from the inside, undressed and got into bed, but for a long time, she couldn't sleep. Her thoughts haunted her.

"What does all of this mean? What has happened between those two? They seemed "inseparable" just a day before. This is all very strange."

*****

The next day, Christine awoke when the sun was already shining brightly through the window. A quiet knock on the door made her open her eyes.

"Who's there?" she asked sleepily, not getting out of bed. Her voice was hoarse and ragged; she shouldn't have drunk all that wine yesterday. Her head ached.

"It is Allan, ma'am," a voice spoke from the corridor. "The Sheriff wants to know if you are alright. He has not seen you since last night. He is worried you might be sick," he said cautiously. "I have everything ready for the trip. What should I say to the Sheriff? When will you be ready?"

"Tell the Sheriff, I will be ready, when I am ready," she said roughly.

"Of course, ma'am, I shall wait for you in the courtyard by the gate," said the voice behind the door and the young man withdrew.

"What is happening to me?" she asked aloud. "Am I becoming like them?"

Christine pulled her legs up to her chest, curled into a ball and closed her eyes. She lay for a long time in this position, her fingers tracing the silver snakes, sliding back and forth over the bracelet. She wished she could open her eyes and wake up at home, back in her own room, but knew that was not possible.

She forced herself to get up and wash. Dressed, she went to the castle square where Allan was waiting for her. She had no desire for breakfast.

Finishing with all the preparations in the next hour, she and Allan left the castle. Christine tried not to look around, the poverty and wretchedness that prevailed in Nottingham affected her already morose mood even more.

Leaving the city behind, she galloped her horse across the field towards the woods. There were no roads leading to the forest, so she couldn't have missed one. Allan rode fast, not lagging far behind.

They entered Sherwood and slowed their pace. Christine was still ahead, she already knew the way. Her stallion had visited the woods so many times before that he walked quietly on. There was no need to hurry. Christine took the reins in one hand and removed the bracelet from her wrist. For some time, she rode tightening her grip over the silver hoop so hard that her hand hurt. Gently swaying in the saddle, she drifted away into thoughts about her life.

She was thinking of Philip, and that after her mother's death she had no one who would have taken care of her, no one but him. She was thinking about Mark: what if that morning she had called him first... if she had stayed in court or in the office with documents, or if from the court she had gone straight home...

"What If... What If..."

Just two words and how much they changed her life...

"What if..."

None of this would have happened. She would have been engaged, she would have been on holiday with one of the most eligible bachelors in London, she would have been happy... or would she? Would she be happy if none of this had happened? Would she be happy with Mark? Sooner or later, his lies would have come out. Then it would have been even more painful, more humiliating. No, it is better this way! Now looking at the situation from the outside, she couldn't understand why she agreed to marry him in the first place.

"Perhaps it is for the best."

In her heart, she wanted to believe it.

"Miss Hawk!" Allan's voice brought her back to reality.

Distracted by her thoughts, Christine didn't notice that she had wandered off the trail.

On the side of the road was a huge stone, and from it the road branched off and went in two opposite directions. Allan was on the left and Christine was on the right side, leading deep into the woods.

"Locksley is this way, ma'am," said Allan, pointing the way.

"Oh?" said Christine in surprise and turned the horse towards him. "What's there?" she asked, not sure why.

"You do not want to go there, ma'am, trust me," answered Allan, a little tense.

"Hm... Why? What's there? The Twilight Zone?" she laughed at Allan's reaction.

The young man didn't seem comfortable even speaking about it.

"People say things about that place. You know, that evil spirits live there. Let's go, they are waiting for us in Locksley."

"Allan, you're a grown man, do you really believe in this nonsense about spirits?"

She caught up with him, their horses now walked side by side.

"It's hard not to believe, ma'am, lots of weird and strange things go on there. We found you there, safe to say, under very strange circumstances. You seemed to have fallen from the sky."

"What?" Christine pulled the reins tight; the stallion reared and almost threw her from the saddle. "Allan what did you say? Where did you find me?" she asked excitedly.

"There in the woods near the South Gates," Allan pointed in the direction of a small path, the very one, where Christine had been just moments ago.

Her heart stopped for a moment, then it started beating again at a furious pace. She didn't dare to believe her ears. Her lips stretched into a wide smile. Fighting the lump that was building up in her throat, she kissed her bracelet and put it into the pocket of her jacket.

"So, to Locksley," she said, and made a hand gesture, inviting Allan to lead the way.

She spurred her stallion and galloped after Allan, glancing behind several times. Somewhere, in that part of the forest was her way home.

Chapter 11:
Locksley

Christine's idea of what a typical English village at the dawn of the thirteenth century should look like did not fit with the actual village of Locksley.

It was a big and well-organised settlement with its own infrastructure: the main square and a place for proclamations, a church, a mill, a forge, a large barn, and about two or three dozen thatched cottages, each with a small garden. And, despite the overall obvious poverty, the village was neat and tidy.

From the shady north side, near to the forest belt, on a mound, stood a big house – Locksley Manor. The two-storey mansion was constructed from thick logs, and the thatched roof was strengthened in some places with long wooden boards.

There was no fence around the manor or the village itself, nor was it necessary. All but one side of the settlement was surrounded by the forest. Warmed and lit by the sun, the southern, leeward side, was occupied by fields and garden beds, which were already covered with green sprouts. Women and older children were working there, while the little ones ran around laughing, playing in the village square, or kicking something in the dirt.

What immediately caught Christine's attention, as soon as they entered the territory of Locksley, were the local residents. In spite of the general poverty, they looked different. These people looked tired and exhausted, but in contrast to what she had seen in Nottingham, their eyes were alive, and more joyful. There was hope in them.

She spotted the owner of Locksley by the forge. His stately figure was hard to miss. With the sleeves of his wide black shirt rolled up to the elbows, Gisborne was sharpening his sword, all the while engaged in lively discussion with a man of advanced age. He noticed the approaching company from a distance and returned to the house to greet his guests at the doorstep.

Having exchanged greetings and having inquired about their journey, he showed Christine to the room prepared for her in the manor. He then retired, leaving her alone, but said that he would come by later to see how she had settled and to enquire if she required anything else for her comfort.

Christine couldn't believe her eyes and ears. What a sudden change! It was less than a day since their last meeting but here, in the comfortable setting of his own home, the master of Locksley seemed less stressed and more welcoming. It was as though the castle walls put an immense pressure on him, and here he felt calm and relaxed. In Locksley Guy of Gisborne was his own self.

*****

Christine was in her room, when she heard the sound of an approaching horse. Soon the rider entered the grounds of the estate. He jumped down from his horse and went straight into the house.

"Sir Guy!" he called loudly.

The owner of the house, accompanied by Allan appeared from one of the rooms.

"Milord," still breathing heavily the rider bowed.

"What do you want?" said Gisborne roughly.

Guy's face immediately tensed. He knew only too well how visits like this usually ended.

"Milord, I have an urgent message from Nottingham. Where can we talk?"

Guy invited him into one of the rooms. Noticing Christine standing on the landing of the second floor, he said nothing and disappeared into the room, closing the door firmly behind him.

"What kind of news?" she thought. *"Could it be that the Sheriff has received a reply from London, and now I am in danger?"* she panicked.

Trying to tread as quietly as possible, Christine went downstairs, but no matter how hard she tried, she couldn't hear a word said behind the door. The men spoke quietly and the sturdy wooden door didn't help either. She could hear the sound of heavy footsteps and the clanking of iron spurs, and she could hear low voices, but couldn't make out the words.

She barely had time to jump away from the door and hide around a corner when, cursing aloud, Gisborne stormed out of the room. Slamming the door behind him, he walked out of the house and went straight to the stables, where, judging by the sounds, he kicked the first things that had happened to be in his way. Christine followed him.

"Is there something wrong, Milord?" she asked, genuinely concerned.

Guy didn't answer. He abruptly turned around nearly knocking her off her feet and returned to the house.

"Allan!" he barked.

"I am here, master, no need to shout," said the servant, trying to defuse the situation. He knew his master too well.

"Saddle my horse, I'm going to Nottingham," he ordered and went to his room.

Ten minutes later, a little calmer and properly attired, he was ready to go. Allan and the messenger from the castle waited for him outside.

"Watch her! Until I am back, she is not to leave the house!" Gisborne ordered mounting the saddle.

He kicked Raven in the sides. The horse whinnied loudly, protesting against such treatment, but obediently turned to leave, and soon, raising clouds of dust, the two riders galloped away from the village.

*****

All day, Christine couldn't find peace. At times, her heart would stop and then, suddenly, regain its rhythm. Her breathing was quick and uneven. She walked aimlessly, wandering around the house back and forth, from time to time exchanging meaningless phrases with Allan.

Her body was in Locksley, but her mind was riding back to Nottingham with the knight in black. She couldn't calm down and feel safe until she knew the reason for him being so suddenly summoned to Nottingham.

Time moved slowly.

She refused dinner, citing fatigue, and retired to her quarters where she paced back and forth, waiting for Gisborne's return.

The sun had gone down but he had not yet returned. About an hour after sunset, Allan wished her good night, and, to her great surprise, asked her quite frankly, if she had any plans to run away. Reassured that she wouldn't make any attempts to escape, he retired to his small room at the far end of the house.

Christine lay in bed but sleep would not come. Thoughts swirled in her head, not letting her rest. Soon, all the servants had finished their chores and retired to their rooms. The manor was plunged into darkness.

*****

The master of Locksley returned home when the moon was shining high and bright over Sherwood. Exhausted and hungry, he took Raven to the stables and went into the house. In the spacious living room, a long-cold dinner awaited him. He quickly finished off the roast partridge, drained the goblet of wine, then pouring himself another and taking the decanter with him, made himself comfortable by the fireplace. He sighed loudly as he sat in the chair. He was very tired.

Trying not to make any noise, Christine exited her room and made her way downstairs. The moment of truth had come. Now it would become clear whether or not her fears were in vain. She quietly stood in the darkness by the door.

The room was dimly lit by candles. Guy of Gisborne sat in the big chair near the fireplace. Light and shadow played on his face; two dark curls fell over his forehead. His gaze was directed ahead, the look thoughtful and focused. He silently watched the flames dancing in the depths of the fireplace.

Guy took a sip of wine and set the goblet on the floor. He wiped his wet palm over his breeches and looked at it – the long slender fingers were shaking. Several times, he clenched and unclenched his fist, but it did not help – his hand continued to shake. He sipped more wine.

Christine's nerves settled. If she had been the cause of his absence, he would have behaved differently. Now, before her, was simply a tired man, trying to dissolve the stress of a long day in a glass of wine. She turned to leave but the floorboard creaked treacherously under her foot. Holding her breath Christine froze in the dark. Guy slowly turned his head toward the sound, but couldn't see anything except the shadows dancing in the moonlight.

"Come out!" he ordered. His hand lay on the hilt of his sword, but then, his mouth twitched into a barely visible smile as Christine came out of the shadows.

"Why are you still awake?" he asked quietly.

"I'm not tired," answered Christine, not lying. "The night is so quiet, I can hear my own heartbeat."

Gisborne smiled again and silently nodded his head towards the second chair that stood by the fire. Christine sat down.

"Silence... Enjoy it, while you can," he said thoughtfully. "This silence will not be here for long. Who knows, maybe tomorrow everything will change."

"What do you mean?" asked Christine, unable to understand the meaning of his words.

Guy didn't say anything, just drained his goblet in one large gulp. His hand reached for the decanter but it was empty. He got up and left the room and soon his footsteps died away in the hallway. Christine was alone. Not knowing what to do, she got up to leave, but the owner of Locksley reappeared in the doorway with a full decanter and a second goblet in his hands. He poured himself more wine, filled the second goblet and handed it to Christine.

"Drink with me," he said as if he had forgotten all decency and manners.

His voice was soft and a little husky. She accepted the wine and took a sip.

"What did you mean when you said about silence in Locksley?" she repeated her question.

"The Sheriff," started Gisborne. Lifting the goblet back to his lips he sipped the wine again and continued, "the Sheriff demands more taxes."

"Taxes?" Christine repeated in surprise, not able to understand what made him so upset.

"Today, we were in one of the villages," he continued, not looking at her. He put the goblet down and looked at his right hand, his fingers were still shaking. "Tomorrow we go to Clun, after tomorrow – Locksley," he picked up his goblet took a long sip.

"But taxes are a very important part of the state income," Christine said, as if trying to justify the Sheriff.

"Do you think I don't know that!" he cut out roughly.

Guy got to his feet and stood with his back to her, leaning one elbow against the mantel.

"Then, what's the problem?"

"Problem?!" he turned to face her, his eyes blazing with anger. "The problem is that the Sheriff collected taxes from Locksley two weeks ago! I cannot demand tax from MY people every time the Sheriff feels like it," he snapped.

Christine felt uncomfortable. Realising that she had just touched an open wound, she rose slowly.

"I'm sorry, if I overstepped my bounds, Milord. It's already late, I think I'd better go."

Not waiting for his answer, she headed for the door. Guy quickly got up and caught up with her, closing the distance between them in one swift motion. He grabbed her firmly by the hand and pulled her into his arms.

"Not so fast," he whispered. His lips were too close to her ear. "I did not say that you could go."

His lips moved to a hairs-breadth from her cheek. A strong scent of alcohol hit her.

"You are drunk!" she tried to break free from his grasp.

"Does it matter?" he would not let her go. "I've seen how you look at me," his lips were searching for hers. "Why waste time?"

"In this state, you are unlikely to give me any pleasure," she said, not stopping her attempts to escape. "You're drunk, and can barely stand," Christine suddenly became very serious. "Let go of me and go to bed."

Obeying, he loosened his hold. Wasting no time, Christine slipped from his arms, ran up the stairs, and locked herself in her room. Gisborne stood alone in the hallway for a moment, and then staggered to his room.

He collapsed on the bed and immediately fell asleep.

The next morning he woke with the rising of the sun and a terrible headache.

*****

When Christine woke up, life in Locksley was already in full swing.

She found the master of the manor in the dining room – gloomy and slightly crumpled, Gisborne was finishing his breakfast.

Ignoring her wishes of a good morning and an enquiry about his health, he got up from his seat and, with a heavy tread, went to the yard where five riders already waited for him.

When Christine was about to sit down to take her meal, Gisborne returned to the house and went straight to the dining room.

"You are coming with us," he said roughly. His voice was hoarse, his tone unfriendly.

"I beg your pardon," Christine raised her eyebrows. "But I..."

"Not to be discussed! An order from the Sheriff!" he cut her off, but added, trying to soften his tone. "We ride in half an hour, Allan will make preparations. We will be waiting for you outside."

Having quickly finished her breakfast, she went outside. Everything was long ready and all the riders except Allan were in their saddles. The last was standing near the entrance to the stables, holding the reins of two horses.

"Thank you," said Christine, when Allan helped her to mount.

"Not to worry, ma'am, I'm always happy to help," he said cheerfully. It seemed of all of the company he was the only one in a good mood.

*****

Most of the time they rode in silence, Allan faintly whistling a cheerful melody. Two men and Gisborne rode ahead, then Christine and Allan, and then three other soldiers completed the company.

It couldn't have been as bad as she had imagined after yesterday's conversation with Gisborne. Only five people, routine administrative work – tax collection. She realised how wrong she was when at the crossroads, they met with the Sheriff, accompanied by twenty heavily armed soldiers.

Christine shuddered in disgust at the sight of his satisfied, arrogant face. Having exchanged greetings the men regrouped and rode on. Soon they reached their destination. Seeing the soldiers, the local residents rushed into their homes, deep inside knowing that even there they wouldn't find sanctuary.

The soldiers rounded the villagers up in the small area of the village square. The Sheriff sat on his horse, not even thinking of getting off. Gisborne's horse was to his right. Since they'd left Locksley, Guy had not uttered a single word; he remained silent, his face was focused, his jaw clenched tightly so that the muscles in his face twitched.

"You know why we are here, don't you?" began the Sheriff, not wasting time on a prelude. "We can do it quickly and peacefully," he nodded toward a large wagon, guarded by two soldiers, "or we can do it the long and painful way," he pointed in the direction of heavily armed soldiers. Half of them had already dismounted, the other half were still in their saddles. "In any case, you know we'll take what we've come for," he said, his mouth stretching into a hideous grin.

*****

For a long time after they had left the village, the screams and cries of the villagers remained in Christine's ears. It seemed as though the smell of fire forever burned into her nose. She wanted to cry but could not allow herself this weakness. Trying to remain calm, she swallowed the lump that choked her.

Once they, again, reached the crossroads, the squad stopped.

"Eeny, meeny, miny, moe!" the Sheriff's finger stopped, pointing to the road leading to Locksley.

Christine noticed as Gisborne tensed, gritting his teeth even tighter.

"Oh, come on, Gizzy, do not make such a face," said the Sheriff. "It's been a very long time, since you invited me over! The day is not over yet, how about we all ride to Locksley?"

"All together?" Guy asked, shooting a cautious glance at the Sheriff's squad.

"Why not?" said the Sheriff. "I am sure these men are tired and hungry as well. You will be able to find something to feed them, will you not?" he smiled hideously.

"Very well," Guy said dryly and bowed his head in humble deference.

He had no other choice but to agree. Christine saw the tension building up inside him. In the morning, he had been gloomy but now he could hardly contain his feelings. His village was in danger and there was nothing he could do about it.

*****

Later, his belly stuffed with food, full and contented, the Sheriff went to the balcony.

"Mmm," he stretched his limbs, "what a good village you have here, Gizzy!"

"Yes, your grace," Gisborne said very quietly. He knew what was coming next.

"Since we're here," Wesley turned to him. "Why waste time? You don't want us to come back again tomorrow, do you?"

"My lord, Sheriff," Guy clenched his teeth, "you said tomorrow. I did not have time to warn them."

"Well, you can warn them now," he answered, and shouted as he leaned over the railings. "Guards! Get all residents to the square, even if you have to drag them by force. Now!" Then he folded his arms, closed his eyes and, as if nothing had happened, lifted his face to the sun.

The soldiers obeyed unquestioningly. Soon all the villagers were gathered in the square. The cries, shouts and noises could be heard from all around, as women tried to calm their frightened children.

When all the residents were assembled, the Sheriff mounted his horse and leisurely rode into the village square. He remained on horseback and addressed people, towering above them.

"Apologies if we have interrupted your daily routines," he said with undisguised sarcasm, "but your master has an important announcement."

The Sheriff waved his hand, inviting Gisborne, who moved forward, with the Sheriff's men were behind him.

"People of Locksley," he began loudly, "as you know, our country is engaged in war. Our King, Richard, is fighting the infidels in the Holy Land."

He tried to speak calmly. At some point, his face became a mask and no longer reflected any emotions. Like a robot, he repeated the words that he had memorised long ago.

"We, as the devoted subjects of His Majesty..." he continued.

"Blah-de-blah-de-blah!" the Sheriff could not resist the temptation to add his sarcastic remark. "If you carry on like that, we will be here until tomorrow morning! Let's speed up the process, shall we? Tax Day! Go and look in your houses for what you are willing to sacrifice in the name of the King and his great cause."

Whispers of indignation rolled among the people gathered in the square.

"Well! What are you waiting for?" the Sheriff waved his hand. "Get on with it, now!"

Someone tried to protest, but was dragged away and beaten by the Sheriff's soldiers. The panic began. The villagers tried to run, to take sanctuary in their homes, but it was easier said than done. With their heavy boots, the soldiers knocked through the thin doors, pulled people out and beat them until they gave up everything they had.

*****

After lunch, Christine was resting in her room. Having heard screams and noises outside, she went outside and ran to the square.

"Sir Guy, what's going on here?" she breathed out, trying to steady her breath.

He said nothing, his face expressionless, like a graven image. He stood motionless staring absently before him.

"Everything is all right, my dear," the Sheriff answered for him. "Internal affairs of the state, you do not need to worry."

"Can you really not do anything?" Christine said, watching how the soldiers destroyed and savaged the livelihoods of Locksley's community. "This is YOUR village!"

"Yes, Gizzy, can you really not do anything? Like, to explain to them that it's useless to resist... My men will take what they've come for either way," the Sheriff began to lose his patience.

Two soldiers ran into the square.

"Your grace, someone has barricaded themselves inside the house on the edge of the village."

"Sir Guy..." the Sheriff turned to Gisborne. "Would you be so kind..." he began, "as to help my soldiers. NOW!" he yelled so loudly, it made Christine jump.

Obeying the orders of the Sheriff, Gisborne started to move towards the house. At first, he walked, but then started to pick up speed and after just a few steps, he ran. His eyes gleamed, his nostrils flared, anger overwhelmed him; anger and hatred for the Sheriff of Nottingham, but also anger and loathing for himself.

Christine ran after him. Having studied his fiery nature over this short period of time, she knew, in this state Gisborne was capable of anything.

"Open up!" his heavy blows shook the thin door. "Open up!" he repeated still pounding.

On the third attempt, with the help of the soldiers Guy brought the door down. Hiding something behind his back and threatening the intruders with a small dagger, there was a boy of no more than twelve years old. He was no match for Gisborne, who easily freed the boy from his weapon and dragged the poor soul to the street.

"What are you doing? He's only a child!" Christine grabbed Guy's arm, trying to stop him, but he couldn't hear anything and shook her off his hand as if she was a fly. Christine flew to the ground.

Gisborne grabbed the boy by the collar of his dirty shirt, dragged him to the square and pushed him onto the dirt before the Sheriff's feet. Following him, the soldiers brought out a big sack that they had found in the house.

"Hmm..." the Sheriff looked at the bag, then at the boy. "Is this not the very flour that was stolen on its way to the castle just a few days ago?"

He looked at the boy, who, even if he had tried, wouldn't have been able to lift the sack, let alone steal it from a moving cart.

"Thief!" said the Sheriff, looking sternly at the boy. He then turned to the people crowding the square. "Do you know what we do with thieves? Guards, take him!"

Gisborne walked away. The soldiers lifted the boy up to his feet and led him to the wagon.

Christine could bear it no longer, pushing the soldiers aside she tried to leave. A strong hand grabbed her not allowing her to move.

"Where do you think you are going?" Guy breathed out heavily. His eyes were as cold as ice.

"Let me go, I don't want to see this anymore!" she tried to break free.

"Oh, trust me, you haven't seen anything yet!" he grinned wickedly.

"You... you..." Christine fought a battle, trying not to say the words on the tip of her tongue.

"Come! Say it!" Guy egged her on. Adrenaline rushed through his veins; he could no longer control himself.

"Murderer!" Christine said quietly looking straight into his eyes.

"Hmm, look who's talking!" he snapped, referring to the alleged purpose of her presence in Nottingham.

"Perhaps," she answered angrily, "but at least I don't get pleasure from it, and I don't kill innocent children." She was finally able to pry his hand away and walked quickly towards the house.

"Good!" he barked as she walked away. "And stay there!"

He returned to the square. The soldiers had already finished loading the spoils. Tied up, the boy was sitting on the edge of the cart under the supervision of the guards.

Guy was very tired. He was exhausted physically and emotionally. He waited for the Sheriff to finally leave Locksley. He wanted to return to the house as soon as possible and to drown this day in wine.

He looked at his people. Today he had betrayed them. Today, he had not stood up for them; he couldn't disobey the Sheriff. His gaze wandered around the villagers and then suddenly stopped. His heart, that just a second ago was pounding like a hammer in forge, had stopped too. A cold sweat broke out on his forehead. Among the crowd, he saw the face – the same face that had come to him so many times in his dreams. It was the very same man, who, every night, pierced him through with his own sword. Pale and haggard, like a ghost, the man stood among the crowd and did not take his black eyes off Guy.

"I will come for you!" said his look.

*****

That night, Christine barely slept, waking up constantly through the night, the cries from the day still echoing in her ears. Each time she woke up, she found it hard to fall asleep again, tossing and turning in her big bed.

When she woke up for the last time, the day was already dawning, brightening the sky over Sherwood with shades of pale pink and gold.

With a heavy sigh, Christine sat up. The last dream had disturbed her, and she cursed herself for it! How could she have such feelings for this cold-blooded murderer! But she couldn't lie to herself; no matter how hard she tried to deny it, she was drawn to him. Undoubtedly, he had an explosive temper, and often he was rude and arrogant, but a few days ago, in Locksley she saw his other side, and it haunted her. In her dream, he was different.

In her dream, he was rough, but gentle at the same time. His hands were strong and skilful, his lips – soft and warm, his kisses – hot. He knew what he was doing and what he wanted. She had no choice but to succumb, but he didn't take her by force – their desire and passion were mutual. They dissolved into one another, again and again, climbing to the heights of bliss.

Christine sat in bed. Her body ached from overwhelming desire, her face flushed as fragments of her vision surfaced in her head over and over again. She could have sworn that she could still feel his lips. Her cheek still hurt as if it was burnt by a fire after gliding over his stubbly jaw.

"This has to stop!" she told herself. "It's just a product of your imagination. This must stop! I've got to get out of this place before it's too late."

She got out of bed, dressed quickly and slipped out into the corridor. The manor was still asleep. Trying to be as quiet as possible, she went downstairs and out into the yard. In the stables, she met Allan.

"Good morning, ma'am, you are up early today," he said with sadness in his voice.

"I could not sleep," Christine said.

"Yes..." he trailed off.

He didn't need to say more, it was written all over his face. Locksley had become his home village too. Trying to show sympathy, Christine put her hand on his shoulder.

"Allan, can you prepare my horse... or show me where the saddle is, and I'll do it myself," she said, constantly looking around, as if afraid of something.

"Is it not too early for a ride, ma'am?" he asked cautiously.

"I can no longer be here, under the same roof as him," Christine nodded towards the house. "It's unbearable. I need to clear my head."

"Yes, of course," he understood. "Give me few moments," said Allan and, yawning quietly, went away.

Christine went to the kitchen and put some bread into a travel bag. Taking a flask of water with her, she returned to the stables, where Allan was already waiting for her.

"Are you going to...?" he asked noting her bag but did not dare to finish. "Ma'am, you cannot..."

"Thank you!" she said softly, ignoring him and gently kissed him on the cheek.

The young man didn't answer; he shook his head almost imperceptibly, and tossed her up into the saddle.

"Where do you think you're going?!" a loud, menacing voice shouted behind them.

Loudly and heavily stepping onto the wooden flooring, Gisborne ran outside and firmly grabbed the reins of Christine's stallion.

"I ask, where do you think are you going?" he repeated angrily.

"Does it matter?!" Christine answered in the same tone. "Anywhere, away from you! You disgust me!" she pulled the reins.

Guy removed his hand. He couldn't argue – he disgusted himself.

"Step aside!" Christine spat, as she kicked the horse in the sides and galloped out of the village.

Riding away from the manor, she nearly collided with a horseman riding in the opposite direction. She had seen this man before; it was a messenger from the castle, but this no longer concerned her. She rode on, looking for the path to the Big Stone, and from there to the South Gates, where she hoped, she would find her way home.

"She'll be back after few hours, or when she gets hungry," Gisborne spat angrily, walking back into the house.

"I do not think so, Milord," said Allan.

"What? What do you mean?" Guy turned abruptly and grabbed his servant by the collar of his jacket.

"Well... I think... she... she..." Allan muttered.

"Speak!" Gisborne roared.

"Sir, it seems to me..." he did not have to say more, Guy understood everything.

With a loud sigh of irritation and anger, he pushed Allan out of the away. The rider from Nottingham stopped at the porch of the house.

"Sir Guy! The Sheriff wants you to come to Nottingham, immediately," he said panting.

"The Sheriff?! What does he want from me again?" thought Guy. *"Were the last two days not enough for him?"*

The pressure that had built up inside him over the past few days needed a release. He could not hold it back any longer. Gisborne turned around, entered the stables and with all of his mighty force kicked the wooden pole. Pain swept through his body, but he didn't care. He once again swung his leg for a second kick but suddenly stopped. He saw something glitter on the ground, amidst the hay. He knelt down and parted the dry grass. Right in front of him on the ground, sparkling in the sun, lay a silver bracelet.

Guy's mouth crooked into a contented grin. He knew exactly to whom this object belonged, but had no plans of returning it to its rightful owner.

*****

That morning, John Wesley was in good spirits. When Gisborne entered the castle grounds, he was still strolling around the carts filled with their spoils. He looked pleased.

"Ah! At last, I've been waiting for you, my boy," he said. "Look at this wonderful haul! Our friends will be very happy!" he was bursting with pride.

"The haul is wonderful indeed," drawled Guy. "And what are you planning to do with those?" he nodded toward the cattle seized from those who had no money to pay to the Sheriff.

"I am sure we will figure something out," the Sheriff said, a nasty grin spreading across his face. "Do not forget, tomorrow is my birthday. There will be guests."

"Yes, of course, I had not thought about that, your grace," said Guy.

"Over the past few days I have noticed this new habit of yours – not thinking!" the Sheriff quipped and laughed.

Guy rolled his eyes.

"Oh, come on, Gizzy, do not be like that," he patted his deputy on the shoulder and beckoned him to follow.

Quickly climbing the stairs, the men went inside. The damp and dark corridors of the castle were cool and refreshing after the hot summer sun.

"I only have one question, my lord," said Gisborne, after a short silence. The Sheriff raised an eyebrow. "What would you do if the King sent a real request for the tax collection?" he asked.

"Well, it is in our mutual interests, you and I," the Sheriff stopped and looked at him, "that such a request does not come," he said, and continued to walk.

They soon reached the Sheriff's chamber.

"By the way, how go the preparations for the assassination of Robin Hood?" he asked as soon as they were inside.

"Excuse me, your grace," of all the questions that the Sheriff could have asked this was the last that Guy had expected, "we still have not had the opportunity. We do not... you yourself know, the last two days, we..." he said apologetically.

"Uh, excuses, excuses!" said the Sheriff. "And what do you two do by night?" he looked at him and laughed again in his hoarse repulsive way. "At least there, I hope, you do not waste your time? Or do you still swoon over that..." the Sheriff pouted his lips and blinked his eyelashes, mocking Lady Marian's image, "if I was a little younger, I would have..."

Guy, yet again, tightly gritted his teeth and bit his tongue. His personal life was no concern of this old man.

"By the way, since we are talking about her, give her this, together with the invitation to the gathering on the occasion of my birthday," he handed Gisborne a big, heavy package.

"To Lady Marian?" Guy was taken aback. "*Why would the Sheriff invite her to his feast?*"

"Miss Hawk! You idiot!" the Sheriff exhaled heavily and shook his head in displeasure.

"I am not sure that Miss Hawk will accept your invitation, your grace," Gisborne said, ignoring another insult thrown by the Sheriff.

"Really? Why would you think so? In any case, try to persuade her. Such a woman would be the cherry on any celebratory cake!" He winked, a greasy smile appearing on his face. "Use your charm, would you? You know how to do these things."

Guy bowed his head and bared his teeth in a simile of a smile.

"Go now, I'm busy," said the Sheriff, turning Gisborne in the direction of the door. "Yes, you can invite your leper girlfriend as well. She will try to sniff around anyway, so better if she does so under our supervision," he laughed again.

Gisborne had gone. He did not dare inform the Sheriff that he would likely not have the pleasure of Miss Hawk's company, as she had left Locksley this morning in an unknown direction.

He took the package outside, ordered it to be attached to his horse and returned to the castle. He couldn't leave without seeing Lady Marian.

*****

"Sir Guy, I cannot accept this," Lady Marian handed back the bracelet.

"Why? Don't you like it?" he asked surprised.

"Oh no, on the contrary, it's very beautiful," she assured him.

"Then why do you refuse?" he would not understand. "My gifts offend you!"

"No! Not at all! I do not want to upset you. Sir Guy..." she did not know what to say. "However, an unmarried girl should not accept such gifts."

"Marian, I have never made a secret of my intentions," his irritation evident in his voice. "You know that I want to marry you! Why, then..."

"Sir Guy, I beg you!" Marian tried to reassure him. "You know my circumstances."

"Circumstances?!" he was beginning to get angry. "You talk as though I do not know of your circumstances! You act as if I do not try to change them! Marian!"

"Sir Guy..." she was afraid of such a sharp and sudden change in his mood. "I did not mean to offend you; I did not mean it that way."

"You know that one word from you would be enough for me to take you away from this place."

"But the Sheriff! He will never allow it."

"If you become Lady Gisborne, he will have no choice but to set you free," he took her hand in his and said, gently looking into her brown eyes, "I'll take you to Locksley, I know you like that place."

"But I cannot," she whispered.

"Cannot what?!" he snapped, suddenly becoming very serious. "Is the prospect of marrying me so disgusting that you're willing to spend the rest of your life in prison?"

A frightened Marian lifted her eyes to him, not knowing what to say.

"I'm starting to get tired of your games, Marian," he pulled her closer, his blue eyes scalded her with cold fire. "Sooner or later, I'll get what I want! Soon, very soon, I will get the land and money, and then I will not need your consent. If you still resist," his lips were very close, "I'll take you by force!" he said enunciating each word.

He let go of her. Marian stood blinking silently. She did not doubt his words in the slightest.

"And yet," his voice suddenly changed becoming soft again, "I hope to have the pleasure of seeing you tomorrow at the gathering, and I would be honoured if you would wear my gift."

He put the bracelet in her hand, bowed and retired.

"Now to Locksley!" At whatever cost he had to find that fugitive, before her absence was known in the castle.

*****

"Is SHE back?" shouted Gisborne as soon as he saw Allan.

"Is who back, master?"

"Miss Hawk," he said, emphasising each word and reining the horse to a dead stop. "Is she back?"

Allan shook his head. Gisborne cursed and was about to dismount when the sound of approaching horses came from behind.

Two soldiers from his personal squad rode towards the manor. On a lead, behind them, galloped a horse; the rider was not in the saddle. Without a doubt, Gisborne recognised that dark stallion with a white star on the forehead. A roar of irritation and anger burst from him. Over the past few days, he had had enough problems and now this.

He dismounted and examined the horse. There were no marks of blood or signs of struggle. The animal too showed no anxiety or distress; there was a flask of water and bread intact in a travel bag. Guy did not like that.

"We need to find her!" he said to the soldiers, his face worried. "The sooner the better..."

*****

Breaking away from Locksley, Christine rode through the forest, away, further and further away from that cursed place. In the time she had spent over the past few days traveling in between the villages, she had memorised the way. Or so she thought.

The trail circled, twisted and turned, forked and then converged again. Sometimes she had to slow down, but she wouldn't stop. However, about an hour after leaving Locksley, the first doubts of the rightness and, most importantly, of the wisdom of her actions began to creep into her soul. Her horse was beginning to tire and the Big Stone, behind which lay her way home, was nowhere to be seen.

Winding its way through the woods, the road came out at the training camp. A sigh of relief escaped her, as she was beginning to doubt that she would ever be able to get out of this thicket.

Returning to the crossroads, for a long while she couldn't decide which way to go – right or left.

"Oh to hell with it! Even if I take the wrong turn, I will always be able to come back."

At least now, she had a rough idea of her location.

As she anticipated, the road led her out of the woods, but seeing a huge field and the city walls further in the distance,

Christine abruptly stopped the horse. She couldn't be seen here! Moving away from the main trail, she entered the undergrowth and rode slowly under the cover of the trees, while maintaining a perfect view of the road.

Finally, after many hours spent in the woods, she reached the place that she was looking for, pulled on the reins, and directed her stallion to the trail that led to the right from the Big Stone.

It was only when the animal refused to go any further, from sheer exhaustion, that Christine realised she was also very tired and hungry. They had left Locksley shortly after dawn, and now the sun stood high above the forest.

Soon, among the rustling of the leaves and the birdsong, she heard the sound of water. Just what she needed. The horse could drink and they could both have a little rest. She dismounted and, taking the horse by the bridle, gently began to wend her way through the trees. Very soon, she found herself in a small clearing near a noisy forest stream. They moved closer and the stallion eagerly dipped his head towards the water. She approvingly patted his neck, and releasing the bridle, walked along the stream, stretching her legs and arms. She drank some water from the flask, washed her face and sat on the grass, lifting her face to the sun.

The summer sun was hot, stroking her face with its warm rays; the water gurgled, and finally, there was peace and quiet. Everything was quiet, too quiet perhaps... This alarmed her. She was very close to the water, and the forest should have been buzzing with life, yet there was silence. She listened. Somewhere very close by she heard the sound of a twig break. The horse looked up from the water and, lifting his ears, began to move restlessly.

"Shh," Christine rose to her feet. "It's okay, it's just the wind," she said trying to calm the stallion, not really believing her own words.

There was another sound.

"Whispering voices?"

She listened, trying to remain motionless. Someone was hiding in the bushes behind her. The question was, who was it? And also, what did they want from her?

With wild cries and hoots, Friar Tuck and Little John jumped out of the trees. They had been watching their victim for a while and, seeing the well-stuffed duffel bag tied to a horse, decided not to waste any more time.

Startled, Christine stumbled and sliding down into the stream got one of her feet stuck in the mud. But that wasn't the worst of it – she let go of the reins and the frightened animal, feeling freedom, instantly galloped away into the forest.

"Hey! Stop!" Christine shouted, in vain.

With some difficulty, she got out of the water and took a few awkward steps toward the forest in a failed attempt to catch up with her transport, but quickly realised it was useless.

"This is not happening!" she moaned loudly. Not even trying to hide her anger, Christine went back to the meadow.

Taken aback, the pair, who had not expected such a reaction, still stood motionless beside the stream.

"Seriously?!" she exclaimed. "Could you have been any louder?!"

She looked at them, hardly able to contain herself. She didn't care who they were or what they wanted from her. Thanks to them, she was now left without any means of transport, and might possibly have lost her only chance of returning home.

"So, who do we have here…" she looked at the failed gangsters with interest. "Priest… and a fat dude… Perfect! Who are you? What did you hope to achieve, if you don't mind me asking? Did you want to rob me – is that it??"

Every time either of the men tried to say something in their defence, she continued to speak.

"It couldn't have been easier! You could've knocked me out, then searched me and then when you didn't find anything you could have just pissed off!" she said, with notes of despair in her voice.

Christine shook her head. She had no choice but to continue her journey on foot. Somehow, she managed to pull her stuck-in-the-mud boot out, put it back on, and with a mocking bow, wished the two men a very good day. She walked in the direction her stallion had galloped away, hoping to catch up with it on the way.

Friar Tuck and Little John remained standing on the bank of the stream scratching their beards. They looked at each other silently, still not understanding what had just happened.

*****

No matter how far Christine walked, and whatever direction she turned, the forest was all around her. At some point, she began to think that she was going round and round in the same place. As if in a mystical closed circuit, she wandered in a circle, not able to find her way out. She was tired. She was starving and needed water, but there wasn't a single living soul around to help her.

What she didn't know was that for the past half an hour, a sole rider was following her hectic movements through the forest. Gisborne watched her while keeping a safe distance. He knew this part of the forest well, so it wasn't difficult for him to remain unnoticed.

He and his men had had to work hard, scouting the woods and talking to the locals, trying not to create unnecessary attention.

In Sherwood, rumours spread very quickly. The last thing he needed were unnecessary questions from the Sheriff.

Nevertheless, he had found her and that was the most important thing. Now, with her under his supervision, he couldn't deny himself the pleasure of witnessing her agony.

When the day was coming to an end, Christine finally managed to get out of the thicket. The trees thinned and she could then see the edge of the forest and a large clearing. She felt as if she had been here before, but she couldn't remember. Muttering curses, and feeling exhausted, she sat on a fallen tree.

Guy, who all this time had been watching her, tensed. He knew this part of the woods, perhaps too well, and he didn't feel comfortable here. In his head flashed the memory of that very day just over two weeks ago – it was in this very place that he first saw Christine. Many things had happened since then.

Now, she was sitting on a tree, her head in her hands. At this point, all of her movement was characterised by obvious fatigue. She raised her head and seemed to be looking straight at him.

"No, it's not possible... She can't see me!"

However, through the green of the trees, Christine's gaze was directed right at him.

"Why!" she asked loudly.

He winced.

"Why!" she asked again, this time louder, still keeping her eyes on the target ahead.

Guy froze.

"Why do I ask you?!" she got to her feet and looked up. "Why?! What have I done?" her words were directed to the heavens above.

A sigh of relief escaped Gisborne – his presence was still unnoticed. Quietly and carefully he began to move forward.

"Why are you testing me? What sins have I committed in my past life that you send me here, to these savages and murderers..." Her feelings raged inside her, her voice broke in a sob, but she didn't care, there was no one here to hear her.

With every step, he came closer to her. "What?! What do you want from me? What should I do? I'll do whatever you want!" she once again raised her eyes up to the skies above her. "Give me a hint, and I'll do it! Anything to get out of this place..." she stopped and wearily sat down again.

Gisborne was already too close. If Christine had lifted her head now, she would have seen, through the trees, Raven and his master's arrogant smirk. Guy made a sound, softly clearing his throat. Christine startled in surprise and looked up.

"Really?!" she exploded, and once again raised her eyes to the sky. "Him?!" staring at the celestial blueness, she pointed a finger in

Gisborne's direction. "What should I do to get out of here?" she asked finally looking at the man standing in front of her. "Shag him?!"

"Need help?" asked Gisborne, his mouth stretched into a wide, smug smile.

"You..." she breathed out with passion.

He did not respond but only bowed in greeting.

"What do you want from me?" she asked in a completely indifferent voice.

"I thought it was you who might be in need of something from me. Help... perhaps? Maybe, to get out of here?" he said with a cheeky smile.

"Oh, just look at him! A knight in shining armour... on his galloping bloody horse, has come to my rescue."

He didn't react to her insults, but grinned impudently. The situation clearly amused him.

"You only have to ask, love... Nicely," he said.

"Love?!" the use of such a familiarity made Christine even more angry. Where had all her iron self-control gone? She could not understand. "How dare you! I am Miss Hawk to you!"

She came closer to his horse. Guy, proudly towering over her, leaned forward and lifted her chin up closer to his face.

"You only need to ask, dear..." he enjoyed every moment of his small triumph.

"I do not need your help!" she pushed his hand away.

"Do you want to go back to Locksley, or not?" he was beginning to lose patience. Her stubbornness was beyond reasonable.

"Go to hell, Milord! To the Devil!" she spat, not being able to control herself; fatigue was taking over and she was losing all reason.

"Oh, you have no idea..." he drawled, his eyes changed, his nostrils began to flare like those of a furious beast. "We are practically neighbors."

"Good! So stay there!" Christine turned away from him, and went back to the tree, but after few steps, she stopped, realising that she was making a terrible mistake. "Please don't leave me here..." she whispered, still standing with her back to him, but it was too late.

Gisborne had turned his horse and, as quickly as the woodland path allowed, rode off in the opposite direction. Christine sat down on the ground.

"Oh, I'm such a stupid idiot!"

The sun had started to set beyond the horizon; evening was falling over Sherwood Forest. She had no choice but to try to find her way back.

"To a village... I am sure I will be able to get somewhere," she tried to calm herself.

Christine slowly rose to her feet – they hurt. It was hard to walk but she had no choice. She couldn't spend the night in the forest.

"Stubborn fool!" she cursed herself, slowly making her way through the trees. "He offered you help!"

Her legs tangled in the underbrush and low branches, but with each step, it was easier to walk, and soon she came out onto the road.

She was surprised beyond belief when, coming out of the woods, she saw Gisborne, standing on the roadside, leaning against a mighty tree. Raven was tied close by and was peacefully nibbling on the fresh grass.

"Look who is here! It took her some time to get out of there," he said as if speaking to his stallion.

"What are you..." uttered Christine.

"Whatever you may think of me, my dear," he tried to look very strict, but his eyes were smiling, "I cannot leave a woman alone in the woods. Even one so stubborn as you. I was not brought up that way."

"Well, it's a credit to your parents," said Christine, coming closer.

"Do you want to stand here discussing the virtues of my parents, or do you want to return to Locksley?" he asked sternly. "I understand that you probably enjoy the beauty of the local scenery, but I have no intention of spending the night in the forest."

Despite her fatigue, Christine smiled slightly. He could have gone a long time ago and left her, but in spite of all the sarcastic comments, he didn't, and offered her help. Only for that, he deserved her respect.

"Very well, you can take me to Locksley," she mumbled at last.

"Excuse me? I did not hear that," he smiled softly back at her.

"You can take me to Locksley," Christine repeated louder.

Guy didn't move. He stood there, looking at the patterns formed over his head by the interwoven branches of the tree. After a pause, he quietly raised his hand to his ear.

"Alright! You can take me to Locksley. Please!" finally she said what he had been waiting to hear.

"That's better!" he rubbed his hands gleefully and went to untie his horse. "You are by far the most stubborn woman I have ever met in my life!" he said, tossing her up into the saddle.

Christine sighed with relief as soon as she dropped into the saddle. Her tired legs thrummed. She closed her eyes, waiting for the horse to go, but the animal didn't move. Guy gently tapped on the toe of her boot.

"You'll have to move," he smiled.

Christine looked at him blankly.

"Move forward. You don't think I'll go on foot, do you?" he asked, smiling up at her.

"But... you... we..." too tired, she couldn't arrange the words into a sentence.

"If we want to get out of the forest before nightfall, you'll have to move. For him, do not worry," Guy patted the stallion's mane, "he's strong."

The animal snorted approvingly and Christine had to comply.

"Forward, forward, a little more," directed Gisborne.

Finally, when she was practically sitting on the horse's neck, he quickly mounted into the saddle.

"Um, good," he drawled, making himself comfortable. "Now you can move back. Do not be afraid, I will not bite," he laughed.

Christine slid smoothly into the remainder of the saddle. Her shoulders touched his chest, his strong legs pressed her thighs to Raven's sides. She could feel his manhood pressed hard against her tailbone.

"I will not bite..." he repeated slowly, his hot breath caressed her cheek. "Unless you want me to..."

Christine, outraged by such impudence, gathered all her last strength and turned to respond to his comment. His face was too close; she recoiled in surprise.

"What?" asked Gisborne, a crooked smile playing on his lips.

One look at him was enough for Christine to realise that he was just teasing her. In the expression of his face and in his eyes, there was no disrespect.

"Nothing," she said softly, turning away. "I think I'll shut my mouth. And keep quiet until we get back to Locksley," she muttered under her breath.

"A wise decision!" the rider behind her chuckled softly. "Probably the first of the day."

This time, a hint of sarcasm had slipped into his words but she felt neither angered nor threatened by it. She smiled and raised her hands in surrender. She no longer had the strength to argue and bicker.

Guy spurred the horse and Raven began to move slowly, gradually picking up speed. At first, Christine was trying to sit straight, but gradually the day's fatigue took its toll. She relaxed and leaned against the man sitting behind her. Resting her head on his shoulder, she quietly dozed off under the monotonous sound of the hooves.

Despite the vicissitudes of the previous days, right now, next to him, for the first time in a long time, she felt safe.

Chapter 12:
These Are My Demons

It was already dark, when hungry and tired they finally reached the village. Even though Raven was a strong and hardy animal, their journey back to Locksley took several hours.

Allan met them at the entrance to the manor, he sighed with relief when he saw Christine unharmed. Not knowing why, he felt as if he owed his master an apology. He could have kept her in the manor, but he had not and, in a way, had helped her to escape.

He helped them to dismount and, after seeing them both to the dining room, where the dinner had long been waiting, went back outside. The animal that had made such a long journey with two riders on its back also needed some love and care.

Christine was sitting in a chair, sipping her wine in silence. She didn't want to eat. Today's journey exhausted her to the point where her only desire was to get to her room and crawl into bed.

"Are you not hungry?" asked Gisborne a little tersely.

He spoke for the first time since they had returned to Locksley. Having quickly swallowed a few mouthfuls of food, he had satisfied his hunger enough to allow him to carve the rest of the leg of the roasted suckling pig with pleasure.

Christine shook her head.

"I'm too tired to eat," she said softly, "but thank you for your concern."

"As you wish," he finished off his own portion and, unceremoniously moving her plate closer to him, set to the second.

Despite the fatigue, Christine staunchly sat at the table until the end of dinner, but it wasn't just because Guy was the owner of the house. He had not abandoned her in the forest and had helped her to get out of the woods. Leaving him alone would be improper and rude at the very least.

After dinner, they moved closer to the fire but exchanged few words. Christine was too tired to try to find any common topics for conversation, and the owner of the manor was too much preoccupied with his own thoughts. He was silent, watching the flames dance in the depths of the fireplace. He still could not rid his thoughts of the words that he had heard from Christine earlier today.

"Why do I ask you?! Why?! What have I done?" again and again flashed through his mind. *"Why are you testing me? What sins have I committed in my past life that you send me here, to these savages and murderers..."*

He could not understand what it all meant. He shot a quick, cautious glance at his guest. She sat across from him, but seemed removed, not aware of him at all. Her face was beautiful, yet very sad; her eyes looked into the void before her. He once again returned to the thought that there was something unusual about her, something strange that differentiated her from all the women that he knew; something in her manner of speaking, in the way she presented herself, perhaps, in the way she looked at him. She was frank, not shy or hesitant. Had she developed these mannerisms because of her profession – he had never met with a female assassin – or was it something else?

No longer able to fight the fatigue that was washing over her, Christine stood up; she wished Guy a good night and walked to the door, but stopped at the threshold.

"Thank you," she said quietly. Gisborne lifted his eyes to meet hers. "Thank you, for not leaving me in the woods."

"I should have done so," he said dryly, "to teach you a good lesson, but I think you've already had one," he turned his eyes back to the fire.

"Yes! Perhaps, but you..." she began, but Guy stopped her, raising his hand. He didn't want to continue this conversation.

"Go," he said wearily, "tomorrow will be a new day. We can discuss it tomorrow, if you still wish to do so."

He was right, to fight over who was right and who was wrong now would have been be a waste of time.

"Good night, Milord," she said, and retired to her room, leaving Gisborne in the company of a decanter of wine, and a dying fire.

Returning to her room, she slowly undressed and, leaving the long shirt on, climbed under the covers. Stretching her tired limbs, she took a deep breath and instantly fell asleep.

*****

A strange sound brought her out of the caressing embrace of slumber. Wide-eyed she sat on the bed. It was dark and quiet, except for the barely noticeable sounds that were coming from the other side of the door.

An uneasy chill ran down her spine.

"What if someone's got into the house... into my room..." adrenaline hit her right in the temple, dissolving the remnants of sleepiness.

She sat upright on the bed staring into the darkness but could not see anything. The night was dark and moonless; shadows played with her imagination, sending her weird images. She closed her eyes and then opened them again; gradually they grew accustomed to the dark.

There was no one in her room. She listened – it was all quiet, but soon she heard the strange sound once again – a quiet moan or a cry, she couldn't say what exactly. It was coming from the back of the house.

Christine stood up and, having wrapped a large knitted shawl around her shoulders, stepped into the corridor. Taking each step cautiously, she walked quietly in the dead of the night, carefully peering into the darkness and listening to every sound. As she crossed the hall, she could hear it more clearly – the muffled cries came out of the room on the other side of the hallway.

A dim light shone from under the door of Gisborne's bedchamber. Wrapping the shawl tighter around her shoulders, Christine stopped by the door. She could hear the hushed moans and sensed some movement inside the room.

"Oh no!" the awareness of her own stupidity hit her, as if a bucket of cold water had been poured over her. "Moans... Sighs... You are such a fool! You imagine all sorts of horrors, and he is just having a good time with one of the servants!" she muttered quietly under her breath.

She suddenly felt extremely uncomfortable with all the awkwardness of the situation, and blushed like a schoolgirl. After everything that had happened today, the last thing she should have done was to eavesdrop at his door, while he was relieving the stress of the day through the satisfactions of basic natural instincts.

Her cheeks began to burn even more; she couldn't help it. She was about to leave, when the sudden loud roar that came from the room made her wince. It wasn't the moan of a man, who had reached the peak of ecstasy – no, it was the cry of a wounded animal that had thrown itself into the last, final battle.

The next moment, all went quiet behind the door; she couldn't hear anything except his heavy breathing. Christine had her hand poised to knock, but didn't dare. Whatever was happening in that room was none of her concern. She stepped back. She had no place here...

A rustle at the door alerted Gisborne to the presence of the intruder.

"Who is there?!" he asked loudly through the door.

Christine paused. She decided not to respond, and sneak back to her room unnoticed, but failed in her attempt. Stepping back, she stumbled over something in the dark. A clay pot, which served as a flower vase, fell crashing to the floor, crumbling into small pieces. In the silence of the night, the sound echoed through the house.

"This is your last warning..." a voice from behind the door sounded eerily. "Who's there?!"

Christine could have sworn she heard the scraping sound of metal. Gisborne had pulled out his sword and was prepared to meet the intruder.

"It's me... Christine," she whispered, clinging to the door and immediately corrected herself. "Miss Hawk."

"What do you want?" asked an unfriendly voice.

"I... I..." she couldn't find the words, that terrible roar was still sounding in her ears.

"What do you want?" he repeated.

"I was awakened by sounds. I heard a groan or a cry... and I..." haltingly, she tried to explain her presence at his door. "I thought... I don't even know what I thought," she said, looking at the dark surface before her. "I can't believe we are having this conversation through a closed door!" she added suddenly.

On the other side, she heard quiet footsteps and then the sound of a metal bolt. The heavy door creaked open.

"What do you want?" he asked, a little gruffly.

Christine opened her mouth to reply to his rudeness, but one look at him made her forget all the anger and resentment.

Barefoot, in breeches, without a shirt, Guy stood in the doorway, clutching his huge sword tightly in his hand. In the dim light of the candles, his face resembled a lifeless mask. He was pale. Dark wet locks fell over his forehead; his face and body were covered with droplets of sweat. He was alone in the room.

Christine peered into his face – horror was frozen in his deep blue eyes. One look at him was enough to understand what had frightened him was in the darkness of his room; it was the "something" which, just few minutes ago, had provoked that terrible cry.

"What do you want?" he asked again, still a little rough, but this time more calmly.

"Are you alright?" Christine ignored his question and asked with a note of sincere concern in her voice.

"Why did you come? You shouldn't be here," he sounded tired.

"You screamed like someone was trying to kill you! I thought someone had got into the house," she tried to look him in the eye.

"You shouldn't have come," he said blankly.

"You look like you've seen a ghost," said Christine finally catching his gaze. "Can I help you at all?" she added softly. Knowing too well that such a gesture would be completely inappropriate, Christine put a gentle hand over his.

"These are my demons!" he jerked his hand away. "I'm to fight them!"

Sleepy, dishevelled Allan appeared on the stairs.

"Sir Guy, is anything..." he broke off when he saw Christine dressed in only her night shirt, with the simple shawl around her shoulders. "Burning the midnight candle, huh?" he smiled.

It didn't take him long to draw his own conclusions regarding her presence outside his master's room at this hour. Gisborne shot him a stern look.

"Excuse me, ma'am, I just did not expect to see you here," Allan said, a little embarrassed, and directed his eyes to his master. "I heard a noise, Sir," he said, trying not to look at the half-dressed woman.

"It's all right, Allan," Guy said quietly. "Miss Hawk here thought there were burglars in the house. She decided to take them down on her own," he looked at her, a familiar note of irony appeared in his voice. Guy smiled faintly.

"Yes, Allan, it was a completely stupid idea," Christine instantly picked up the tone of the conversation and turned an innocent face to Allan. "I thought there was someone in the house and came to check, and in the dark, I stumbled over this," she patted the wooden cabinet. "Something fell off and seems to have woken half the house," she gave the master of Locksley a long look.

"I thought I heard screams..." Allan rubbed his sleepy face.

"Oh, that was me as well," she continued in a childlike manner. "In any case, if there were any intruders in the house, they have likely fled by now, frightened off by my clumsiness," she smiled.

Allan seemed to believe her story, or maybe not, but at this early hour, he didn't seem to care about the details, he wanted to sleep. Everything was in order, there were no strangers in the house and that was the most important thing. He bowed and wandered off to his room to continue his interrupted sleep.

"I am grateful to you..." began Guy.

"Not at all," she replied dryly. The lovely, friendly smiles, which she, only moments ago, had so generously bestowed on Allan, disappeared from her face. "You can go and fight your demons, Milord."

Having said that, she returned to her room. Neither she nor Gisborne returned to sleep for a long time; for a long time they lay awake in their beds, peering into the darkness of a moonless night.

*****

The singing of the morning birds revealed the start of a new day to him. Rising at dawn, he saddled Raven, and, not speaking to anyone on the estate, rode off straight to Nottingham. There was no need to wait for an invitation from the Sheriff, Gisborne knew too well that sooner rather than later a messenger would call on him directly; besides, taking into account the night's incident, he didn't want to stay in Locksley.

To Guy's great regret, the Sheriff was not in need of his company. Preparations for the evening's celebration were well advanced with His Grace running throughout the castle ensuring that the decorations, tables, candles, indeed everything, was being completed to his high standard. He was having rooms readied for any guests who decided that they would stay over. He was making final preparations for the dinner, and therefore the presence of his deputy was quite unnecessary.

Direct and to the point, as ever, the Sheriff informed Gisborne that his presence wasn't required and sent him back to Locksley, reminding him to convey his invitation for the evening celebration to Miss Hawk.

Guy didn't feel like going back just yet and instead rode to the training camp. Having checked on the work of his soldiers, he practiced archery and combat with them. But even there he had no peace.

He sought solace in a walk through the woods but knew that sooner or later, he would have to go back to Locksley.

"What will I tell her? How will I look her in the eyes after what happened last night?"

He had to go back to Locksley, but, no matter how hard he tried to persuade himself to do so, he could not.

Guy of Gisborne – the fearless knight, who over his lifetime had witnessed so much. He had participated in many battles and the word "fear" was not in his vocabulary, nor was he familiar with the feeling that this word described. At least, that was what any who knew him would think, but last night, he showed his weakness. Last night, he showed his fear. For the first time in all these years, another living soul had seen him in such a state, yet despite what had passed between them, despite their scrapes, arguments and disagreements, she didn't betray him. She made it look like a joke, she took all the blame and humiliation, she stood up for him, and protected him in front of his servant.

Last night, when she looked at him, when she touched his hand, for the first time in many years he had felt something real. Was it possible that someone genuinely cared for him?

In his life, there were so many lies and pretences, so many false emotions, that the simple act of human compassion shown to him by a complete stranger threw him off balance. Yet he could not hide from her forever, thus, after circling the forest for a few hours, he made his way back to Locksley.

*****

"What's going on here?" asked Gisborne surprised, when, on his return, he found his servant crawling under the bed in Christine's room. Meanwhile the resident of the room herself was busy shaking the clothes in her closet.

"We are looking..." Allan peered out from under the bed, "and what exactly are we looking for, ma'am?" he turned to Christine.

"My bracelet," she replied, not looking at him. "I'm sure I've left it somewhere in here," she opened the closet again and began to go through the folded clothes. "It couldn't have gone anywhere."

"But if you've left it there, maybe I can get out from under here?" asked Allan, with a plea in his voice. "There is nothing here but dust!" he added sneezing loudly.

"Yes, of course," Christine smiled and stretched her hand out, helping him up, while continuing to survey the room. "Come out, come out wherever you are..."

"Missing something?" asked Gisborne, knowing perfectly well what was going on.

"My bracelet with the two intertwined snakes," she repeated and once again rummaged through the cupboard. "Looks like those..." she paused and motioned her head pointing behind.

Guy quickly glanced under the blanket, and then looked about the table and underneath it.

"Well, it's not here," he said, finishing his impromptu search in less than a minute. "Leave us," he added addressing his servant.

Exiting the room, the young man went straight to the kitchen – all the searching exercises had made him very hungry.

"Here, this is for you," Gisborne handed Christine a large bundle as soon as Allan disappeared behind the door.

"Ough!" she uttered quietly.

Their relationship could not have been called friendly, so the last thing she expected from him was a gift. She smiled softly and a little shyly at him, but curiosity got the better of her and, not being able to fight it, she opened the package.

Inside she found a neatly folded velvet dress. The black and gold bodice was decorated with inserts of blue silk. The same silk patches were sewn into the sleeves, making them very long, and elegant. The long black skirt was adorned with gold embroidery. Pinned at the waistline of the dress was a small bag containing a cameo strung on a blue ribbon to match the silk inserts on the sleeves.

Christine was at a loss for words.

"Sir Guy," she managed at last. "It's very beautiful! I don't know what to say... I don't know what I've done to... you shouldn't have..." the smile never left her face.

"It's not from me," he said a little absently. "The Sheriff asked me to deliver it to you with an invitation to tonight's gathering," he bowed respectfully.

"Sheriff? Why am I not surprised?" her enthusiasm vanished as soon she heard his name. "Still doing your boss's dirty work?" she added, unable to resist the jab.

"I'm doing what I am told," he said gruffly, the expression on his face changed instantly.

"That's right, you do what you are told," she repeated his words, looking him straight in the eyes.

An uncomfortable silence fell in the room. They looked at each other, not taking their eyes off one other; Christine gave up first.

"Well, if I may say so... At least your snake of a Sheriff has good taste," she said thoughtfully. "But he shouldn't harbour any hope of me wearing it or being there."

"The Sheriff asked me to convey his invitation and insisted that you would honour him with your presence. There will be guests."

"And he hopes that I would be their entertainment?!" retorted Christine, not letting him finish. "That's not going to happen, even if I am taken there under escort. You can take it back," she scooped up the dress and loaded it into Gisborne's hands, "and you can convey to his grace, that he can shove it up his..." she paused, the words, that hung dangling from her tongue wouldn't have been proper for a lady. "Well, I'm sure you'll work out what to say."

Christine made a face, picked up her jacket and headed for the door. But just before exiting the room, she stopped at the threshold and turned to him.

"I don't want to deprive you or the Sheriff of the pleasure of my company," she said sarcastically, "but I have other plans for today," she added, then walked down the stairs and straight out.

"Pray, do not tell me you are going to run away again," Guy grinned, catching up with her in the stable.

"Don't even think you can get rid of me that easily!" she quipped, skilfully saddling the bay. "I think I will linger around for another day or so, and then who knows."

"As you wish," said Gisborne, automatically checking that she had fastened the saddle properly. "In any case, what do you want to do in Sherwood? For a woman, even of your profession, it may not be safe to travel alone. There are outlaws."

"Oh, I am well aware of that," said Christine. "Besides, I met two of them yesterday."

"What? Why didn't you tell me about that? What did they want with you?" he said, concern in his voice. "You should not go into the woods alone. Take a few of my men with you, just in case," he added.

"Nothing major happened," she assured him. "They wanted to rob me, but only managed to scare off my horse," she added. She noticed how, at these words, Guy calmed down a little. "But I honestly think your guards would be overkill. Besides, if we are planning to proceed with the Sheriff's request and sort out Hood," she continued, "don't you think, it would be better if I go and explore a little on my own, rather than dragging a company of soldiers with me? What do you say? Good plan?"

She had to use all of her charms to convince Gisborne that it was necessary for her to ride into the woods alone. Christine wanted to go back to the tree she saw yesterday, to explore the forest further. She hadn't deserted her hope of returning home for a moment.

"Very well," agreed Guy finally. "Only this time, please try not to get lost," he said with his usual sneer. "Today I will be busy and will not be able to come to your rescue."

"Don't worry, Milord, I'll be fine," said Christine, mounting into the saddle. "Besides, as you know, I can protect myself," she winked at him, clicked her tongue and spurred the horse out of the village.

*****

Taking advantage of the turmoil that reigned in the castle, Marian had managed to sneak out. With the help of her friend, a tavern owner, she easily found herself a horse, and soon raced across the field toward Sherwood and the outlaw's camp.

Noting the girl from afar, Robin went out to meet her. He was determined to catch her before she got any closer. Marian knew the location of the camp too well and Robin couldn't risk it. It was not often she managed to escape the castle unnoticed. The last thing he needed right now was a tail: a guard, or even worse, Sir Guy of Gisborne himself. Robin knew first-hand who this man was and what he was capable of; Gisborne was not to be trifled with.

"Marian, what are you doing here?" he said meeting her off the road a few hundred yards from the camp. He looked concerned, constantly glancing around.

"Oh, Robin!" the girl threw herself on him. "You sound like you are not happy to see me at all."

"Easy, easy," he laughed softly, "you'll strangle me."

"I missed you," she said unable to understand the reason for such a cold reception, "it's been a week since you last came to the castle, and I'm sure you've quite forgotten all about me?" she pouted.

Convinced that no one was watching, Robin picked her up in his arms and kissed her.

"How could you think such a thing, my love? Not a minute has passed without me thinking about you," he looked at her, his eyes sparkled. "But you know yourself, a man in my position cannot be too careful."

"Oh Robin!" she said once again, wrapping her arms tightly around him.

"You didn't answer my question," he said, sitting down with her under a big oak tree. "What are you doing here?"

"Well, I told you – I've missed you."

For a moment she paused, considering whether she should be offended and make a scene, but as with other of her spontaneous fancies, this one soon passed and, forgetting immediately what had upset her in a first place, she carried on cheerfully.

"I have got a wonderful idea!" she exclaimed and began to quickly convey her plan to Robin, jumping from one thought to another. "The Sheriff collected the taxes the other day, right? The money is still in the castle, but I'm sure tomorrow it will be gone from Nottingham!"

Robin listened to her attentively, imitating genuine interest.

"What makes you think that?" he asked, encouraging her enthusiasm.

"I overheard a conversation between Wesley and Gisborne! Today, guests will gather for the feast. They will be the Sheriff's supporters, the other traitors and conspirators, those who want to kill the king – Buckingham, Winchester and others. So... the Sheriff has said that tomorrow, after the celebration, they will divide the money between themselves – and we won't see it again. My plan is, today, when the Sheriff and the rest are at the gathering, you and your gang will get into the castle and steal the money!" she finished proudly.

"Bravo!" applauded Robin and added, with notable sarcasm in his voice. "Great plan! If I remember correctly, neither of your brilliant ideas ended well... The last time we barely managed to get away," his voice became very stern. "I have told you so many times, Marian, you should not get involved in this."

"But Robin, I am sure this time, it will all work out!"

"Don't you think, my love," he spoke again, his tone softened a little, "that the Sheriff's guests won't come alone, but with guards and soldiers? And don't you think that on this occasion the number of guards in the castle will be increased? If only it was as simple as you say," Robin pulled her close and hugged her shoulders.

"But I thought..." she murmured.

"Leave it to me, Marian," he put a finger to her lips.

"The castle is so busy with people preparing for the celebration, that , I'm sure you would be able to sneak in and out and no one would ever notice," she said removing his hand, she would not be appeased.

"I see you too have already started the preparations," said Robin and pointed to the bracelet shining on her wrist. He was still smiling, but by the tone of his voice she could clearly hear he was upset.

"It's just a gift, it does not mean anything to me," Marian tried to pull down her sleeve, in an attempt to hide the jewellery.

"It may mean nothing to you, but I'm sure it means a lot to HIM. Do you think I don't know who it is from?" he said, angrily.

"I'm sorry, Robin, I didn't think you would react like this," Marian tried to calm him down.

"Well, how do you expect me to react? My beloved accepts such gifts from another suitor!" he was angry.

"He's not a suitor!" she got to her feet and walked away. "But it is not easy to refuse him! And then, you know on what conditions I am living in the castle... and my father..." her shoulders began to shake.

More than anything, Robin hated it when she was in this state. He knew too well the reasons why Marian remained in the castle, and why she accepted gifts and courtship from Gisborne. But sometimes simple male jealousy took over, when he realised that, being an outlaw, he would not be able to give her security. Stability and security that could be offered by that bastard Gisborne.

Not saying a word, he slowly walked over and hugged her.

"I'm sorry, my love, I was wrong," he said quietly.

"Look," Marian turned to him and, still sniffling, removed the bracelet and put it away in the inner pocket of her cloak. "Here, you see, it does not mean anything to me."

Robin hugged her tightly and held her close to him. Holding each other in their arms, they stood there for a while, until their lips met in a passionate kiss.

A voice from behind made them both jump. A woman walked out of the trees, holding a tall bay stallion by the bridle.

"That explains a lot," she said as if to herself, a broad smile decorating her face. "Good afternoon, Lady Marian."

Trying to protect his beloved, Robin shielded the girl and took a few steps toward the intruder. His hand slid to a small dagger that hung on his belt, but the woman did not move an inch and stood as if rooted to the ground, still grinning widely.

"Robin Hood, if I'm not mistaken?" she asked. "Just the man I was looking for!"

Christine stretched out her hand in greeting.

Chapter 13:
The Gathering

Not wasting time on unnecessary preludes and presentations, Christine quickly moved on to more important matters. She didn't have the luxury of spare time; her deception could be discovered at any moment.

"I'm sure you've heard about me, and are aware of the purpose of my presence in Nottingham," she said quietly.

"I'm afraid I haven't yet had the pleasure," Robin answered respectfully.

"Hm, I was quite sure that our little friend here would have brought you up to date with on all the latest news and events."

Robin didn't reply and only shook his head.

"Alright, we will have to do it another way then," she muttered under her breath. "I'm here to kill the King!" Christine declared, staring straight at Robin Hood. "And you too, for that matter," she smiled and bowed her head.

Robin stood motionless, his fingers tightened around the hilt of his dagger.

"Well, at least that's what the Sheriff thinks," she carried on, "and it is in my best interest that he continue to do so for as long as possible," added Christine, still not releasing his gaze.

"But..." Robin hesitated. "If you are not part of the plot, and you were not hired by Prince John to kill Richard, then what are you doing here?"

"That, my friend," exclaimed Christine, "is a very good question! To which, I, unfortunately, do not have the answer."

Robin stared blankly at her.

"I happened to be in the wrong place at the wrong time and I need your help... I need your help to get back home."

"Robin! Do not believe her!" cried Marian, grabbing Robin's hand. "I've seen what she can do! And Sir Guy also said..."

"Yes?!" asked Christine, genuinely surprised. "And what exactly did he say, if I may ask?" she peered behind Robin.

"He said that you are good, whatever that meant," Marian replied, as if ashamed of her words.

"Well, I am flattered," Christine smiled, "but let's not talk about it. What you saw, Marian, was part of a show, if you can call it that. I had to play along with the role, defined to me by the Sheriff. What do you think they would have done with me if they knew the truth?" she looked at her. "I think you, of all people, do not need to go too far for an example?"

Marian didn't answer; the expression on her face spoke for her.

"Precisely!" Christine replied.

For a while, they all stood in silence; Marian calmed down a little and now her face looked more curious than scared.

Christine stretched out her hand to Robin once again.

"Can I trust you?" she asked, looking straight into his eyes. "Can you help me get back home?"

Hesitating for a moment, he nodded and held out his hand in response, and the three of them slowly strolled in the direction of the outlaws' camp.

*****

"Good afternoon, gentlemen!" said Christine loudly; inside the cave that served as the gang's camp, she addressed the already familiar priest and big man. "Glad to see you again!"

Startled, Friar Tuck dropped his spoon and stumbled over the cauldron, nearly setting fire to the hem of his robe.

"Do you know each other?" Robin asked. "Little John, you did not tell me that you met the lady."

"Uh... We..." they mumbled.

Little John retreated slowly and soon disappeared into the storeroom, leaving the Friar to answer for both of them.

"Well, it's really hard to call it a proper meeting," Christine laughed. "They tried to mug me," she winked at Tuck, who, pretending that he didn't understand what she was talking about, continued to stir something that was boiling in a large pot, while occasionally shooting her cautious glances.

"What!?" Robin was aghast. "I have told you not to do anything like that! It could put us all at risk."

"Robin, we just wanted to..." the Friar tried to come up with an excuse but Christine did not let him finish.

"Mmm, what's that divine smell?" she broke in and walked straight towards the fire. "I hope you can find an extra portion for a guest?"

Giving her a long look, Tuck thanked her silently for steering the conversation in a different direction. The last thing he wanted right now was a row with Robin.

Ragout of wild birds had always been Friar Tuck's specialty. Christine could have sworn that she had never eaten anything tastier in her life and didn't stop praising the cook, who gratefully accepted the compliments.

Having finished their lunch, Robin and Christine retreated to the cave's improvised storerooms. He sat on a chest of coins and Christine, slowly pacing the room back and forth, began her story.

"I understand that what I am going to tell you now will sound very strange and you most likely will decide that I have gone completely mad. I can hardly fit it all into my head myself, but you have to believe me."

"Very well," said Robin, his face became serious. "I am listening."

"As you know, I'm not from around here," she said, "but, the problem is, I am not just not from around here, I'm also from a different time," she paused, giving him the opportunity to process what she had just said.

Robin did not move but his eyes widened.

Christine told him everything. When she finished her story, Robin sat in silence for a long time.

"Right..." he drawled after a long pause. "Wow! What a story!" he added, rubbing his sweaty neck. "It sounds unreal!" he paused again. "Ok, I believe you!" he said at last. "What do you want me to do?"

She sighed in relief.

"Thank you, Robin! There is no one else who knows Sherwood better than you do. I'm sure you can find the place where I crossed over to your time. I've told you everything I remember, all that I know. Only I'm afraid I do not have much time. I'm not sure how long I will be able to fool them," she said and added with a pleading voice. "Please, Robin, please help me to return home."

"Ok," said Robin. "I'll do my best."

*****

"So, what's the story with you and Gisborne?" Christine asked as soon as she and Marian rode a safe distance away from Robin's camp.

"What do you mean?" asked the girl, her face flushed bright red.

"I mean, you don't love him, that's pretty obvious," Christine squinted at her, "but I've noticed you flirting with him so many times, deliberately provoking him, giving him false hope."

"I... I..." stammered Marian, "how do you know?"

"Well, I'm a woman, aren't I?" Christine laughed. "I know how these things are done. I sometimes resort to such tricks in my work," she smiled. "But, poor fellow, he really believes that he has a chance with you. He is quite determined."

"Oh! Like I do not know that," she said, her face changed. "Sometimes he surprises me with his attention and tender care and sometimes scares with his unrestrained and explosive character. Sometimes I am really scared," said Marian, looking up at Christine.

"Yes, I agree, he does seem to have a problem with his temper," Christine laughed. "But I think that's because he is alone. From what I understand, he doesn't have any family?" she asked. "And this snake of a Sheriff only adds oil to the fire, so to speak, pulling all the right strings."

"Have you noticed that too?" Marian asked, surprised. "Sometimes I feel very sorry for him, but I cannot do anything. The Sheriff..." she did not finish.

"The Sheriff! The Sheriff is a subject for an altogether different discussion," Christine smiled. "There's something very strange going on between those two," she trailed off and then, after a short pause, continued. "But then I saw Gisborne in Locksley, I saw him with his people. He is happy there. And the people seem to love him too..."

Chatting along, they had soon left the woods and, having crossed the field, entered the city. The entrance to the castle was decorated with festive flags, but in the square in front of the castle a structure had been erected that didn't match the planned celebration – the gallows. In front of it, as always, a large throne-like chair had been placed, for the Sheriff to sit in. The head of the region himself, together with his deputy – Guy of Gisborne – watched the scene from the balcony of the upper gallery.

"I do not like that... Oh, I do not like that at all, Gisborne," he said, pointing to Christine and Marian entering the castle square together. "I hope our Miss Hawk will not contract anything from your leper girlfriend," he laughed hoarsely and winked at his servant.

Gisborne pulled his usual sneer but the expression on his face changed as soon as the Sheriff turned away from him.

The women looked up and acknowledged the Sheriff and his deputy with most respectful curtseys, then left their horses in the stables and entered the castle.

"You live very well for being under house arrest," said Christine, examining Lady Marian's room.

"Yes, I know, I can't complain, Sir Guy has seen to it that I am made very comfortable, but it's not me I am worried about. My father... the Sheriff keeps him in a dungeon," she said.

"Yes, I've heard about the plot," Christine mused and then suddenly stopped; one of the objects in Marian's room attracted her attention. "What's that?" her eyes widened. "Is that what I think it is?" she asked, pointing to a small opened chest with two large compartments, which were filled with various jars, boxes, pouches, thin sticks, and brushes.

"I honestly do not know what it is. Sir Guy gave it to me last Christmas," said Marian, indifferently. "He said that it's very popular in London among young women."

On the table in front of Christine, was a medieval make-up kit.

"It is a good gift! It might be a little early for you though. Although..." she sat Marian in a chair, "we can enhance a little of the beauty which is already there," she smiled.

Christine finished applying Marian's make-up and arranged to meet with her later at the celebration. She took the chest and, with the intention of returning to Locksley, left Marian's room. She did not get far before she was noticed.

"Trying to sneak out?" a nasty voice croaked behind her. "Where from and where to, are you going?" demanded the Sheriff. His deputy stood in the middle of the hallway, barricading the way, his face wore one of the haughty grins she was now used to, his arms were crossed over his chest.

"I'm going from Lady Marian's room in the direction of the stables and from there back to Locksley, your grace," said Christine, bowing her head and bestowing upon the Sheriff a sly smile.

After her meeting with Robin, she was in an excellent mood. Having noted the sarcasm in her answer, which Christine had no intention of hiding, the Sheriff smiled languidly.

"What's in the box?" asked Guy, already knowing the answer to his question. Much to Christine's surprise, the tone of his voice and his facial expression were much friendlier than she had had the pleasure of witnessing over the past few days.

"It's a secret!" said Christine, raising her eyebrows innocently. "A woman is entitled to her own little secrets, is she not?" she smiled sweetly at him.

Guy tried to look serious, but his smiling eyes betrayed him, he could barely maintain a straight face, trying to keep the smile off it.

"Well, regardless of where you are heading off, you will have to stay in the castle a little longer. I've planned something, an event, so to speak, to kick-start the celebration," the Sheriff made a distinctive sign with his hand, "I would like you to attend."

"Obviously, I have no choice but to obey, your grace?" she raised her brows questioningly.

"Obviously," he replied dryly. Once again, he tried to smile, but his face looked more puzzled, as he could not understand her joyous mood; clearly there was something going on, but he could not figure it out just yet.

Mimicking a polite bow Christine followed the Sheriff and his deputy, the smile never leaving her face.

*****

They walked out of the castle, once again into the courtyard square.

People had already started to gather around the gallows. Four hooks were attached to the scaffold. The executioner examined his tools, making sure that all the equipment worked as it should.

After about half an hour, the entire square was crowded with people.

"I think it's time to begin, shall we?" the Sheriff laughed, calling Christine and Gisborne to follow him. All three walked out to the platform. The Sheriff took his place in his chair, Guy and Christine stood behind him.

"What does this all mean?" she whispered quietly. "What's he up to?"

"I have absolutely no idea," Gisborne replied, confused.

They didn't have to wait long. Very soon the Sheriff raised his hand and, calling the crowd to silence, spoke in a calm and matter-of-fact manner.

"People of Nottingham! As you know, today is my birthday! And as you know, on this festive occasion a big gathering is to be hosted in the castle," he paused for a moment and then continued. "I am sure you also know that I am a just and fair master, so on the occasion of my birthday, I have decided to gift you all a little present as well!"

He paused again; Guy and Christine looked at each other in confusion.

"On the occasion of my birthday, I have decided to pardon some of those criminals – some of those miserable lowlifes, who are sitting in the dungeon."

A hum of approval rolled through the crowd that had gathered in the square. The Sheriff concluded his speech and made a sign to the executioner. Seven people were taken up to the gallows, among them were a few young men, a woman, a man of about fifty and a boy. Christine recognised him; it was the very same boy who the Sheriff's soldiers arrested in Locksley a few days ago.

"Those, whom we pardon, will be decided by chance. The others will go..." he nodded toward the gallows, then rose from his seat and walked up the wooden scaffold.

"Eeny, meeny, miny, moe," his finger stopped at the only woman. "You are free, my dear, you can go," he said and waved his hand. The woman froze, paralyzed with fear. "Unless, of course, you want to stay," he added with a malicious smile.

Having finally realized her good fortune, the woman showered him with gratitude, throwing herself to the Sheriff's feet, trying to kiss his boots. The guards dragged her to the side and down the stairs into the crowd. In disgust, the Sheriff shook his leg, wiped the boot with a piece of cloth he snatched from the executioner and continued.

"Eeny, meeny, miny, moe," he spoke again and this time his hand stopped at the man of about fifty. The Sheriff grimaced. "I'm sorry, Edward but you know, my friend, I cannot let you go," he made a disappointed face, and shouted loudly. "Guards! Take him back to the dungeon, if you please."

"That is Lady Marian's father," said Guy quietly.

"Eeny, meeny, miny, moe," repeated the Sheriff, for the last time, pointing to one of the young men. "You are free, my friend. The rest hang!"

Christine shuddered. The prisoners began to cry, but the castle guards were quickly at hand. One man tried to escape, but was immediately hit in the face with a shield, and fell heavily to the ground. The boy from Locksley was not moving; he stood still, not fully understanding what was going on.

"Milord," Christine turned to Gisborne, "that boy, he's from your village, would you not do anything?"

"What do you want me to do?" he asked absently.

"I do not know... Anything! He will hang..." said Christine with a plea in her voice.

The guards pushed the prisoners closer to the executioner, who one by one placed bags and ropes on their heads. Finally realising what was about to happen, the boy from Locksley had shoved the nearby guard and ran.

"Gisborne!" shouted the Sheriff. "Get him!"

"Guards!" pausing a moment, Guy called out absently.

"What are you waiting for!!!" shouted the Sheriff. "Get him!"

Guy did not move; his eyes were fixed on the crowd.

"Gisborne!" the Sheriff cried again, but one of the guards was faster, he launched an arrow after the fleeing prisoner, which had no trouble finding its target and pinning it the ground.

Gisborne was silent, his face frozen in horror. He stood, not daring to take his eyes from the square. From the crowd of people gathered, a man was looking back at him – the same man that he saw in Locksley a few days ago, the same man who now, so many times, came to him in his dreams, only now, it was not a dream. The man stared back at him, his eyes were full of tears, pain, and hatred. They warned that the payback day was near.

Guy turned pale, he felt dizzy and grabbed onto a chair for support.

"Are you okay?" Christine asked, noticing how suddenly his face had changed. "What happened?" she got worried seeing him in this state.

He didn't respond, he was still staring into the crowd, as if afraid to look away.

"What's wrong?" she pulled down his arm.

Gisborne looked at her. Fear froze in his eyes. Last night, she had seen the same expression.

"Say something! What? What did you see?" she asked again. "I can't help you unless you tell me what's wrong."

For some time he stood silent and motionless – lost and scared. But just as quickly his expression changed, becoming cold and aloof.

"Why do you think I need your help?" his voice, matching his expression, was cold. He slowly removed her hand. "I don't need help!" he snapped.

"It's obvious, Milord, you don't need anyone's help!" she said passionately. "You are too proud and too stubborn to accept help, let alone admit that you need it!"

Having said that, Christine returned to the stables, untied her horse and walked it to the castle gates; her good mood had vanished, but she had promised to meet Lady Marian at the party and was not going to break that promise.

*****

Back in Locksley, Christine still couldn't decide whether she wanted to go to the celebration or not. She didn't want to see the Sheriff's nasty face but the promise given to Marian left her with little choice.

After washing her face and styling her hair, she started on her makeup. The chest borrowed from Lady Marian contained everything she needed – powder and rouge, eyeliner, rose and lavender oil and lots of different small things, the purposes of which Christine didn't understand.

She made herself comfortable in a chair and set to work. After about half an hour she looked stunning, so much so that even the maid who came to help her with her dress couldn't help but marvel.

Christine tried the dress on and, having worked out how all the lacing and ties fitted together, took it off and packed it carefully into a large saddlebag. To ride to Nottingham in a dress like that, even in a man's saddle, would have been impossible.

She set off from Locksley in the direction of Nottingham, when the sun had almost drowned behind the forest line.

The main road through the field to the city was lit with dozens of huge torches. There was a long queue of coaches, carts and solo riders heading in the direction of the castle. The host, along with his deputy, greeted his guests on the steps of the main entrance.

"My dear, how glad I am that you have accepted my invitation!" exclaimed the Sheriff when he saw Christine walking up the stairs.

"I was under the impression that you were not going to grace us with your presence, even if..." said Gisborne. "I cannot recall the exact words you used," he quipped, bowing his head in a most polite greeting.

"I wouldn't miss it for the world!" Christine replied, vigorously.

She bowed to the Sheriff and grimaced at Gisborne, noticing as the corner of his mouth curled up in a slight sneer.

"But I was hoping you'd wear my gift," said the Sheriff.

"Your grace, I would have gladly arrived in the full attire, but you didn't send for me and the only means of transport I had was my horse," she said, pouting her lips slightly. "It would have been very inappropriate to ride through Sherwood in such a beautiful dress," she smiled and her long eyelashes fluttered several times.

The Sheriff broke into a silly smile. Guy, on the contrary, was barely able to contain himself trying not to laugh aloud. There was no doubt she knew how to turn a man's head and how to use her feminine wiles. Now, even in her normal clothes, she looked stunning. The old debaucher, the Sheriff, did not understand what had happened but continued to smile with a little silly look on his face.

Leaving the Sheriff of Nottingham in the company of his deputy, Christine went to change in the room previously assigned to her in the castle. She didn't rush, planning a spectacular, grand entrance when all the guests had already gathered and taken their places at the tables.

She changed into the dress, fixed her hair, released a pair of playful curls at her temples and around her neck, and went to the grand hall.

The celebration had already begun; one after the other the guests toasted to the host. She took a deep breath and stepped to the staircase leading to the hall. Tall and graceful, with her head held up high and a haughty arch in her eyebrow, she slowly began her descent. The dress given to her by the Sheriff emphasised all the best features of her figure.

The noises in the hall died down and a hundred pairs of hungry eyes turned to look at her, watching her every move. The Sheriff was the first to come to his senses. He walked up to meet her at the bottom of the stairs, took her to the table, sat her in a chair to his left, and then went to the other end of the hall, to exercise his duties as a host and to accept greetings from his guests.

"I thought you said you would not come, even if the Sheriff dragged you under escort," said Guy, softly. Sitting to her right, he said it very casually, not even looking up at her, but she could see he was smiling.

"I changed my mind," she said smiling slyly back at him. "We women tend to do it more often than you think, and I, above all, am a woman," she added, with a faint smile, "and only after that, am I anything else," she turned to her companion, raised her goblet in salute and sipped the wine. The drink was tart and too strong for her taste.

"Undoubtedly," he smiled, "and probably one of the best representatives of your sex," he added a little awkwardly, raising his goblet towards her.

"A compliment!?" that, she did not expect. *"From anyone else, but not from him!"* she thought. "I can't see Lady Marian, where is she?" she said suddenly and emptied the contents of her glass in one gulp.

"She will be here later. Why do you ask?" asked Gisborne, surprised as he refilled her goblet.

"Well, I can't flirt with you, if my rival is somewhere nearby, can I?" she said, looking straight at him.

Guy choked on his wine; in an instant, his face transmitted a kaleidoscope of feelings.

"I'm kidding..." Christine laughed, patting him on the back, helping him to cough it through. "She's always around you, so I was surprised that she's not here yet."

"It's not funny," Gisborne suddenly became serious; he got up from his seat and walked over to the Sheriff at the other end of the hall.

The celebration went on, the wine flowed. The guests ate and drank, praising the host. The time rolled past midnight yet no one was going to diverge from the party. Very soon, the tables were pushed aside, and the musicians started to play lively music. Those guests still able to stand on their feet, joined in the jolly dance. Among the dancers Christine noticed Lady Marian. Although she moved with the beat of the music, her face was tense, her eyes wandered amongst the guests until finally, they met with Christine's.

Marian separated herself from the dancing mass and strolled towards Christine. Smiling, Gisborne walked to meet her.

"Lady Marian, I am very glad that you have decided to come," he said, raising her hand to his lips.

Though he enjoyed Christine's company, the appearance of Lady Marian evidently improved his mood. Watching them, Christine only shook her head.

After that day's conversation with Christine, Marian felt uncomfortable accepting Guy's advances; she freed her hand and sat at the table next to Christine. Not parting with his glass, Guy walked to the wall behind them, and stood leaning his back against it.

"I'm very sorry I am late," said Marian. "I went to see my father in the dungeon. Oh, he has suffered today!"

"Yes, I can imagine, the Sheriff put on quite a show."

"Let's not talk about it," said Marian, not willing to discuss the matter in Gisborne's presence. "You look exceptionally beautiful this evening!" she said bestowing a compliment on Christine.

"Thank you," Christine smiled in return, "I have to admit, I feel great too! But to tell the truth, the wine that his grace is offering us today is so disgusting! Though, I think, I might have drunk a little more than I intended to," she laughed softly.

Trying to contain her giggle, Marian lifted her hand to her lips. In the bright light of the candles, the snake-head bracelet sparkled on her wrist.

*****

Christine's face changed when she saw the silver snakes resting comfortably on the girl's wrist.

"What a beautiful bracelet, Lady Marian! Where did you get it, if I may dare ask?" asked Christine, the words themselves slipped from her lips.

"Oh, do you like it? Sir Guy gave it to me!" said Marian, proudly displaying her jewellery.

"Indeed... Sir Guy..." echoed Christine and turned to face the man standing behind her. "Amazing beauty, is it not, Sir Guy?" she looked at him, struggling to remain calm, barely containing her anger.

He said nothing. What could he say, what excuse was there to offer? He should not have taken her bracelet. No! He should not have given it to Marian, for now she was bound to hate him should she find out that her present was stolen from another.

Gisborne silently strolled to the table and poured himself wine. He emptied the goblet and filled it up again, then returned to his place, and stood there resting his back against the wall.

"It must have cost you a fortune, Milord!" said Christine drilling him with her gaze. "It's an exquisite piece. One cannot find anything like that in these parts," the smile had vanished from her face, her eyes blazed with cold fire.

Unable to withstand her direct gaze, Guy lowered his eyes. He took another sip of wine and walked back to the table. He stood silently, trying to figure out how he was going to get out of this situation, but the thoughts ran away from him.

Marian, Lady Marian. It is all for her, all for the sake of this girl I love, the girl I want to see as my wife. I shower her with gifts and attention, but she remains cold and indifferent to me. All because of this outlaw – Robin Hood! Why does she still have feelings for him? They were engaged to be married, but he left her. He went to war in search of fame and recognition. When he returned, he had nothing left! I've got his estate, his title, and his lands. I now have everything that he ever had. Everything, except her. But never mind, I will be patient! Soon, it will all change. Soon she will succumb, soon she will be mine. She, first of all, should be thinking about her own welfare and the welfare of her father. A girl like her would not be able to live in the forest, along with outlaws, vagabonds, and dead souls. Just a little more time and Hood will be done with! Richard will never return from the Holy Land, Prince John will become King of England, and I will be rewarded for my faithful service."

Basking in his dreams he sneered, the corner of his mouth curling up as he slowly sipped his wine. In his thoughts, he dreamed of the day when Robin Hood would be dead or sent away from Nottingham forever, into exile. The day when he would marry Lady Marian, and then she would belong to him.

A sharp pain in the left cheek brought him back from his peaceful reflections.

Christine stood before him, with an expression on her face the like of which Gisborne had not seen till now. He did not immediately realise what had just happened, but the way his cheek burned, didn't leave him any doubt.

Everything went silent. The musicians stopped playing and the Sheriff nearly choked on the grapes he was eating; wide-eyed, Lady Marian was not moving either.

"You had a mosquito on your face, Milord," Christine said loud enough for all to hear and moved her foot, cold-heartedly crushing an imaginary insect.

"How dare she!" Guy felt overwhelmed with rage. While he was trying to master his disoriented wits and work out what to do next, Christine, as if nothing had happened, turned to the Sheriff.

"If your grace will excuse me," she said, "I would like to go back to Locksley, I'm tired."

"Well, why? Back to Locksley! There are many rooms prepared in the castle," he said.

"Thank you for your hospitality, but I think I'd better go," she said softly and added in a changed voice, directing her words to Gisborne. "I am suffocating here!" she then softened her tone again and, turning back to Wesley added, "Perhaps, I've drunk too much wine; the fresh air will do me good."

Not waiting for an answer, she headed for the exit. Gisborne caught up with her at the stairs. He was tense, his face flushed and his eyes were blazing with fire. The overall dimness of the hall gave him an even more devilish look.

"I'll escort you back," he spat through gritted teeth.

He grasped her hand and in a sharp, slightly rough move, pulled her to the side, behind a large pillar, so no one could see them.

"Let me go, Milord!" Christine said, her eyes burning with anger.

"I cannot let you go alone..." he managed with a malicious smile, still not letting go of her hand. It cost him a great effort not to allow his temper to win over his mind. "You cannot ride a horse in such a state," he said.

"Perfect! In that case, I'll walk! Would you let go of me already!" she struggled to free herself from his grasp.

"You cannot go alone on foot through the woods at this hour," he chuckled with yet another devilish sneer.

Never in his life, had he seen such a stubborn woman, and, powered by alcohol, her stubbornness reached a completely new level. He was no longer angry; the situation was starting to amuse him. However, seeing her resolute spirit, he tried to convey to her the absurdity and stupidity of her intentions, but where alcohol was present, common sense no longer prevailed.

"It is not safe..." he began again.

"Outlaws? Even better! Is that not what we all want – to get rid of Robin Hood?" she looked at him with her big eyes. "Maybe I'll get lucky tonight, and I can do the job you couldn't, and finally get out of this damned place," she added, still unsuccessfully trying to free her arm.

"With such an attitude, you will be lucky if you manage to get out of the city in one piece! Foolish woman!"

Her stubbornness went over any limits. Gisborne finally slackened his grip on her hand. Christine had been waiting for it and, not losing another moment, briskly climbed up the stairs and disappeared into the hallway.

Guy came back to the table and drained his goblet in one large gulp.

"Such a woman! Fire!" Wesley croaked behind him. All this time he had been watching the scene with great interest. "You should have looked at her more closely, my boy."

"What?" Guy breathed out surprised.

"She's not a girl like your Marian. Oh, no... she's a woman, fiery and passionate. If I were you!" his face broke into a dreamy smile. "If I were you, I'd have followed her," he added giving his deputy a meaningful glance.

"She clearly said she wanted to be left alone," he replied.

"You're an even bigger fool than I thought, Gisborne! You do not understand women at all!" the Sheriff rolled his eyes. "She said that on purpose. Women always say the opposite of what they want and think. If she said you must go away, you most certainly should go after her," the Sheriff pushed him for speed. "Go... go, before she changes her mind."

*****

In a slightly lurching gait, cursing the Sheriff, Guy of Gisborne and Medieval England altogether, Christine wandered through the endless corridors of the castle, trying to find her way out.

Finally, she heard voices and soon was able to see a few guards standing next to the entrance into the stables, having a lively discussion about what was happening in the castle that evening. She didn't want to go in their direction but had no choice – it was the only way out.

Trying to stay as straight as possible and not make eye contact with any of them, she strolled forward. Seeing her, the men began to chatter, pointing in her direction and, as soon as she was close enough, one of the guards whistled after her, inviting her to join their festive mood.

At this point, she should have ignored them and carried on but the alcohol in her blood cried the opposite. She turned and in a slow, smooth movement, came close to the guard. The man broke into a smug smile, already picturing in his mind the sweet moments that awaited him when, after drinking some more wine, he would retire with this beauty to one of the dark corners.

"You must be careful, my friend," Christine whispered in his ear, in her most seductive voice, yet loud enough for his friends to hear. "Your friends," her lips were slightly parted, she slowly ran her finger down his face, outlining the line of cheekbones and chin, "your friends may assume that you're blind..." she paused, and suddenly her voice become unfriendly, gaze cold, "if you whistle, mistaking a Lady for a dog!"

Pushing him aside and taking one of the jugs of wine that stood next to them, she walked towards the door.

The guards laughed loudly – all except one.

"Hey, you! Where do you think you are going beautiful?" he shouted, trying to restore his bravado in front of his mates, as he caught up with Christine.

He tried to grab her arm, but she moved aside and in a swift move felled him, sending him tumbling to the ground.

"You'll pay for this!" he shouted as she walked away.

"Always at your service," cheerfully replied Christine, dropping into a deep bow before sauntering out into the street.

If only she had known that very soon, she would seriously regret her actions. Might she have acted differently, or, perhaps, everything that was happening to her was destined?

Chapter 14:
The Attack

Despite the late hour, life in Nottingham was still in full swing.

In the tavern near the castle, the townspeople shouted toasts for the Sheriff, King Richard, Prince John, Eleanor of Aquitaine, the innkeeper, and others. After the amount of alcohol that had been consumed by that time of night and, for as long as the owner of the tavern continued to fill up their cups and goblets, it didn't really matter whose health they were drinking to.

"Miss Hawk!" a familiar voice called behind her.

Christine, who was already past the tavern, turned sharply and began to scan the faces of the people crowding the street.

"Allan! What the hell are you doing here?" she asked with the heat of passion, when, among the people, she saw the familiar face of Gisborne's servant.

"Excuse me, ma'am?" he stared at her, surprised, not expecting such a tone.

"I'm sorry, Allan, don't pay any attention to me. I'm not myself," she said frankly. "Walk with me."

Because her words sounded more like an order than a polite request, the young man was left with no choice but to obey.

"Mmm, that's better!" she said with notable relief in her voice. Taking his arm, she hung on to it. "I feel a little tired today."

"Somehow I doubt you are tired," Allan smiled, looking at the flask of wine in her hand.

"You know, maybe you're right," Christine laughed joyfully. "To tell you the truth," she whispered into his ear, "this wine tastes disgusting! The Sheriff apparently decided to pocket more money, so he was offering this... I don't even have words to describe it," she lifted the flask, took another sip, grimaced and laughed again.

They walked slowly through the streets of the city.

"Oh, yes! By the way, I've found my bracelet!" she said after short a pause.

"Really? Where was it?" asked Allan, with keen interest. "We searched the room from top to bottom!"

"It was... Ooh, it was..." she looked around and leaned into his ear. "It was on Lady Marian's wrist!"

"I don't understand!" said Allan, looking at her blankly. "How did it happen to be there?"

"Your dear master gave it to her!" Christine said. Then she continued, not letting Allan speak, "Yeah! Gave! After he had stolen it from me! But shh... It's a secret! Obviously, it must not be known by any living soul," she took another sip from the flask.

"I don't understand. Why would he do that?" Allan couldn't help but wonder.

"Well, all's fair in love and war, as they say," she said. "However, he lost this battle way before it began, but unfortunately, still refuses to accept it."

Having walked through the town they reached the city gates, where Allan bowed to Christine.

"I'd love to walk you back to Locksley," he said, "but I have orders from my master to wait for him in the castle. Are you sure you will make it to the village?"

"Why of course! What could happen to me in the middle of the night... in the dark forest full of outlaws," she smiled and winked at him.

"Well, exactly!" laughed Allan in response.

"I'll be fine!" she said and added in a conspiratorial tone. "Besides, all the notorious villains are still in the castle at the gathering," she laughed softly. "Through the field, into the forest, a few miles straight, the third turn to the left and from there it is not far to Locksley."

And so, they parted. Allan went back to the castle, and Christine wandered off towards the woods, across the field lit with torches.

Reaching the verge of the field, she looked back at the city far behind her and entered the forest.

It was very difficult to walk, her legs tangled in the hem of her skirt and every now and then her long sleeves entangled themselves in the undergrowth.

"Stupid dress..." she muttered under her breath.

She reproached herself for hurrying away and leaving her clothes in the castle, but what she could do now? It was too late to go back, and the last thing she wanted was to see the arrogant faces of the Sheriff and his henchman.

*****

The high moon shone bright lighting up the forest path, the summer sky was covered with a myriad of stars, and the mighty trees guarded both sides of the road. Scooping her dress up with one hand,

and holding the flask of wine with the other, Christine walked slowly, quietly humming a gentle tune. The night was peaceful and quiet.

The sound of a twig snapping nearby made her wince. She turned – there was no one on the road. Not paying too much attention to it, she strolled on, but as soon as she started to move, she heard the sound again. This time it was not behind her but directly to her right.

Looking around warily, Christine quickened her pace. Whoever was hiding in the trees, sped up as well. A chill ran down her spine. Peering into the darkness, she tried to see something behind the trees, but in vain.

"Robin?" she called quietly, "Little John... Friar..." nobody answered. "Robin, this is not funny!" she said into the darkness, trying to sound as serious and as calm as possible, but her voice trembled. "If you are trying to scare me, you've won, I am scared. That's enough!"

"Going somewhere, beautiful?" the voice spoke behind her.

Her heart bumped loudly against her rib cage, nearly jumping out of her chest, ready to break free. Christine spun around. On the road, in front of her stood a man – the very same guard, who, so recklessly, she had laughed at earlier that evening. The guard wasn't alone; two other men came out of the trees.

They had been following her since she left the castle; it was not hard for them to continue to follow her quietly through the woods. The guard was determined to receive what was due to him.

Pulling a brave face, Christine tried to calculate her chances – there were not many!

"Are you afraid that you won't be able to satisfy me and decided to bring some friends to help you out?" she cried tightening her grip around the neck of the flask.

Offence, it seemed to her at this precise moment, was her best option and a chance for defence. Carefully, step-by-step moving forward, she walked towards him, slowly closing the distance between herself and the man before her. Her gaze moved quickly from the man to the road, from the road to the trees and back. She was trying to estimate her chances of escape, knowing full well, there were not many.

"If there is something that you want, you just have to ask," she said, trying to crack a smile.

She was close enough; surprising her opponent and, with all the force that she could manage, Christine hit him in the face with the flask and ran.

"Get her, quickly!" the man shouted, after a moment of confusion.

Realising she wouldn't get far on the road, she dived into the woods. Leaves whipped her face, her dress tangled in the undergrowth. Picking up the hem of her dress with one hand, she ran as fast as she could, neither knowing nor seeing where she was running to, yet knowing too well her pursuers were close behind. She could hear the men crashing through the trees and from the sound of their voices she knew they were quickly coming after her.

Christine didn't get far; stumbling over a fallen tree, she tumbled to the ground, issuing a muffled groan as she fell. She wasn't able to get up – her pursuers were too close, and almost immediately surrounded her.

"Gotcha, beautiful!" said the man looming over her.

Rough hands grabbed her by the shoulders, restricting her movement. The man dropped straight on top of her, pinning her to the ground. Christine felt his stinking breath on her face. In the bright moonlight, he looked like a wild beast, going for his prey.

A moment later, he was kissing her vigorously, trying to stick his tongue in her mouth. Christine had no intention of giving up without a fight, screaming and wriggling like a snake, she tried to escape from his strong grip, but it wasn't easy to do. Her dress and the amount of wine she had consumed significantly limited her abilities.

"Don't just stand there! Hold her!" the man ordered his friends.

They tried to grab her legs, but she kept kicking, pushing them away.

"What are you waiting for!" he snapped.

After a brief struggle, they managed to hold her legs to the ground. Christine could barely move.

The man continued to kiss her violently; his mouth moved across her face, neck and shoulders, the weight of his body was pushing against her. She could feel his erect penis pressing hard against her stomach. His hand was trying to get under her skirt, but to do so would have meant loosening his grip.

In an instant, the man turned his attention to her chest and, grabbing the front of the dress, pulled it furiously. Through her cries, Christine could hear the sound of tearing fabric. She froze, taken aback as her attacker stopped as well, when instead of soft white skin and naked full breasts, under the dress he found an undershirt.

Using this moment of confusion to her advantage she, with the sound of an angry cat, dug her nails into the attacker's face. Roaring with pain, the man grabbed his face. That was enough for Christine to push him aside and repeat her attempt at escape, but even in this state, it wasn't difficult for one of the other guards to catch up with her. Disoriented, Christine ran in the wrong direction and found herself face to face with one of her pursuers.

"My dear lady," he said with a malicious sneer. "You have nowhere to run."

Christine found herself surrounded once again. The man shook her by the shoulders and pushed her to the ground. Barely managing to remain on her feet, she tried to fight back but the other two were behind, grabbing her by the arms.

"The harder the struggle of the battle, the sweeter the triumph of the victory," he said grinning impudently and, with mighty force, kicked Christine in the guts.

Desperately gasping for air, she went limp in the strong arms of the men that stood behind her. They released her hands, and with a muffled groan, she sat down on the ground. Gathering her last strength, she tried to stand up, but a sweeping blow to her face sent her back down. Unable to stay on her feet, she fell; the metallic taste of blood filled her mouth. The strong hands roughly grabbed her hips and turned her onto her stomach, a hard male body was now on top her, pushing her face into the dirt.

"My friends and I will now use you like the whore that you are," the guard growled into her ear.

Cheered by his friends, he continued to tear her dress to shreds, trying to get to his final prize. Exhausted, Christine could no longer resist. Her voice was hoarse, and now she could only sob quietly; tears flowed from her eyes in an endless stream.

She had almost surrendered to her fate, when the voices behind her began to fade and the man attacking her grunted one last time and went limp, pinning her further to the ground. Gasping for air like a fish in the shallows, he was helplessly opening his mouth, and moments later, lifeless, he fell to the ground beside her. Everything went silent, except for the fast, quiet steps behind her.

Afraid to move, Christine lay on the ground, not breathing. The footsteps stopped beside her. Someone knelt next to her, and a pair of strong hands gripped her waist. Gathering her last strength, she again attempted to escape, but failed. Holding her firmly and not allowing her to move, the man turned her on her back and lifted her off the ground. Only now, did he speak.

"I'm here... I've got you... you are safe..."

The familiar voice was quiet, soft, and almost soothing.

Out of the darkness, the blue eyes of Guy of Gisborne looked at her.

"Guy!" was the only thing Christine could whisper through her tears before clinging to him as tightly as she could.

His strong arms wrapped around her shoulders, shielding her from the night's horror. She couldn't speak, not that it was necessary. He understood everything. Kneeling beside her, he took her in his arms, like a small child.

"Shh, it's alright..." he comforted Christine. "I've got you..."

Sobbing silently, she threw her arms around his neck and laid her head on his chest. The rhythmic sound of his beating heart calmed her. She closed her eyes. Gisborne sat on the ground and, rocking from side to side, held her in his arms, gently, barely touching, stroking her hair.

When Christine stopped sobbing, he pulled away, loosening his embrace.

"Are you alright?" he asked, gently brushing the hair off her face. "Are you hurt?"

"My pride..." she replied softly.

"You know what I mean. Did they do anything to you?" he asked concerned.

"They... ripped my dress..." Christine sniffed, trying to pull the torn bits of sleeve and top back on her shoulders and over the undershirt. "The Sheriff will be upset..." she said, and tried to smile.

"I am glad to see that, despite everything, your sense of humour is still with you," Guy smiled back at her.

His face was calmer now. He rose to his feet and held out his hand, helping Christine up.

"Will you be able to walk?" he asked, removing the dry leaves from her hair.

"I think so," said Christine and then moaned in pain as she tried to take the first step.

Guy gently put his arm around her waist, giving her the opportunity to cling to his shoulder. Christine said nothing, but looked at him gratefully.

"My horse is not far," he said, pointing the way.

"Did you... kill them?" Christine asked hesitantly, after a short silence.

Only now, did she see the lifeless bodies of the other men who attacked her.

"Yes," he said quickly, "I couldn't take any chances."

She simply nodded in response.

"Do you know them?" she asked suddenly.

"No. They came with Lord Winchester," said Guy.

"What if they are missed... and people start looking for them?" she asked concerned.

"Of course they will be," he said quietly, "and they will be found, should someone really want to. Nobody will suspect anything, you should not trouble yourself."

"I suppose you've done this before?" Christine asked, although not sure why.

Guy didn't say anything. He had done this before and not only once or twice. At first, it was hard, then easier, and over time it had become one of his routine duties. Over time, he learned to turn off his feelings. Over time, it became easier, but for those he left lying in the small clearing, he felt nothing. Like cutting into soft butter, his sword neatly entered one, then another, he cut the throat of the third man and watched silently as Christine's attacker quickly bled to death.

*****

Raven was indeed tied to a tree quite close to the clearing where the three men had first attacked Christine.

Guy tried to toss Christine up into the saddle, but after several attempts, gave up the idea. Her leg caused her a lot of pain and, although she was trying to make a brave face, she was badly shaken.

"Alright..." he said finally. "Locksley is not too far from here, we will walk."

He untied his horse, whispered something into his ear and pushed the animal to the side. Raven whinnied and galloped off in the opposite direction.

"He'll find his way home," Gisborne said, without any doubt.

He allowed Christine to rest for a while and then wrapped his arm around her waist once again as they slowly walked towards the village.

"I understand the horse," began Christine, with a tone of disbelief in her voice, "but are you sure you'll be able to find your way back in this pitch-black?"

She calmed down a little, her voice became softer; she almost stopped trembling.

"Trust me," he said with a light smile. "Locksley is no more than a mile from here. Soon we will be able to see the lights of the village."

They walked in silence until Christine noticed a wide meaningful grin spreading across his face.

"What?" she asked. "What is it?!"

"I think tomorrow, I will need to have a serious conversation with the Sheriff," he answered with a mischievous look in his eyes.

"About what?" Christine breathed out cautiously.

"Since you arrived, getting you out of scrapes and troubles has become my daily routine," he smiled, glancing at her sideways. "I think I need to ask him to increase my pay for saving your..."

"My arse?" she finished for him and smiled.

"I thought I'd put it in a slightly different manner, but literally speaking, yes!" he laughed softly.

For the first time since they met, she heard him laugh. It was a deep hearty sound.

"Philip laughs exactly like that..." flashed through her mind.

Deep inside she knew that it was neither the time nor the place, but by talking to her, he distracted her from thinking of what just happened.

"I, by the way, could have dealt with them without your help," she said, maintaining his playful tone.

"Yes, I saw that!" he laughed again.

"I just shouldn't have drunk so much of that crap the Sheriff calls wine."

"You just should not have left the castle alone and should have taken advantage of my offer," he said, giving her another sideway glance.

"To walk me back to Locksley? Is that what you mean? Somehow, I doubt we would have had a different result should I have accepted your offer," she smiled. "If there weren't so many people at the Sheriff's gathering, you would have strangled me right there. And if not there, then as soon as we were both out the door..." she stopped and looked at him, her lips curled into a faint smile.

"You're right..." he said slowly and then suddenly become very serious and added, "I really wanted to pay you back for what you had done. It cost me a lot of effort not to do so, but a good slap across the face or a flogging would have done you good. To cool your ardour and love of adventures," he raised an eyebrow slightly.

She gave him another faint smile and then they walked in silence, until with a loud sigh, Christine dropped to the ground.

"I can't. I can't walk anymore," she uttered.

One look at her was enough to know she wasn't lying.

"We're almost there," he said and gently took her in his arms.

Christine no longer had the strength to fight the fatigue. She put her head on his chest and closed her eyes. Her head rose and fell with his each breath. Listening to the rhythmic sound of his heart, she descended into slumber as he carried her back to Locksley.

*****

Christine didn't notice how they reached the manor. She opened her eyes when Guy gently lowered her onto the bed. She heard as he left the room and, pulling her legs in, trying to wrap herself in the scraps of the dress, she turned on her side, and once again succumbed to the drowsiness.

She woke up when the door of the room creaked quietly. Gisborne walked in and strolled to the bed. Slowly and carefully, he took off her boots and began to untie the braid and laces of something that, just a few hours ago, represented her dress.

"What are you doing?" she asked still half asleep.

"I am taking off your clothes," he said.

"Where am I?" she muttered, trying to raise herself onto her elbows and look around.

"You are in my room," he said quietly and continued with the task at hand.

Freeing her from the remnants of the dress and leaving her only in the undershirt, he slowly unbuttoned his jacket and placed it at the head of the bed. Then took off his sword belt and put them next to the jacket.

"What are you doing?" still not able to understand what was happening, Christine asked again.

"Now I am taking off my clothes," he replied with a soft smile.

"And you too!" were the only words she uttered, instantly making a conclusion about his plans. "Well, if that's what you intend to do, please be gentle..." she no longer had the strength to resist. "At least you look better than those thugs from the forest and it may not be as disgusting..." she murmured and, exhaling heavily, lay down on the pillow, meekly surrendering to her fate.

Guy said nothing. A corner of his mouth quivered into a slight grin. He shook his head and gently taking Christine into his arms, walked out into the corridor.

"What are you doing? Where are you taking me?" she tried to protest again.

"You know, Miss Hawk," he said, ignoring her question. His voice sounded very official, but light sparks shone in his eyes. Guy continued to tease her, and seeing her in such a confused state, received immense pleasure from the process. "The Sheriff is right," he smiled, "there is too much noise from you!"

*****

Christine shivered in surprise when her foot touched the hot liquid. She slowly opened her eyes. A sigh of relief mixed with pleasure escaped her, as he lowered her into the bath filled with hot water.

The air around was hot and humid. A few burning candles gave the room an intimate dim light. She sank in; only her head and neck were floating on the surface.

"Have you decided to drown me, Milord?" she asked with a light smile. "Drown me and make it look like an accident?"

Behind the high walls of Locksley, away from the night's horrors, she calmed down a little and spoke to him as before. Now she was teasing him, yet by his reaction, she knew he enjoyed it as much as she did.

"To tell you the truth, the thought had visited me more than once," said Guy.

He tried to look serious, but could barely keep the smile off his face. He liked seeing her like this. Her eyes sparkled as before, she smiled again, yet he knew it would be some time before she would be able to leave the events of this night behind.

The corner of his mouth quivered stretching his lips into a soft smile as he rolled up his sleeves and sat down next to the huge trough that served as a bathtub. He took a small cloth, dipped it into the water and began to wipe the dirt off her face. His touch was gentle and careful, as if he was afraid to hurt her even more.

"I can't believe you've made me a bath, and now are coddling me. After all that I've done to you," she mumbled quietly.

"Well, although I have to admit that the prospect of making you pay for all your previous insults looks, at this moment, very attractive," he gave her a long look, "I think you've had enough adventures for one day."

Guy continued to wipe her face and neck, from time to time rinsing the cloth in water.

"I just... I thought you might want..." she trailed off. Not lifting his eyes to hers, Guy arched an eyebrow. "To take advantage of the situation..." she said hesitantly, not thinking of the possible consequences.

"If you insist..." his hand slowly slid into the water.

Christine shuddered when his long fingers wrapped tightly around her ankle. She tried to draw her leg back, but could not move. Guy looked up at her. She had seen this gaze before, his eyes burned with fire. She swallowed.

"Will he really do that?"

Gisborne looked at her as if evaluating what was offered to him and lifting her leg out of the water slowly, pushed the wet shirt aside. Christine froze, unable to move, her chest rose and fell with each heavy breath; mixed emotions overwhelmed her. She didn't know whether she would resist or succumb if he attempted to take her. However, in just a few brief moments, the expression on his face and in his eyes had changed. Catching her confused and frightened gaze, he smiled slyly. Now it was he who fooled her.

"It looks much worse than it actually is... Just a scratch, it will heal in a few days," he said, lowering her leg back into the water. Christine released a loud gasp, not even trying to hide her relief. "And as for your question, why do you think I ought to do it?"

It was some time before she answered.

"It just seemed to me that a man of your time wouldn't decline an opportunity to..." she stopped trying to find the best word to put politely what she was trying to imply, "to get pleasure..."

"Pleasure?" he laughed again, very loudly this time. "Whatever do you mean by the words a "man of my time"... By the way, what exactly do you mean by that?" he gave her another long look and continued. "First of all, you should see yourself! You look worse than a tramp from Fleet Street!" he pulled another dry leaf out of her hair. "I, like a "man of my time"," he smiled, repeating her own words, "have a sense of self-respect, not to... get pleasure, as you put it, with just anyone."

Christine opened her mouth in surprise. Even in the dim light of the room, he could see her cheeks blazed with red. She buried her face in the palms of her hands.

"Do I really look that bad?" she asked peering through her fingers.

"Disgusting!" he laughed again and getting up to his feet, walked to the fireplace and threw a few more logs in.

For a while, there was silence in the room. He stood by the fireplace adjusting the wood with a poker, while Christine enjoyed the warmth of the water.

"And what's the second?" she asked suddenly.

"What?" he turned to her startled by the unexpected question.

"You said what was the first, but never said what's the second," she looked at him with a slight smile.

Not really knowing why, he'd waited, yet dreaded this question.

"You..." he hesitated, "you are not to my taste..." muttered Guy and turned to the fire.

There Gisborne lied. He stood in silence looking at the fire, not daring to raise his eyes back to her, afraid that his eyes would betray him and give away his lie. She was very much to his taste, and over the last few days, he had been thinking about it more than he should have been. She was beautiful, smart, she knew her own worth, was able to present her advantages, and at the same time was not afraid to accept her shortcomings.

Christine sighed and, releasing dozens of bubbles, sank under the water. When she emerged, his face was very close. Startled, she jerked her head back and almost bumped it against the side of the bathtub.

"Was that a sigh of relief or disappointment?" he asked with a slight grin.

"I don't know," once again looking him straight in the eye, she said in a soft low voice, "I haven't decided yet..."

Unable to bear her direct gaze, he looked away. Never in his life, had a woman looked at him like that. Something inside him was telling him that she had already decided, but he did not dare to believe that what he read in the bold gaze of her blue eyes was true.

"The fire is dying, I'll get more logs," he said quietly and left the room.

For some time Christine was alone. Soon Jenny, the daughter of the house cook, came in, bringing a few large buckets. She scooped out two buckets of the cooling water and replaced it with more of the hot. Christine sank in so that now only her face was floating on the surface. Taking a deep breath, she closed her eyes and sank to the bottom, letting the water swallow her completely.

Upon returning to the room, Guy put the wood on the fire and sat down next to the bathtub. He looked at her, in the dim light of the candles there was something unreal in Christine, something mystical. He looked at her face; with her dark hair floating around her she looked peaceful, as peaceful as when he first saw her in the woods. A lot had happened since then.

Without lifting her head, Christine opened her eyes and looked at him. Their eyes met. Over the past few days, his face had become almost dear to her. She smiled and rose to the surface.

"Wine?" asked Guy and handed her a goblet. "I think you might need it."

*****

They talked and drank wine, Guy filled her cup more than once. Despite the events of the day, they genuinely enjoyed each other's company.

"I'm sorry I hit you," said Christine.

"No need to apologise," answered Guy. "I think I got what I deserved. But I was so angry with you!"

"For the first time in my life, I see a man admitting he was wrong!" Christine's eyes widened in surprise. "This deserves a toast! Cheers!" she smiled and loudly clinked her goblet on his.

"In any case, what's the story with your bracelet?" he asked, refilling her cup.

"Have you decided to get me even drunker, Milord?" she smiled and took another sip. "Mmm, what a heavenly taste, can't be compared to the rubbish that was offered today by the Sheriff."

"This is our house wine, I am glad you like it," he said. "But you haven't answered my question," he looked at her. "Tell me: what is that female secret, which I got slapped in the face for."

"There are no secrets. It was a gift, a very dear one to me," she said and suddenly become very sad.

"Mm," he nodded, "from your... man?" his expression changed as well. *"Of course, there is someone in her life,"* he thought, *"it cannot be otherwise. There is someone who she will return to when this is all over, someone who is going to hold her in his arms as I did today in the woods, someone who is going to feel her every heart beat and her warm breath on his face."*

"No!" she laughed softly. "It's not as romantic as you think. It was a gift from my mother. She gave it to me when I was sixteen. Shortly thereafter, she died, and it is one of few things that I have left to remember her by," staring straight before her, she took another sip from the cup. "When she died, I got a tattoo that resembles the shape of the bracelet. You have seen it," she added a little embarrassed. "We were very close."

"I am very sorry. I did not know," he said sincerely.

"Another apology?" she opened her eyes even wider. "You astonish me, Sir Guy of Gisborne. One apology from a man is a record, but two and in one night! Maybe, you are not as bad as you want to seem."

"I'll get it back to you," he promised. "I know how important and dear those small things, which we cherish in the memory of loved ones can be," he said, there was sadness in his deep blue eyes. "I also have something that is left from my mother. It is a ring, and one day I hope to give it to the girl who would agree to become my wife."

"And by that girl, you, of course, mean Lady Marian?" Christine asked. "She will never marry you."

"Why do you think so?" he asked with a genuine interest.

"I thought I already told you my opinion," she raised an eyebrow.

"And yet," he insisted.

"She doesn't love you, that's to start with, but more importantly, you don't love her either, and you know that better than I do. You will satisfy your hunger and then lose interest and become bored with her eventually."

"You are well versed in men," he chuckled softly, "have you known many?"

"If that is your way of asking if I am a maiden, the answer is NO and I don't think it's gonna come to you as a shock," she laughed. "I'm a woman. Yes, there were men in my life, and yes, I know what you want. Well, most of you anyway."

Guy felt uncomfortable continuing the conversation and paused briefly. No matter how much he enjoyed her company, they had already spent more than an hour here and, although the maid had brought and poured in more hot water, it was nearly dawn. He was very tired and wanted to sleep, but after the amount of wine she had consumed, Christine was feeling cheerful and very chatty.

"I think it's time you get out, otherwise you run the risk of becoming unwell," said Gisborne, touching the cool water, and rising to his feet.

Obeying him, Christine got to her feet as well. The water rushed down her shirt into the tub. The wet fabric clung to her body, outlining her every curve – breasts, waist and hips – leaving very little room for the imagination. She looked up at him mischievously and playfully bit her lower lip. Christine knew exactly what she was doing.

Trying not to look at her, he handed her a big cloth that served as a towel. Christine took it, then turning her back to him she slid the towel under her undershirt and wrapped it around her hips. She then pulled off her wet shirt and threw it down into the tub.

Standing with her back to him, she began to hum a slow melody, gently moving her hips and hands to the rhythm of the song. She sneaked a peek at him a few times, to make sure she was achieving the desired effect. Guy stood motionless, mesmerised, watching her every move.

She continued her dance, then opened the towel and continuing to glance back at him, slowly slid it over her body upward. She wrapped the towel around herself and turned to face Guy. Her eyes sparkled; her face bore the same playful smile.

"I've told you, Milord, I know what men want," she raised her eyebrows a little and bit her lip again.

If, up to this point, Gisborne had had any doubts about her innocence, what he saw before him, dismissed them entirely. She teased him, knowing full well what she was doing and what effect she had sought to achieve.

"You won, I believe you," he said, trying hard not to look at her. "It's late," he extended his hand to her.

In response, she made a face like an upset child, who was being sent to bed ahead of her time, and continued to move her hips smoothly, still humming that very same slow melody.

"Miss Hawk," he was trying to sound as firm as possible, realising too well it would be very difficult to get through to her after the amount of alcohol she had consumed.

"Alright, alright!" she said and stretched her hand out to him but, as soon as she lifted her leg, she lost balance and plopped back down into the tub with a small yelp, covering Guy with a splash of cool water. "Oops!" she giggled softly.

Guy gave her a disgruntled look, pulled off his wet shirt, threw it on the floor and, still not saying a word, held out his hand to her once again. Giggling, Christine obeyed and got to her feet once again, water gushed down her towel.

He held her by the waist and, lifting her with ease, swung her across the tub and lowered her onto the floor beside him. She was so close that she almost bumped into his shoulder. His strong hands still held her waist.

As soon as she was next to him, her face changed instantly. Her expression became serious, slightly lost and confused. She couldn't take her eyes off his broad muscular chest. So many times before, she had caught herself thinking how much she wanted to run her fingers over his skin, to feel its warmth.

Not lifting her eyes to him, holding her towel with one hand, she lifted her free hand and gently, even shyly, touched him. He startled, but to her surprise didn't take her hand off. Slowly, barely touching, as if caressing him, she ran the tips of her fingers over his chest. His skin was soft, hot.

Perhaps it was the effect of the wine or the result of her earlier emotions, the fact that she found him very attractive or maybe everything together, but Christine felt overwhelmed by the strong physical attraction. Just one look at him was enough to make her head spin, butterflies fluttered in her stomach, the tension rose in her abdomen, and everything trembled inside her.

She smiled faintly and looked into his eyes. Still a little shy, feeling like a fifteen-year-old girl on a first date, she touched him again, this time less self-consciously, her movements were bolder. Her fingers slowly caressed his skin, tracing his shoulders and strong arms, her fingers ran across his chest as she slowly walked around him.

Breathing heavily, Guy stood motionless. Every muscle, every cell in his body was tense. He did not know what to do, but knew he would not be able to control his desire much longer; the fire of passion that faintly kindled inside him now began to burn with full strength. When she was behind him, he could have sworn he felt her warm, soft lips touch his skin. Her hand slipped onto his belt, then further down and glided over his buttocks. What happened next, he could not have expected.

She was in front of him again and looking up into his eyes and holding his gaze, she opened her other arm, allowing the towel that was covering her body to fall freely to the floor. Gisborne swallowed hard. Still holding his gaze, Christine took his hand and gently put it on her waist.

"What..." he tried to speak, but she put her finger to his lips.

"Shh..." she whispered. "Don't say a thing and do not move, Sir Guy of Gisborne. I am seducing you."

Her hand was still gliding across his chest and shoulders then sank slowly to his stomach and stopped on the belt. She ran the tip of her finger over his muscular abdomen, along the line of his breeches. As if in a spasm of electroshock, Guy jerked involuntarily.

She took a step closer so now her breasts were touching his chest, barely but just enough that he could feel the warm touch of her skin on his. Panting heavily Gisborne clenched his teeth, his fingers digging hard into her waist. She closed her eyes and moaned quietly from pain and pleasure.

She slowly raised her eyes to his. Her fingers eagerly and greedily explored his face; barely touching it, she outlined his eyebrows, hairline, nose and lips. She breathed deeply and frequently and with every new breath, her chest rose and fell and her hardened nipples pressed against his hot skin. She felt how with every new touch his body became more and more tense. Guy could hardly contain himself; she was ready too.

Christine gently kissed his chest. Her lips slowly slid from his shoulder up to his neck, sending the surges of electroshock pulses all over his body. Her soft kisses moved further up to his face. Guy could no longer remain idle, wrapping his hand tightly around her waist and pressing her hard against his body, he lifted her face up to his. Her hot breath burned his cheek. He bent his head down ready to take her lips that longed for his kiss.

Their lips almost touched when the soft creak of the door made them both cringe and, as if from a dream, they snapped back to reality. Moving quickly, Guy turned towards the sound, shielding Christine with his body. Jenny, the housemaid was at the threshold of the room. "What?" he asked roughly, his voice was hoarse, throat dry.

"Milord," she bowed, "I wanted to know whether you have any other orders for me."

"No," he answered curtly, still breathing hard, "you can go to bed."

When she was gone, he turned to Christine. Intoxicated, she looked at him helplessly, not knowing what was happening. Trying not to look at her naked body, Guy wrapped her in a dry towel.

"Come, let's get you to bed," he said quietly, taking her into his arms.

"Yes... very good idea," she murmured in response.

She laid her head onto his shoulder and burying her nose into his neck once again gently ran her lips over it.

Guy carried her to his room and laid her gently on the freshly prepared bed. Christine fell asleep as soon as her head touched the pillow. She curled up and pulling her feet up to her chest, breathed evenly, making a soft sound as she breathed. Guy covered her with a blanket and went away to her room.

He pulled off his boots and lay on the bed on top of the covers. He was hoping to fall asleep instantly, but the thought of her gave him no peace. His body ached; his shoulders, chest, and neck – just visited by her lips – were burning. He could not stop thinking about her. The Sheriff was right – she was a real woman.

Guy lay in bed aimlessly staring at the ceiling, catching himself again and again in the thought that he would have given much just to, once again, feel her soft hands, her gentle kisses. Having tasted desire, he wanted more. He wanted to possess her completely.

Trying to rid himself of these thoughts, he turned on his side, but even then, he had no peace. He breathed in the floral scent that came from her pillow and her image again was alive in his head. He hugged the pillow and closed his eyes, but sleep never came.

The sun was beginning to rise over Sherwood Forest, a new day was dawning in Locksley.

Chapter 15:
Who is Mark?

The next day he did not go to Nottingham.

Not wishing to leave her alone in Locksley, Guy left orders with Jenny to notify him as soon as Miss Hawk woke up and engaged himself in the local administrative affairs. The devastation that had been left after the recent visit of the Sheriff and his soldiers demanded his attention. Guy hoped that the physical work would distract him from the memories of last night. He was wrong. Again, and again, his thoughts returned to the previous day, playing it over and over in his mind, savouring every detail.

A face slap...

He runs through the forest, a heavy sword gripped tightly in his right hand...

Her voice changing to a scream, her muffled moans, and sobs...

She is in his arms, frail, agitated, frightened.

A few hours later, they are in Locksley. She is safe. She is close...

Her lips...

Quickly finishing his daily routine, he returned to the house and went straight to his bedroom where, earlier that morning, he had left Christine. Finding her still peacefully asleep, Guy took off his jacket and lay down on the bed beside her. Making himself comfortable, he shifted the weight of his body onto one elbow, rested his head on his hand and, studied her face while she slept.

*****

With a blissful moan, Christine stretched her limbs. Reaching out, she found another pillow and brought it closer, clutching to it tightly. It had been a long time since she had slept this well, and if it wasn't for a terrible headache, she would have felt quite rested and refreshed. She stretched again, curving her spine slowly, and then tightly wrapped herself in the blanket. Not opening her eyes, she rolled over and buried her face into a man's shoulder.

"Good morning, dear," she purred. "I had such a strange dream!"

She nested comfortably, hiding under the covers. The man didn't answer, but she could hear his soft chuckle as he moved slightly away from her.

"Tell me," she continued muttering from inside her hiding place, struggling through each new word, "why every meeting of the Law Society ends up in a competition of who can drink the most? My head is killing me!"

She once again started to toss and turn inside her cocoon, trying to make herself comfortable and reduce her suffering. She pulled one hand out from under the covers, laid it on the man's chest and moved her head onto his shoulder.

"Mmm, so much better," she purred, smiling.

She wrapped her hand around his neck and started to slide her fingertip up and down, tracing the lines of his face – cheekbones, and chin. She felt how, from her light soft touch, his mouth stretched into a pleased smile.

"Did I drink a lot yesterday? I don't remember anything after I left Philip. Thank God, our flight is at eight and we don't have to rush," she sighed with relief. "We can spend all day in bed," she added and, in a catlike manner rubbed her face against his shoulder.

She briefly dozed but the pain, like a heavy hammer, started to pound in her temples again.

"Mmm, my head," she said, retreating to her pillow. "Mark, honey, be a dear and bring me a Nurofen," she said, curling up and pulling the blanket over her head, naively hoping it would help to numb the pain.

The man next to her did not move.

"Mark... please!" she moaned. "I understand that you probably receive immense pleasure witnessing my suffering," she again moved closer and began to slowly push the man that was lying beside her towards the edge of the bed. Not that it worked – he didn't move and Christine decided to choose a different tactic. "Please..." she began in her most seductive voice. "As soon as I'm better, I'll be very, VERY grateful. You know I can be..." she freed her hand from under the blanket and gently laid it on his groin.

The cold touch of the smooth leather breeches was not exactly what she'd expected to find there, and she jerked her hand back.

"What?!" she exclaimed, throwing the blanket off her head and peering out. Dressed as usual in black leather pants and a loose shirt with lace ties on his chest, Guy of Gisborne lay on the bed beside her, his head propped up on his right hand. Grinning widely, he looked at her with a hint of enquiry in his eyes.

"Who is Mark?" he asked in his soft velvety voice. His blue eyes smiled cunningly.

Wide-eyed, Christine tried to say something, but the words and thoughts treacherously fled from her head in all possible directions with no intention of returning back to her. She helplessly opened her mouth, trying to start several sentences, none of which she managed to finish, the words refused to come out.

"Oh no!" she breathed out finally.

Guy said nothing. His grin grew into a broad smile; he found the expression on her face very amusing.

"Oh no!" she whispered again, shooting a quick glance under the covers. It was not difficult for her to draw conclusions about how the previous evening had ended. "So, it wasn't a dream..." she said with a plea in her voice and eyes.

"Looked quite real to me," he said, still smiling unashamedly.

Christine pulled the blanket up, trying to cover herself, although in her current state it did not really matter. She was in his bed, and she was completely naked.

"You have not answered my question," said Guy, still smiling slyly. As if nothing had happened, he got up, walked around the bed and sat down on the other side, next to her. "So, who is this Mark?" he repeated his question. "If I have a rival, I need to know who he is," he was trying to be serious, but the expression on her face at that moment made him smile.

"No one! He's no one..." said Christine, finally able to squeeze out a few words, as she moved away from him.

"You know, it's very rude," he spoke again in a low voice, "to spend a night in bed with one man, and in the morning to call him a different name," he raised an eyebrow, his eyes demanded an answer.

"Oh, please! I beg you!" she said helplessly. "What happened yesterday? Please, you have to tell me!" she pleaded. "I don't remember anything after I parted with Allan. You... have you..." she did not finish, not daring to ask the question.

"Oh no! On the contrary!" he chuckled. "You tried to seduce me, ma'am," he bowed his head, got up from the bed and walked to the window.

He stood there with his arms crossed on his chest; his statuesque figure overshadowed the entire window.

"Seduced... or tried?" asked Christine, quietly.

She didn't know why she was asking this question, her presence in his bed made it unlikely to be the second option. He turned slowly. His blue eyes caught hers. He came closer and sat back down next to her. He gently lifted her face by the chin and pulled her closer to him. Christine froze, horrified and wide-eyed in confusion and anxious waiting. He leaned in, close enough that she could feel his breath on her face. She felt goose bumps across her entire body.

"You were very, very persuasive" he whispered into her ear.

"Oh my God!" Christine leaned back against the pillows and closed her eyes, pulling the blanket up to her chin. "What did I do?" she asked cautiously.

"You..." he paused and, raising an eyebrow, gave her a long look.

No further explanations were needed; his lustful gaze spoke for itself.

"Did I really?" she asked, still refusing to believe.

He nodded. This was the answer she dreaded. Christine swallowed. He smiled cunningly. Guy knew that eventually, he would have to tell her the truth, but for the moment, he could not resist the pleasure of tormenting her.

"To save your reputation, I, probably, will have to marry you now..." he sighed in disappointment. "Poor Lady Marian, I'm not sure if she will be able live with it. She so much wanted to be the mistress of Locksley."

"What? Marry?! What?! No!" Christine protested.

"Am I such a bad candidate?" he asked, with genuine amazement and surprise. "Yesterday you thought differently."

"Yesterday I was drunk! I didn't know what I was doing..." protested Christine. "You... you... I don't even like you!" she said, and bit her tongue.

In vain she tried to convince herself of that, but the way her heart skipped a beat at the sight of his blue eyes, and how butterflies began to fill her stomach when he was near, proved otherwise. She looked away.

"Am I really that bad? Is there nothing good about me?" he asked.

He narrowed his eyes slightly. He was still smiling when suddenly, as if yielding to compulsion, he lifted his hand, the back of his fingers lightly touched her shoulder and slid down to her elbow. He knew he shouldn't do it, but, as if some unseen power was prompting him, he could not stop himself. As he touched her, he felt as though an electric impulse pierced through his body, making it tense; his memory reproduced the events of last night.

All morning, he hadn't been able to stop thinking about her, pawing through fragments of his memory, putting her image together, like the small pieces of a puzzle. He could not forget how her soft hands caressed his shoulders, how her warm lips gently, explored his body, how her sweet hot breath touched his face. If only she knew how much of an effort it had taken him yesterday not to succumb to the temptation.

"If it was not for Jenny," he thought.

Now, looking at her lying in his bed naked and vulnerable, he once again found himself wanting to feel her touch. His breathing quickened, the fire again began to blaze in his soul. The warm waves of desire flowed through his body, he felt the tension begin to build in his groin. He shook his head, trying to shake off these thoughts.

He was still gazing at her with desire when someone knocked on the door.

"Sir Guy, I'm sorry to bother you, can I speak with you?" Allan's voice spoke from the hallway. Gisborne slowly got up from the bed and went to open the door. The young man couldn't help but peek inside. "Good afternoon, ma'am," he said cheerfully. "I can see you were able to make it safely back to Locksley after all."

"Afternoon!" Christine repeated after him horrified. "What time..."

She had no time to say anything else; Gisborne went out and shut the door behind him. Christine got up and, wrapping the blanket around her, came closer to the door, but couldn't make out what they were saying.

"Prepare everything, I will set off immediately," said Guy. Stepping back into the room, he nearly bumped into her, his face expressed displeasure. "The Sheriff has requested my presence in Nottingham," he said, looking past Christine who, standing in the middle of the room, tried to cover her naked body with the bed cover. "I should be back for dinner, but if not, don't wait for me."

He bowed stiffly and, with a heavy gait, walked back into the hallway, leaving her standing in the middle of the room. His change was remarkable. Five minutes ago, he was cheerful and happy, smiling and joking but now, going to Nottingham, he was cold again. His face was tense and stressed.

As soon as he disappeared around the bend of the staircase, Christine, not waiting another moment, slipped across the hall into her room. On her bed, she found her clothes – breeches and shirt that she had left in the castle – someone had brought them back for her from Nottingham.

She got dressed but then went back to bed. Her head ached from the strain and a hangover. She lay there, staring at the ceiling, trying to remember what had happened last night, but in vain. The question of how she ended up in his bed remained unanswered.

*****

Having reached Nottingham, Gisborne went straight to the Sheriff, who waited and greeted him happily. His cat-like smile decorated his face.

"Before we move on to the important political matters," he said, coming closer and taking his deputy by the hand, as soon as Gisborne crossed the threshold of his room, "tell me, did you get lucky last night, eh?"

"Yes," lied Guy, his answer was short. He knew what Wesley was hinting at but decided it would be better that the Sheriff not know the details.

"Ahh! That's my boy!" the Sheriff proudly patted him on the shoulder. "Was I right, huh? Good?" he longed for details.

"Yes, you were right, your grace," replied Gisborne dryly. "But I do not think you have invited me here to discuss how I spent the night," he added and bowed his head respectfully.

"Alright, alright! Oh, well done! I knew you would not disappoint me!" he once again patted his shoulder.

Gisborne moulded a smile to his face.

The Sheriff invited him closer to the table, where maps and papers were scattered in a familiar mess. Guy obeyed and walking closer he stood nearby, shifting his body weight from one foot to the other.

"The money is divided and distributed among our friends," began the Sheriff, handing him the ledger. "Tomorrow they will be leaving," he continued, "you will have to arrange their safe passage through Sherwood. Use only your squad. I am sure you have enough people to provide them with a convoy. You only need to take them as far as Sherwood's border. From there they can go as they will. This is first," he walked around the table and began to rummage through the papers.

Surprisingly for both of them, the door to the Sheriff's room swung open and Lord Winchester stormed in.

"Wesley, is there any news for me?" asked the middle-aged man as he stepped inside.

"Ah, and this is the second," the Sheriff muttered to Gisborne and then turned to the man, who had so unceremoniously sauntered into his room. "You do not need to worry, your grace, my best people are dealing with it," Wesley bowed and then rudely turned his back on his guest.

Guy looked at him blankly.

"I'll explain everything when he goes away," the Sheriff said quietly. "I will let you know as soon as there is any news, your grace," he added, hinting to the visitor that he should leave.

As soon as Lord Winchester left the Sheriff's chambers, Wesley turned to Gisborne.

"Three men from his personal guard did not report for duty this morning. They were seen leaving the castle late last night and heading towards Sherwood," muttered the Sheriff. "I sent a small squad to search through the woods. They were found about a mile from Locksley. There are signs of a struggle. It doesn't look very good... one has a scratched face and, then, my people also found this," the Sheriff produced a piece of cloth from the sleeve of Christine's dress. His face was worried. "I did not want to upset the old man, not just yet... Do you know anything about it?" the Sheriff looked at him with keen interest.

"Yes," said Gisborne shortly, as he bowed. "I killed them," he added quietly and coolly.

"Hm, did you just!" the Sheriff raised his eyebrows. "You should not have, really," he said patting his beard. "Reason? Just do not tell me that you had a fight over a girl," he added with a joke, fiddling with the piece of blue fabric.

"They followed Miss Hawk into the woods and attacked her, trying to..." he paused. "I got there just in time."

"Hmm... we, of course, can't let anything happen to our dear Miss Hawk until she does what she was invited for. Witnesses?"

"None," briefly replied Guy. "Everything was done cleanly, no one will suspect anything, you know me."

"Of course, of course, I do not doubt you, my boy," the Sheriff approvingly patted him on the shoulder. "And the girl? What if she talks?"

"I doubt she would," Guy hesitated a little. "I do not think she remembers much of the previous evening."

"Including this?!" laughed the Sheriff moving his hips back and forth. "I hope you fully enjoyed your victory!" he laughed out loud.

Guy bared his teeth in a forced grin.

"Well, what's done is done. We will have to come up with a story of some sort and blame everything on Hood. He, in any case, is going to be hung soon enough or be otherwise disposed of, so a few extra corpses will not change his fate," he laughed again loudly and winked at his deputy.

Gisborne was not amused; he walked silently to the window.

A few moments later, the door to the Sheriff's bedchamber opened again, and a guard, gasping for breath, appeared on the threshold.

"Your grace," the man bent in a deep bow, "a messenger from London with a letter from Prince John!" he stepped aside.

The young man entered the room, bowed to the Sheriff and handed him an envelope sealed with red wax.

Breaking the seal of the royal arms, the Sheriff opened the letter and quickly scanned the paper. His face changed instantly. He glanced at the letter a few more times as he silently paced across the room and back again. Then he stopped at the table, poured himself a glass of wine and gulped down the contents in one breath.

"Tell me, what you make of this," he said, and handed the letter to his deputy.

Guy looked down at the piece of thick yellow paper. In wide, sweeping handwriting, there were only a few sentences written on it.

The message ended with the royal seal and the monogram of His Royal Highness, Prince John.

Gisborne's eyes moved quickly through the lines on the paper once again. He read the letter for a third time, and then lifted it up to the light and tried to look through it as if looking for hidden messages – there were none. The letter was limited to just the few lines written in it.

"I do not understand," he said after a moment of silence, handing the letter back to the Sheriff.

"Yes..." Wesley murmured quietly and again began to fiddle with his short beard. "This is all very strange... the Prince invites me to London to discuss how we should proceed with our plan of action... I thought that the plan was already in action!"

The Sheriff began to pace the room from one side to the other, muttering something under his breath. He stopped at the window and folded his arms, and then began to rock slowly back and forth, rolling from heel to toe and back again. He was thinking.

"Who is she, Gisborne? Who is she, I am asking you, hmm?" he rattled. More than anything, Wesley hated it when someone was trying to outsmart him.

"Who, your grace, who are you talking about?" Gisborne could not understand.

"That woman, Gisborne! That woman who lives in your house!" he hissed, losing his patience. He took a few steps forward and now, standing very close to Gisborne, he looked up at Guy. "Who is she? What is she doing here, eh?" his small bulging eyes demanded an answer.

He once again began to measure the room with his quick short steps.

"She's a spy!" he said jumping back at Gisborne. "Yes, yes... She is a spy sent to us by Hood. Oh, that explains why she became friends so quickly with your leper girlfriend!" the Sheriff was furious. "Or it could be even worse, she could be working for Richard himself and sent him all the information about our plans!" he said to himself and then looked up at Gisborne. "How could we be so blind, so blind!" emotions overwhelmed him.

Only now, Gisborne understood the Sheriff. Over the past few days, his attention had lain elsewhere; he had forgotten about the real reason for Christine's presence in Nottingham.

"Your grace, I am sure there is a reasonable explanation," he said finally.

"Yes, maybe you're right," said Wesley thoughtfully. "Tomorrow I will go to London! You will stay here – keep a close eye on her until I'm back."

They both walked out of the room into the hallway.

"Ah, Lady Marian, how fortunate!" said the Sheriff when he saw the young girl trying to hide in the shadows of a nearby doorway. "Just the person I needed! Pack up your things," ordered the Sheriff.

"Pack up my things, your grace?"

"Yes, my dear, enough of you sitting around idly! Tomorrow morning, you and I are setting off to London," he said.

"To London?" she repeated after him.

"My dear, it occurs to me that since yesterday you seem to have some problems with your ears? Or am I not making myself clear?" he shouted angrily.

"No, I'm sorry, your grace. But London? Sir Guy..." Marian turned to Gisborne, but he did not react.

"Don't look at him, my dear, your lovely eyes you will not save you this time. You and I are going to London. End of story!" he snapped. "And besides, I thought that you might want to take this opportunity to plea for your precious daddy before the Prince?"

Left without any other option, the girl agreed, and promising to be ready early in the morning, retired to her room.

"So, it's done..." muttered the Sheriff going back to his room.

Guy followed him obediently.

Having received his last orders from the Sheriff, Gisborne bid him good-bye and rode back to Locksley. In Wesley's absence, he was instructed to take on the responsibilities of the Sheriff of Nottingham, as well as the duties of the head of the region. However, his main task was to keep an eye on Christine. The Sheriff was hoping that his deputy, using his charm, would be able to extract important information from her. Guy did not like this approach, or the blessing of Wesley to use any means possible.

*****

Spurring Raven mercilessly, Gisborne galloped back to Locksley. In his head, he could not believe that all this time Christine might have been spying for Robin Hood, or, even worse, for the King himself.

"Was it all a cover-up, a lie?"

Now, her frequent trips to the forest had a completely different meaning for him.

"But she got lost... for a person of her profession, if she really was the one who she claimed to be, it would have been unlikely. She was attacked... It cannot be that she agreed to that knowingly; it cannot be that the attack was staged to divert our attention, to dull our vigilance..."

Her screams were still loud in his ears. She trembled and shook in his arms when he saved her from the attackers.

"No! It can't all be a lie. Did she use me? If the Sheriff says so, then it must be the truth, the Sheriff has never lied to me."

Yet deep inside, Guy still refused to believe it. His inner voice kept telling him that, perhaps, things were different to what they seemed at first glance but how exactly, and why, he could not understand.

He rushed his stallion to Locksley; he needed to see her, he needed to look into her eyes, to get a confirmation or to disprove his suspicions.

Reaching the doors of the manor, he abruptly pulled up Raven, threw his leg over the horse's head, jumped off the saddle and stormed into the house. He ran up the stairs and without knocking, walked into her room only to find that she wasn't there.

A loud sigh of irritation escaped him. Loudly stomping on the wooden floorboards, he went down into the stables. Neither Christine nor her horse were there. In anger, he kicked the first thing that got under his feet and, returning to the house, hurried into the kitchen.

"Did she really lie to me all this time?" he still refused to believe. "Where is she?" he asked gruffly.

Jenny, who had not seen her master coming in, jumped in surprise.

"Who, M-Milord?"

"Miss Hawk..." he hissed through tightly gritted teeth.

"She went out for a ride into the woods wi..." she was not able to finish.

He heard the clatter of the hooves of the approaching horses and stormed outside.

As he ran outside, he saw Christine approaching the house. With flushed ruby cheeks and a sparkle in her eyes, she was sitting in the saddle trying to catch her breath, her hair was untidy from a fast ride.

"Where have you been?" he asked. His tone was harsh and rude.

"And a very good evening to you, Milord," she said, getting down from the horse.

"Where have you been?" he repeated the question and, grabbing her by the arm, dragged her the rest of the way down.

"What the hell do you think you are doing?" Christine protested, trying to free herself.

"Where have you been?" clearly pronouncing every word, for the third time he repeated his question. The anger began to overcome him.

"I... was... out... in the woods!" mimicking his tone she said, one eyebrow raised.

"Do not play with me!" he shook her lightly. "What were you doing there?"

"None of your bloody business! What kind of interrogation is this? Let me go!" Christine struggled in his hold.

"Or what?" Gisborne asked tightening his grip around her hand. "You will use one of his tricks?"

"Release me, now!" she ordered. Her expression changed. Her eyes blazed with anger. Obeying, he unwittingly opened his hand. "What's wrong with you!?" Christine pushed him aside. "I've been riding in the woods with Allan," she said angrily scalding him with her fiery gaze.

"Allan?" he breathed out.

Christine said nothing, staring him right in the eyes. Having heard his name, the servant peered out of the stables.

"Sir Guy, did you call me?" he asked.

"Where have you been just now?" Gisborne threw over his shoulder still looking at Christine.

"We went to Sherwood, Sir. Miss Hawk had a headache, so we rode out to get some fresh air. She asked me to accompany her. She did not want to go alone."

"And you have not lost sight of her at any time?" he asked slightly confused.

"No, Sir, not for a moment. We were together, but... what happened?" asked the young man.

"The Sheriff..." muttered Guy. "The Sheriff said..."

"The Sheriff! Why aren't I surprised!" exclaimed Christine. "What does he do to you?" she said, unable to restrain herself. "What powers does he have over you? You make the impression of a reasonable, sensible man, you are not alien to feelings, emotions and common sense, but every time... every time you come back from the castle or if you speak with him, you turn into a monster!"

She shook her head in disappointment, abruptly turned around and entered the house. Quickly climbing the stairs, she disappeared into her room, slamming the door behind her.

Guy followed her. How dare this woman speak to him like that? He raised his hand to push the door and enter the room, but hearing her angry mutter inside, stopped.

She was right! She was right in everything except for one thing – he was not becoming a monster, he was one already. He had become one long ago, and there was no hope for him, no turning back. The Sheriff of Nottingham was the only person who understood and appreciated Gisborne, who needed him; without him, the Sheriff would not have gotten his current position.

Guy smiled to himself, basking in the thoughts of his own significance and importance, but then the smile went from his face. No matter how hard he tried to reassure and console himself, he was a monster – a fearless, cold-hearted, senseless, heartless monster!

But there was something else that affected him even more. Like a sharp arrow her words pierced through his soul.

"You make the impression of a reasonable, sensible man, you are not alien to feelings..." he repeated.

And there she was right again, sometimes, in his moments of weakness, his human qualities and feelings tried to break though, but he always managed to bury them back, deep into his soul, where no one could see them – no one but her. As if she could see through him, through the layer of that brutal and cold mask he wore all the time, as if she could see deep inside him, into those parts of his soul, which he so carefully concealed from everyone. The parts of him, which were invisible to everyone – except her. Could it be that there was still hope for him?

Hesitating for a moment, he softly knocked on her door.

Chapter 16:
I Have To Thank You

Despite his expectations, Christine refused to speak with him; she did not even open the door.

"I don't want to see you," were her only words.

There was nothing else for him to do but to return to the dining room in the hope that she would calm down a little and come out for dinner. Then, he was sure, he would be able to speak with her. However, she did not come out and Gisborne had to dine alone. He did not have an appetite and after a nibble, he pushed the plate away and poured himself a glass of wine.

He was very tired. Last night he did not sleep – first, there was the Sheriff's gathering, then the forest, then Christine. He managed to get to bed at dawn but even then, he could not sleep as his thoughts had swirled in his head.

Now he was alone in the room. Without witnesses, he did not have to follow the rules of etiquette. He closed his eyes, stretched out in a chair, and slowly sipped the wine, enjoying the silence, broken occasionally by the crackling of the fire and soft cracks of the bursting pine bark.

Gisborne was trying to work out what he should do next.

"Go to sleep or try again to speak with Christine?"

Tomorrow he would have to get up at dawn and ride to Nottingham, to get the last instructions from the Sheriff before he left for London. Despite the fact that today the Sheriff had dedicated sufficient time to the task, Guy knew that Wesley would not deny himself the pleasure of, once again, reading to his deputy a lecture on how the fair head of the region should act. If, to summarise his monologue in just a few words, the motto of John Wesley, the Sheriff of Nottingham, was to put into the dungeon and hang anyone who in anyway resisted or undermined his authority.

The second but no less important task for tomorrow, which Guy should not forget about, was to escort the departing guests. He divided his men into several groups and gave them all the required instructions – all but one. Allan, his faithful servant, was entrusted with the most important task – staying in Locksley and not letting

Christine out of his sight. Even though Guy still refused to believe the Sheriff's accusation, one could not be too careful.

He, himself, would have to accompany Lord Winchester, and convey him to the borders of Sherwood. Firstly, because the man would carry away the largest share of the money and Guy could not risk him meeting with Hood's gang, and secondly, because thanks to Gisborne, Winchester's company was three men short.

"Tomorrow I will spend most of the day in the saddle again," thought Guy stretching his tense and cramped muscles.

Yet, despite the appealing prospect of getting back to his room and plunging into a deep sleep, Guy, as if driven by an invisible force and pushed by his inner voice, climbed up the stairs and walked straight to Christine's room.

He stood there for a while, listening to the sounds inside the room and then knocked softly. There was no answer. After a brief pause, he knocked again, this time more insistently. On the other side, he heard footsteps.

"Miss Hawk," he said softly, his hand lay on the wooden barrier separating them.

Uncontrolled by him, his heart quickened its pace.

There was a rattle of the metal bolt and with a slight creak, the door opened. Their eyes met. Christine looked at him; her gaze was cold.

"What do you want?" she asked quietly.

"I thought you did not want to see me," he said, his lips stretched into a barely perceptible smile.

"I do not want to see you," Christine replied dryly.

"Then why did you open the door?" still smiling, he asked in his soft velvety voice.

Raising an eyebrow, Christine made a motion to shut the door in his face, but Guy stopped her, quickly placing his leg into the doorway.

"What do you want?" she asked blankly.

"I've come to apologise."

"I don't think I want to hear your apologies," she answered, not changing her tone.

"Why?" asked Guy, surprised.

"Because you'll apologise now, but what will happen tomorrow? Tomorrow you will go back to the castle, speak with the Sheriff and he will once again make up some crazy stories, and what'll happen then? It will go around in circles. Why waste time on it in the first place?" her voice was still cold.

Despite the late hour, the house was still buzzing with life, one of the servants appeared on the stairs behind him.

"Can I come in?" he asked quietly.

"This is your house, Milord; you can go where you please. You don't need to ask my permission," she said and stepped aside, letting him into the room.

"You are still angry with me," Guy walked in and, closing the door behind him, crossed the room and stood by the window.

"Angry? No," she said, still standing in the middle of the room. "I am disappointed," added Christine looking him in the eye.

"Disappointed?" repeated Guy, his brows flying up in surprise. "To be honest, I am not sure which one is worse," he said, lowering his eyes. Her direct gaze made him uncomfortable.

"Anger fades away fast," quietly replied Christine. For a fraction of a moment, it seemed to him that her voice became softer, calmer. "But after disappointment, as well as the betrayal, it's very difficult for one to restore faith and trust."

Guy knowingly shook his head and turned to the window.

"I should explain myself," he began, looking into the darkness. "Today the Sheriff received a letter from the Prince."

Christine was lucky that Guy didn't see how, at these words, her face changed. Her heart almost jumped out of her chest. It took a moment for her to pull herself together.

"Letter?" she asked trying to speak in an even voice.

"Yes, the content of it was somewhat vague, and the Sheriff suggested that you... that you could be a spy... I came back to talk to you, and when I did not find you in Locksley..." he paused.

"You assumed that the Sheriff was right?" she attempted to smile.

It was not, however, a happy smile, more of a laboured smile that was followed by a sigh of relief. The situation was far from entertaining.

Robin... why does he take so long? Are there so many places in Sherwood that fall under similar description? I need to meet with him and the sooner the better.

Today she was very close to failure.

"I may, perhaps, repeat myself," she said, "but you give off the impression of a sane, normal person. You know compassion, but you need to very carefully reconsider your inner circles, the people you spend your time with! You are alone, and HE tries to play on it," she spoke with passion. "Several times I've seen that other side of yours, no matter how hard you try to hide it, probably believing that others will take it for your weakness. Emotions and feelings are not a weakness, on the contrary. The ability to feel and show empathy and compassion makes one stronger and you know that. Here in Locksley, you are different, but as soon as you cross the threshold of the castle..." she paused.

Guy listened attentively, silently agreeing with everything she was saying.

"I understand that it's your job, Sir Guy, but ask yourself – why are you with him? Because you are alone and have no one to turn to? For this reason, you concentrate on the material side of the matter. Do you think that wealth and fame will make you happy? The fame of a ruthless, merciless, heartless and cruel murderer? Think again before it's too late! He destroys what little humanity is still left in you! While this man is around, you will sink deeper and deeper into this swamp, until it is too late," there was a faint note of tenderness in her voice. "Here in Locksley you are loved and respected, you care about your people. I've seen it more than once. I'm sure that others will respect you as well, if they are given a chance to see the real you, not this mask that you wear all the time," Christine came closer to him and put a gentle hand on his shoulder. Looking into his bottomless blue eyes, she added, "Sir Guy, you're not a bad person, no matter how hard you want to convince everyone otherwise. You can be happy."

Having said that, she moved away from him and sat down on the bed. For some time, Gisborne stood by the window, looking into the night sky, thinking about her words.

"Everything will be different! I promise!" he said finally, turning to Christine,

"I would very much like to believe that, but judging by what I have seen so far," she shook her head.

"The coming days will be the perfect chance to revive your faith in me," he said, the light of hope shining in his eyes.

"Coming days? What do you mean?" Christine asked.

"Tomorrow morning the Sheriff is leaving for London to meet with Prince John. There and back, it will take him about a week," Guy said. "While he is away, he's delegated to me his post of the Sheriff of Nottingham," he added proudly.

"That is... wonderful news!" Christine said, making a brave face.

Her heart was pounding at a furious pace, adrenaline rushed through her veins. A week! She must get out of here as soon as possible!

*****

Guy rose at dawn, ate a quick breakfast, and rode off to Nottingham, leaving Allan to keep an eye on Locksley; however, both men were well aware that the only person whom Allan had been assigned to watch over was Christine.

As soon as Raven, carrying the black rider, disappeared from sight, Christine slipped into the stables. She saddled her horse and within ten minutes was ready to ride to Sherwood. Time was mercilessly running away from her. Like sand in an hourglass, day after day, hour after hour, each minute could decide her fate.

"Ma'am?" suddenly a voice spoke behind her. "You know I have orders to keep an eye on you."

"Allan," she breathed out, "I need to leave. Alone! I can't explain it, but please don't say a word, I'll be back soon, I promise."

Not waiting for his answer, Christine mounted her horse and galloped away in the direction of the outlaws' forest camp.

It wasn't difficult for her to find the place in the woods. Only now, she realised that the camp was based very close to Locksley. Without a doubt, Robin didn't want to go far away from his native village. Besides, it was also more convenient to monitor the movements of his enemy – Guy of Gisborne.

Tightly surrounded by trees, the cave served as a safe haven for the outlaws. Christine dismounted and went inside. Not wanting to risk leaving her horse outside, she took it with her. Whinnying loudly, the restless animal tried to protest – the dark, damp cave was not to its liking, but despite the protests, it had no choice but to obey.

Unfortunately for Christine, the cave was empty. Neither Robin nor the other members of the gang were anywhere to be seen. Hoping that Robin and his men would come back soon, Christine decided to wait. After waiting for an hour, with still no sign of Robin returning to the camp, she had to go back to Locksley.

*****

As if he had not moved since she left the village, Allan met her at the stables.

"Thank God you're back!" he exclaimed.

"Allan, please," she replied.

"Where have you been? You know what he will do to me if he finds out that I let you out alone!"

"I don't think you want to know where I was," she said.

"On the contrary! If I have to cover for you, I need to know where you and I have been today," said the young man.

Christine knew that Allan was right and his frightened face was further proof to it. Yesterday she had experienced for herself how bad with jokes Gisborne could be.

"I went to Sherwood," she said, hoping that this response would satisfy him.

"Miss..."

"Well," sighed Christine, there was no point in denying it, "I went to see Robin Hood, but it's..." she couldn't finish.

"Oh no!" Allan's hands flew up to his face. "I hoped you wouldn't say that! So, master was right about you." Rubbing his neck, he added, a little disappointed, "So, you really are a spy."

"No, Allan, no!" Christine tried to calm him down. "I'm not a spy! You have to believe me. I can't tell you more, but I beg you."

Christine moved closer to him and gently touched his shoulder, urging him to look into her eyes.

"Please believe me," her eyes were full of despair. "I... I... I am lost..." she tried to find the right words to explain. "I need to go back home..." she spoke quickly, her feelings almost overcoming her, "Robin... Robin promised to help, and now, that the Sheriff has gone to London, I'm afraid I don't have much time."

"Very well," he said, not knowing why. There was something in her eyes that told him she was not lying. "Alright, but I'll go with you," he said quickly, saddling up his horse.

"But you can't!" protested Christine. "I can't take you to Robin's camp!"

"Do not worry," he smiled, "I know where it is."

"What? How?"

"It's a long story," said Allan, "I'll tell you as we ride."

*****

From her conversation with Allan, Christine found out only six months ago, the young man had been in, as he, himself, called it, Robin Hood's gang, but was kicked out for his treachery.

In one of the raids on Nottingham Castle, Allan was caught and, in spite of his attempts to talk himself out of trouble, ended up in prison. Guy of Gisborne took up the gruesome task of beating the truth out of him, and carried it out gleefully. After spending a week in prison, in the gentle and caring hands of the Sheriff's deputy, Allan could no longer bear the torture and finally admitted everything. To save his life, he agreed, then and there for a small fee, to feed Gisborne information about the outlaws' plans – which route to avoid for the transportation of money, when to send a bigger convoy and so on.

As soon as Robin found out about his betrayal, Allan was kicked out of the camp and the gang all together, and he had no choice but to seek employment with Gisborne, who, after brief negotiations, gladly took him in. When Robin learned about this, his first wish was to send Allan to his ancestors, but Marian did not let him take on this sin and made Allan swear on his own life, that he would never betray their secrets.

Since then, Allan A'Dale had served his new master well but continued to keep the location of the outlaws' camp and, most importantly, the relationship between Robin Hood and Lady Marian a secret.

"So, ma'am, if I am to risk my life, I want to be sure it's worth it," said Allan tying his horse to a tree. "That I am doing the right thing, you know?"

As he said, he well knew the location of Robin's hideout. He rode up behind the cave and showed Christine where to leave her horse so it would not be seen from the main road.

"Very clever!" smiled Christine and patted him on the shoulder. "Thank you, Allan, you're doing the right thing," she added, as soon as they stepped into the darkness of the grotto.

They spent about half an hour in the cave before Christine started shivering. Seeing her trying to keep warm and, wrapping a light jacket tightly around her shoulders, Allan went to the storeroom, and bringing out a few logs, quickly made a fire and invited Christine to come closer and get warm.

Soon their patience was rewarded and in the distance, at the entrance to the cave, they heard the sounds of laughs, happy chatter and the rattling of metal.

"Nice work!"

"I can imagine his face when he finds out..."

"Well done, lads! Tonight, we will count and divide the money. Tomorrow we will take it to the vil..."

The voices fell silent. Christine heard careful slow steps – Robin had noticed the fire. A small group of people, led by Robin Hood, came into the front room of the cave. Expressions of surprise, mixed with relief, appeared on their faces when they saw Christine.

"We have a guest, boys!" Robin laughed, but his face and happy mood changed as soon as he saw Allan. "What is he doing here?" he asked, not daring to take his eyes off of his enemy. "Is Gisborne here with you, too?" he added, cautiously looking around. "I knew there was something wrong, it was too easy to steal the money."

"No, no, Robin! It's not what you think," Christine tried to reassure him.

"You are not welcome here, Allan. You leave now," Little John did not miss the opportunity to add a word and threatened Allan with his club.

"Hey, hey, good men, I'm with her!" Allan raised his hands in surrender. "Gisborne left me to watch her. If he finds out that I let her go... my life is at stake as well!"

"Robin, it's true! That's why we're here. Listen," Christine spoke very quickly, trying to stick to the important facts. "The Sheriff has received a letter from Prince John that puts my stay here in jeopardy. I am afraid I may have very little time left. I need to get out of here before he comes back! Did you find anything?"

"Miss, not even a day has passed since we last spoke," said Robin a little confused.

"Really? I don't know how much time has passed, I just know that I don't have much of it left," she sat down on one of the benches. "Today? Can you start the search today?"

"I'm not sure we will be able to do anything within the next few days, especially after today's attack on Buckingham's convoy," he pointed towards the two large trunks held by the Friar. "And then there are a lot of soldiers in the woods after, after what happened last night."

"Happened last night?" repeated Christine. "What happened?"

"Don't you know?" he asked. "Last night when Nottingham celebrated the Sheriff's birthday, three people from the personal guard of Lord Winchester were killed... the Sheriff, of course, said nothing to him and is making a fake search, although it is clearly murder and professionally done."

"Murder?!" Christine could not believe her own ears.

"Yes, a woman was attacked in the forest", said Robin, taking one of the chests from the Friar, "not very far from here. We heard the screams but when we arrived to help, there was no one, but three bodies," finished Robin and, grunting quietly, carried the chest into the next room.

Christine sat open-mouthed. How was it possible that something like that had gone unnoticed by her? She was in the forest last night; she was walking through the woods... And then, as if on a screen, the picture appeared before her. She was that woman! It was she, who screaming at the top of her voice, was calling for help. She shook her head, trying to get rid of the terrible vision.

After a moment of silence she finally asked, "When can you start Robin?"

She tried to pull herself together, but the faces of the people who attacked her were still there in her mind.

"Tomorrow, if we are lucky," he said. "We will need to wait until it all calms down a bit."

"What are you looking for?" asked Allan. With his natural curiosity, it was uncommon for him, not to be aware of the latest events.

"I asked Robin to help me to find a place in the forest," replied Christine. "I hope that there will be something there, something that will help me work out how I can return home."

"You mean that place at the South Gates," Allan asked blankly, "the one where we found you?"

Christine nodded absently.

"Then why look for it?" he said. "You should have asked me long ago, I know where it is."

"What?!" Christine's eyes widened.

"I know that place," he answered surprised, not being able to understand her reaction.

"Well, of course!" she exclaimed. "You've said that before! How could I forget, Allan, you were with him!"

Christine couldn't contain her joy. She almost strangled the young man in her tight embrace.

"C'mon," she grabbed his arm and dragged him after her, "Can you take us there?"

"You mean, right now? No, out of the question, we cannot go now. It is too far away, and besides, we need to get back to Locksley. Gisborne will be back soon."

"Well, then, tomorrow? In the morning, okay?" she insisted.

"Tomorrow we have a training day," he said, "and then in the absence of the Sheriff, I am sure, the master will have some extra work for me."

"Oh, Allan," she pleaded, "the Sheriff will be back and... We cannot wait!

"In three days, there will be a wedding in Locksley," said Allan thoughtfully.

"Wedding? What wedding?" Christine could not understand. "What has a wedding to do with anything?"

"I can ask Sir Guy to grant me leave and take Robin to the place where we found you," he explained.

"Oh, perfect!" Christine said happily. *So, three days!*

*****

Back in Locksley, Christine went straight to her room. She was too excited to feel hungry.

Once alone, she sat on the bed, but couldn't sit still. Thoughts raced through her head, chasing and overtaking one another. She tried to calm down and put everything in order.

The Sheriff's gathering.

The Forest.

The Attack.

Gisborne.

Allan and his news.

The pressure was too much, her head began to hurt, she felt as if it was about to split in two.

"He saved me," she murmured. "After all that I've done to him. He saved me. He killed for me and didn't say a word."

Was the Sheriff aware of it? She didn't know, she had no idea if the Sheriff knew who had killed those people in the forest? What punishment could have awaited Gisborne for that?

Now the events of the previous night passed before her eyes. The amount of wine consumed and the shock of the tragedy itself had blocked out the memories, but now it was all there.

She remembered how they had walked back through the forest, how with his talk he had tried to distract her from the thoughts of what had happened. How he had held her in his arms and then how long they talked. She remembered the warmth of his caring hands, holding her in the soundless night, the soft gaze of his blue eyes and his gentle voice. But that was not everything that she remembered. Her face flushed.

Christine felt hot from the memories of his beautiful athletic body, his soft, hot skin, and her lips gliding across his chest. Her hand rose up and she touched her lips.

"*I kissed him...*" her breathing quickened. "Oh, my God..." she said softly, sensing how at the thought of him, the desire began to burn slowly, filling her with its warmth.

*****

Soon, from outside, came the sound of hooves and whinnying of horses. An incredible sense of relief filled her heart when she heard his voice again.

"You can go to the house," Guy turned to the horsemen who arrived with him, "and tell the cook that I ordered her to feed you. Rest here a while and then return to the castle. The fact that these outlaws have taken their toll today, does not mean that they will not try it again, or that they will not attempt to raid the treasury while the Sheriff's out of town."

His commanding voice sounded tired, he looked exhausted, too. The last few days spent without rest and sleep had caught up with him. Against his black clothes and dark hair, his face looked very pale, almost ghostly. He dismounted and handed the reins to Allan. Gisborne pulled off his leather gloves with his teeth and tucked them under his belt. Christine, who had been watching him all this time from the door of the manor, couldn't help but smile. There was something special in this ordinary gesture of his, something that made her heart beat faster.

He undid his jacket, closed his eyes and rubbed his tired neck. A soft moan escaped him when his strong fingers began to knead the tense muscles.

"Long day?" she asked softly.

His expression changed instantly, as soon as he heard this ordinary question. A corner of his mouth lifted in a light smile. Turning his head slightly, Gisborne sent a glance to the owner of the voice. Christine smiled in return. Not saying a word, he nodded his head affirmatively.

"Then, why don't we go inside," she said, inviting him into his house. "You will sit by the fire, I will bring wine, and you can tell me how your day was."

"I have a better suggestion," he said, smiling wearily. "We go inside, I will sit in the chair by the fire, you will bring wine, and then tell me how YOU have spent your day."

They entered the house and walked into one of the rooms. Guy pulled a chair closer to the fire and made himself comfortable, stretching out his long legs. He knew that he ought not to sit like that in the presence of a woman, but with her close by he felt different. Around her, he felt that he could be himself.

Christine brought wine, filled their goblets and sat down opposite him.

"So, what were you up to today?" he said and closed his tired eyes.

"Well, nothing interesting really," she said, smiling, "I went for a ride, and then returned to Locksley."

"Went for a ride alone?" he opened one eye and looked at her.

"No, Milord," she smiled. "Allan accompanied me all the time. He's a good lad."

"Good?" her comment aroused a lively interest in him. "Do you like him?" Gisborne sat up in his chair.

"Yes, of course," replied Christine, without a moment of hesitation, but seeing the reaction of her companion, immediately clarified it with, "Oh, I guess I didn't put it correctly. He is a good and faithful servant who honours the interests of his master. He is a good lad," Christine repeated her phrase with emphasis on the last word.

"And is that all?" he asked, his face visibly brightened.

"That's all!" she nodded her head affirmatively. "He's too young for me, if that's what you mean," she looked him straight in the eyes. "And besides he's not my type."

"What is your type?" he raised an eyebrow quizzing, demanding her to voice aloud what he already saw in her eyes.

Christine didn't have time to answer; they were invited to the dining room. The maid brought a starter, but neither of them seemed to have an appetite and didn't touch their food.

"What else did you do?" he spoke again.

"Wandered about the village, watched the people and listened to what they talk about," Christine fibbed.

"Yes? And what do people in the village talk about?" he asked with interest.

"They say that there will be a wedding soon," she began steering the conversation.

"Wedding? I haven't heard about that," he said taking a sip from a cup.

"Yes, Allan said he wanted to go. I think he likes one of the local girls and wants to try his luck."

"I hope the girl whom he fancies is not the bride?" Guy chuckled loudly.

"I don't know, he didn't tell me," Christine smiled. "But even so, why couldn't he make his feelings known and try his luck. Who knows, maybe she is not indifferent to him but is forced to marry another."

"What else are people saying?" Guy changed the subject of conversation.

"People say that there was an attack in the forest last night," said Christine. She could see the tension grow as she spoke these words. "The attackers were killed..." she added.

"Those lowlifes got what they deserved!" Gisborne said coldly.

An uncomfortable silence hung in the room but, after a brief pause, Christine spoke again.

"I have to thank you, Sir Guy," this time she addressed him by his first name. "I did not expect anything like that from you, especially after all the insults I have thrown at you."

"You have insulted me, yes, and you will answer for those insults to me only," his voice was stern. "I will not let anyone hurt you until I get my satisfaction from you," he added, the corner of his mouth rose in a sly grin; in the dim light of the candles his eyes gleamed with mischief.

Christine smiled in response, and, not expecting it from herself, got up from her seat, took a turn around the table and walked over to him. She touched his face and softly kissed his bristly cheek, involuntarily inhaling his spicy masculine scent. The smell of strength and power – enveloping, a slightly bitter flavour, made her head spin, provoking the memories that she was trying to silence and forget.

"I am sincerely grateful to you," she whispered, her lips were still close to his face. "I am happy to accept whatever punishment you may think fit, Milord."

Christine bowed her head and in a smooth, catlike gait walked back to her chair. As she returned to her seat, she didn't take her eyes off him. Guy couldn't help but smile.

"I believe the attack is not the only thing that you have remembered from last night?" he said, not letting go of her gaze.

Christine noticed how his breath quickened. She nodded in response and lowering her head, looked at him. A dark wavy lock fell over her eyes.

"I have to apologise, I behaved indecently. I don't know what came over me. Although, I have to admit, I do find you very attractive," she said frankly. "It took great effort to control myself..." she gave him a long immodest look.

"So, what you did yesterday, you mean to call "controlling yourself"?" he seemed genuinely surprised. "Well, then my dear, Miss Christine..." he looked at her. From his formal tone, Christine nearly choked on the wine, though she couldn't deny that she liked the way her name sounded coming out of his mouth. "My dear, Miss Christine Hawk, you can practice your training in self-control any time," he continued. "I'll be glad to help, but the next time you have to be a little more... inventive."

His mouth stretched into a satisfied smile. Christine tried to maintain a cool face, but it didn't work, and the next moment, they both burst out laughing.

"You have to forgive me," she said still laughing so much that she was almost crying.

By the time the main dish arrived they had both rediscovered their hunger. Guy took a piece of meat from his plate. Christine watched him with interest; his expression showed a kaleidoscope of emotions, but enjoyment of food wasn't one of them. With great effort, he tried to chew through the overcooked pork and, barely managing to swallow the piece down, winced involuntarily, sending half a glass of wine immediately after it.

"Is it really that bad?" asked Christine.

"Jenny is a good girl," he said softly, "but she can't cook."

"Then why do you keep her?" Christine asked. "Surely there is someone in the village who can cook you a decent meal."

"Her mother, my usual cook, is ill, and, in the meantime, her daughter is replacing her. I hope she gets better soon; I am not sure I will be able to survive on this for long," he pushed his plate away, took another long sip of wine and rinsed his mouth, trying to wash away the aftertaste.

"Alright, alright," smiled Christine. "You don't even have to beg me. To show you my gratitude for you having saved my life..."

"And not just once," corrected Guy.

"Ok! To show you my gratitude for you having, more than once, saved my life," she laughed. "Tomorrow, I'll cook you something nice," she leaned back in her chair and saluted him with a goblet.

"You?" his blue eyes widened in surprise. "Don't tell me that, amongst the other talents that I have had the pleasure of witnessing, you can also cook! Miss Hawk, you surprise me more and more!" he exclaimed.

"I'm full of surprises!" said Christine playfully, and rose from her chair.

She walked to him again and, barely touching his shoulder with her fingers, softly whispered into his ear in her most seductive voice. "As for pleasures, Milord, you haven't seen anything yet."

She teased him and knew that he liked it. Her warm breath touched his cheek. Guy turned toward her voice. Her lips were very close, her eyes were holding his. His breathing quickened, he swallowed hard.

"Good night, Milord," she whispered softly, almost touching his lips with hers.

Before he could say anything, Christine pulled away from him and turned to leave. At the door, she turned back and, after giving him another long look, went to her room.

After she left, Guy moved back to the fire. Sitting in the room alone in silence, watching as the flames slowly devoured the logs, he thought about the woman who lived in his house.

He didn't know who she was, or how she lived before their paths had crossed in Sherwood Forest less than three weeks ago. Was she sent by the Prince to kill the King, or, by some other strange coincidence, did she just happen to be in the forest? Was she really the same kind of ruthless murderer as he, or was it all a lie, a game? He did not know.

But he did know one thing – the feelings that started to come to life in his soul when she was close to him, when she looked at him – those feelings were real. She was here, so close but at the same time out of reach. She made it clear that she was attracted to him, but at the same time, she was unassailable.

"To catch such a fox, one must be a skilful hunter," he thought, silently staring into the depths of the fire.

For a long time, the soft smile still hovered about his lips.

Chapter 17:
Getting To Know You Better

With great responsibility, Christine addressed herself to the task of cooking Guy a delicious dinner. As soon as she was up, she made herself presentable and went to inspect the kitchen.

Guy was right; in the absence of her mother, Jenny clearly felt the tensions of her new duties creeping up on her. She tried her best to keep everything under control, but whatever she attempted to do, she failed. The presence of Christine threw the young girl into an even greater panic.

Having considered what was available for her to cook with, Christine quickly made up her mind as to what would be served that evening. She cut pork into large chunks, seasoned it with salt and pepper, and layered it with rings of onions. She told Jenny to put the meat under the press and into a warm place but away from direct sunlight. She smiled gently at the girl, noticing her sniffle and bitter tears. Christine wasn't sure if they were caused by the onions or the awareness of her own incompetence.

Once she had finished with the meat, Christine went to the blacksmith, and after spending a considerable amount of time trying to explain to him what she had in mind, she finally gave up and drew a rough design of a barbecue grill on the ground. Having set a clear deadline for her order, the barbecue had to be made and delivered to the manor no later than at six o'clock that evening, she went back into the house.

*****

The whole time Christine was in the village, Guy had watched her, with great interest, from the balcony of the manor. He was surprised by the degree of confidence and easiness with which she was able to speak to people who she met for the first time in her life. How a few well-chosen words, spoken at the right moment, were all she needed to achieve the desired result.

Walking back into the house, Christine found Gisborne at breakfast.

"So!" she said happily. "Orders for dinner have been made. What are our plans for the day?"

"Orders?" Guy repeated surprised. "I thought that you, yourself, would be cooking me a dinner."

"Why, of course I will, I never said I wouldn't be," she said, sitting down at the table across from him. "But you don't want me to cook it now, do you? By dinner time, it will all be cold and I will not achieve the results I want."

"And what results do you want to achieve, if one may ask?" he said, cutting off a piece of cold meat; a light smile hovering about his lips.

"It's a secret!" she smiled in reply.

"Ah, as I can see, you are full of secrets," said Guy.

"You have no idea..." she said a little wistfully, and for a moment he sensed that in her thoughts she was somewhere else. She then added, lifting her eyes back up to him, "So, what's the plan for the day?"

"I'm going to Nottingham," he said slipping another slice of meat into his mouth. "On this day of each month, the Sheriff deals with complaints from the residents of the district and sorts out local disputes. Now that he is away..." he did not finish his sentence. It was obvious from his tone that the prospect did not appeal to him.

"Just please, do not be like Wesley," pleaded Christine. "Listen to what people have to say and be fair in your judgment."

"Is your faith in me reviving?" he asked with a smile.

"I'm sure you'll do just fine," she smiled in return. "And what then? Or do you plan to spend your whole day in Nottingham?"

"I don't know yet, but if so," he raised a brow, "will you miss me?"

"Why, of course! I'll miss you very much!" she laughed. "I love our fiery arguments."

"Very well, then," he smiled softly back at her. "Why don't you come to the training camp? I'll be there as soon as I finish at the castle. Then you can teach me some of your tricks."

"You just need to ask, Milord," Christine bowed her head and then added, arching her brow a little. "Nicely."

Guy grinned. Christine had repeated the very same words he had said to her on the day when she had tried to run away and ended up lost in Sherwood.

*****

When Christine arrived at the training camp, Gisborne was still not there.

She sat on a bench for a while and, when she eventually got bored, went into the tent to begin her warm up. She only managed to complete a few exercises when she heard the soldiers in the compound shouting in unison, welcoming their commander. Guy of Gisborne, accompanied by Allan A'Dale and several armed horsemen, proudly entered the camp. His eyes gleamed happily, his face bore a satisfied smile.

Staying on his horse, he greeted his soldiers, and for some time, his gaze wandered over the gathered crowd, as if looking for someone. His face became anxious – he could not find her.

But wait, there she was! Behind everyone, near the entrance to the tent was Christine. Her hair was untidy, and her shirt stuck out from under the belt of her breeches, but even so, she looked very beautiful. The light summer breeze played in her hair, the bright sun illuminated her face, and her blue eyes seemed almost transparent.

Guy slid down from his horse. He gathered the soldiers and, after giving them their first tasks to practice, walked over to Christine.

"Someone's in a good mood!" she said, immediately noticing the sparkle in his eyes. "One dares to assume that your day at the castle was a success?"

"Yes!" he said, unable to contain himself. "But I will need to return to the castle tomorrow. There is something I need to finish."

"Tomorrow?" repeated Christine. "You astonish me, Milord, but please, don't lose your vigilance. Although the Sheriff has left you in charge of his office, he may not appreciate your efforts."

"The difference between me and Wesley is that I can and do want to help people, he can, but does not want to. For him, and the purpose that he pursues, the situation is good as it is." Christine nodded in agreement. "I will help these people, whether the Sheriff likes it or not," Guy said determinedly. "After what I saw and heard today... I never imagined the situation in the region to be as bad as it is. I don't really understand why Wesley bothers to organise these meetings if, in the end, everything remains as before."

"I think he has to somehow justify the high taxes. So, he creates an appearance of caring," said Christine

"Yes, perhaps you are right," Guy said, a little wistfully, his gaze was focused.

Although he wanted to continue this conversation, the duty of military chief and first deputy of the Sheriff of Nottingham demanded his attention. He took off his jacket, threw it on the bench next to her, and went to join his soldiers.

Gisborne's squad scrupulously followed the instructions of their master, practicing attack, defence, archery, and fencing. Christine sat on the bench, basking in the summer sun and enjoying the view as Guy exercised with his men. There was something hypnotic in his movements; he wielded a large heavy sword with such ease and grace.

"Miss Hawk, you look as if you want to join us," he said out of breath, and lowered his sword to the ground. A pair of dark curls fell across his forehead and over his eyes.

"Thank you, Milord, but I'd rather stay where I am," she smiled. "First of all, with that weapon, I am no match for you, and second, I have a much better view from here," she narrowed her eyes a little.

Gisborne smiled, he knew exactly what she meant.

"And what is your secret weapon, ma'am?" he asked, grinning.

Christine got up and slowly entered the arena. She moved close to him and with a light soft touch, gently brushed the hair from his forehead.

"My secret weapon?" she smiled seductively. "I thought you'd already worked that out," she said looking him straight in the eyes.

A light smile touched his lips.

"Leave your sword here and follow me," she said with a slight arch in her brow and a commanding tone in her voice. "I am going to teach you something."

With a smooth gait, she walked into the tent. Guy didn't need a second invitation. He followed her as soon as she disappeared inside. Seeing this, Allan whistled, for which he received a burning glare from his master, and as a punishment was sent off to train on one of the wicker men.

*****

They stood opposite each other at arm's length.

"So, Milord," she tilted her head to the side, "what do you want me to teach you?" her candid gaze challenged him.

"Anything Milady wishes," he bowed. "I am your humble student."

"Very well," she smiled, "then we will start with the basics. Grab me from behind."

"Excuse me?!" his eyes flung open in surprise. He did not expect such a turn of events.

"Sir Guy..." smiling, Christine shook her head, "I think you are jumping to the wrong conclusion as to what I am about to teach you."

She walked behind him and wrapped her arms around his arms and torso, restricting his movement.

"Like this," she said, "and stay on guard."

Gisborne obeyed. Grinning, and barely touching her, he circled his arms around her.

"Sir Guy..." Christine said, insisting that the effort shown on his part would not be enough.

Guy tightened his embrace, pressing her harder against him. The floral scent from her hair hit his nose. He felt slightly dizzy. Memories of that night came alive in his head once again, he found himself not wanting to let her go. His hands cupped her even tighter.

The only thing he felt, before he ended up lying on the ground, was the slight movement of her hips. Christine was standing over him.

"I warned you, Milord, stay on guard," she said sternly and stretched her hand out.

"What have you done? I did not even..." Guy said, taking her hand as Christine helped him up.

"Remember? Never underestimate your opponent," she smiled. "I'll show you a few tricks, but if you want to learn, you have to stop looking at me as if I am a woman."

"You are a woman..." he replied softly, a barely visible smile appeared on his face.

Not saying a word, Christine arched her brow. He nodded in reply.

Gisborne took everything that Christine had to show him seriously – kicks, movement, twists, lunges, undercuts. Several times, he found himself on the ground again, before anything had started to happen. Accustomed to working a heavy sword, he found it very unusual to fight with only his legs and arms.

"Try not to overdo it," Christine said, after another lunge. "Your body isn't used to such exercise You could hurt yourself."

"I'll be fine, you need not worry about me," was his only reply. "Continue!"

He was eager to learn more.

About an hour later, it was Christine who begged for mercy. Her student's progress was immense.

"Have mercy! I can't do it anymore!" she pleaded, getting up on her feet once again. Having overcome the first awkwardness, Guy had immersed himself in the techniques of martial arts. "We have to finish our training unless, of course, you want to go without dinner!" said Christine, shaking the dust off her trousers and tidying her disheveled hair.

*****

"What is that odious thing?" chuckled Gisborne looking at the barbecue parked in the front yard of the manor.

Christine, on the contrary, was very pleased with blacksmith's work.

"It's perfect!" she said, rubbing her hands. "Take it to the backyard, if you please, and light a fire in it."

"Me?" he asked surprised.

"Why, of course, Milord! I cannot see Allan anywhere and, I hope, you don't think I'll be dragging this heavy thing anywhere?" she looked at him sternly.

"Yes, ma'am," he smiled and, having picked up the iron structure easily, he carried it through the kitchen to the backyard.

Guy lit the fire and sat down on a bench in the garden, watching his guest. From the knives offered by Jenny, Christine had chosen the most suitable and comfortable one to work with, then sent the maid away and began to chop vegetables, softly humming a tune.

Like a flamingo standing on one leg, she rested her right foot on the shin of the left leg, and while continuing to work with the knife she maintained perfect balance. Not interrupting what she was doing, she shifted from one leg to another and continued with her task. When she had finished with the vegetables, she put them into a large bowl, and went outside to check the fire, taking the plate of marinated pork with her.

"I see that you can manage a knife well," Guy noted when Christine began to stir the burning logs. "Is it your choice of weapon in your work?"

"In my work?" she looked at him as though she couldn't understand the meaning of his words. "Oh, that! No, it is too messy. I don't like to get my hands dirty and then there is no guarantee. Poison, in my opinion, is much better! You just need to get close enough," she winked at him and began to put the pieces of meat on skewers.

Guy sat motionless, closely watching her every move, in his eyes was a mixture of bewilderment and fear.

"I'm kidding!" Christine laughed. "I'm kidding! God, you should've seen your face just now."

The wood burned out slowly and turned into hot charcoal. Christine carefully laid the skewers on the grill.

"I think I saw something like that when I was in the Holy Land," Guy said.

"I thought you might have, it's a shish. It's an Arabic dish, although they don't eat pork," said Christine, turning the meat, "they use mainly lamb or chicken."

"Have you been to the Holy Land?" he asked cautiously.

"Yes, I was in Jerusalem," replied Christine, without hesitation, "but it was a long time ago, when my mother was still alive." For a moment, there was sadness in her eyes. "Right!" she shook her head as though shaking off sad memories. "The meat will be ready in about fifteen minutes," she said, turning the skewers. "You should go and wash."

"Whatever for?" he sounded genuinely surprised and took a tone of offence at this suggestion.

"Trust me, you do not want me to say why out loud," Christine smiled slightly.

"Say what..." he insisted.

"You asked for it, Milord," Christine tried to find the words, but could not and blurted it out as it was, "You smell..."

Gisborne gritted his teeth. He had to fight his inner self. Downing the retort, which was choking him, he swallowed the words. Whether he liked it or not, she was right, again, and, although, after what had been said earlier, he did not want to leave her alone with food, he rose obediently, looked at Christine, then at the meat sizzling on the charcoals, and went to his room. Her words, much like merciless hammers, banged in his head.

"'Poison, in my opinion, is much better! You just need to get close enough'". Is that what she was doing all this time – getting closer, gaining my trust?"

*****

When washed and dressed in a clean shirt, Guy entered the dining room, the table already set. Two large candlesticks stood in the centre, two plates and goblets were on the sides. A large bowl with salad of fresh vegetables and a plate of freshly baked bread rolls stood on the right and left sides of his seat. Baking the bread was the only task that Christine entrusted to Jenny.

The aroma of grilled meat was wafting through the house.

"Ah, you are just in time," Christine appeared in the doorway, carrying a huge dish of meat. "Please sit down. No, wait, no, please pour the wine first."

Obediently Guy filled the goblets and took his seat.

"Take whatever you like," said Christine bringing the dish closer to him. "Don't be shy, I know you're famished," she added, seeing that he had only taken two pieces, and placed some more onto his plate.

She placed the dish on the table and sat down in the chair opposite him.

"What should we drink to?" she asked, raising her goblet.

"To trust," he said looking her in the eyes.

"A very good toast! To trust!" she repeated his words and saluted him with her goblet. "Now, please, tuck in, I'd like to know what you think," she said and leaned back in her chair.

Guy smiled and was about to put a piece of meat in his mouth when he saw her empty plate.

"Will you not eat?" he asked cautiously.

"Oh, no, I'm ok – had some when I was finishing. I needed to make sure it was properly cooked," she answered.

"I'm not hungry," he said suddenly, pushing his plate away. His friendly tone had changed.

"What?!" Christine shouted. "What do you mean, you're not hungry?"

"If you do not eat, I am not eating either," he answered a little sternly.

"Do you really think that I've decided to poison you?" she finally realised.

Gisborne didn't reply – his silence was more eloquent than any words.

"Oh, for Christ's sake!" Christine cried.

She moved her chair with a loud creak and, muttering something angrily under her breath, walked quickly around the table, speared a piece of meat from his plate onto the knife and sent it into her mouth. Savouring the taste, she chewed it holding his gaze and then swallowed, accompanying this process with moans of pleasure. She stared at him.

"Satisfied? Or do you want me to take a bite from each piece? Unbelievable!" she exclaimed, throwing her hands up, and returning to her place.

Guy lowered his head, trying to hide a smile.

"Just look at him! Now he's laughing!" said Christine referring to an imaginary audience. "And I don't see anything funny about it!"

"You look adorable when you're angry," he said smiling.

"Adorable?!" she protested again but, seeing his light blue eyes and a gentle smile, added in a soft tone, "Now, will you eat, please? I, by the way, have spent half a day on making it."

"Half a day?" still smiling, Guy arched his brow.

"Well, maybe not half," Christine agreed, "but I really wanted to please you, so, please, don't make me beg you. I will have some as well, to keep you company," she put two small pieces on her plate, "Bon Appetit!"

Christine watched happily as Gisborne devoured his dinner. The smile never left her face.

When he finally realised that Christine wasn't planning to poison him, he enthusiastically got to work on his food. She had not lied when she promised to surprise him, the food tasted very good and unusual. While he was eating, Christine didn't take her eyes off him. Quietly sipping her wine, she didn't say a word, giving him the opportunity to fully enjoy the taste.

Finishing with the meat, Guy leaned back in his chair.

"Mmm..." a low moan of satisfaction was the first sound he managed.

"I'm glad I was able to please, Milord," she said, smiling.

Christine called Jenny to clear the table and re-fill the decanter. She then invited Guy to sit by the fire. Full and satisfied he stretched out in his chair.

"You were right, I've never tried anything like that!" he praised her once again. "I'm afraid to ask what other skills you have in your arsenal."

"Many!" she smiled.

He looked at her for some time, studying her face and then said suddenly, "Can I ask you something? It's been occupying me for a while."

"Shoot."

"On that morning, after the Sheriff visited Locksley, why did you try to run away?"

"What makes you think so... that I tried to run away?" she asked making an indifferent face.

"Have you not?" he raised an eyebrow. "I thought that was quite obvious."

"Well, you're wrong..." she said trying to maintain calm. "I just needed to clear my head but I got lost after my mount was scared off by the outlaws," her heart was racing with her thoughts.

"That does not sound very convincing, you know that, don't you?" he smiled softly at her.

"Besides, the Sheriff wouldn't be happy if I left without doing his bidding."

"Unless you're not the one the Sheriff thinks you are..." he said holding her gaze. "I've been watching you and sometimes," he paused, "sometimes you wonder off into your own thoughts and act very strangely."

Christine looked at him not daring to take her eyes off his, taking slow deep breaths, trying to steady her pounding heart.

"Sometimes, you look like you don't belong here, like you've been taken out of place."

"Out of place and out of time..." she thought, still not saying a word.

"And then again there was the letter from the Prince... Who are you?" he asked suddenly.

"I am me," she answered cautiously, carefully considering her next words. "I am a woman who tries to make a living in a man's world."

"I have never met a woman like you before."

"Where I come from, a woman is valued for more than her beauty and her ability to bear children, not that that's unimportant. In this world, one has to adapt to survive and get ahead in life."

"And where is this magical place that you have visited us from?" asked Guy with interest.

"I was born and raised in London," she answered trying to steer the conversation in a different direction.

"Sounds much more interesting than the London I know of," he grinned. "What about your family?"

"I have none. My mother, as you know, died some years ago and I never knew my father. I'm on my own."

"You are not married?"

"Nope."

"Why? Honestly, I find it hard to believe that a woman with qualities such as yours is not married," he added cautiously, as if a little hesitant.

"I presume my profession and work doesn't help much," said Christine.

"And what exactly do you do?" he asked continuing his impromptu interrogation.

"I... people come to me when they have problems, like your Sheriff now. I act on their behalf... I'm well paid for what I do, so I can provide for myself."

She hoped that her answer would satisfy his interest and prevent any further questions on this subject. She was wrong.

"So, there is no one in your life who..." he paused.

Under any other circumstances, he wouldn't care, but he found himself wondering and slowly realising that he wanted to know everything about her.

"No," she answered shortly, "there's no one waiting for my return."

"Even Mark?" he asked cautiously. This character haunted Guy from the moment Christine had called him by his name.

"Mark?" Christine laughed. "That shagging bastard, who can't keep his pants on? I apologise for my tone but I seriously doubt that, after our last encounter, he will be missing me," saying this, she smiled at the memories that surfaced in her mind.

"That morning when you woke up in my bed, you thought differently," said Guy softly.

"That morning, I thought that this was all a dream," she sighed. "Mark and I were going to announce our engagement on the day..." she trailed off struggling to find words, "on the day that I travelled here."

"You were? But you did not? Did something prevent it?" he asked.

"You could say that. I caught him with another woman," said Christine looking him straight in the eye.

"I'm sorry to hear that, but perhaps you have misinterpreted?" his face became serious.

"When you find your fian... betrothed, practically naked in the company of a barely dressed woman, it's very difficult to misinterpret."

"I understand, I'm sorry to hear that," he said. "What did you do?"

"I walked away," Christine said, without expressing any emotion. "Oh, yes! But I did break his nose before that," she added with passion.

At these words, Guy burst out laughing, but immediately recovered.

"I'm sorry but even knowing you for this short amount of time, for some reason, I can well imagine that," he said, trying to compose himself.

Still very calmly, Christine replied, "At that moment it seemed to me the only appropriate reaction," her eyes glistened with looming tears. "Apparently, I wasn't good enough for him." Hiding her tears, she turned her face to the fire, but even so, Guy could see she was upset. He was deeply sorry that he had brought the subject up. "Perhaps, it was my fault," she said. "I knew what kind of man he was when I agreed to marry him. I've known him for years and knew well enough he was a "Don Juan" and "Lovelace" but I thought he'd changed. He promised me he had, and I really wanted to believe it. I was wrong. People rarely change..."

Christine swallowed the lump that was building in her throat. The wound was still fresh. She looked away from the fire to the man sitting across from her. The gaze of his deep blue eyes was tender and full of compassion; a desire to come close and hold her tight, and then never let her go. Christine smiled faintly.

"Perhaps it's for the best," she said softly. "But let's not talk about it any more. On that day, I cried out all the hurt and humiliation. So, to once again answer your question – no! There's no one who would be waiting for my return."

She finished her wine and lifted her eyes to him. Guy smiled in return. He enjoyed her company very much and, although, there was no romantic attachment between them, he was inexplicably drawn to her. He sensed there was something common between them.

A thought went through his mind, *"If, there is nobody waiting for her, maybe she would want to stay in Nottingham?"* However as quickly this thought came to him, he, just as quickly, brushed it away, *"Who am I to her to ask her to stay?"*

Still deep in his thoughts, Guy lifted his hand to the decanter and a sharp spasm of pain shot through his body. His face twisted into a horrible grimace. With a loud sigh, he dropped his hand.

"What happened?" Christine jumped up to her feet. "Do not tell me I have actually poisoned you!" she added walking to his chair.

"My shoulder, it seems..." he said, holding his hand and still wincing in pain.

"Ah, I warned you," smiled Christine, "Do you want me to have a look?"

"No," he replied, not knowing why. "I'm sure everything will be fine in the morning. You'd better sit next to me and tell me more about yourself. We have known each other for three weeks, and I know so very little about you," he added.

"It's late, you're tired," said Christine.

She, too, was tired, although more emotionally than physically. Memories of Mark and that day opened an unhealed wound. She tried to keep calm and make an indifferent face but deep inside it hurt so very much, she needed time to be alone.

"Tomorrow is a new day," she said after a pause. "If you don't change your mind, I'll tell you more tomorrow at dinner. Good night."

"Miss Hawk," he called, when Christine was already at the door.

By her tone and body language, he sensed that she wanted to leave as soon as possible. Was it something he had said, or something that he should not have said? There was no doubt, something saddened her, but he did not understand the reason.

"You are upset," he said, getting up from his seat. "Have I said something to hurt you?"

"No, it's okay..." she lied. "I'm just tired."

"I don't think I thanked you for the delicious dinner," Guy came closer and, gently taking her hand in his, placed a soft kiss on the back of her hand. "Thank you," he said, looking into the depths of her eyes.

For some time, he just held her hand in silence, perhaps a little longer than he had originally intended. Looking into her sad eyes, he wanted, just like on that night in the forest, to hold her close, to shield her in his arms, to protect her from all the hurt and pain, to say that no matter what he would be there for her. He always wanted to be there for her.

Guy was about to speak but got anxious that his actions would scare her off – how would she react to his confession, when no more than just a few days ago, he had been telling her about his passionate love for Lady Marian? However, what was happening inside him at that very moment was nothing like the childish infatuation for that girl. His feelings for Christine were much deeper, much stronger. Pausing for another brief moment, he let go of her hand.

"Good night, Milord," Christine smiled briefly and left the room.

*****

Gisborne stood by the window, greedily breathing in the cool night air, reflecting on the events of the day, when someone knocked on his door. He opened it without asking who it was. Christine stood at the threshold.

It had been no more than half an hour since they parted but now she looked different. Her hair was pulled back in a high bun, her face a little paler, yet the sadness, which he had seen when she bid him good night, was no longer there.

"I am sorry, Sir Guy, but I can't leave you to suffer in pain. You have to let me look at your shoulder," she said softly, "besides, I feel guilty about it."

Not saying a word, he smiled and stepped aside to let her in.

Christine sat him down on a chair near the fire and began to gently move his hand, raising and lowering it slowly. After each movement, she asked if he felt any pain or discomfort. Satisfied that there was no dislocation, no stretching, Christine started to gently probe the surface of the shoulder and the blade, where Guy complained about the pain, with her fingers. It was all going well, until with the next touch he gritted his teeth, but didn't utter a sound.

"Does it hurt?" asked Christine feeling a small bump underneath his shirt. He nodded. She moved her fingers around the bump. "Nothing serious, your muscles are just very tense. I'll be back," she said and left the room.

She returned quickly, carrying two small glass bottles of oil, one rose and the other lavender, from Lady Marian's chest.

"Take off your shirt and lie down on the bed," she said.

"Excuse me?" he asked confused.

"Do you prefer rose or lavender oil?" Christine asked, not paying the slightest attention to his words. "A small massage will help to relax your muscles and relieve the pain."

Guy stood in the middle of the room not knowing what to do. Christine looked at him with a cunning smile on her face.

"What?" she asked. "I've seen you without a shirt before, Milord. You, as I understand it, have already seen me without any clothes on," she turned her back on him. "So, by the principles of your time, we are practically husband and wife," she said, and added after a pause. "If it will make things easier for you, think of me as a doctor. So, rose or lavender?"

"You said it again," he uttered quietly.

"Said what?" Christine shot a quick glance over her shoulder.

"Again, you said about my time. As if you and I live in different..." he said a little absently.

If she had been facing him at that very moment, he would have seen the sudden fear that reflected in her eyes. Her heart bumped loudly inside her chest and stopped for a moment, the bottle of rose oil slipped through her fingers and hit the floor, shattering into dozens of little pieces. Fragrant liquid spilled on the wooden surface.

"How clumsy of me," Christine said, looking down at the tiny pieces of glass scattered across the floor. She tried to speak as calmly as possible, but everything trembled inside her. "Lavender it is, then," she continued, still ignoring his comment, still not looking at him. "Lie down on the bed," she said, and then turned back to him.

Guy obeyed. He pulled off his high boots, took off his shirt, and lay down on his back, with his hands behind his head. When Christine turned to face him, he lay there with a wide grin on his face.

"And what part of your body do you expect me to massage?!" Christine couldn't help but laugh, finding him in this position. "Lie on your stomach, Master Gisborne, rest your arms beside your body and try to relax."

She rolled up her sleeves and, leaving the oil to warm by the fire, took a large bed sheet and covered him with it; she then began to apply light pressure to his back, rubbing his tired muscles through the cover. She continued this for several minutes, and, from her every new touch, his body stiffened and tensed even more.

"Now, that you more or less know what awaits you, I'm going to ask you again, to try to relax," she said removing the sheet from his back.

Guy flinched when the soft heat of the oil touched his skin. Rubbing it in, her hands slid briefly over his broad shoulders. The scent of lavender hit him in the nose, urging his body to relax and surrender to Christine's power.

He stiffened again when the bed bent slightly under him and her knees pressed tightly against his hips, yet as soon as she resumed her work, after the first few touches, a soft moan of pleasure escaped him. Christine smiled.

"Oh heavens!" he moaned quietly. "Where did you learn to do that?" he managed, barely able to speak.

Her strong fingers, like sharp needles, pierced through, penetrated deep into the skin, bringing him heavenly pleasure.

"I was not always..." Christine paused. "I have had to learn to master many skills. One never knows what may come in handy."

"I'm afraid to ask what else you were doing," he uttered quietly.

"A lot of different things, Milord," she chuckled softly. "A lot, except the one which you just imagined," she laughed.

Her elbows slipped on his shoulders, increasing the pressure. Following the momentum of her body, she leaned over and whispered in his ear.

"Now, stop talking."

Her hands swiftly and smoothly moved over his shoulders, neck, and back, rubbing the stiff muscles. She strengthened the pressure as her hands glided over him, not leaving even the smallest part unattended. Guy continued to utter soft moans. No matter how hard he tried to contain himself, groans of pleasure uncontrollably escaped from his lips.

"Don't resist. Surrender to your feelings and try to relax, then there will be more effect," Christine whispered, once again seeing how Guy was struggling to stay awake, trying to keep his heavy eyelids open.

It seemed he had only been waiting for these words. Yielding to her skillful hands, his body went limp, and he began to drift off, floating away from reality; further and further away with her every move. Gradually, his breathing became even, and he fell asleep.

Like a child, he slept making quiet snoring sounds. Dark curls fell over his eyes and covered half of his face, Christine gently brushed them away. His expression was calm, yet his eyes sometimes shifted under his eyelids, but even now, while asleep, he continued to radiate masculine beauty. Unable to take her eyes off him, Christine sat on the bed for a while looking at his peaceful face.

She then rinsed her hands and closed the shutters to shield the room from the cool night wind. She was about to leave, when Guy, who just some moments ago had been sleeping so peacefully, became restless. Muttering something vaguely and shuddering, Gisborne was now violently tossing in his bed.

Not knowing what to do, Christine came closer.

"Guy," she called quietly, leaning over him, "Sir Guy, wake up," she gently touched his shoulder.

With a loud cry, Gisborne broke from his nightmare. With eyes wide open, unaware of what was happening, he locked his hands on the first person he saw before him. His eyes were full of terror and hatred. He was determined to finally deal with the ghost who had been haunting him these long weeks.

Frantic, he squeezed his hands tighter and tighter around Christine's neck. She unsuccessfully tried to disengage his fingers, her mouth working like a fish gasping for air.

"Guy... Guy... It's Chr..." she managed to whisper, already losing consciousness.

"Christine!" at the last moment, sanity returned to him.

Seeing her eyes pleading for mercy, he slackened his grip and drew back. Clutching her throat, struggling to breathe, Christine fell, exhausted, on the bed.

"I'm sorry, I'm so sorry! Miss... Oh, Christine..." Guy helped her up. "I... I do not know... What..." he looked into her frightened eyes.

He was trying to find the words but couldn't find any reasonable explanation for what had just happened. Unable to speak Christine stared at him blankly.

"I'm a monster!" he muttered quietly and sat on the edge of the bed; his head in his hands. "You're right, I'm a monster! And there is no turning back for me."

"You just had a nightmare," she said finally, her voice was hoarse and very quiet. She was struggling through each word.

"My whole life, my whole life is an endless nightmare that haunts me! A nightmare from which I cannot wake up. Every day, I'm afraid it will break into my reality and consume all the humanity that is left of me," he said without looking up.

Christine got up and walked over to him.

"It was just a dream," she said, lightly touching his shoulder.

"If you knew..." Guy looked up at her; his blue eyes were full of tears.

"It's okay, it was just a dream," she said again.

She laid one hand on his shoulder, her other hand brushed through his hair.

"If you only knew..." he whispered.

Unable to overcome the desire, he firmly grabbed her by her waist and pulled her close, burying his face into her stomach. For a while, he sat silently. His arms locked in a tight circle around her. She felt his shoulders shudder, his breathing was laboured and inconsistent, and soon her shirt was wet from his tears. Trying to comfort him, Christine stroked his hair and shoulders, whispering sweet words.

"Do you want me to stay?" she asked, when after a while, having calmed down, he let go of her.

"What do you mean?" he looked at her blankly.

"I can stay with you, here in the room... until you fall asleep," she said, once again running her hand through his wet hair.

"But, what would the servants think?" he hesitated.

"Do you really care what your servants would think? We are grown-up people, you don't have to bother with such nonsense," she said.

"It's you that I am worried about," he answered.

"I couldn't care less what they would think," Christine said. "Do you want me to stay?"

"Yes," he breathed out and smiled timidly, "thank you."

Christine brought him cold water to drink and to wash his face, and helped him to get comfortable on the pillows. He turned on his side and closed his eyes. She sat beside him, put her hand on his shoulder and also closed her eyes. Listening to his breathing, Christine started to hum a quiet tune. He smiled faintly at the sound of her voice and soon fell asleep. The smile never left his face. When he began to shudder again, Christine took his hand in hers and softly brushed her other hand through his hair.

He didn't wake up and, gradually, sank into a deep sleep, this time without dreams. His breathing became deep and even. His face expressed peace and tranquility.

"Good night, my black knight," she whispered and kissed his forehead.

Chapter 18:
The Wedding

Wrapping the knitted shawl around her shoulders, Christine walked out on to the balcony.

The morning was bracing. Despite having already risen from behind the forest, the sun had not yet had time to warm the air.

Birds were chirping in the green, the air smelled of forest freshness; peace, quiet and tranquillity were all around her – it was an ideal morning. Nothing, it seemed, could make it better. She lifted her face up to welcome the new breeze that came from the forest, allowing it to ruffle her long locks, still unkempt after the night.

"Good morning, Miss Hawk!" called a soft velvety voice.

Christine leaned over the railing. Gisborne was standing outside the house. Dressed, as always, in the same black breeches and leather jacket, he was looking up at her, his lips twitched in what was now a so-familiar-to-her cocky, smug grin.

A little sadly, she smiled back at him. She would miss him when she returned home. If, she did ever return home. These thoughts developed into an ache deep inside her chest; very deep inside, such a dull, moaning pain. She didn't know what upset her the most; the inevitability of her return, the possibility that she may never return to her time, or the fact that she would never see his face again, his large sky-blue eyes, and his bold smile. She tried to brush off the sad thoughts.

"Good morning, Milord," she said, smiling softly in the golden light of the morning sun. "How's your shoulder?"

"Very good, thank you," he said and enthusiastically moved his arm in different directions.

"Judging by your mood, one may presume that you slept well last night," Christine smiled.

"For the first time in a very long time," he said, patting the neck of his horse. "It seems you are not only healing my body, but also becoming a medicine for my soul," he said, and then stopped as if he instantly regretted his words. "I slept like a child," he added quickly, trying to avoid her eyes.

"I'm glad I could be of help."

She smiled, but behind the smile, everything froze inside her, *"Did he really just say that?"* she did not dare believe what she had just heard. *"Did he really... No, it's impossible..."* she shouldn't think about it! Christine changed the subject. "I see that you are ready to go. What is your plan for today?"

"I have to be in Nottingham to finish yesterday's business, and then I will come back to Locksley," once again, he patted Raven's mane and mounted into the saddle. "Tonight at dinner, I hope to hear more about you!" he said and looked up.

Before leaving Locksley for the day he, wanted to see her face just once more, as if trying to remember her face to the smallest detail and keep it in his memory. Guy looked at her and then abruptly turned his horse; he gave Raven a hard, brisk kick in the flanks and galloped away.

*****

Christine was in the kitchen making preparations for dinner when a noise and stir in the village attracted her attention. She wiped her hands on a piece of cloth wrapped around her hips – her own version of some sort of medieval apron – and climbed up to the balcony to see what was happening.

On the far side of the village, she saw a company of riders and a cart that had brought a small group of people. The Master of Locksley, accompanied by Allan, was leading the party. Stopping at one of the houses on the edge of the village, Gisborne spoke to his companions, pointing first in one and then in another direction.

Even from a distance Christine could see the focus on his face. He was handing out instructions to his soldiers, who obeyed him unquestioningly.

Unable to fight her curiosity Christine left the house and walked towards the rider in black, who was still proudly towering over everyone on his raven stallion.

"You are back early, Milord," she said, taking Raven's bridle.

"I have not yet returned," he said, a barely visible smile playing about his lips.

"Oh, I thought, I saw..." she did not finish and started to look around.

"Who are you looking for?" he asked amuzed.

Following her example, he too began to look around, trying to figure out whom she had lost. Curious, his soldiers mimicked his actions.

"Why, the Master of Locksley, of course, a man who looks exactly like you. I saw him from the manor and came out to ask how his day was, but, if you are saying he hasn't yet returned, then apparently I was wrong." Smiling, Christine glanced at him sideways.

At these words, Guy burst out laughing. The people of the village stopped their work and glanced at Sir Guy in surprise and curiosity; they had never seen him this open and joyful before. He slid down from the saddle, tied his stallion to a fence, and stood next to Christine.

"I like your wicked sense of humour and your sharp tongue. I could get used to it," he said, still smiling.

"Is it just my sense of humour that you like?" she asked, but regretted her words immediately. "I'm sorry, I shouldn't have said that," she felt awkward.

"No, not just that," said Guy, looking at her slyly. "However, this is neither the time nor the place for this conversation. We will continue it later, over dinner," he bowed his head.

In reply, Christine arched an eyebrow.

"Anyway, what's going on here?" she asked, feeling the time had come to change the subject.

The village was still bustling. The soldiers, along with several local residents, were energetically discussing the placement of big logs, straw and stone.

"This is what I told you about yesterday," he said, carefully surveying the process.

"You just said you didn't finish some business and had to return to Nottingham," said Christine, unable to understand what he was referring to.

"I have moved two families to Locksley," he said, sotto voce, as if embarrassed by his words. "Their houses were destroyed during the last tax collection that the Sheriff..." he paused, "They had no place to live and there were two empty houses here."

Christine couldn't believe her ears.

"What a wonderful idea!" she exclaimed. "It's very noble of you to allow them to settle in your village."

"I told you that I want to help people," he said.

"I didn't doubt you for a second, Milord," said Christine, giving him a long look.

Guy's lips stretched into a satisfied smile.

"So," he began, after a brief pause, in his velvety voice, "what have you been up to this morning?"

"Oh, I've been very busy too! With very important things!" she said, proudly tipping her nose up high.

"I can see that," he laughed softly, looking pointedly at her.

"What?! Is something wrong?" her eyes widened.

"Your face is covered in flour," he whispered into her ear.

Her cheeks flushed.

"Oh, I can imagine how silly I must look right now," Christine muttered, trying to wipe her face.

"You look very lovely," he smiled. "Allow me."

Guy gently, barely touching her face, wiped the rest of the flour from her cheek. Unable to overcome the desire, his hand touched her hair, removing an unruly curl that clung to her lip.

"There, much better," he smiled again.

"Sir, we've finished!" said one of the soldiers, breaking the idyll.

"Well then, I won't keep you any longer," said Christine. "You have a lot of work, and I have things to do as well."

"Yes, I think we will be here for the rest of the day," he said, estimating the level of intended work.

"If you want I can take him home," she said nodding toward Guy's stallion. "The day is promising to be very hot, there is no need for him to fry out here in the sun," she moved closer to Raven. "Will you come with me? Yes? Will you come with me? Good boy!" she patted his muzzle.

The animal snorted affirmatively and stamped his hoof.

"Careful, he does not like strangers. He is a bit headstrong," warned Gisborne.

"Just like his master?" she smiled, still stroking the horse's muzzle. "He seems to be lacking some female attention," Christine laughed when the horse buried his snout into her chest.

"The animal or its master?" Guy asked with a cunning smile.

"Both, Milord," she said, smiling in response. "You may perhaps, remove that as well?" she said pointing at his jacket. While they spoke, Guy had, several times, rubbed his sweaty neck. "I am sure you will feel much better without it."

Quickly undoing the straps, he took off his leather jacket and handed it to Christine, who carelessly threw it over the horse's neck. With a light touch, he tossed her into the saddle; she put the jacket in front of her and lowered her eyes to Guy.

"I hope you don't mind? I've wanted to ride him for a long time now."

"Not at all, please," he grinned, "besides, he himself does not seem to mind," said Gisborne, as he noticed the stallion begin to shift from one leg to another, eager to go.

Christine turned the horse and, gently swaying in the saddle, rode off in the direction of the manor.

Gisborne watched her, enjoying the view of her smooth back and rounded hips, hugging the blue-black sides of Raven.

"How I envy that horse," said a voice from behind him.

"Yes, I do, too! I'd pay a lot to get in between those lovely legs," said the second voice.

"She can ride me anytime she wants," laughed the first voice.

Guy turned to his soldiers, right at the moment when, a man was vigorously moving his hips, imitating a sex act.

"Don't you have anything else to do?" he snapped angrily. "Allow another thought like that about the Lady to pass your lips again and you will regret it dearly, trust me!" he said and kicked one of them in the arse.

*****

A few hours later, the sun gained its full power; there was no escape from its merciless rays.

Christine walked the stallion into the stables, took off the saddle, gave him some fresh water and then returned to the kitchen to finish preparing dinner. The dough was ready for baking, the large chicken was cut into portions, marinated, and awaited its turn. The meat left from the previous night was finely chopped and, together with the grated cheese, transformed into a version of a medieval pizza. In the absence of tomatoes, Christine had no choice but to improvise with the products at hand. God alone knew what would come of it.

In between hiding in the cool of the house, she went out to the balcony several times and watched the latest developments at the far end of the village.

With his sleeves rolled up high, Gisborne worked tirelessly together with his soldiers. By joint efforts, one of the houses had been almost completed and prepared for the new residents.

Finishing with the first cottage, the men moved to the blacksmith's house and took shelter from the scorching sun under the canopy of his forge. Even from afar one could easily see how the hard work had exhausted their bodies. The soaked-through shirts had been removed long ago and either thrown on the fence or tucked under their belts. The heat wasn't receding; even in the shadows, there was no escape from its relentless hit.

Having prepared a tray on which there was a large carafe of a cold drink made from apples and mint, a couple of clay cups and a towel, Christine went in the direction of the forge.

The men, who, engaged in lively conversation, had tried to find shelter from the day's heat, noticeably brightened when they saw a female figure approaching them. One in particular, more so than the others, was pleased to see her again. It had been only a few hours from the moment they had parted but he caught himself thinking that even within this short period of time, he had missed her greatly. Despite his hands being kept busy repairing the house, her image had never really left his thoughts.

Now, she looked even more beautiful than this morning. Her shirt was flowing freely above her breeches; her sleeves were rolled up to the shoulder, exposing toned arms. A pile of dark hair was pinned high at the back of her head, with a few locks gently curling around her graceful neck. In this outfit, with a carafe and mugs in her hands, she looked as a mirage would to weary travellers in the desert.

"Sir Guy," she bowed as she crossed the threshold of the forge, "I have brought you a drink," said Christine, filling his cup.

He drained it in one gulp and asked for more. Flinging his head back, he emptied the second. His Adam's apple bobbed seductively with every gulp. Refreshing liquid ran from his lips to his neck and fell on his chest.

Christine handed him a towel and lowered her eyes; she looked away, trying hard not to stare at his naked torso. Guy wiped his mouth and face, then his neck and chest. Christine offered the remainder of the drink to the other men hiding under cover of the forge. They gratefully divided the remaining two cups between them and thanked Milady for her kindness.

Taking away Guy's towel, Christine moved directly in front of him with her back blocking the view of the others.

"Invite them to the house," she whispered.

Guy could not make out her words, and just looked at her.

"Invite them to the house," she said a little louder and made a sign with her eyes.

"The heat is unbearable," Gisborne said as if to himself, and then added, turning to the men who, like himself, had desperately tried to seek refuge under the canopy of the forge, "let's move into the house."

"That is a wonderful idea!" Christine exclaimed, turning to the men. Her fingers lightly brushed over Guy's hand. "The house is cool, you can relax and refresh yourselves, and in few hours, when the heat subsides, you can return to your work," she added, helping the blacksmith to his feet. "But I beg you, please put the shirts on," she smiled at the soldiers and their master, "there is a young girl in the house, I'm not sure it would be appropriate for her to be under the same roof with half-naked men. You will embarrass her."

"And you, ma'am? Will we embarrass you?" asked one of the younger soldiers.

"You have nothing that I haven't seen before and nothing that would embarrass me, young man" she threw over her shoulder.

She took the blacksmith by the arm, and together they went in the direction of the manor.

Gisborne chuckled softly.

*****

As soon as they stepped into the house, the soldiers were sent into the kitchen and left in Jenny's gentle care. The girl blushed deep red to the roots of her hair every time one of the young men addressed her.

Leaving the guests, Gisborne retired to his room. Christine and the blacksmith settled in the big hall.

"I did not have a chance to thank you for your excellent work," she said seating the elderly man into the chair.

For his age, the blacksmith was still in good shape, but the heat was getting the better of him as well. He sat, breathing heavily, and continuously wiping sweat from his forehead.

"I'm glad I could be of service, ma'am," he answered.

She poured him a refreshing drink and sat in the chair opposite. The man drank and sighed again, the coolness of the house was bringing him back to his senses.

"You know," he began cautiously, "people in the village talk..." Christine lifted her eyebrow and looked at him. "People talk about you and Sir Guy," he began again, but stopped. "This house has changed since you have come here. It lacked a woman's touch."

It was at this moment that Guy, having just come down the stairs, heard his name and stopped at the door, hesitating, not daring to enter.

"There are enough female servants in this house," Christine answered, pretending she did not understand the blacksmith's inference.

"You know what I mean," the man looked at her. "For a long time I've not seen the master in such good spirits and cannot remember when I last heard him laugh as much as in the past few days, and I have known him since he was a boy. He was a good, sensible lad."

"He's still a good man," said Christine. "A lost one, perhaps, but I'm sure he'll find his way."

"I am old and have seen a lot in this life," he continued, "whatever is happening between you two..."

"There is nothing between us," Christine interrupted him.

"Whatever is happening between you," ignoring her, he continued, "he's changed! You helped him to change. I hope you will stay here."

He looked at the woman in front of him, noting how from his words, her mood had suddenly changed.

"Unfortunately, I cannot stay," Christine replied, sadly adding, as if speaking to herself, "I can't stay here, I have to go back."

Guy entered the hall. His face was tense; he was trying to make sense of the conversation he had just overheard. Christine had made it clear that she was not going to stay in Nottingham. He had to try to persuade her to change her mind.

"Ah, Sir Guy," said the blacksmith, getting up from his chair, "I am sorry I took your place. Please, sit down."

"No, it's alright," Gisborne replied wistfully, his head was too preoccupied with other thoughts to worry about an occupied chair.

"I was just telling your guest, what a positive impact her presence has made in this house," said the blacksmith, bluntly.

Christine breathed loudly, her eyes, a little frightened, wandered over the men in the room.

"Yes, you are right," said Guy still bemused.

"Sir, do not consider this impudent," the blacksmith spoke again, "but let me invite you and your guest to my son's wedding tomorrow."

"Wedding?" Guy repeated surprised. "Oh, yes, Miss Hawk has said something about that," he added. "I'll be glad to come, but I cannot answer for her," he turned to face her, a question in his eyes.

"Sure, I'd love to come!" she replied smiling. "Where will the wedding be?"

"The ceremony will take place in the local church at sunset, and then the celebration will be in front of our house," said the blacksmith.

"Not a lot of room for a wedding gathering," Guy grinned, returning to his usual self. "I have a better suggestion, what if you have the celebration here, at the manor? After the ceremony in the church, bring all your guests to the house. There is enough room in the backyard to put out tables. After sunset, we will light fires," he seemed pleased with the thought.

"Guy! It's a great idea!" exclaimed Christine, but immediately recovered. "Please forgive me, Milord."

Guy's lips twitched in a light smile.

Watching the man and the woman in front of him, the old blacksmith, too, could not help but smile.

*****

The afternoon passed quickly. The sun began to sink behind the forest, the heat gradually subsided, and the men were able to return to their work.

Knowing that a nice, quiet dinner in the manor was no longer on the agenda, and to support the men in their work, Christine and Jenny tripled the amount of food prepared for Guy's dinner and without further delay, also set to work.

When the food was ready, the women, taking the trays of food and flasks with drinks, went to the far end of the village. Their arrival was greeted with joyful cries. Food and the long-awaited rest had cheered up the tirelessly working men.

They ate, praising Guy's guest. Christine smiled softly, watching the speed at which the men had emptied the trays.

The summer day was long, but even so, the men still had to work late into the night. The result of this long day was that both houses were completed and the new residents of Locksley, bowing low to the ground to their new master, having gathered all their simple belongings, had settled into their new homes.

*****

When the work was finished, Guy returned to the manor. He felt very tired, but his fatigue brought him satisfaction.

For the first time since he had become the master of Locksley, he was able to do something that he really wanted to do without worrying that the Sheriff might disapprove, or discourage the idea. For the first time in a very long time, he finished the day without feelings of regret, remorse and self-loathing.

Whatever was in her past, whatever secrets she kept in her present, the old man was right. Since Christine's arrival in Locksley Guy had changed. Since she had entered his life, he felt as if his strength had returned to him. But what was more important, was the desire to prove, at least to himself, that in spite of all the tricks of the Sheriff, he was still alive. Under the cold blackness of his clothes there was still a beating heart – a heart full of compassion, empathy and love.

"Love," flashed through his mind again. *"Christine,"* just the thought of her caused a light smile to appear on his face.

So he thought, sitting in front of the fire in the hall of his manor, watching the hot flames, flaring brightly for a second and then fading again in the depths of the fireplace. He was still sitting in the chair when the pressure and fatigue of the day took their toll on his strong body. His eyes closed, his fingers unclenched, and, with a loud thundering sound, his silver goblet fell to the floor. Yet even that noise didn't disturb his deep, profound sleep.

He woke up late, long after the fire had died and the ashes cooled. The manor was deep in darkness, there were no sounds. His boots had been removed and placed by his side, a small stool was placed under his feet, and he, himself, was covered with a warm blanket. Guy smiled. Even in these simple, little gestures, he felt her gentle care.

He took his boots and blanket and went upstairs. Not knowing why, he walked up to her room and listened – it was all quiet inside. He pushed the door; it was unlocked. With a soft noise, it opened easily letting him in. Curled up in bed, hugging her pillow tight, Christine was fast asleep. He carefully brushed the hair away from her face, and looked at her peaceful beautiful face, then left, firmly closing the door behind him.

He did not think he would sleep at all, but he fell asleep as soon as his head touched the pillow.

That night Gisborne slept without any dreams.

*****

In the morning the noise and stir returned to Locksley, yet, even this did not prevent Guy from sleeping through until lunchtime.

His tired body and weary soul had finally found their peace and rewarded their owner with such a deep and profound sleep, that even the preparations for the evening's celebration, which began in the manor early in the morning, could not take him from the caring embrace of Morpheus.

He woke up and had lunch, then went to Nottingham, where exercising the duties of the County's Sheriff, he met with representatives of the local nobility and discussed the plan for preparing the County for the coming autumn and winter seasons. Sorting out the affairs of the state took hours, but even though he barely had time to get back to Locksley, check on his new residents and prepare for the ceremony, Guy was cheerful and happy and remained in the same mood till the end of the day.

At about seven o'clock in the evening, he and Christine walked to the local church, which was decorated inside and out with white flowers and ribbons.

"You look as if you are going to the archers' competition, not to a wedding!" laughed the blacksmith, noticing Christine from a distance.

"I'm afraid, my wardrobe is somewhat limited," she threw her hands up and smiled back at him.

"A woman must always look like a woman, especially at such an important event as a wedding!" he said strictly. "Haven't you heard the saying: one wedding leads to another? You never know who you might meet. Maybe here you will meet your future husband," he looked at her and barely noticeably winked to Guy.

"I very much doubt that," said Christine with notable sarcasm.

"You never know what fate has in store for you," he said. "Believe me; I know of what I speak. Alice," he called and looked around. "Alice!" he shouted loudly and muttered something under his breath. "Where is that old woman when I need her?"

The stout woman of approximately fifty, lively and youthful, despite a face with deep wrinkles, exited the church.

"What are you yelling about, you old devil! Lord, forgive me!" she said and bowed to the church. "Why are you yelling?"

"Alice, we need to do something about this," he stepped aside, revealing Christine, who, barely suppressing a smile, just shook her head.

With oohs, sighs and gasps the blacksmith's wife walked around her.

"Oh, this is terrible! Terrible," she chirped, and then clasped the younger woman's hands. "Come, come, my dear," she said, and led Christine away.

*****

The sun began its slow descent behind the forest, gradually moving towards the horizon, immersing Locksley in the evening haze. The guests gathered outside the church, and those especially impatient went inside to take their places closer to the altar.

Guy's absent glance wandered through the crowd. He was hoping to see Christine, but she was nowhere to be seen. He had not seen her since the moment the blacksmith's wife took her away.

Gisborne sighed loudly.

"Come in, Sir, I have prepared the best place for you," said the blacksmith, when the church doors were opened wide, and a big wave of guests poured in. "Are you looking for your lady friend?" he asked, seeing the confusion on Gisborne's face. "I am sure she will come soon enough."

The guests went in, filling all the space inside the church and leaving only the aisle leading from the door to the altar. The noise of eager anticipation filled the space of the small village church. Guy and the groom's father stood on the right side of the priest; the place on his left hand was still empty.

Everything went silent, when the bride, accompanied by her maids, stepped over the threshold and slowly began her walk down the aisle. The girls walked to the altar, and leaving the bride with the groom, moved aside. Guy felt uneasy, shifting from one leg to another, studying the faces of people, when the blacksmith laid his hand on his shoulder. Still smiling he nodded toward the altar. Looking up, Guy finally saw her.

In a long dress made of light fabric, to match the clothes of the other bridesmaids, Christine, with the rest of the girls, was standing to the right of the priest. The only decoration to her dress was a leather belt that gently circled her waist. Her dark hair was decorated with fresh flowers and flowed over her shoulders. Gisborne could not take his eyes off of her – in this simple dress, she looked more beautiful than in the expensive gown gifted to her by the Sheriff. Noting his bold look, Christine smiled and bowed her head slightly.

The ceremony was so beautiful that it moved Christine almost to tears. There was something enchanting in the way these two young people said their wedding vows, promising to protect, and to care for, to maintain loyalty and to love each other until death do they part. Watching them from the side Christine knew that, for them, these were not just words; it was a promise, which both intended to keep until their last breath.

In her mind, she tried to imagine herself and Mark standing at the altar before the priest, saying these words but, hard as she tried, she couldn't. Life had shown her that Mark was not one of those who would make such a promise, and even if he did, would not intend to keep it.

Christine listened to the priest's words, and her eyes wandered over the people gathered for the ceremony – men and women, young and old. Their faces expressed genuine joy for the two at the altar.

It seemed that people were somewhat different in this time; they were able to love more sincerely, without any conditions or reservations. For all the hardships and difficulties of life, their love was simple yet strong. How little they needed to be happy – to know that the person one loves lives and lives for him.

Moving from one person to another, her eyes stopped on the man who stood to the right of the groom's father. From what she had been able to see during her stay in Sherwood, Guy of Gisborne was the man who would give such a promise – to love one till the end of days – and would not only keep such a promise but also wouldn't hesitate to give his life for the person he loved.

Her mind was still drifting far away, consumed by her thoughts, when their eyes met. They looked at one another as if their souls were engaged in a silent conversation. They couldn't take their eyes from each other, until the priest had announced the couple before him to be bound before God, and allowed the groom to kiss his bride.

Cries of congratulations rolled amongst the crowd and echoed through the church, with happy, cheering people pouring out into the street. Showering the newlyweds with greetings, the crowd moved towards Locksley Manor.

*****

In the back yard of the manor, under large canopies, the freshly laid tables awaited the guests. Fires were burning. The musicians were tuning their instruments.

Christine looked around: the bride and groom took their central places, their parents and close relatives scattered around but

Guy was nowhere to be seen. She was about to go to the house when a soft, deep voice spoke to her.

"So, this is where you've been hiding from me all evening."

Her heart leapt. "I didn't know you were looking for me, Milord," she turned to him and smiled.

"I wanted..." he trailed off, looking away from her.

"What did you want, Milord?" Christine tried to catch his gaze. Inside her chest, her heart was pounding so fast, it was as if she was afraid to hear his words.

"I wanted to say... you look stunning, Milady!" he bowed his head and took her hand in his. For some time, he was silent, never taking his gentle eyes off her and not letting go of her hand. "I have something for you," he finally said.

Releasing her hand, he pulled a small velvet package out of his pocket and handed it to Christine.

"A gift? For me?" she asked, untying delicate lace.

In the dim light her face lit up, when opening a velvet flap, inside it, she saw the bracelet given to her by her mother.

"I promised I would return it to you," he said softly.

He took the bracelet and gently put it on Christine's wrist.

"Thank you! You don't know how much this means to me!"

Her eyes shone with overwhelming feelings. Christine gently caressed his face and kissed his cheek. Guy smiled in response. Still holding on to her hand, he looked into her eyes.

"I... I wanted..." he was about to say something, but before he could finish, he was interrupted by the groom's father.

"Come, Sir, it's time to begin," he said, beckoning for Guy to follow him.

Still holding Christine's hand, Guy obediently walked after him, but soon he had to let her go, as her place was prepared on the opposite end of the table with the other bridesmaids and relatives of the bride.

Taking their places, the guests began to fill up, raise, empty and re-fill their cups, toasting the bride and groom, their parents, and for their long and strong union. Soon the meat was ready and served to the tables. After a short break, the toasts continued. Guests raised their cups, wishing the newlyweds healthy children and importantly, a male first-born, comfortable home and good health. Under the joyful cries of the guests, the bride and groom again and again found themselves in each other's arms, sealing their bond with passionate kisses.

Christine joined the others in their celebration joyfully. From time to time, her gaze wandered off to the other side of the table, where from his seat, the master of Locksley was watching the scene. Sometimes their eyes met and, smiling, they engaged in a wordless conversation, as if at that moment no words were necessary or important.

Having satisfied their hunger and thirst, the guests joined in jolly dancing. The newlyweds and the bridesmaids, with their dance partners, swirled around the campfires to the rhythm of the cheerful music. Seeing that Gisborne was alone, Christine walked towards him, but before she could reach him, one of the women grabbed her arm and pulled her toward the dancing crowd.

With undisguised pleasure Guy watched how, smiling and laughing, Christine, along with all the guests, whirled in the dance. She didn't care that she didn't know the steps and wasn't always in rhythm with the dance; she enjoyed every moment of it.

Soon tired guests returned to their places, and to give them a chance to catch their breath, the musicians began to play slow melodies, one after another.

The bright moon rose over the manor, the black night sky was covered in a myriad of stars. The fires provided light and drove away the cool of the night. The bridesmaids, having rested after a quick dance, started to sing a sad song about a young lad who went to war in a distant land and the maiden awaiting his return. While the girls sang their song, the father of the groom walked across to them.

"Dear guests! Can I have your attention, please?" he said, as soon as the girls finished their song and the guests had rewarded them with cheerful applause. "You know that this wonderful celebration would not have taken place if our dear host – Sir Guy of Gisborne – had not invited us to take advantage of his wonderful home! Let us thank him for his generosity, and raise our cups in his honour. To Sir Guy of Gisborne!" he said, then lifted his cup, and drained it in one gulp.

People began to shout out Gisborne's name and toasts to the health of the host rolled around the tables. Christine joined in on the well-wishes and, turning to him, saluted Guy with her cup.

"Dear guests! Can I have a moment of silence, please!" the blacksmith spoke again. "We also know that our master is hosting a guest in his house," he turned to Christine and at the same moment another hundred eyes turned in her direction, the hum of voices echoed over the tables. "Today in conversation Sir Guy had mentioned that his guest is not only an exceptionally beautiful lady, but also has a beautiful voice. Sir Guy also said that she came to us from a distant land, so let us all ask her, on the occasion of our celebration, to gift us a song of her land.

At these words, Christine's throat became as dry as a desert. Seeking support, she glanced in Guy's direction, but he only smiled, giving her a daring look.

"Song, song, song..." shouted the guests while Christine frantically tried to figure out which song, of those that she knew, would be suitable for the occasion.

"Alright, alright!" she said, trying to remain calm.

She walked to the musicians and quickly hummed the tune of the only song that came to her mind.

"Unfortunately, I didn't actually come from a distant land," addressing the guests, she said in a low voice. "Like all of you, I was born and grew up in England. Maybe, a different England to the one you know. This is a song my mother used to sing to me when I was a little girl. She used to say it is an old English folk song."

Christine paused. The soft chatter around the tables quietened. She closed her eyes and taking a few big breaths began to sing:

Where are you going? To Scarborough Fair?
Parsley, sage, rosemary and thyme,
Remember me to a bonny lass there,
For she once was a true lover of mine.

After the first verse, the musicians picked up the tune and began to play along with the melody. Hearing the music, Christine smiled; she opened her eyes and continued:

Tell her to make me a cambric shirt,
Parsley, sage, rosemary and thyme,
Without any needle or thread work'd in it,
And she shall be a true lover of mine.

After the second verse, unable to resist the charms of the beautiful melody and Christine's magical voice, the bridesmaids came to dance, slowly circling the yard in rhythm with the music.

Tell her to wash it in yonder well,
Parsley, sage, rosemary and thyme,
Where water ne'er sprung nor a drop of rain fell,
And she shall be a true lover of mine.

Tell her to plough me an acre of land,
Parsley, sage, rosemary and thyme,
Between the sea and the salt sea strand,
And she shall be a true lover of mine.

Tell her to reap it with a sickle of leather,
Parsley, sage, rosemary and thyme,
And tie it all up with a tom-tit's feather,

And she shall be a true lover of mine.

Tell her to gather it all in a sack,
Parsley, sage, rosemary and thyme,
And carry it home on a butterfly's back,
And then she shall be a true lover of mine.

Where are you going? To Scarborough Fair?
Parsley, sage, rosemary, and thyme,
Remember me to a bony lad there,
For he once was a true lover of mine.

The girls continued to dance while Christine, finishing the last verse, once again ran her eyes over the faces of the people around her. She needed to see him; she needed to feel his eyes on her. This song touched the notes in her heart that for the past few days she had so helplessly tried to suppress. She tried to ignore how her heart quickened every time he was near her or when his deep velvet voice spoke her name. How butterflies began to flutter in her stomach when she saw his eyes smiling and his lips curving into his favourite slightly arrogant, cocky smirk. The feelings were too strong for her to fight. As she tried to calm down, a storm was raging inside her. It was neither her place nor her time, but no longer able to resist, she wanted to sing the last words of the song to him.

The song ended. The music stopped, and then there was silence. Her heart skipped few beats and pounced when their eyes met again. Never before had Guy looked at her like that! The look they shared froze into a complex range of emotions. He looked at her as if in this garden and in this house, they were alone, as if no one else existed in this world – none, but them.

Enthusiastic applause and cheerful cries forced her back to reality. Christine helplessly blinked several times. Her face looked troubled.

"What a beautiful song," said the blacksmith, clapping his hands loudly as he turned to Christine, "and how beautifully was it sung!"

Out of nowhere, there were two cups in his hands, one he put into Christine's hand, who was still looking around slightly confused.

"Dear friends, let us raise our glasses, and thank the Lady for her beautiful song. To the Lady of Locksley!" he shouted loudly, raising his cup high up.

"To the Lady of Locksley... to the Lady of the house... to the Lady of Locksley," drifted between the tables.

Her eyes wide opened, confused and frightened Christine looked at Gisborne, who, following the example of his guests, also raised his cup.

"My Lady," he moved his lips, looking straight into her soul.

"No! It is not so!" Christine protested, turning to the blacksmith. Her heart pounded in her chest, wishing to break free. "I'm not the Lady of Locksley. Things are not..."

"What's wrong, my dear?" asked the blacksmith, with a cunning smile. "Don't you love him?" his words sounded more like a statement than a question.

"I... I cannot... It cannot... This should not..." she muttered disjointedly. Strained, her heart was ready to burst; her gaze was flying between the blacksmith and the man sitting at a table under a canopy of trees. "No... This cannot be," she whispered again shaking her head, and, giving Gisborne another long look, she disappeared inside the house.

"What happened?" asked Guy, walking towards the blacksmith. "What happened to her?" his face was concerned. He was about to go after Christine, but the blacksmith caught his arm.

"Leave the girl be. She needs to be alone."

"Why? What happened?" Guy asked again, concerned.

"Everything is fine, Milord. She's just realised that she is in love," said the blacksmith with the same cunning smile.

"What?" Gisborne exclaimed, afraid to believe what he had just heard. "What are you talking about?"

"Sir Guy, the whole village has long been talking about it. It seems that it is only for the two of you that it remains a big secret."

"You've gone mad, old man!" Guy said, still refusing to accept what the man was saying. "I dare not believe that a woman like her could care for me."

The old man only smiled.

"You are like two little dying embers, smouldering, burning slowly alone. Put you two together, and there will be hot fire..."

Gisborne had not heard him finish; leaving the blacksmith, he was already running towards the house.

*****

He found her in the living room, by the fireplace. She stood silently, absently looking into the flames, lost in her own thoughts. She was sad, for a moment he thought she was crying, but there were no tears.

As he stepped into the room Christine turned to the sound. Her slightly bewildered, disconcerted look spoke louder than any words he'd heard before, and yet he still couldn't dare to believe that what he read in her eyes was true. For him there was only one way to make sure.

Unable to wait any longer, in two large strides Guy crossed the distance between them. He wrapped one arm around her waist, pulling her closer; his other hand ran through her silky hair.

Christine smiled faintly. His hand gently touched her cheek, brushing the hair off her face. His blue, almost transparent eyes wouldn't let go of her gaze, piercing through into the depths of her soul. She didn't move, just sighed softly. Her lips parted.

He tried to fight the feelings, suppressing himself; the last thing he wanted now was to scare her. Not taking his eyes from her, he slowly moved his face closer to hers. Her hot breath burned his lips, breaking down the walls of his self-control, crushing them into the dust. No longer able to restrain his urge, his need for her, he kissed her carefully, holding back a little. He waited for her reaction.

She didn't push him away. On the contrary, her lips, warm and moist, parted to meet his. His head began to spin like that of a young boy who kissed a girl for the first time. Releasing her lips, he pulled back to look at her beautiful face once again; to make sure that he wasn't dreaming it all.

It wasn't a dream. She was with him, right now and right there, she was in his arms. Her eyes were full of feelings that mere words could not express.

"Oh, Christine," he whispered.

His breathing grew heavy. Wrapping his arms tighter around her waist, he drew her closer to him, kissing her once again, deeper and harder this time. He held her tight, afraid to let go, afraid if he loosened his hold, he'd lose her forever. But she had no intention of leaving him. Circling her arms tightly around his strong neck, she kissed him back, releasing all the passion that was bottled up inside her.

The tension between them grew stronger with every passing second. From the two dying embers, the fire of passion had broken out and was now blazing with hot flames.

At some point, they stopped to catch their breath.

"We must not," she whispered quietly, resting her head on his broad chest.

"Christine, please," panting, he could hardly speak, his deep voice resonated in her head. "I cannot stop thinking about you."

"We should not," pleading she lifted her eyes up to his.

She freed herself from his arms, and ran out into the hallway then quickly up the stairs and into her room.

Closing the door firmly behind her, she leaned against it. Her heart was pounding in her chest like a caged bird that thirsted for freedom. Her lips were sore from his passionate kisses; her lower abdomen sung and ached. Christine hadn't felt such a desire for a long time.

"God, what am I doing... what am I going to do?" she murmured, clasping her head between her hands. "I fell in love with a man 800 years older than me! I am not even sure this is all real."

She lied to herself, trying to extinguish the thought of him. Yet deep inside she knew that everything that was happening to her was real. She knew that the man who had kissed her just now wasn't a figment of her imagination. Like her, he was flesh and blood.

A soft knock at the door startled her.

"Christine, please, let me in," his deep, sensual voice spoke from the other side of the door. "I need to see you," there was a tone of despair in his voice.

Her fingers lay on the bolt of the iron handle. She hesitated, knowing that if she opened the door, there would be no going back. Taking a deep breath, she pulled the ring.

She opened the door and stepped aside, letting him into her bedroom. When she shut the door behind him, she was once again in his arms, their lips locked in a deep, passionate kiss. This time, there was no tenderness, only hunger, urge and need.

A moment later, she was lying on the bed, feeling the weight of his body on top of her. Not that she minded, her hands moved over his shoulders, back and buttocks, while their lips continued to enjoy each other. Christine moaned with longing, feeling his hardened symbol of manhood pressing hard between her thighs.

"I can't bear it anymore," she whispered, not letting go of his lips.

"Just one word," he could barely utter, "just one word and I will leave..." he said, panting heavily, resting his forehead against hers. "Do you want me to leave?" he asked, pressing harder against her body.

"No," she whispered almost inaudibly. "I don't want you to leave," she arched her back, to feel his erection even stronger.

He kissed her deeply, his tongue exploring the depths of her mouth. She pressed herself against him, wishing to dissolve into him, to merge into one.

"Will you have me?" he asked, barely restraining himself.

Christine looked up at him. In his eyes there was thirst and longing, a hunger, the kind of hunger no food would satisfy.

"Yes!" she replied, kissing him softly.

He stood up and held out his hand. Helping her up from the bed, Guy brought her closer to the fire. Light and shadow from the flames played on her face. In the dim light of the room, she seemed even more beautiful, surreal.

He gently pulled out the pins and flowers that decorated her hair, his fingers sliding along its soft silk.

"You are so beautiful!" he whispered with passion.

He brushed the hair from her shoulder and gently pressed his lips against her collarbone, slowly moving along her neck, to her lips. Barely touching her lips with his, he stopped and rested his forehead against her cheek. His hot breath, like a gentle fire, caressed her face. His strong arms wrapped tighter around her waist, bringing her closer to him. He pulled his face away from hers.

"I wouldn't dare take you by force... But now, if at any point you'd want me to stop," he said, his voice deep, "I'm not sure I'll be able to."

He looked at her, longing in his eyes. Christine said nothing. The desire and passion that was burning in her gaze spoke for her. In response, she touched his cheek and gently locked her lips with his.

As soon as their lips parted, his mouth slid back to her neck. He slowly and avidly consumed it with his lips. Christine sighed with a groan. His strong hands were on her shoulders, sliding down, pulling down the sleeves of her dress, pushing it lower to her hips. He pulled back to enjoy the sight of her naked body. Pressing her hard against him with one hand, he cupped one of her breasts with the other.

Her skin was soft and warm, exactly as he'd imagined. From this sense of closeness, the fire of passion was now raging inside him. Like a thirsty traveller finding cool water, he eagerly clung to her breast, devouring it with his lips.

Sighing with every breath, Christine ran her fingers through his hair and tugged at it gently. Guy groaned in response, lightly clenching his teeth around her nipple.

Their lips once again united, Christine floated in an ocean of endless pleasure. She grabbed at the fabric of his shirt pulling it over his head, and then crushed her hot body against his chest. His strong hands were, once again, around her in a tight circle and then slid down her waist and thighs, pushing the dress further down.

Tightly clinging to her body, the fabric of her dress, slowly descended down her rounded hips and slid to the floor. Guy took a step back. That night, after the attack, when under the influence of alcohol she had tried to seduce him, he had not dared to look at her. Now she was before him in all her glory.

"I can't believe that you're mine," he whispered, once again taking her into his arms. With their lips linked, and their bodies close, hot and sweaty, he could barely cope with desire. Still holding her close with one arm he began to untie the laces on his breeches.

"Don't rush," she gasped, "we have all the time in the world," she added, placing a soft kiss on his lips. "Allow me."

Christine dropped her hand down and ran the tip of her finger over his stomach, along the belt line. Guy jerked as if pierced by an electric shock. It was the same simple movement she'd used on the night of the attack; it had had a great effect on him then and now it did again. His erection became stronger, his body screamed to be free.

Sensing this, Christine, softly caressing his lips with hers, undid his laces and sank down, running her hands over his strong muscular legs, helping him out of his breeches. Releasing him from this unnecessary piece of clothing, she placed soft, gentle kisses on his thighs, one, then another – her lips moved higher and higher. Following her mouth, her hands glided up and stopped on his buttocks.

A deep, animal-like groan came from depth of Guy's chest as her soft moist lips touched his hot hardened flesh.

"Oh heavens..." he breathed out.

This woman took him to the heights of bliss; a bliss, the existence of which he could never have imagined.

Christine looked up at him and smiled lustfully, a devilish fire was burning in her eyes. With every move of her lips and tongue, his body tensed more and more, his heart was beating at a furious pace, ready to burst into hundreds of pieces. Finally, she let go of him and stood up.

"I want you to love me," she whispered kissing him hard on the mouth, running her fingers through his hair. She couldn't bear it anymore, she wanted to feel him flesh to flesh.

He didn't need a second invitation, he had waited long enough for these words. He easily picked her up into his arms and carried her to the bed. Placing her gently onto the soft sheets, he covered her body with thousands of kisses, not neglecting even the most secluded corner of her being. There was no point in waiting any longer, they were both ready. She wanted to feel him inside; he wanted to possess her body and soul.

With their lips still locked, Guy raised himself up allowing Christine to guide him in. He entered her with a soft, deep moan. Their bodies – arms and legs – hot and wet, were intertwined. They were losing and finding themselves in pleasure over and over again. In unison with his movements, she arched her back to meet him, allowing him to plunge deeper into the secrets of her essence. His movements were rhythmic; he pierced her again and again, first slow and smooth, then fast and slightly rough.

Not trying to restrain her feelings, she moaned with pleasure, and when she reached her highest point, she wrapped her legs around his hips so tight they almost cramped. He followed her into ecstasy, and expressed his peak with a loud moan that came from the depths of his body.

Exhausted, they fell asleep instantly, holding each other in their arms. After a short sleep, they enjoyed discovering one another, yet again reaching the summits of bliss. She wished this man would never leave her, and that this night would never end.

When they finally fell asleep, a new day was dawning over Locksley. Tired, their bodies entwined in a simple pattern – her head rested on his chest, her hand and leg wrapped around his hips. Even in his sleep, he held her close firmly, not wanting to let go even for a single moment.

*****

A soft knock awoke her.

"Miss... Miss Hawk," on the other side of the door a voice spoke quietly.

Trying not to disturb the man sleeping next to her, Christine climbed out of bed. She threw a blanket over her naked body and opened the door.

"Allan, what happened?" she said softly and glanced back.

"We found the place, ma'am, there, at the South Gates..."

Her eyes widened. She wanted to say something, but could not squeeze out a single word. With all of the events of the previous day, she had completely forgotten that Allan and Robin had gone to the South Gates in search of the place of her crossing.

"Ma'am, are you okay?"

"Yes..." she managed to mumble. "But are you sure, Allan? There can be no mistake?" she still refused to believe it.

"Yes, hill, cave everything as you had described. Robin will take you there. He is waiting for you outside Locksley. I have already prepared your horse," he said.

"Alright, I'll be ready in five minutes," she said at last.

Christine returned to the room and dressed quickly. Guy was still fast asleep. She kissed him, barely touching his lips with hers. A slight smile appeared on his face.

At the threshold, she looked at him once again and exited the room, leaving Guy in the arms of a profound sleep.

Chapter 19:
Gisborne

Christine walked out of the dark cave, and into the light of day.

The smell of damp and stale water still tickled her nose. She felt a little dizzy and lifted her face towards the light summer breeze. For several minutes, she just stood at the cave's entrance keeping her eyes closed, listening to the sound of the wind, feeling its light touch. A few minutes had passed before her eyes fully adjusted to the bright daylight. She opened them slowly.

She raised her head and looked up. The green leaves hid the clear sky from her sight but the sun was still shining brightly through. Its rays made their way through the dense pattern of the branches and twigs high above her head, happily sparkling on the surface of the water and the rocks at the bottom of the stream that flowed out of the cave. Birds were chirping blissfully amidst the abundance of green foliage. It was humid, the day promised to be hot.

She had never experienced such a mixture of feelings – joy, anxiety and sadness. Her heart contracted, then stopped, and then began to pound again at a furious pace. Overwhelmed by emotion, she was gasping for air.

Thoughts, like an endless stream, rushed through her head. It was the place! Not a month had passed since she woke up in this very cave, barely understanding what was happening to her, but now everything was clear in her mind – as if projected on to a screen the picture was clear before her eyes.

She remembered the rain, the severe thunderstorm that had crashed through the sky, trying to tear it apart. She remembered the rainbow and the light – the light that came out of the giant tree in the middle of the clearing, the light that drew her in with its vivid tints, the light that mesmerised her and invited her to enter into the unknown.

On that day of the twentieth of June, the year two thousand and fourteen she walked through a sphere of bright, pulsating light and exited on the other side, in another time, and in another place – into the completely different reality of medieval England.

Everything was exactly as it was on that very day; except for one thing – there was no light inside the cave. There was nothing there to suggest how she could cross back over.

She walked through the cave to the very end but couldn't find an answer to the question that had been tormenting her all this time – how was she going to return home?

Christine stood on a hill, surrounded by dense green foliage, trying to organise her disordered thoughts.

"Perhaps, this is how it all ends? Maybe I am stuck in this time forever and am never destined to return home."

Thinking about her home, her time, and Philip, brought her thoughts back to the previous night.

Her chest ached; the feelings were overwhelming. She tried to drive the thoughts away but the blacksmith was right, she really had fallen in love with Gisborne. She didn't mean for it to happen but the warmth that spread inside her chest when he looked at her, when she heard his voice, or even now, when she was simply thinking about him, indicated otherwise.

Undoubtedly, he was handsome and had the body of a Greek god, and, as proved by the previous night, was a skilful and attentive lover, but it wasn't just a physical attraction. She loved him with all her being: his smile, his eyes, his explosive and obstinate character, the way he laughed – sincerely and heartily, the way his eyes lit up when he spoke of something dear and important to him; when, with his sleeves rolled up, he was doing something for his village and for his people.

He had gone down a long and difficult road in life, trying to achieve recognition and a successful position, such as that which he had at the Sheriff's side. He hadn't always chosen the right path and means to seize his fortune but, in spite of all the cruelty and harshness surrounding him, he hadn't lost his innate goodness.

Thus, her thoughts swirled in her brain, as she carefully walked down the slope. At the foot of the hill, whistling a tune, Robin waited for her. He always seemed cheerful and carefree but his gaze was focused on the surrounding forest.

"Well? Did you find what you were looking for?" he asked with a keen interest.

"Yes. And no," said Christine. "It is the place, and somehow I should be able to get back home, but I still can't figure out how," she spoke with notes of uncertainty in her voice. "You know, when I crossed, there was light! A very bright light – like a fireball. I went through it and then found myself in the cave."

"What kind of person walks through burning balls of fire?!" Robin glanced at her sideways.

"What kind of person runs around the forest with a bow and arrow and steals money from the rich?" Christine retorted.

"Touché," Robin smiled, and they both laughed.

"I don't know, it's all very strange. Perhaps I'll never get out of here," Christine shook her head.

"Perhaps it's not your time yet," he said.

"What do you mean?" Christine asked, surprised.

"Well, if you came here, then it was meant to happen."

"I ended up here on account of my own stupidity," she said. "If I had not gone through the light... If I had not..."

"If..." repeated Robin. "But you did, and now you're here, so it was meant to happen."

"Meant for who, Robin?!"

"I am sure that with time everything will fall into place," he said.

"Oh, time! Time is something that I don't have! The Sheriff will return any day, and what then? I must get back!" she said, and at these words sadness flashed in her eyes.

"Somehow, you don't seem to me, too happy about this prospect, neither do you look like a person who really wants to go home," said Robin, noting how her expression had changed. "It seems to me that something is still holding you here... something or someone," he winked cheerfully.

Christine only smiled in response. Slowly, they reached the road and stopped to untie the horses.

"What I cannot understand," said Robin mounting onto the saddle, "is what you women see in him?"

"He is not as bad as he seems, Robin," Christine smiled.

Talking away, they slowly rode towards Locksley.

"You probably want to say he was not so bad, until he got together with the Sheriff?" he grinned. "Guy was a good lad, if it wasn't for that snake... you know he killed his mother."

"What? Who?" her eyes widened. "What are you talking about?"

"Wesley, I'm talking about the Sheriff Wesley. Well, back then he was not the Sheriff of Nottingham, but a bastard and a scoundrel all the same!" said Robin, gently swaying in the saddle. "That was many years ago. I do not think Guy knows about it, otherwise, he would have dealt with him by now."

"How do you know that? Tell me, please," asked Christine.

"Well, there is not much to tell," said Robin. "Guy's father, Sir William of Gisborne, from the Gisborne estate, was killed in the war."

"Gisborne estate?" she repeated. "I have never heard of it, Guy never spoke of it."

"There is nothing left to speak of now, really, the manor is in ruins. People laughed at him. Sir Guy of Gisborne bears the name of an estate that does not exist."

"What happened?" pressed Christine. She wanted to know everything.

"For as long as his father lived, Gisborne was one of the richest estates in the district, almost as good as Locksley in its structure and significance. William Gisborne was a member of the Council of Nobles and a highly-respected man but, when he was killed, the estate began its decline. His wife, Guy's mother, was a very beautiful woman, and John Wesley, at that time he was still a nobody, wanted to marry her so he could get his sleazy hands on the lands and estate. She, of course, refused him," he paused.

"What happened then?"

"Then... Then, he would not leave her alone and often visited her in the hope that she would change her mind. She continued to refuse him, and one day he decided to take her by force... He killed her. I do not know whether it was done deliberately or by accident but, to cover it up, his people burned the mansion to the ground... half of the estate went with it. The family was deprived of any means or livelihood," he paused again.

"What about Guy? Where was he? Why didn't he do anything? Couldn't he have protected her?" Christine showered him with questions.

"He was not at home at the time. He and I were sent to London to study and when we returned there was nothing left of the house and estate."

"But if you weren't around, Robin, how do you know all this?"

"His sister told me everything when we returned," Robin said.

"Sister? He never said he had a sister. God, how many more surprises?"

"That's the last, I promise," Robin laughed. "Guy and Juliana never shared much love for one other. She was always very jealous of her mother's love for him and thought he was to blame for her death. When they were left without their parents and means, Guy married her off to a wealthy nobleman. To be more accurate, he sold her to him. She now lives in France. Since then I have not heard from her."

"That is terrible! Poor Guy!"

"He is not so innocent," said Robin.

"Well, I agree, but your story does explain a lot. I cannot believe that the Sheriff... Although, why am I surprised? During my short stay here, he manifested in all his glory," she wrinkled her nose in disgust.

They rode in silence the rest of the way. Christine considered, played in her mind, over and over again, what she had just heard from Robin. Now, knowing Gisborne's story, everything finally fell into place.

When they reached the borders of Locksley, Robin spoke again.

"We'd better part here. I don't think my presence is welcomed in this place. Besides, you do not want them to see you with me," he winked. "I will send someone to watch at your cave, just in case if..." he paused.

Neither he nor Christine knew what "if" was supposed to be.

"Thank you, Robin," she held out her hand and, having said her goodbyes, galloped her horse along the road leading to the village.

*****

Christine was unfastening the saddle of her stallion when two hands settled on her hips, glided over her waist and firmly pressed her back against a strong male body.

"Good morning, Milady," a velvet voice murmured into her ear. "Where have you been?"

"Good morning, Milord," she purred, placing her hand over his.

She turned her head towards him and nestled it under his chin. Burying her nose in his neck, she inhaled his scent.

"I went for a ride," she said softly, her lips barely touching his Adam's apple.

"For a ride, where to?" he asked, tightening his hold on her. His deep voice resonated in her head.

Christine felt his hot breath in her hair.

"I rode in Sherwood," she said softly, and still staying within the protective ring of his embrace turned to face him.

Now her arms wrapped around him. Her face was smiling to meet his, her eyes gleamed with soft light.

"I thought that you had decided to run away from me, Milady," freeing one hand, he gently touched her hair, removing a stray lock from her forehead.

His blue eyes studied her face.

"No... Not yet," she answered, melting in the pleasure of his touch. "I needed to clear my head, and you were fast sleep, I didn't dare to wake you."

"I must admit, when I woke up this morning and did not find you next to me; I thought that I had dreamed it all. And if it was not for your dress on the floor..."

Christine did not let him finish. Her fingers slid through his hair, her lips gently touched his.

"I beg your pardon, Milord," she breathed out stepping back, "I could not resist. I interrupted you, you were about to say something," smiling, she bit her lip.

"Does not matter," he whispered, returning her kiss.

His hands moulded her harder against his chest, Christine could hardly breathe, not that she minded, melting into his strong embrace, full of raw passion, which he could hardly contain.

"What are your plans for today?" asked Christine, when Guy released her lips and loosened his hold. "Again, to Nottingham?"

"No, for today I only have one plan," he said softly, his lips curled into his favourite smile. "It includes me, you and much fewer clothes," he added, moving away the collar of her shirt.

His soft lips touched her shoulder then slowly slid to her neck, making his way to her lips. Throwing her head back, Christine moaned softly, feeling the tension beginning to rise inside her.

In one quick movement, Guy lifted her off the ground and backed her against the stable wall. Her long legs wrapped tightly around his hips. Eagerly devouring each other, they shared a long, passionate kiss. Guy was struggling to maintain his composure and was fighting the urge to take her right there. He lowered Christine to the ground and, for some time, remained motionless, holding her in his arms. His breathing was ragged, each exhale was lost in her hair.

"I think," he finally spoke. His voice was hoarse, his breathing raced along with his heartbeat. "We will postpone my plan, for a little while."

"For a little while?" asked Christine.

"Yes, for a little while," he repeated, with a promise in his tone. "Now that you're dressed, I want to show you something."

*****

They had given Jenny instructions for dinner, saddled the horses and, around noon, the two riders left Locksley, having taken with them a bit of cheese, cold meat, a flask of wine and a large blanket.

After wandering along the forest trails for a little more than an hour, they finally reached a small clearing. Guy swung out of the saddle and tied the horses, he took the supplies and, holding Christine's hand, directed her onto a small path leading into the depths of the forest. Cautiously looking around and peering into the shadows cast by the green leaves, Christine followed him.

Soon, Guy led her out of the forest to a small, brightly lit hill, underneath there ran a fast forest creek. From the hill, over a stream, they could see a lush valley. In a small corner of the valley could be seen a former settlement, now a heap of ruins with burnt logs and stones scattered about.

Not saying a word, Guy spread the blanket, put a bag with food at one end and invited Christine to sit next to him.

One look at his face was enough for Christine to understand what this place was. In the valley at the bottom of the hill was what used to bear the proud name of Gisborne Estate.

He poured himself some wine, saluted the ruins and drained the cup. His blue eyes were focused on the landscape in front of him.

"What is this place?" Christine asked cautiously.

"This," he sighed heavily, "this is my family's estate – Gisborne... or rather what is left of it," he refilled his cup.

"This was your home? What happened?" after her conversation with Robin, she wanted to hear his version of events.

"Some outlaws tried to rob the house, they started the fire. It..." he trailed off, "it took my mother's life," he continued to drink his wine.

"Do you know who did it?" Christine asked hesitantly.

"No, some lowlifes, I suppose. There were many of them at the time. If I knew who had done it, I would have dealt with them long ago," his face froze, his expression reflected his anger and hatred.

"Even now, it is very beautiful," said Christine, placing a hand on his shoulder.

"You should have seen this place in all its glory," he said dreamily. "The time will come, and I will reclaim the rights to this land and restore the manor, and eventually all the estate... but for now..." he took a long sip from his cup.

"For now, Locksley is your Gisborne?" asked Christine, handing him her cup.

"Yes," he smiled.

*****

They made themselves comfortable on the top of the hill and had a lunch of bread, cheese, and cold meats. As they ate, Guy told Christine the history of his family. She listened with lively interest, asking questions from time to time.

From what she had heard from Robin earlier and what Guy was telling her now about his life, she was able to put together, more or less, a clear picture of what seemed his uneasy and unhappy circumstances. However, what struck her even more, was that, not even once, while he spoke of the hardships he had endured, did he look to her for pity. On the contrary, when he was telling her about the last five years of his life in Locksley, a trip to Acre and other dirty work that was entrusted to him by the Sheriff, she sensed in his tone hatred and contempt for himself.

"It was hard, and, at first, I often wondered about the righteousness of my actions," he said, "but I had no one to turn to for help or advice. The Sheriff, however, continued to whisper sweet promises. Oh, he has paid me generously for my work!" said Guy, with passion. "At first I was performing some simple errands and small tasks, but then the work became more... delicate and demanding, if I may put it as so. Many times, I wanted to get away from him but then I was so deeply caught up in this mess, in his plots and intrigues, that it was too late. You see, in my life, there was no one who could direct me to the right path. Eventually, I stopped asking questions. Silencing the voice of my conscience, I silently and implicitly followed his instructions and did the work that was entrusted to me. I wanted to revive the family and the honour of the name of Gisborne."

"Well, now a lot of things make more sense. At least, it is understandable why you hang out with this serpent of a Sheriff," said Christine.

"No, there is no excuse for my actions," he shook his head. "All these years, people looked at me as a ruthless and cold-blooded killer, who does not and never had anything human in him, but then you came into my life," he looked at Christine tenderly, his hand gently touched her cheek. Guy moved closer and, lightly caressing her skin with his lips, kissed her wrist. "Oh, I hated you!" he said with passion.

"What? Why!?"

"The very moment the Sheriff said that the Prince had sent someone else to do the job that I failed to complete two years ago, I began to hate that person."

"Oh, you're talking about that."

"Then we found you in the forest... On that day, something happened, as if my life had turned upside down," he remembered that very first day and smiled at his thoughts. "I was going to prove my importance to the Sheriff; but the more I got to know you, the stronger were the feelings in my heart."

Guy moved closer to Christine, his hands wrapped around her in a tight embrace, pressing her harder to himself. She leaned her back against his chest and rested her head on his shoulder. Her arms were on top of his.

"At first, while you were still unconscious, it was just an interest, a curiosity; then after our first encounter..." he smiled again, "it was hatred, but as time went by, other feelings began to blossom inside me," he kissed her neck, cheek, then found her lips. "I have long refused to believe what was happening to me, but that unfortunate night after the Sheriff's gathering put everything in its place. Walking out of the castle, I went after you with one purpose – to make you pay for all the insults that you have levelled at me, but when I saw what happened to you, I did not think twice and rushed to your aid. I don't regret my actions," he turned her face to him. "The thought that something might happen to you was unbearable to me," he added, holding her to closer to him.

Their lips locked again in a gentle kiss.

"Come," said Christine, as soon as he let go of her lips. Freed from his embrace, she rose to her feet. "I want to have a closer look at your ancestral village."

Slowly, they descended into the valley. Not willingly at first, but then with great enthusiasm Guy told her how things were organised within the estate at its prime.

"I am sure that you will be able to restore this place to its former glory, if not better," she said.

Gisborne said nothing and just held her closer. Christine nestled her head on his chest, her arms locked around his waist. They stood in silence for a while. Then he lifted her face to his and looked into her bottomless blue eyes.

"When I look at you, when you're close to me," he finally spoke. His velvety voice was full of tenderness. "I feel a certain something..." he ran his hand through her hair. "When you are next to me, I feel I can defeat anyone who dares to challenge me! When you are next to me, I am not afraid of anything!"

Christine touched his face, and there, on this, the estate that once bore the proud name of Gisborne, they shared a deep, passionate kiss.

*****

The sun continued to shine mercilessly, and the air became very humid. Christine and Guy returned to the hill.

"If we're not planning to go back just as yet," said Christine, "let's move our picnic under the trees over there," she pointed towards a small grove, where, under the canopy of the trees, they could shelter from the scorching sun.

Once in the shade of the trees, Christine sighed in relief and rubbed her wet neck under her hair. With a mass of hair such as hers, the heat seemed stronger and more intense to withstand. She broke off a piece of high straw, slipped it under her hair and tried to tie it up in a ponytail.

"No, do not do that," Guy caught her hand, his fingers slid through her hair, enjoying its softness. "That is so much better."

"I'm too hot," Christine said smiling and repeated the attempt.

"If you are hot, Milady, I have another suggestion," he took a step closer and started to pull her shirt up from her breeches.

"What are you up to?" she smiled cunningly.

He said nothing, just raised an eyebrow. There was devilish look on his face; a soft fire was gleaming in his eyes.

"What? Here?! What if someone sees us?" Christine said, looking around.

"Someone like a squirrel or a hare?" he whispered in her ear, continuing to work her shirt up.

Pulling her closer, he helped himself with a second hand. Once her shirt was discarded, Guy pulled off her undershirt, accompanying the process with a long kiss. Christine followed his lead, and a moment later, two naked torsos met in a hot embrace.

Releasing her lips, he took a step back and looked at her boldly, surveying her beautiful rounded form. One glance at her was enough for a fire to flare up inside him. She looked at him; her eyes demanded more.

Guy pulled her closer abruptly, hungrily, almost crushing her to himself. He wanted to feel her hot skin on his. Quickly freeing her from the remaining clothing, he gently laid her down on the blanket and his soft lips, yet again, ventured on a quest to discover the secrets of her body. Yielding to his caresses, she threw her head back and moaned softly.

Gisborne stopped as his eyes caught a small patch of pale pink skin at the base of her throat. He knew immediately what it was. A picture flashed through his mind – Christine, lying on the sand of the arena in the training camp and he, towering above her, pressing the tip of the dagger to her throat, ready to pierce through it.

Christine opened her eyes.

"What's wrong?" she asked, noting the change on his face.

Guy didn't answer; his fingers gently touched the scar on her throat. Christine shivered.

"Does it still hurt?"

"No," she answered shortly and took his hand in hers.

"I am a monster," he withdrew his hand, moved away from her and sat on the edge of the blanket.

His head hung low. Christine got up on one elbow and gently touched his shoulder.

"I'm a monster!" he repeated.

"Don't you dare say that," Christine sat up and turned his face to hers, "Do you hear me? Don't you dare!" she peered into the depths of his blue eyes. "You are a good man, Sir Guy of Gisborne and do not listen to anybody who would tell you otherwise. You are a kind, gentle and caring man, that's why I love you," she kissed him softly.

"What did you just say?" he asked when their lips parted, his eyes widened.

"I said you are a good man," she replied with a soft cunning smile.

"No, not that, what did you say after?" he looked at her in disbelief.

"I said I love you," she said, her voice and eyes were full of tender feelings.

"Oh Christine!" he whispered, circling his arms around her in a tight embrace. "I, long ago, lost the hope of ever hearing those words."

"I love you," she repeated again and smiled.

"Will you forgive me?" he asked and, once again, softly touched the pink scar on her neck.

"I have a few ideas how you can make amends," she smiled and lay down on the blanket, pulling him down with her.

His lips devoured her. Hot waves rolled over their bodies, the tension from the desire and passion that had been building up inside them demanded release.

They reached ecstasy together. With a final plunge, Guy gave a loud roar and went limp, his body crushing her to the ground. She encircled her long legs around his hips, not allowing him to move, trying, for as long as possible, to extend the pleasant feeling of unity and wholeness.

*****

Spent, they lay in each other's arms. Christine nestled her head on his chest; listening to the rhythmic beat of his heart. Her legs entwined with his, the tips of her fingers played with the smattering of hair on his broad chest. His one arm glided over the surface of her shoulder, the other rested on her hip.

Christine looked up at his face. His eyes were closed, his face expressed calmness and serenity; a smile froze on his lips. She got up on one elbow and moved closer. Barely touching his face her fingers traced the outline of his nose, chin and lips, lingering on them slightly longer, she completed her study with a gentle kiss.

"You are so beautiful," she whispered, kissing him again.

Guy answered her kiss and rolled over to his side, pressing her to the ground, looming over her. Not for the first time since last night, she once again found herself in this position, not that it bothered her. She received immense pleasure finding herself in his strong arms over and over again.

"As in my dream..." at the memory, her lips quivered in a soft smile.

"What? Why are you laughing, love?" he asked, surprised, and removed a hair from her face. "Am I doing something wrong?"

"No," she ran her hand over his bristly cheek. "I just remembered a dream," she said, her cheeks flushed a little.

"A dream?"

"Yeah," she smiled again. "That night after the Sheriff visited Locksley and after you and I... argued once again, I had a dream."

"Was I in it?" he asked with keen interest.

"Oh yeah!" she breathed out.

"Sounds interesting," his lips touched hers. "I really, really want to hear it," he said, kissing her again.

His mouth wandered off to her neck, slid to her collarbone and further down to her breast. Christine got up on one elbow, and whispered into his ear the most delicate details.

"Mmm," he gasped. "We should definitely try it."

Her hands slid down to his back and stopped on his buttocks. When she touched him, he was once again ready to conquer the previously unknown heights of bliss.

This time was different, his movements were smooth and slow. He was enjoying the warmth of her body and her soft skin. Her beautiful face reflected a kaleidoscope of feeling, as he slowly moved his hips. He wanted to love her again and again.

"I love you," she whispered, as the tension inside her was climbing to its peak. "I love you so much that it scares me."

Hearing these words, he tightened his embrace, pressing her to his body even harder. Having reached their highest point, they did not let go; their lips continued to enjoy each other while their bodies remained motionless.

*****

After a short rest, they washed in the stream and dressed. The sun, although beginning to move slowly toward the forest, was still merciless. The leaves on the trees drooped from its relentless rays. The air was heavy and very humid.

"I think it's gonna rain," said Christine as she walked up the hill from the water. "The heat has been holding on for so many days."

"I don't think so," Guy said, raising his eyes to the skies. In the blue heaven above him, he could not see a single cloud.

They ate. Now it was Christine's turn to talk about her family. Trying hard to avoid any specific details, she told him about her mother, her death, about Philip and her life in general. She wanted to tell him more, she wanted to tell him everything, but didn't dare.

As she spoke, Guy looked at her tenderly. Listening to her melodic voice, he found himself thinking that over the last few days, he had not thought about Marian, not even once. The woman who sat beside him was made for him, even more so, she was destined for him. She was the one he wanted to spend the rest of his days with.

His fingers slipped into his pocket and found a small round object. Smiling at his thoughts, he held it tight in his fist and pulled his hand out.

"Come with me," he said, standing up, holding out a hand to her.

They walked to the edge of the hill that overlooked what remained of his family estate. He stood behind her and held her tight against him. For a while, they stood in silence, and then he spoke.

"Christine, the past few days, I think, have been the happiest of my life. I have never felt more alive than during the time we've spent together," he paused, trying to choose his next words. "I know that this may be too much, and I have no right to ask," he turned her to face him. "I do not even know where to begin... I've never felt anything like this," his blue eyes caressed her with his soft gaze. "Stay with me!" She looked at him wide-eyed, he spoke again, "I do not want the Sheriff to return. In the past few days, I have changed so much that I would not be able to look at him without disgust or contempt."

Christine sighed, realising that sooner or later the Sheriff would return to Nottingham, and she felt as if the weight of a heavy burden had fallen onto her shoulders.

"But... you do not know me," she said a little absently.

"I know you and love you just the way you are," he said looking into her eyes. "You have accepted me in spite of my past, and I do not care what you have done before you came here. I love you now and I will love you forever. It feels as though my heart is ready to burst out of my chest."

"Guy..." she began. "I need to tell you something..."

"No, wait, let me finish," he did not let her continue. "When the Sheriff comes back, I'll go to Acre. If they want to get rid of Richard, I'll do it. I will do what they want and, when I return, we will go away. Together! Just you and me!" he spoke vehemently, fighting his overwhelming emotions. "We can go away to France, my sister lives there... to Normandy or we can stay in England, whatever you want. I do not care where we live, as long as you are with me."

Not letting go of her arm, Guy got down on one knee. A small amethyst sparkled in the rays of the bright sun as the ring slid onto her finger.

"I ask you to stay with me and share my life. I ask you to be my wife."

"Guy... I..." she hesitated, not knowing what to say.

She had the most tender feelings for him, but to become his wife, to stay in this barbaric time, where for open opposition to the ruling power people's heads were chopped off without hesitation, and where every second person was suspected of treason and sent to the gallows, she could not.

"Do not answer me right now," he said, rising from his knee. "But, please, think about it!"

He kissed her lips softly, but being too shocked, Christine stood absently and did not respond to his kiss.

A bright flash of lightning above their heads startled them. Through the trees, they could hear the thunder rolling towards them, the horses neighed nervously.

"It's gonna rain," she mumbled, as if waking from a dream.

They didn't notice as the sky darkened. Strong wind buffeted out of nowhere and drove the black clouds towards them. Still consumed by her thoughts, Christine stood at the edge of the hill, while Guy was packing.

"Before returning to Locksley, we need to get to Nottingham. I hope we will make it there still dry," he said, when they mounted into the saddles.

The first drops of rain began to fall.

*****

The rain caught up with them as they rode.

Ruthlessly dousing them with water, the skies opened above their heads with each new roar of thunder. They were soaked to the last thread, but continued galloping their horses. They were almost out of Sherwood when the rain began to subside. The sky slowly cleared away the black clouds, releasing the sun from its dark prison.

"Christine, look," said Gisborne and nodded his head towards the forest. His face expressed surprise and delight.

Christine looked up into the sky – the view took her breath away. In the sky above the field stood the multi-coloured arc of a double rainbow.

"I've never seen such a beauty!" said Guy.

"Never?" repeated Christine. "I saw something like that no more than..." she paused. Now everything fell into place. She uttered a quiet laugh. "Some say if you see a double rainbow, you should make a wish and it will come true!" she said and added, squeezing harder into the sides of her stallion, "I will race you to the castle!"

Guy was surprised to see such a sudden change. Since they had left Gisborne she was not herself, and had barely said a few words; now she was laughing as if nothing had happened. He grinned and, kicking Raven in the sides, chased after her.

Christine was the first to ride into the castle yard, Gisborne followed not far behind. He quickly swung himself out of the saddle, took both stallions by the bridle and led them into the stables. Holding Christine tightly by her waist, he helped her down, and immediately took her into his arms.

"Did you make a wish, Milord?" she asked, when Guy released her lip after a long soft kiss.

"I have only one wish, Milady," he gently touched her face, "and you know it."

"Do you believe in destiny?" she asked suddenly.

"Do you?" he said, avoiding her question. His eyes were full of tenderness and love.

"Yes... I think I do, now," she said quietly. "I believe that everything that happens to us is destined to us from above, and the people that we meet, we meet for a reason..." she lowered her eyes and paused briefly and then took a deep breath, again she looked up at him.

"Shh," Guy placed a finger to her lips, seeing the sadness taking over her face again. "You talk too much..." he said, leaning closer.

"Sir Guy!" a voice called behind them.

"Allan?! What are you doing here?" Gisborne and Christine asked in unison.

"Oh, thank God you're here!" he said. "You just saved me a trip to Locksley, I was about to ride after you. The Sheriff is back and urgently wants to see you!"

At these words, Christine froze in horror.

"The Sheriff is back in Nottingham!"

Adrenaline shot through her, almost knocking her to the ground.

"Are you all right, love?" asked Guy, noting her pale face. "The Sheriff is in Nottingham! We did not expect him back so soon, but it is for the best! I'll speak with him right away," he ran his hand through her hair and kissed her forehead. "I'll be back soon! Wait for me here."

Christine grabbed at his arm, trying to stop him, but her body wouldn't obey. Her legs were shaking and numb; her pulse was pounding in her temples. Gathering all her strength, she ran after him.

"Guy, please, don't go," she pleaded, having caught up with him on the stairs. "I have to tell you something important!"

"I think I'd like to hear that too!" a hoarse, nasty voice spoke from the top of the stairs. "But let's create for our Lady a more comfortable environment for a conversation, shall we?" The Sheriff's lips stretched into a sinister, cold-blooded smile. "Guards!" he yelled. "Please, take Miss Hawk to the dungeon!"

Chapter 20:
The Escape

"I told you! I warned you! Did I not warn you?!" the Sheriff thundered inside his room, covering the distance from the wall to the door and back with his short legs.

Gisborne stood by the window with his arms folded across his chest, silently watching as the sun made its routine descent behind Sherwood Forest. Breathing loudly, he was trying to silence the feelings that raged inside him, wanting to break free.

"Gisborne! Would you care to say something, eh?" the Sheriff yelled as he stopped right behind him.

Guy gritted his teeth tightly. He took a deep painful breath and, trying to keep an indifferent face, turned to the man who so persistently demanded his attention.

"What do you want me to say, your grace?" he squeezed through clenched teeth and lowered his head in a respectful bow.

"Well, have the decency to say something, at least!" the Sheriff blurted out. "I have been talking to you and circling around this room for the past few hours and you could not care less!"

"Then, perhaps, your grace, must be very tired," Guy said indifferently, bowed his head once again and turned back to the window.

"What! How dare you!" the Sheriff started to rage again but stopped, noting the state his deputy was in. "There, there, come, sit here."

Gisborne obeyed unquestioningly. The Sheriff sat him down in his big throne-like chair and stood behind him. His hands lay on Guy's shoulders.

"Hurts, huh?" he said, leaning closer to his ear.

Gisborne was silent, only his cheekbones clenched tighter. His body was as tense as a cord, ready to snap at any moment.

"Well, well, my boy, I warned you, women are contagious..." Wesley whispered into his ear, and started to massage his shoulders, first slowly but gradually increasing the pressure. "I know it hurts... You can feel the cold metal of a blade twisting in your back, piercing right through you..."

Guy closed his eyes. The pain was unbearable. He still could not believe what the Sheriff had told him about his trip to London and his meeting with Prince John. Now it was clear why he had not wasted any time with his return.

"All this time... All this time when she smiled at you, she laughed at you behind your back!" circling Guy, like Eden's snake in the apple tree, the Sheriff continued to whisper into his ear. "She betrayed you... all this time flirting with you, she mocked you."

His fingers tightened their grip, digging deep into Guy's shoulders, adding a physical pain to the unbearable suffering of his soul. Gisborne groaned in pain. His rapid breathing become more frequent, his nostrils flared with each new breath, his eyes filled with hatred.

"Yes! Yes, my boy..." encouraged the Sheriff. "You are beginning to feel it... Lies! Deceit! Betrayal!" the words, one after another flew out of his crooked-tooth mouth. "She will pay for this. You know, she will have to pay for her lies," like a swamp adder, he hissed into the ears of his deputy. "What do you want to do with her now, hm?"

"Oh, she will pay for her treachery!" breathed out Gisborne, getting up to his feet.

The job was done! Wesley knew what strings to pull far too well. It was not the first time he had played with Gisborne's mind.

"Good!" he said, releasing his grip on Guy's shoulders. "Go! Go, my boy, and enjoy it thoroughly!"

*****

In the deepest bowels of the castle, exhausted, Christine sunk down to the damp floor of the prison cell. Her calm exterior was deceptive, everything raged inside her.

By order of the Sheriff, the guards grabbed her and dragged into the dungeon. She tried to resist, tried to get her footing, she tried to call for Guy's help, but as if paralysed, he remained indifferent and motionless.

She had spent the first half hour banging on the bars of her cell, appealing to his common sense, but beyond the dungeon, her cries would not reach him. God alone knew what the Sheriff had told him, what stories he had invented, which mortal sins he had accused her of. The rest of the time she was in prison she tried to figure out how to get out of this situation.

There were no windows. To her right and left were similar cells, but they were empty – there were no other prisoners in this part of the castle. An armed guard was sitting next to the inner door. While she was dragged in, she had seen two more outside.

"Even if I manage to get out of the cell and neutralise the first guard, how would I cope with those outside? The men are well armed."

She again tried to shake the door but it would not budge.

Despair began to take over. For a moment, she closed her eyes and buried her face into her hands.

"Think! Think!" she ordered herself. *"There must be a way out!"*

There was a faint noise behind the door, and then it opened.

"The Sheriff has ordered me to bring some bread and water to the prisoner," she heard a familiar female voice.

With a clay cup and a bowl in her hands, Lady Marian Norton appeared on the threshold of the dungeon. Her face was calm.

"Come in," the guard stepped aside. "Be quick."

While Marian was walking down the stairs, her face was expressionless but, as soon as she came closer to Christine's cell, her feelings broke through.

"What happened?" she whispered, clinging to the cell bars. "I could not believe my ears when I heard the Sheriff. He says that you are a spy and accuses you of treason!"

"Marian, I'm not a spy! I swear it! I know it all sounds very strange, but please..."

She wasn't able to finish. The door opened again and the Sheriff's deputy walked in. His heavy steps echoed loudly in the silence of the prison as he quickly ran down the stairs.

"Lady Marian," he raised one eyebrow. She was the last person he expected to see in this part of the castle. "What are you doing here? You know you cannot be here," he said sternly.

"Sir Guy, I... I... I just wanted to take some food to my father," she managed at last.

"Pray, do not tell me that you got lost again," he sneered. Marian did not sound convincing.

"I guessed I must have taken a wrong turn," she murmured quietly, trying to smile.

"You should not be here! Get out, unless you want to end up in the neighbouring cell," said Gisborne roughly.

"Find Robin!" whispered Christine as Marian was preparing to leave the dungeon.

Marian nodded almost imperceptibly and hurried off before Gisborne got a chance to fulfil his threat.

"Leave us," he ordered the guard, as soon as Marian had disappeared behind the closed door.

"Guy," clinging to the bars, Christine breathed out as soon as they were alone. Gisborne said nothing. He held his head up high. His blue eyes scalded Christine with their ice-cold gaze. "Guy, what's going on? What does this all mean?" She could not believe the sudden change in him.

"How dare you speak to me!" he snapped.

"What?" Christine was taken aback, she had never seen him like this before.

"You betrayed me! You lied to me!" in the shadows of the prison, his eyes were blazing with anger.

"What do you mean, I betrayed you? What have I done?" she pleaded.

"You said you were sent by Prince John!" he said, barely able to control his anger.

"No!" protested Christine. "I have never said that!"

Guy looked at her blankly.

"I never said that," Christine peered at him through the bars of the cell. "The Sheriff suggested it... I had no choice but to play along!"

"You've lied to me!" he raged. "All this time you have been lying to me!"

"I was not lying!" she cried out. "Well, I was not exactly honest, I do not deny that, but I have never lied to you!"

Guy looked at her, still unable to make any sense of her words.

"You are accused of spying and conspiring against the Sheriff," he said after a pause, his voice was stern, matching his gaze.

"Conspiring against the Sheriff?" she repeated. "What are you talking about?"

"All this time, you were trying to gain my trust. All this time you have been passing information to our enemies! Who are you spying for, hm? Robin or perhaps for Richard himself?" he paused for a moment and then continued. "Now I understand why you refused to go to the Holy Land, you had a job to spy on us here!"

"What the hell are you talking about? Have you gone completely mad?" Christine broke down. "What has that snake told you? What kind of crazy stories has he made up?" she was beginning to lose her temper. "This is exactly what I've been telling you. As soon as he returned, everything is as it was before! It has been just a few hours since he returned to Nottingham, and you, again, are turning into a monster! What's wrong with you Guy? Do you really think..." she shook her head disappointedly. "I guess I was right, people never change."

For some time, Gisborne was silent, absently looking ahead.

"Just now, she's admitted that she is not an assassin, and was not sent by the Prince... Who is she, and what is she doing here? What does this all mean?" After a long pause Guy spoke again, "Do you know what the most serious crime is?" he did not wait for her reply, answering for her. "Betrayal! I trusted you!"

"Betrayal?" echoed Christine. "I do hope that the Sheriff provided sufficient evidence of my guilt, and thoroughly explained what exactly my crime is. You keep talking about betrayal, but have not yet stated what it is that I have done."

"Who do you work for?" he said, not paying attention to her words. "Who do you spy for? Who are your accomplices?" one question after another fell from his lips.

"I don't work for anyone," Christine said angrily.

"Who do you work for?" Gisborne asked again. "What is your real name?"

"You know my real name!"

"Who do you work for? If you will not speak..." he paused.

"Then what?" she blurted, horror froze in her eyes. "Are you going to torture me? Like you did with Allan?"

"How does she know about Allan? Could it be that the Sheriff is right, and she is indeed associated with outlaws?" he shuddered at the thought.

"What is he doing with you?" the expression on her face changed; her voice became softer. "I saw the real you! This isn't you!"

A shadow of doubt crept over his face.

"Who do you work for?" he asked, yet again.

Guy turned to the door. He couldn't look at her, he could not see her eyes pleading with him. He loved her more than anything in this world, but the pain inflicted by the lies and deceit fabled by the Sheriff was much stronger.

"Do you want to hear the truth?" she asked suddenly. In the flash of a moment, her face became very serious. "I can tell you the truth."

Guy turned to face her.

"But I'm not sure you will be able to handle the truth. Even I no longer understand what is happening," said Christine holding his gaze.

Guy tensed. In his heart, he wanted to hear the truth but was afraid that what she might say would confirm the accusations of the Sheriff and her betrayal.

Christine did not take her eyes off him. She knew she would not be able to get through to him unless she told him the truth. Time or no time, she may never get another chance to do it – the Sheriff was serious in his intentions.

"I live in London," she began. "Is that what you want to hear, huh? I work for a man called Philip Laferi, I have told you about him. I work for a company "Laferi and Partners". I am not an assassin, nor am I a spy! I am a barrister, a lawyer, I defend people in court! I live in Kingston, it's one of the boroughs of London... but I think its name is somewhat different now," she frowned trying to recall the ancient name of her hometown. "Chingestune... or Kingeston... oh God I can't remember... Never mind, you should've heard of it – it's an ancient place where some of the Saxon Kings were crowned... But of course, it's very different in my time."

Guy stared at her blankly. What she was saying made absolutely no sense. Seeing his confused face, Christine took a deep breath. The time had come for her to tell him her true history.

"I was born in London, on the twenty-first of April, in the year one thousand..." she paused trying to cope with her overwhelming feelings, "one thousand nine hundred and eighty-five..." she paused, seeing how his face changed. "I was born 800 years from now. In my time, London is vast and has millions of people living in it. England, Scotland, Wales and Northern Ireland are not at war with one another, there is only one queen, and everyone is happily and peacefully living together as one great United Kingdom..."

Wide-eyed, Gisborne continued to stare at her. She did not look crazy, yet what she was saying did not make any sense.

"I know it sounds very strange, but please believe me because I'm telling you the truth!" her big blue eyes begged him to trust her. "I wanted to tell you, I swear! Even today several times, but I was afraid... I was not sure how you would rea..."

She could not finish. The heavy door of the dungeon opened and the short figure of the Sheriff of Nottingham appeared at the top of the stairs.

"I have decided to come down and check on you, my lovebirds," he laughed. "Did you manage to get anything interesting out of our guest here, Gizzy?" he asked, giving Christine a cold stare.

"No," muttered Guy, still trying to make sense of her words.

"Well, that's a pity. It will be a great loss," Wesley folded his hands in prayer and lifted his eyes to the ceiling. He stood there for a while, muttering something quietly, and then spoke again. "Well, will you do it? Or shall I, just for the occasion?" he said turning to his deputy. "Come, come, don't be shy. For the crimes..." the Sheriff patted him on the shoulder encouragingly.

"For the crimes committed against the Sheriff and the state..." spoke Gisborne. He held his head high. His face did not express any emotion. He spoke the words, which he knew by heart, for he had spoken them so many times before. "For the crimes committed against the Sheriff and the state, for the treachery and betrayal, you are sentenced... to death," it took him some time to say the last words.

"What?! Have you gone completely mad! I'm not a spy!" Christine protested.

"You will be hanged tomorrow at sunset," he added quietly and turned to leave.

"Tomorrow?" her emotions got the better of her. "Why wait till tomorrow? Perhaps the honourable Sir Guy of Gisborne will do us the honours, take his big sword and kill me right here and now?" her voice broke into a cry. "Guy, what's going on with you?" her fingers gripped the cold metal bars of the cell, she looked at him, her large eyes were trying to get through to his senses. "Just a few hours ago, you asked me to be your wife..."

"Wife!?" whistled the Sheriff. "I think I came back just in time. You will thank me later, my boy," he winked at his deputy.

"You are so much better than this! I saw the real you. Do not let him..."

"Blahdy-blahdy-blah!" the Sheriff mocked her and made a face. "Come, before I burst into tears from this charade," he pushed Gisborne to the exit. "And you, my dear, are a very good actor!"

All her efforts were in vain. Christine helplessly sunk down to the wet floor of the prison cell. Her last hope remained with Marian. Would she be able to reach Robin in time?

*****

"What's the matter Gizzy?" asked the Sheriff, as they climbed out of the dungeon.

Standing on the balcony, Guy greedily inhaled the cold night air. He tried to pull himself together but his feelings overwhelmed him, his head was spinning from his disoriented thoughts.

"Pray, do not tell me that you have fallen for her tricks?" the Sheriff looked at him incredulously. "You know, women cannot be trusted... Take your leper girlfriend, Lady Marian, although I must say this one is a much better act!"

Guy was silent, still trying to digest what he just heard. What she had said seemed unbelievable to him.

"Could it be that she was telling the truth?"

Many times, before, he had noticed the strangeness in her words and behaviour, and the comments about him belonging to this time, as if she belonged to another...

"This is impossible!" he tried to persuade himself.

As much as the Sheriff tried to convince him otherwise, Guy still refused to believe that what had happened between him and Christine was a lie.

"Your grace," he turned to the Sheriff. "I would like to speak with her once again."

"Whatever for?" the Sheriff looked at him with surprise. "We know that she is not the one whom she claimed to be. What else do you want to know? Well, come-come, you did not tell me, what were you up to while I was away? You can skip the marrying bit, I already know that," he laughed in his disgusting voice.

"But think," insisted Gisborne, "you have caught her off guard, she is scared... No matter how skilful she might be in her intrigues, she is a woman and vulnerable," he gave the Sheriff his most charming smile. "I think I can get her to talk, but please allow me to take her to Locksley."

"To Locksley? Why, is the prison cell not good enough for you? I must agree, not the most romantic of places for a date but the most suitable for the occasion," he laughed again.

"Exactly, but she is different. While you were away, I was able to get to know her. I'm sure that using my charm and her feelings for me, I can squeeze more information out of her."

"Feelings, you say," the Sheriff started to pace gallery back and forth.

His footsteps echoed in the stillness of the night. He, of course, wanted to finish with her once and for all, without going into specific details, but his natural human curiosity prevailed.

"Very well," he said, at last, rubbing his hands. "Only mind you!" he took Gisborne by the lapels of his jacket and pulled him closer. The Sheriff's eyes gleamed in the night. "No tricks! At sunset, she will return here, or, you will take her place," he made a gesture with his hand, throwing an imaginary noose over his deputy's neck.

Gisborne knew that look, more than once he had witnessed this silent promise. He said nothing, only bowed humbly and hurried into the dungeon of the castle.

*****

All the way from Nottingham Castle to Locksley Christine was silent.

She had not uttered a word from the moment the two guards took her out of the cell and walked her outside, where she was put in a closed carriage. One of the guards took his place with her inside the cart. He sat across from her, pointing his long spear at her chest.

She could not see what was going on outside the wagon, but it was not difficult for her to recognise the heavy footsteps as they approached the cart and the quiet jingle of a sword as Gisborne mounted his stallion.

"Get a couple of torches," in the stillness of the night his voice sounded menacing, "we don't want any surprises on the road."

"Yes, Sir," an obedient voice replied to him.

Christine heard as quick, short footsteps approached the cart from the other side.

"Did you hear me? No tricks," she shuddered upon hearing the Sheriff's disgusting voice. "Remember, Gisborne, you are my right hand..." at first, the voice was loud and could be heard from afar, but as it moved closer with each step, it grew quieter. "You're my right hand, Gisborne," now the voice was very close. "If you want to get ahead in this life and to achieve a good position, I have to be sure that I can trust you!" he finished almost in a whisper. "I am waiting for your return at sunset, otherwise, well, you know…"

Guy didn't answer. The wagon swayed and slowly rolled down the stony road.

Christine couldn't see anything but, by the sounds that surrounded her, she knew that they had left Nottingham, and had moved onto a country road.

Her journey to medieval England was ending exactly as it had begun just over a month ago. Accompanied by a rider in black, she was taken away, into the unknown.

They drove straight for a long time, and then the cart turned left.

"Are we going to Locksley? What for?! What do they want from me?"

Christine could only hope that Marian could get to Robin in time.

*****

When they reached the village, the cart drove up to the manor and stopped at the entrance. By the time the soldiers pulled Christine out of the wagon, Gisborne was nowhere to be seen. They took her into the house and, leaving her alone in the room, went outside to guard the exit.

With an expression darker than storm clouds, Gisborne entered the room. Not saying a word, he came inside and locked the door behind him. He looked at her. His bitter glare made Christine's heart freeze. She spoke first.

"Is this really necessary?" she asked quietly, raising her hands, chained by heavy cuffs.

"It's a precaution. I've seen what you can do," he replied coldly. "Whether I take them off or not, depends on how you intend to behave."

"I'm not going to attack you," she shook her head at his official tone, "I am too tired to even argue with you. What do you want from me?"

"I want you to tell me the truth. Speak, I'm listening," he said, leaning against the door in his favourite pose, his hands entwined across his chest.

"I have already told you everything, whether you believe me or not, I don't care. I just can't understand why you've brought me here. If, by the order of the Sheriff, you are going to torture me, prison would have been a far better place."

"I'm not going to torture you!" he snapped. "I want to know the truth!" throwing her a stern look, Gisborne started pacing the room. "I asked the Sheriff to let me bring you here. I was hoping that here you would tell me the truth," he looked into her eyes.

He came closer and unfastened the shackles. With a rattling noise, they dropped to the floor. He grabbed her firmly by the shoulders.

"Don't you see? I'm trying to save you!" he caught her gaze, but her eyes expressed nothing.

"Trying to save me? I don't think so," said Christine, her voice was cold. "If you were trying to save me, I wouldn't be here. The only person you are trying to save right now is yourself! You hope that I will say something that would confirm your suspicions of my betrayal, and then tomorrow, with a free conscience, you will watch as I am strung up on the gallows. You hope that there will be at least one fewer ghost in your sleepless nights. I don't think so!" Christine broke from his hold and walked away from him, leaving Guy standing in the middle of the room. "I have told you the truth! I understand that it all sounds more than unbelievable, but how could someone make up all of this?"

Christine looked at him, trying to see behind this mask, but, absorbed in his own thoughts, Guy stood motionless.

"I don't know how I ended up in your time," she hesitated. "I do know now, but don't know why and what for... Don't you think that I was in the same state of shock as you are? To find oneself in an unknown time, in this barbaric place!" her emotions overwhelmed her. "The Sheriff mistook me for someone else... What else could I have done? On that first day, when you came into my room, I thought you had come to kill me, just as some moments before, I had watched you kill an unarmed man..." she spoke desperately, trying to get through to him as if she was trying to get through a giant wall built by John Wesley. "I had no choice but to play along with this charade... What would have happened to me, if I'd said that I wasn't the one you mistook me for?"

At these words, Guy looked up at her, the fear in his eyes answered for him.

"Exactly!" she continued. "I would have already been hung. I had no choice but to play along."

"There's always a choice," he said quietly.

"Unfortunately, there was none for me! From the first day, all my thoughts were about how I could get home... Then the Sheriff sent me to Locksley and I began to know you better. I fell in love with you..." she tried to look him in the eye. "I didn't plan for it, it just happened, but I don't regret it... I don't regret anything."

He listened to her but dared not raise his eyes to hers. Gisborne stood staring at the dying fire. Christine went over to him and turned his face to hers.

"I do not regret anything," she said again, then moved closer and tried to kiss him.

Guy did not push her away, but avoided her kiss.

"Do not think that you will be able to fool me again!" he said. "All this time you have lied to me! How can I believe you now?"

"For the hundredth time, I did not lie to you. I just didn't tell you the whole truth!"

Despite all her efforts, it was impossible to get through to him. The Sheriff had done his job well. The seeds of doubt and mistrust had been planted in Guy's heart, and had now broken through to the surface, bearing fruit.

"You betrayed me!" he repeated yet again.

And then Christine lost her temper and let her anger out.

"Oh, Milord! Just look at him, he has been betrayed. You are surrounded by people who tell you everything but the truth!"

"What are you talking about?" he looked at her blankly.

"Do not make such a face! You know exactly what I'm talking about!" she raised her eyebrows. "Your dear Lady Marian is using you and your feelings for her, to ferret out information and send it to Robin. Your right hand, Allan, is well aware of that, and besides, he knows the exact location of Robin's camp, but will never tell you! And your master, the Sheriff of Nottingham. Oh, he is worthy of a separate discussion," Christine looked at Guy. "You're lecturing me about honesty and loyalty; ask the Sheriff who killed your mother."

"What?!" he breathed. *"How does she know all this?"* What do you mean, ask the Sheriff? How would he know?"

"Oh, he knows, alright!" Christine evaded a direct answer, still not daring to tell him the truth.

"Stop playing with me!" Gisborne grabbed her by the shoulders and gave her a little shake.

"Let me go!" Christine struggled to free herself from his hold.

"You tell me the truth right now or I will..."

"Or what? You'll kill me? I was so wrong about you, noble Sir Guy. I thought I saw the real you, the alive you. How mistaken I was. You have long been dead, and your place is among your ghosts," she shook her head.

"Who killed my mother?" he uttered quietly, releasing her shoulders.

He raised his eyes to Christine; there was fear – he was afraid to hear the answer.

"Your master, John Wesley, the Sheriff of Nottingham," she said quietly, "but I think you have guessed that already. If you do not believe me, ask your sister."

"Marian, Allan, Wesley, Juliana how does she know all of this?" like a bolt of lightning, her words struck Gisborne.

"Whatever fate awaits me now," she spoke again, "I will accept it, but do not let him destroy you as he destroyed your life. Don't let him kill what little humanity is still left in you!" she pleaded, a lone tear slipped from her eye and rolled down her cheek. Christine walked away from him. "Take me upstairs," she spoke to one of the soldiers guarding the exit. "I will be in my room until it is time to return to Nottingham."

With that she was gone. Gisborne was alone, helplessly standing in the middle of the room with a dying fire as his only companion.

*****

The fire had long died, the ashes grown cold, and the candles burned down. The room was cold and damp, the dawn of a new day was colouring the sky.

Guy was alone in the dark room, but did not feel the cold. His body was exhausted, but he didn't want to sleep. His soul was torn into thousands of pieces.

Over and over again he was thinking about her words. In his thoughts, he returned back to the events of recent weeks. Like putting together a large puzzle, piece by piece he was trying to construct the whole picture. He found he still couldn't believe her but he couldn't find any other explanation, no matter how crazy or absurd it may be.

How does she know all this, about Marian, Allan, but most importantly about his mother? How could he have been so blind, not seeing what was happening in front of his own eyes?

Several times, he wanted to go to her, but could not force himself to make the first move. What would he say? How would he look her in the eyes, after all that he had done today? He demanded something from her that he himself could not give her – trust. She had every right to hate him now, she must hate him... But he couldn't ignore the flame that was slowly burning inside his chest.

"Sir Guy," a soft female voice called his name.

Gisborne blinked a few times, as if waking from a long sleep.

"Marian? What? How did you get here?" he asked wearily, turning towards the voice. "You know what the Sheriff would do if he found out that you had left the castle. Why did you come?"

"I have come to ask you..."

"Come to ask me," he interrupted her grinning. "What do you want to ask of me?"

"I came to tell you that you are making a mistake about Christine," she sank to the floor beside him. "Things are not as they seem. In fact," she took his hand, "as strange as it may sound, please believe her. Everything she says is true!"

"Is everything that she has said the truth?" he asked.

"Yes," said Marian.

"Even the fact that you were using my feelings and feeding information to Robin Hood?" he raised his eyebrows.

Her face flushed deep red.

"Yes..." she replied timidly.

"That my faithful servant, Allan, knows about this and covers up for you?"

"This is true as well, Milord" said Marian.

She knew that by confirming this she would likely be putting the noose around her own neck, but she had no choice. If she chose to deny it, Gisborne would never have believed Christine.

"She's right," he smiled wearily. "I am surrounded by traitors and hypocrites!"

"Whatever she told you, Sir Guy, it's all true," she caught his eye. "You must listen to me."

Taking him by the hand and holding his gaze, Marian told him everything she knew about Christine and her crossing into their time, about her meeting with Robin Hood, and the search for the cave. Guy listened in disbelief. What she was saying had no logical explanation but at the same time, strangely, put things in their own places.

"How do you know all this?" he asked, as Marian finished her story.

"Robin told me," she said calmly.

"Robin?!" repeated Guy, surprised. "Even if all of this is true, why did she trust him, but did not say anything to me?"

"I don't know," she shrugged, "perhaps she was afraid that you would not believe her, and everything would turn out exactly as it is now."

"Yes... I think you are right, Marian..." he muttered, stood up and began pacing the room. "She did not lie to me!" his eyes sparkled with hope. "I cannot believe it! She really loves me! I must to talk to her!" he cried, running out of the room.

"Sir Guy!" Marian hurried after him in a vain attempt to stop him.

Gisborne ran up the stairs taking a few steps at a time.

"Stand aside!" he commanded the soldier guarding Christine's room.

He pulled the handle, trying to get in, but the door was locked from the inside.

"Christine! Open the door, please! I need to talk to you," he banged loudly on the door, but on the other side, there was no answer, no movement.

"Sir Guy," having caught up with him, Marian caught his arm, just as he was about to pound on the door once again.

Unable to understand what was going on, Guy stared at her absently.

"She's not there," Marian said quietly.

"What? What do you mean she is not there? Christine, open the door!" once again, he banged on the door.

"Guy," Marian took his hand, "she is not there," she repeated looking into his eyes. "Robin is taking her back to the crossing."

"What?" breathed out Gisborne. "No! She can't leave!"

He ran out of the house.

"Where did he take her?" were his only words as he jumped into the saddle.

*****

"I think it's time to say goodbye!" said Christine when she and Robin came out of the cave.

Bewildered, the forest outlaw still could not believe what he had just seen.

"It's incredible!" he said, a little lost. "Now I understand what you meant! I'm not sure I would have been able to resist the temptation."

"I hope you would," a little sadly, Christine smiled. "Trust me, you do not want to end up in my time."

"Is it that bad?" he asked.

"No, not that bad," she said, "just different, very different."

"But are you sure that the passage works in the opposite direction? How do you know that you will get home?" he asked suddenly.

"I don't," Christine shook her head. "But I don't think I have any other choice but to go through the light and hope that on the other side..."

She was suddenly sad. In her mind, she knew she had no place in this time, but her heart ached at the thought of the man she had left in Locksley. She felt a strong moaning pain inside her chest knowing that she would never see him again; would never see his eyes, his smile; would never hear his soft, deep, velvety voice, whispering her name; would never again feel his strong arms holding her close to him.

She thrust these thoughts away, and reached her hand out to Robin.

"Thank you, thank you again for everything, Robin!" she said.

"Good luck! I hope you will be able to find your way home."

Christine hugged him and, having said her goodbyes, took a deep breath, and turned to the cave entrance. Suddenly she stopped.

"Robin, can I ask you for a favour?"

"Yes, ma'am," he said cheerfully, predicting what she might ask of him.

"I wanted to ask you," she began a little timidly. "Not today, perhaps tomorrow, or when it all is settled down... Please tell him..."

She couldn't finish. Somewhere close by they heard the loud neighing of a horse and the sound of a struggle. Then, for a moment, everything went silent. The silence was followed by a loud noise that ripped through the quiet and serenity of a morning Sherwood. It was not a cry, but the roar of a wounded beast.

Fearful, Christine looked at Robin. The voice was familiar to them both.

Not hesitating for a second, they ran in the direction of the sound. Jumping over fallen trees and trying to avoid low branches, they rushed through the undergrowth as fast as they could. Guy's stallion galloped past them, almost knocking Robin to the ground – it was not a good sign.

They ran to a small clearing. What appeared before them pleased Robin to some extent, however Christine stopped and gasped for air, horrified at the image before her.

On the ground, in a pile of dry leaves lay Gisborne, an arrow stuck in his back. Growling in pain, he struggled to get up several times, but each and every time he fell down again helplessly, releasing a deep groan. His face was twisted with pain.

Above him stood a middle-aged man. Christine thought she had seen him before but couldn't remember where. In the man's hands was Gisborne's sword. The man held it up high with the clear intention of killing his enemy. He was resolute but at some point hesitated – it was one thing to shoot an arrow at an armed rider but he couldn't plunge the sword into the wounded, helpless man lying at his feet.

Gathering all his strength and courage, he raised the sword above his head ready to make his final, fatal blow.

"Stop! Wait!" the words flew out of Christine's mouth.

The man didn't immediately realise what was happening. He was so consumed with his act that he hadn't noticed Robin and Christine enter the clearing; he had hoped to settle his accounts with Gisborne without prying eyes,

Still holding the sword up high, he slowly turned toward the voice.

"Stop!" Christine repeated.

"What?" Robin could not hide his surprise. Raising his eyebrows, he looked at her. "I'd love to see that..."

"Robin, stop it, please!" said Christine, with a plea in her eyes. "Do you know this man?" she whispered.

Robin nodded.

"Luke," he turned to the man in front of them, "whatever has provoked you to this, believe me, what you are about to do, will not solve your problem."

With undisguised hatred in his voice and anguish in his face, he sobbed, "He killed my son!"

"What?! When?!" Christine was taken aback. "Guy, is this true?"

"No!" groaned Gisborne, wincing in pain.

"It was him, who took my son from Locksley. It is because of him, my son was put in prison! Because of him, he was killed. It's all because of him!!!" shouted Luke, still trying to hold the sword high above his head.

"Let him go, please," said Christine, trying to speak calmly. "Once you cross that line, you will not be able to live in peace. The knowledge that you have killed a man will haunt you forever."

"He is not a man!" he shouted, tightly clutching the sword in his hands.

"Do you think the Sheriff will forgive you for the murder of his deputy?" once again Christine spoke, trying desperately to reason with the man. "He, to some extent, relates to Gisborne as to a son... He will never forgive you for this! Who will take care of your family, if you are gone?"

Luke lowered the sword a little – there were tears in his eyes. He couldn't kill a man. He had long planned it and thought that he had considered every detail. He thought he would be able to avenge his son, but he could not take a human life, even the life of such a ruthless murderer as Guy of Gisborne.

While Christine was trying to talk him out of the intended act, with small and silent steps, Robin cautiously moved towards him. For some time, all three stood silent; not moving. Then, Christine spoke again.

"You've got the blood of your enemy, he is wounded..."

Talking to Luke, her eyes were constantly on Guy as she was trying to assess his condition. Christine was well aware that, regardless of the outcome of these negotiations, they would have to act quickly if they were to save Gisborne's life.

"Maybe he won't recover from these wounds," she said. "Let the heavens decide his fate. Don't let this sin be on your conscious."

The man could no longer hold back his tears. Hard as he tried, he still held the sword high up, but his hands were shaking. Robin, sensing that the end was close, took a few cautious steps in his direction.

"Luke..." said Robin.

The villager, so consumed by thoughts of his revenge, did not pay attention to Robin, who managed to get very close unnoticed and was now standing right behind him. Startled, Luke winced and lowered the sword slightly, but he was still was not ready to let it go.

"Luke," Robin spoke again, "she is right. Do you want to teach him a lesson? Then, spare his life! Let him live and let this day be forever a reminder of his actions."

The man continued to lower the sword; it was too heavy for him to hold and there was little strength in him left. He sighed heavily.

"I'm sorry, Jane," he said quietly, as if, in his head, he was addressing his wife. "I'm sorry, but for the sake of our son, I have to do this!"

The man raised the sword high, and with a loud cry of hopelessness and desperation, brought it down on Gisborne.

Chapter 21:
The Last Goodbye

The wild cry thundered through Sherwood Forest – a terrifying, deafening cry that could only be produced by a father, holding the body of his dead child in his hands.

What followed next happened so quickly and was so well-coordinated that one would have thought that these people's actions were pre-planned and rehearsed down to the second.

With the agility of a cat, Robin leapt forward and caught Luke's hands, grasping them tightly, not allowing him to lower the sword to pierce his prey through. Fear flashed in the villager's eyes. In an instant, he realised what he was doing; he was becoming that which he hated. A murderer! The sword became heavier in his grip; his body was rigid but his arms were losing their strength.

In the same moment, Christine ran to Guy, grabbing him by his jacket; straining to pull him aside. His great height and bulk worked against her but, sensing her intention, Guy tried his best to help. With a deep groan, he managed to lift himself off the ground. Together they created enough momentum to move his body out of the threat of direct impact.

Robin lost the struggle to stop the descent of the sword, which came crashing down, plunging itself deep into the soil.

Luke dropped to his knees next to the weapon. He could no longer hold back his tears and, burying his face in his hands, wept like a child.

Resting his hands on his knees, still trying to catch his breath, Robin stood right behind him.

"You've made the right choice," Robin patted him on the shoulder, and added, looking into his tear-stained eyes, "Come, I'll walk you to the village," he helped the man up on his feet. "I'll take him to the village and come back," he said, shooting a quick glance in the direction of Christine and Guy, who still lay motionless on the ground in a pile of dry leaves.

No one answered him.

"Just begging you lovebirds, no fighting and none of your naughty business," he said in a slightly parental tone. "I know the two of you!" he smiled.

There was still no answer but Christine had raised her hand in reply. Taking Luke by the elbow, Robin went in the direction of the nearby village.

Pinned to the ground by a heavy male body, Christine lay panting. Her wide eyes looked far ahead to the heavenly blueness yet she could not see anything before her. Her head was too busy, trying to process what had just happened to enjoy the surroundings and the beauty of the morning.

Her heart was pounding in her ears in a hectic rhythm. As Gisborne's body had crushed her to the ground, she hurt her coccyx, and could now feel a nasty ache spread through her body.

Guy lay on top of her yet hadn't moved at all since Christine had pulled him away from the blow. His face was only millimetres from hers but she couldn't see him. He lay with his nose buried in her neck, his dark hair stuck to his forehead. Only his heavy breathing indicated that he was still alive.

Trying to get his attention, Christine made a sound as if clearing her throat. Guy didn't say anything.

"Hey, are you alive there?" sounding a little annoyed, she tapped him on the shoulder.

He was silent. The only answer she received was a barely perceptible movement of his head. He was too weak for anything else.

"Right..." she muttered, fumbling underneath him. "I understand that you are probably enjoying the moment and want to prolong the pleasure for as long as possible, but..." she would not give up her failing attempts to free herself. "You are bloody heavy!"

Still muttering something softly and grunting as she moved, she began to crawl out from under him. Gisborne moaned in pain, her movements causing him great discomfort.

Having finally managed to free herself, Christine sat beside him. She leaned her back against a tree, spread her legs wide, closed her eyes and sat there for a moment, enjoying the feeling of freedom. Gisborne still did not move.

She looked at him and froze as she saw the arrow that stuck out from his back. She had completely forgotten about it!

"Guy," she called and touched his shoulder, "how serious is that?" there were notes of concern in her voice when he again did not respond to her question. "Guy, speak to me!" Christine begged.

Gisborne stirred a little, letting her know that he was still conscious and could hear her, but he could not answer – his breathing was ragged.

Christine leaned in closer and gently touched the arrow; Guy didn't make a sound.

"How serious is your injury?" she asked again. "Can you feel it?" Gathering all of her courage, she pressed a little harder on the arrow.

"No," Guy answered in a croaked voice.

"And like this?" she pressed her fingers around the place where the shaft of the arrow stuck out through his clothes.

"I feel your touch..." he said, swallowing hard.

"The pain, do you feel any pain?" she got angry.

"No," he uttered quietly.

"I don't even know why I'm still here with you," she murmured angrily. "If it weren't for you, I would have probably been home by now, sipping coffee in my garden..."

"Then why did you come back?" struggling through each word, he asked quietly.

"I don't know..." she said thoughtfully and slid her hand under his collar.

Slowly, she moved her hand lower and further down under his shirt, carefully examining the surface of his back with her fingers.

A frown creased her forehead – all seemed fine. She felt no wounds, no dampness of blood – nothing that she had expected to find there. As she reached the place where the arrow had pierced his jacket, she paused for a second gathering her courage, trying to steady her heartbeat, and then, taking a deep breath, she moved her hand down.

"Nothing!" she gasped. "There is nothing!" she repeated again. On the inside of the jacket, she could feel the tip of the arrow as it stuck in the tanned skin. "I do not understand, then why do you," she could not finish, afraid of her own thoughts.

"I did not say... that my wound was on my back," he muttered quietly.

"What?! Why didn't you..."

Only now, her eyes caught the bright scarlet-red spots that adorned her shirt and breeches at her waist.

"Oh no," she could barely manage and jumped up to her feet.

Pacing the distance from one tree to another, Christine tried to think, but her thoughts were running away from her. The bright crimson bloodstains on her shirt clouded her vision and thoughts. She once again looked down at her clothes. Her eyes froze in horror. Guy was bleeding heavily.

By the location and intensity of the stains on her clothes, she could only guess how much blood he could have lost by now and how serious was his injury.

"I need to turn you on your back otherwise..." she paused, afraid to say the words. "Otherwise, you'll bleed to death. Can you hear me?" she added, helplessly trying to keep calm.

Guy moved his head a little, nodding slightly. He said nothing, but Christine felt his body stiffening as he prepared to move.

"On the count of three," she said.

She pulled the arrow from his jacket and got down on her knees beside him. She grabbed him firmly by the shoulder, her other hand was on his hip.

"One... two... three!" she counted quietly and abruptly pulled him over.

A deep groan, which escalated into a wild roar, echoed through Sherwood Forest.

"Are you trying to kill me?" were the first words he said as soon as he was on his back.

"Yes! And would've done it gladly!" Christine retorted. "Oh, I should've just left you here... to God's will."

She was angry, but her anger lasted for only a few seconds. She softened her tone as soon as she saw his pale face.

"I'm trying to help you," she added quietly.

Her voice was stern, but there was no hatred in it. Guy tried to sit up, but she laid a hand on his chest.

"Lie still, I need to examine your wound," she added softly.

Trying to prepare herself for the worst, Christine was quickly undoing his jacket. Her fingers did not obey, slipping over the buckles and rivets smeared with blood. It seemed this simple process took her forever. Finally, she managed to undo them and, taking a deep breath, opened the edges of his jacket.

For a moment, she could not utter a single sound. Christine exhaled slowly and cast a quick glance at the pale face of the man, helplessly lying on the ground. Guy closely followed her expression. She didn't have to say anything; her eyes voiced the words that were stuck in her throat.

Under his jacket, his light shirt was soaked with blood, and now was a deep crimson-red colour. Just above the belt, there was a large cut.

Pulling the shirt up, she tried to get it out from under his belt but her hands slipped on the fabric soaked with blood. She grabbed the shirt by the sides of the cut and ripped it apart, exposing his bloody torso.

"Oh, my God..." she whispered quietly.

First, his opponent had aimed for the heart but Guy was able to repel this attack. On the left side of his chest was a scratch. The few drops of blood that were fresh some time ago had already dried out – it was no longer a threat. On the right side, everything was more serious. This blow Gisborne could not escape. On the right side, under the ribs, the flesh was torn; the deep incised wound was oozing blood.

Unable to speak Christine looked at the wound and then lifted her eyes back to Guy's pale face. Her hand flew up to her mouth; tears flowed from her eyes.

"Is it that bad?" he asked quietly.

"It does not look very promising," she said, swallowing her tears.

She rose to her feet and began to pace back and forth quickly. There was not a moment to lose but she had absolutely no idea what to do in this situation. Every drop of blood was accounted for; every minute could decide his fate. She shot another quick glance at him – one didn't have to be a doctor to realise that they did not have much time.

*****

"Everything is going to be alright," Christine tried to soothe him, although the words were addressed more to herself, than to the man lying on the ground.

She dropped to her knees beside him. Stroking his hair, she was repeating the exact same phrase over and over again.

"I'm not so sure about that," he opened his eyes and looked at her tenderly. "It looks like I have lost this battle with my demons," he said, closing his eyes again.

"No!" she said angrily. "Stop it! I'm sure you've been through much worse."

Delving into her memory, she tried to remember anything of her first aid course: how to assess the condition of the wounded and seriousness of the injury and most importantly, what to do about it. Medicine had never been her strong side, which was probably one of the reasons she was so attracted to Mark, who, in spite of the peculiar nature of his odious character, was an excellent doctor and surgeon.

"Tell me what to do," she turned to Gisborne, but he said nothing.

He lay breathing heavily, his eyes were closed, his chest was rising and falling slowly as he struggled through every breath. His pale face grew even paler.

"We must try and stop the bleeding!" exclaimed Christine, glad she was able to come up with this wonderful idea.

She quickly took off her jacket and shirt, tore off the sleeves and rushed to the stream she had seen close by. She washed her hands, took a bit of water with her, and then ran back to the clearing.

She wiped his face and lips. Feeling a touch of coolness, Guy opened his eyes.

"Everything is going to be alright," she said again, looking into his eyes. "Guy, do you hear me?" He only blinked. "I'll have to leave you for a while, I'll go to the stream and come back," she was trying to catch his wandering gaze, "and then I'll try to bandage your wound... Robin will be back soon, I'm sure he'll know what to do."

She folded her jacket, rolled it tightly and placed it under his head.

She wiped his blood-stained body and several times ran to the water, washing the dirty cloth in the running stream. She took off his belt, tore her shirt into long strips, folded them tightly and pressed them against the open wound. She managed to squeeze the belt under his torso and then pulled it over, fastening a makeshift bandage tightly around his belly.

"It should stop the bleeding a little," she said, as Guy once again whined in pain.

Christine sat down beside him. She pulled her jacket from under his head, made him comfortable on her lap and gently ran her fingers through his hair. No matter how angry she was for what had happened last night, her feelings for him were much stronger.

"You are going to be ok," she said again, brushing the dark curls off his forehead. "Do you hear me? Robin should be back soon," she tried to calm herself. "I hope he will bring help."

"Thank you," Guy opened his eyes. "Thank you for coming back, I know I don't deserve this."

"Don't say that," she replied. "What were you doing here in the first place?"

"I... came... after you," he said, pausing after each word.

"Came after me?" Christine asked. "Whatever for? Pray, do not tell me you wanted to bring me back to the Sheriff?" she smiled.

"No, not like that," he struggled. "I wanted to apologise and..." he paused again, swallowed hard and then continued, "I know that I have no right... and, you should probably hate me right now, but I wanted to ask you, not to leave me."

"You wanted to ask me to stay?!" she asked in surprise. "A few hours ago, you were about to hang me, and then you rush after me to ask me to stay? You have to make up your mind, mister!" she retorted.

"I have. I know what I want," he breathed out.

His cold fingers lay on her hand.

"Really? Are you sure about this? Will you not change your mind again as soon as you cross the threshold of Nottingham Castle?" she could not resist.

"Please, Christine, let me speak. I am afraid I don't have much time," Guy interrupted her. "I was wrong. When you left, I did a lot of thinking," he paused to catch his breath. "It was not so easy to understand and believe in what you'd said but after speaking with Marian everything suddenly made sense. Why did you not just trust me? I am sure if you..." he clenched her hand tighter.

"If I would have told you the truth, is that what you mean? Do you think things would have been different?" she shook her head.

"Please," he paused again, struggling through each word. "Before you came to Nottingham, I was dying, I was almost dead. My body was full of strength but my soul was slowly dying. Drop by drop, life was running away from me with every evil act that I committed for the Sheriff. When my mother died, the whole world turned away from me. There was no one left who would show compassion, who would care for me, who would love me," he paused again, gathering his strength. "At some point, the Sheriff became that person, or so I thought. He did a good job convincing me of that. I was longing for something, yearned for something in my life, not knowing what that was. I wanted to satisfy my carnal desires, but first and foremost to satisfy my ego. It seemed to me then that it was the meaning and purpose of my existence. Everything changed when you came into my life..."

He looked at her, his blue eyes full of tender feelings.

"You brought me back to life. You showed me love that I thought I would never feel again," his hand touched her face. "Christine, I love you! I have never loved anyone before in my life like I love you. My heart is overwhelmed, it feels like it's about to burst," he raised her hand to his dry lips. "I love you. Even if it's the last time that I am destined to say these words..."

"Shh... please do not say that," she tried to calm him.

"I'm glad... I'm glad that these last moments I will spend with you..." he closed his eyes.

His body relaxed and went limp. His breathing became even.

"Please stop talking like this, you are not going to die..." she said, stroking his hair. "You will see, everything will be fine. You will be fine. You will get through this."

"This end was destined for me. Sooner or later I would've had to pay for all the evil that I've done," he opened his eyes, his lips curled into a slight smile. "My demons have finally got me. I have to answer before God for all my sins... but as long as you are with me, I'm not afraid of the end, I don't regret anything..." with a little groan, he pulled her closer and their lips touched in a soft kiss.

"I swear, I wanted to tell you," Christine spoke when he released her lips and went limp in her lap. "I wanted to tell you everything. Yesterday, several times, after I returned to Locksley, but I did not know where to start," her fingers brushed through his hair. "Then at your family estate, when you asked me to stay with you, I didn't know what to say, but not because I don't want to stay with you..." she kissed him and looked into his blue eyes. "Believe me, there is no one in this world who I would've wanted to spend the rest of my days with. I believe, in you, I have found a soul mate. We are so different, but at the same time, we are so much alike, like two halves of one whole," she stroked his hair as she spoke. "I would've loved to stay with you, and under any other circumstances, I wouldn't have given it a second thought, but I cannot! I cannot stay here," she looked around and shook her head.

"Then at least, please, do not leave me until my heart stops beating in my chest..." his cold fingers touched her face. "Will you stay with me?"

"I promise!" Christine smiled, tightening her embrace, holding him closer to her. Tears glistened in her eyes. "I promise I will not leave you until..." she wiped the tears from her cheek. "I will not leave you until I'm sure you will get better." She placed a soft kiss on his dry lips.

"Tell me about your world, about your time," he asked, closing his eyes again.

"I'd love you to see it – my England and my London. I am sure that you would have liked it," Christine smiled.

Listening to the sound of her voice, Guy dozed off. A peaceful smile appeared on his pale face. His breathing was steady and calm.

"Please..." tightly clutching him to her, Christine raised her eyes to the heavens. "I haven't asked you for anything since my mother died... You took her away from me, perhaps there was a reason for that," she was trying to order her thoughts, "but I ask you, let him live! Please! Let him live! Give him strength! Even if I will never see him again, let him live!"

She kissed his damp forehead and closed her eyes. Uncontrollable, heavy tears rolled down her cheeks. She sat silently, slowly rocking him back and forth, holding him close to her.

*****

She didn't know how long she had waited. Her back and legs felt numb and tired. She moistened Guy's lips with a wet cloth, wiped the sweat from his forehead and constantly watched his breathing.

Soon she heard voices from behind the trees. Robin, Little John and Friar Tuck came out into the clearing.

"Robin! Finally! Thank God you're back!" Christine exclaimed. "Have you not brought the doctor?" she asked, looking around.

"I brought John and Tuck," he answered a little confused. "I just met them in the village."

"Robin, he does not need a priest! He needs a doctor!"

"I thought..."

He was about to speak, but Christine did not want to listen.

"Friar, you have an understanding of medicine, don't you? Can you help him?" with a plea in her eyes, she turned to him. "His wound is deep," Christine looked at him. "He needs help!"

"Yes, I understand a little," he replied, bending over Gisborne.

Christine carefully rested Guy's head on the ground and stood up. Gisborne sighed deeply and loudly when the priest began to untie his bandage. His breathing quickened as a spasm of pain swept through his body and reflected on his pale face.

"Well, what do you say?" she asked, when Tuck put the bandage in place and re-fastened the belt.

"We are all in God's hands," he said folding his hands in prayer. "Now, we just need to pray for his soul."

"What?! No!!!" exclaimed Christine. "How can you say that? Robin," she turned to the outlaw, "is there really nobody who can help him?"

Robin did not reply.

"Oh, I understand… There are people who could help, but neither of them would want to help," Christine shook her head. "In this case, you are no better than him!"

"Maybe…" Robin began but paused, the thought that struck him seemed completely insane.

"Maybe, what?" asked Christine, ready to seize any opportunity.

"No, it's a stupid idea," Robin said.

"What, what did you think of?"

"I thought maybe you could take him with you? You know, to your time," Robin asked cautiously.

The idea was not as crazy as it seemed; Christine, herself, had thought of that, but the risk was too great.

"I don't know… I don't even know if I myself will be able to get back, and even if I can, that is no guarantee that he would survive the crossing… No, I cannot take the risk, but, if…" she paused. Her breath quickened. She stared at Robin. "Well, of course! Of course, Robin, how did I not think of it before?" she said, staring off absently in front of her.

Robin blinked a few times and exchanged confused glances with his friends. Whatever insane idea had just slipped into her mind, he had absolutely no clue.

Muttering something quickly under her breath, Christine paced back and forth. Her head began to ache from the overwhelming excitement. For all the time she had known Mark, she had never wanted him to be with her as much as at this very moment.

"Well, of course!" she repeated aloud and laughed. "Robin, if I can get back to my time, there is someone who, I am sure, will be able to help. I will try to bring him here, but I need you to watch him," she nodded her head towards the man lying on the ground. "Get a fire burning! Boil water! Bring something to dress the wound! If I manage to get there and come back, we will have very little time…"

"Alright," Robin replied curtly. "Little John, Friar you go to village, and try to get what she asked for, I will stay here and watch him."

Tuck and Little John looked at each other blankly. They didn't relish the prospect of running around Sherwood in an attempt at saving Gisborne's life. Ignoring them, Christine rushed to Guy.

"Guy... Guy, can you hear me?" she called softly, dropping to her knees beside him.

It took her considerable effort to bring him back to consciousness. He slowly opened his eyes; they were almost transparent; his face was pale and emotionless like a wax mask. He had already accepted his fate.

"I have an idea of how we can fix you!" Christine spoke, not even trying to conceal her excitement. "I have to go... Shh," she did not let him speak, locking her lips with his. "I know, I promised to stay, but I can't leave you here to die! You have to promise me, do you hear me? You have to promise me that you will hold on until my return. Alright?"

In response, he sighed heavily and loudly.

"Perfect!" Christine smiled. "I love you! I will be back, I promise!" she said hardly believing her own words, then she kissed him again and got up to her feet.

"Good luck!" said Robin, and stretched out his hand in farewell. "I promise, we will do our best."

"Thank you," said Christine, and hugged him tight and rushed through the forest, praying that the magic light was still there.

Her prayers were answered. The sphere of light was still there, shining at the far end of the cave, but the light had dimmed noticeably. The passage began to close. There was not a moment to lose.

*****

She ran through the forest.

It seemed she had never run so fast in her life. At first, Christine wasn't sure if the crossing was a success. For some time, she stood in the clearing, anxiously looking around, looking for something, anything; a little sign that would prove her right.

A smile lit up her face when over her head, she heard the cracking sound of helicopter blades. There was no doubt – she had made it back! Christine lifted her eyes to thank the heavens and ran.

It wasn't difficult to get out of the forest and soon she found the path leading to the central part of the park. From there it was close to the exit. It had been over a month since she was here but she remembered the way as if she was here just yesterday.

To her great surprise, the car was still in the parking bay in front of the school office. She ran to the school and got her bag and car keys from the locker where she had left them a month ago and rushed back to the car. On the windshield of her Mini, she found a note. The wind and rain had battered the piece of paper quite badly but she could still make out three phrases that were written on it.

"Really?!

"We are not a national carpark! Next time I will charge you by the hour!"

"If you don't collect your scrap, I'm selling it at the auction!"

All three phrases were written in the same handwriting but at different times, the irritation and bewilderment obvious in the slant of the writing. Christine just smiled and tore the note off the windscreen.

"Christine? Thank God! Where have you been?! Everyone is looking for you!" the worried voice of the school's mistress spoke behind her. "Are you all right?" the voice called again when Christine did not respond.

"I'm fine," she said a little absently. "I was... no matter where I was... I'll explain later, I need to get home as soon as possible," said Christine, getting into the car and starting the engine.

"You are welcome!" shouted Monica, alluding to the never voiced gratitude for the safety of Christine's car.

Pushing the gas pedal hard to the floor, Christine only raised her hand and sped away.

*****

In her house, everything had remained the same – exactly as on that fateful day of June the twentieth, when she had left it. A small suitcase stood by the entrance, her passport and a plane ticket still lay on the dresser by the mirror, and if it was not for the large heap of letters and brochures that had covered the floor by the door, no one would have guessed she had been absent for over a month.

As soon as she was in, she rushed upstairs. Her phone was where she had left it – on the nightstand. Not that it surprised her, the battery was dead. Cursing, she plugged the phone into the wall socket, then ran downstairs to the kitchen, and rummaged through a small cabinet with the medical supplies, unloading bandages, cotton wool, iodine, painkillers, and antiseptics. She left everything on the kitchen table and returned to the bedroom.

She sat on the bed, absently staring straight ahead. Thoughts swirled in her head, not giving her mind rest – the sense of reality slowly begun to sink in. The question "what to do next" was now pulsating in her temples.

She was home.

"Has all that horror really ended?"

She wanted so much to leave that cursed place and to return home, to her own time. She was home at last!

"What now?"

Everything that had happened to her in the last month seemed unreal – some strange endless nightmare, which she was finally able to wake from.

She was home, but what to do now, she did not know. Should she forget everything and return to her previous life? The blood pounded in her ears, sending painful impulses to her temples. Trying to release the pain, Christine tightly clasped her head in between her palms.

Succumbing to the voice of reason, she knew, there was no place for her in that time. Everything there was foreign to her. She must forget it all! Forget everything and return to her normal life as though none of this had happened. That seemed the easiest and the only right decision. Her mind insisted on that, but her heart uttered a violent protest. How could she forget all of that? Eight hundred years in the past, the man she loved, was slowly bleeding to death.

The phone on the bedside stand hummed softly, producing its first signs of life. Christine lifted her eyes to it – the screen showed a missed call.

"Only one?" surprised, she pressed the call-back button.

"Welcome to voicemail service," an electronic voice replied on the other side. *"You have one hundred and forty-two voice messages."*

She didn't have time to listen to all one hundred and forty messages, not that it was necessary. From the first ten, it was quite obvious who had left the other one hundred and thirty.

At first Mark's tone was hesitant, his voice quiet. He called again to beg for forgiveness, knowing it was unlikely she would speak with him unless he tried to sound as polite as possible. In subsequent messages, his voice was more concerned – for some days now she had not got in touch. He asked her to, at least, get in contact with Philip. In the last message that she listened to before disconnecting the voicemail, he sounded frightened, agitated and anxious. One call or message from her would've been sufficient to tell them she was ok, but she would not answer to his pleas.

Christine closed her eyes and took a deep breath. Guy's pale face surfaced in her mind. She exhaled slowly and dialled Mark.

"Christine? Is that you?! Where are you? Why..." instead of a greeting, Mark bombarded her with questions.

"Hello, Mark," she said quietly.

"Christine, where are you?"

"I need your help," she said, ignoring his questions. "There has been an accident..."

"What? What happened? Are you all right? Are you hurt!?" he asked anxiously.

"I'm fine, but someone else is badly injured," she said trying to remain calm. "He's hurt, his liver might have been damaged, and he has lost a lot of blood... I need your help."

"From what you describe, this person might need a morgue, not a doctor," he said with a quiet snigger. "Where are you? Have you thought of calling an ambulance?"

"I thought you were a doctor!" she retorted but stopped. "I'm sorry, I just... I can't call the ambulance! There's no time to argue, I need your help! Come to my place as soon as you can, get your bag and equipment, everything that you need to close and stitch up the wound. He needs blood as well and, probably, an IV."

"I guess it is useless to ask what's his blood type?" asked Mark.

"Yes, it is," said Christine calmly. "How fast can you get to me?"

"Well, lucky you, I'm in Parkside hospital now. Be there within an hour."

"Thank you, Mark, please hurry," she said and dropped the call.

Now she only had to wait. She put the phone on the nightstand and looked up. Her eyes caught her own reflection in the mirror. She looked terrible! Her dishevelled hair was sticking out in different directions, her skin and clothes were stained with blood, her face was haggard and pale, dark circles under the eyes. She pulled off her dirty clothes, threw them into a corner by the door and went to the bathroom.

After a shower, she made herself a coffee. Only now, she realised how much she missed this life-giving, regenerating drink. The hot liquid slowly poured into her, preparing to distribute energy boosts to all parts of her body. Christine knew that it would take a good half an hour before she would feel its invigorating effect.

She poured herself another cup and drank it slowly, aimlessly drilling the landscape outside the window with her eyes. Now she could only wait and hope. Wait, for Mark to come; hope that he would come soon; hope that the passage would still be open; hope that Guy would still be alive.

Time moved slowly. It had been only fifteen minutes since her conversation with Mark, but it seemed like an eternity had passed since the moment she crossed back and got home. Now, sitting on the bed in her bedroom, she went through her memories of last month's events over and over again. Should she decide to tell this to anyone, she would be sent directly to a psychiatric hospital. Sherwood Forest, the Sheriff, Robin, Guy... her heart ached. For her, he was not just a memory.

She looked at her watch again. A half an hour passed since her conversation with Mark.

"Why is it taking so long?"
Fatigue began to take over. Christine rested her head on the pillow. A second later she was fast asleep.

*****

She ran through the dark corridors towards the light. She knew neither where she was nor to where she was running. The only thing she was sure of, someone was chasing after her.

On both sides of the hall, there were doors. In a vain attempt to escape from her pursuer, she pulled the handles, one after another. One of the doors opened.

Christine ran into an elegantly decorated hall, where people in old-fashioned clothes were drinking, dancing, and raising toasts. As she entered the room, the music died, and all the voices in the hall went silent. From the far end of the room, the Sheriff of Nottingham was looking at her, and, with his chin lifted high, Guy of Gisborne was standing by his side. An arrogant sneer decorated his face.

"Get her!" shouted the Sheriff and, with their weapons drawn, the   guards   moved   towards   her.

A moment later Christine was out of the room.

There were doors again and an endless darkness of corridors. Trying to find her way out, she ran forward, trying to break free. Behind another door, she saw herself. Exhausted, she was walking through the woods, someone invisible was watching her. A moment after, darkness began to thicken around her, getting ready to devour her. Christine screamed, she wanted to shout out, to warn herself about the approaching danger, but as hard as she tried, her scream was soundless. She closed her eyes in despair.

When she opened them again, the forest was gone, and she was back in the dark corridor. She saw light ahead and rushed towards it, but the darkness that surrounded her would not let her go, thickening around her. Behind another door, there was a room. She felt like she had seen these modest furnishings before – a bed, a wardrobe, a window overlooking the forest. Christine hurried back to the door and managed to lock it just a moment before it was shaken by the first terrible blow – that "someone" who pursued her was close behind.

Leaning her back against this saving barrier, she prayed to the heavens that this "someone" would not be able to break through. There was a blow, then a second and then the third blow threw her hard to the floor. She ran back and pushed against the door, realising that she would not be able to hold on for long. Her strength was leaving her.

She was tired and could no longer resist. She slowly stepped back and stood in the middle of the room, ready to accept her fate.

With one last mighty blow, the door shattered. The darkness poured inside the room consuming her...

Christine's eyes flew open and she stared at the ceiling of her bedroom. Breathing heavily, she sat up on the bed.

"It was all a dream! Could this all be just a dream?"

The last month spent in preparation for the hearing had worn her out – she was exhausted physically and mentally. No wonder she started to have nightmares. Returning from Mark's, she probably just fell asleep and slept through as the storm was thundering outside.

"Yes, of course. It is exactly what must have happened!" she reassured herself.

She rubbed her eyes and looked around. Everything in the room looked the same, everything but one – in a corner on the floor lay a pile of bloodstained clothes.

A loud knock on the door made her jump.

"Christine! Open up!" a familiar voice called from the street. "Christine!!!"

She went to the window. With his doctor's satchel over his shoulder and a large bag in his other hand, Mark Laferi stood outside, pounding heavily on her front door.

Everything froze inside her – it was not a dream...

*****

"You cannot park here!" protested Mark, when Christine drove off the road and parked her Mini by the small forest path.

She didn't say anything, but gave him a long look.

They took the bags out of the boot, and she walked Mark towards the clearing, trying hard not to pay attention to his disgruntled muttering behind her back. Before they came out onto the clearing, Christine stopped.

"I'm sorry Mark, I have to do this."

She took a scarf, covered his eyes, and tied it around his head.

"What are you doing?! Care to explain what's going on!" he was indignant, trying to remove the blindfold.

"Please, trust me," she said, keeping the scarf in place. "I don't have time to explain, we need to hurry."

She took one of the bags, and taking him by the hand, led him after her. Having made a few extra hundred steps around the perimeter of the clearing, she led him to the tree. The passage was still open, but the light that some time ago was still shining brightly, had now begun to fade.

*****

The bright light blinded her.

As they walked through the light, they felt the change in atmosphere, as if the heat mixed with the cold, as if the scorching hot sun was followed by the ice-cold northern wind that scalded them at the same time, as if thousands of small burning hot and icy needles were simultaneously piercing their bodies. When the light disappeared and darkness consumed them, Christine did not stop. She was moving forward, holding Mark's hand tight she led him behind her.

As they walked out of the cave, she took off his blindfold.

"Be careful on the hill, it is quite steep," she warned.

Mark stood still.

"Mark, please!" Christine pulled his hand.

"What does this all mean!? Christine, what's going on? Where are you taking me?" he sounded annoyed and angry, pulling his hand from hers. "I am not taking another step until you explain what's going on!"

"There is no time to explain," she pleaded. "There is a man waiting for us. He needs your help. He could die, while we argue here, please, Mark, trust me," she held out her hand.

"Ok," he said and followed her, hesitantly.

They began their descent down the slope. Confused, Mark was looking everywhere, trying to figure out where they were; he saw nothing besides the green trees, blue sky and the dense forest. The green that surrounded him now was no different from what he saw just moments before.

Once on the flat surface at the foot of the hill, Christine ran, dragging him along.

"Robin! Robin!" she called, wading through the leaves.

When a familiar voice replied to her, she knew they were close. Soon the flames of the fire became visible through the trees.

When they reached the clearing, Christine smiled softly at Robin and patted his shoulder. She put the bag by the fire and knelt down beside Gisborne.

"How is he?" she asked brushing the wet hair from his forehead. "Guy... Guy, can you hear me, dear..."

Slowly he opened his eyes.

"Christine..." he spoke, his lips barely moving. "You're back..." a light smile appeared on his pale face. "I did not think I would ever see you again."

"Shh, don't say that," she kissed his dry lips. "I promised that I would return... Everything will be fine! I brought the doctor, he will fix you, and you'll be as good as new, you'll see!" her eyes watered, tears rolled down her cheeks.

Christine looked at Mark, who, still lacking the comprehension of what was happening, stood by the fire, cautiously looking around.

"Mark..." she called and waved her head calling him closer.

"Christine, who are these people?" he whispered, dropping to his knees beside her. "Have they kidnapped you? What's going on here?"

"Mark, can you help him?" she asked, ignoring his question.

"Who is this guy? What's going on here? Where have you been all this time?" he asked again.

"There's no time for this now, Mark. I'll explain later. Please help him, he's gonna die!" she pleaded.

For all the time he had known her, Mark had never seen her like this. Not saying a word, he got up and walked to the fire. He dragged his bags closer to the wounded man and then quickly and methodically began to lay out his tools. He sterilised his hands, put on the gloves and untied the bandage.

"He's lucky to still be alive," he said dryly, examining the wound. "The wound is deep and serious, but not fatal. The liver is intact, but he is in traumatic shock and has lost a lot of blood."

Mark took off his gloves and pulled a small bottle and a pack of sterilised syringes with a needle out of the bag.

"What is it?" asked Christine.

"Morphine," said Mark filling up the syringe with a transparent liquid. He touched Guy's belly choosing the best place for injection.

"You cannot inject that!" terrified, Christine grabbed his arm. "He's lost too much blood. His heart will not cope."

"Christine!" snapped Mark. "I thought you called me because I can help. So...let me do my job!" he replied sternly but added, in a calmer tone, "Trust me, I know what I'm doing. If you want, you can sit here, but be quiet!"

Christine let go of his hand, allowing Mark to continue his work. She sat by and placed Guy's head on her lap.

Gisborne clenched his teeth and issued a muffled groan, as the needle pierced through his skin.

"There, there, buddy," Mark patted him on the shoulder, "you are as strong as an ox. As soon as the sedative starts working, we will patch you up, as requested by our fair lady."

He winked at the man lying in front of him and glanced at Christine, who, at this moment, could not appreciate his sense of humour.

"Hey, you two, don't just stand there idly, come over here!" Mark shouted, addressing the men that stood by the fire.

Little John and the Friar were taken aback by such a commanding tone. Here, in the depths of Sherwood Forest, Mark was calling orders like he did in his own operating theatre. Pulling packs with blood and the IV out of the bag, he began preparations. The bag with the IV was connected to a plastic tube and fixed to the back of Guy's hand, then given to Little John, who was placed to stand by Gisborne with his hands lifted up high.

With a sharp scalpel, Mark cut through the sleeve of Guy's jacket and prepared him for the transfusion. Placing Friar Tuck next to Gisborne, opposite Little John, he handed him a bag of blood and connected a small plastic tube to Guy's vein. He noted the time. Opening and closing the valve of the drip, he started to infuse new blood in small portions, constantly watching Guy's breathing and pulse.

All seemed to be going well. The morphine had worked and Guy began to drift off. The blood and IV fluid slowly went down the plastic tubes. Everything went quiet – only the crackling of the wood fire was occasionally breaking the silence of the forest.

Mark put on the gloves. He treated the wound with antiseptic, then armed himself with a surgical needle and a thread, and began to sew up the cut. He was attentive and focused, carefully doing each stitch he slowly worked his way through the deep wound. While he was working, the first bag of blood ran out and Mark connected the second. All the while Christine sat silently, holding Guy close to her.

Soon everything was done – the wound was sewn up and Mark had treated the stitches with antiseptic and applied a pressure bandage. The whole time Mark was working over Gisborne, no one uttered a single word. As if spellbound Robin, Friar Tuck and Little John watched him work. For an hour after he finished, he did not leave his patient's side, carefully watching his pulse and checking the flow of blood and the IV. The sedative was doing its job; Gisborne was fast asleep. His chest rose high and fell with each deep breath. His breathing was calm and steady.

Once both containers were empty, Mark removed them and put them into his bag. He took out three packages with IV and handed them to the Friar, explaining how to connect the tubes, how to set the drip, how to treat the wound and stitches and, when and why to give a painkiller.

Having once again examined the dressing, Mark packed his tools and turned to Christine.

"I did everything you asked; now we have to go," he said, holding out his hand to her.

"I'm not going anywhere!" protested Christine. "I'm not going anywhere until he gets better!" she repeated, making no attempt to get up from her place.

"He will be fine," replied Mark calmly. "Trust me on that but we have to go home."

"I'm not going anywhere! I can't leave him!" she shook her head.

The idea that she would have to leave him again seemed unbearable.

"Christine! He will be fine, I promise!" Mark knelt next to her. "I didn't ask you any questions, you asked for my help and I helped... But whatever is happening here, we have to go home. My father needs me... and you too," he paused.

"What do you mean?" Christine looked at him.

"Philip is ill," Mark replied shortly.

"Ill? What do you mean ill? How... What happened? I don't understand..."

"While you've been gone, we didn't know what to think," he gently took her hand into his. "We were... I was... looking for you, but you were nowhere to be found. We thought you were upset and just needed some time off, but as the time passed, there was no news from you," he lowered his eyes and fell silent for a moment but then continued. "Father said it was all my fault... we argued... his heart..."

"What happened with your father?" asked Christine, unable to believe her ears.

"He had a fall," Mark said.

"Oh no, Philip!" whispered Christine.

"He's in a coma," said Mark. At his words, Christine gasped. "He is very weak; we are keeping him on life support."

"It's impossible! He was alright..." her hand flew to her mouth.

"I've done two operations already. Tomorrow I must operate again. If this attempt is not successful, we will have turn off his life support," sadness shadowed his face. "If it comes to that, I'm sure he'd want you to be there."

Christine carefully rested Guy's head on a small bag, got to her feet and walked away. Mark wanted to go after her but she stopped him. She needed some time alone.

She buried her face in her hands and sobbed quietly, swallowing her tears. Why was fate so cruel to her? Only a few hours ago the man she loved more than anything in this world, was bleeding to death in her arms. And now, when he was on the mend, a new blow – the man who became her mentor, who helped her and supported her through the most difficult time in her life, lay dying.

She didn't know what to do. Her heart and soul were crushed into tiny pieces. Her choice lay between the devil and the deep blue sea – to leave the man she loved or the person who had replaced her father. Either way, she couldn't win.

She felt a gentle hand on her shoulder.

"It's time..." said Mark.

In response, she just shook her head. She took a few deep breaths, trying to calm her racing heart, walked back to Guy and knelt down beside him.

"Guy, I know you can hear me," she said softly, swallowing her tears. "I kept my promise... I leave knowing that you will be all right. But before I go, there is one thing I want you to know," she smiled. Her fingers traced his face. "No matter what happens, no matter how life works out for you, I want you to know that you are a man who was truly loved," she whispered and kissed him gently. "You deserve all the love and happiness in the world, and I'm sure one day you'll find them," she pressed her lips against his. "I love you and will love you until the end of my days."

Christine took off her bracelet and placed the silver snakes on Guy's wrist. She knew it was time for her to go, but she couldn't leave him yet, she could not force herself to make this final step. She looked at him again, trying to save his image to her memory.

"Goodbye my love. I will never forget you," she whispered swallowing the lump of tears, "I will love you forever."

She kissed him one last time, rose to her feet and walked over to the men who were silently standing by the fire.

"Will you tell him? Promise that you will tell him, okay?" she asked Robin.

"I promise!" he said.

"Thank you, Robin, thank you for everything!" she hugged him. "John, Friar, thank you. Look after him for me, please?"

"Christine, it's time," Mark said, holding out a hand to her.

One last time she looked at Gisborne. Brushing the tears away, she took Mark's hand, and together they walked towards the cave.

*****

"Who were those people?" asked Mark, as he helped Christine into the passenger seat of her car. "Have you been with them all this time?"

"It doesn't matter," she replied indifferently. "I'm here now."

"That wounded man, did something happen between you two?"

"It doesn't matter," she repeated, her fingers traced over the ring given to her by Gisborne. "I'll never see him again."

She swallowed hard and closed her eyes, the tears rolled down her cheeks. As soon as they crossed back into their time, the glowing orb flared and disappeared, vanishing into the unknown. The passage had closed. For her, there was no turning back. Her body was driving in the passenger seat of the car; her heart and soul remained forever in Sherwood Forest with the man she loved, with her black knight.

Chapter 22:
The New Life

All the way to the hospital, Christine was quiet. So much had fallen on her shoulders within the past twenty-four hours; there was no strength left in her. She was exhausted physically but more so emotionally, and too tired to talk. All of Mark's attempts to get her talking had been in vain, he hadn't been able to extract a single word from her.

She sat in silence, aimlessly staring ahead, preparing herself for what she was about to see in the hospital, but as hard as she tried, what actually appeared before her eyes, shook her to the core.

Like a stuffed puppet, Philip was lying in a large bright room. Endless wires, tubes, and cables were connected to various parts of his body. Aside from the monotonous beeps and sounds of the medical equipment, the room was quiet. The bellows inside the huge ventilating machine was rising and falling noisily, delivering oxygen to his depleted body.

Seeing him like this, Christine sighed loudly and sank into a chair beside his bed. His bulky body had shrunk and seemed to have lost a third of its size. The skin on his hands and face had dried up and looked like ancient papyrus, his cheeks were sunken, his grey hair that once had a beautiful silver shine had turned yellow, and now was the colour of fallen autumn leaves.

"Oh, Philip!" Christine said, taking his wrinkled hand in hers. "Please, forgive me..."

These were the only words she could say before, once again, tears began to flow from her eyes. Seeing him like this brought back memories of her mother's last days. Having rested her forehead against his hand, she cried, quietly swallowing her tears.

A hand gently fell on her shoulder.

"Is he going to be alright?" asked Christine. "Please promise me, that he will be alright," she turned to the man standing behind her.

"I can't," he said quietly. "I cannot promise that."

Christine looked at him. He held a hand out to her and helped her up. Seeing her tear-stained eyes, Mark pulled her closer and wrapped his arm around her.

"I can't promise that," he spoke stroking her hair, as she quietly sobbed into his shoulder. "But you know, I will do everything within my power," he added, raising her face to his. "I promise!"

He pulled her closer and kissed her cheek. His lips moved and brushed against hers, his arm wrapped tighter around her waist.

"What the hell do you think you're doing!?" Christine broke from his embrace and pushed him away.

"I just... I thought..." mumbled Mark.

"You thought that because your father is in this condition, I am just gonna jump back into your bed?" her tears dried up instantly.

She stepped aside.

"I've missed you," he said calmly. "I was worried that something might have happened to you," he came closer and tried to touch her face. "Christine..."

"You were worried! I seriously doubt that!" she smiled, avoiding his touch. "Mark, we have known each other for many years! The only person you were worried about is yourself; or rather the fact that you were caught at the crime scene, so to speak, and you weren't able to talk yourself out of trouble."

"Christine, please don't say that," he sounded genuinely hurt, "you know I love you!"

"I can't believe we are having this conversation when your father is dying!" she snapped.

"Of course, I love you," Mark did not give up. "But in my own way," he smiled.

"That, I can believe," she softened her tone. "By the way, how is your new girlfriend?"

"Ugh, it's all over. Finito! She dumped me, when she realised that I love you."

Christine smiled and shook her head in response.

"You don't love me, Mark and never have. You loved the idea of me in your life. I was one of the trophies that you wanted to win to fluff your own ego."

She, once again, glanced at Philip and turned to leave.

"Where are you going?" Mark asked.

"I want to go home. I am very tired," Christine said.

"I'll take you," said Mark. "Give me five minutes, wait for me in the hall."

As Christine turned, she saw a young girl who, all this time, had been standing in the doorway. Her lustful, horny look said it all. Mark opened the door to one of the rooms and let the girl in first. Christine rolled her eyes.

"Five minutes? You are losing your touch," Christine smiled. "Do not worry, I'll get home," she added, walking away from him.

"Christine! It is not what you think," he caught up with her as she was about to enter the lift.

"I don't think anything, Mark. Your personal life is no longer my concern," she smiled tiredly and patted him on the shoulder. "What time is the operation tomorrow?" she asked, changing the subject.

"We start at eight-thirty," Mark said a little scattered.

"I'll be here at eight. See you tomorrow," Christine smiled indifferently. "And try to get a good rest. He needs you," she added, as the elevator doors closed.

*****

The next morning at eight o'clock, Christine was in the hospital. By the time she arrived, Mark was already there, waiting for her in his office, looking fresh and trying to be cheerful. Having clarified the few final details and provided last minute instructions to his assistants, he went to prepare for the surgery. He was serious and focused. His father's life, in the literal sense of the words, was in his hands.

The whole time Mark operated, Christine spent in a waiting room. Unable to stay in one place, she paced the perimeter of the room and consumed one cup of coffee after another. Her heart, which had already been beating at a furious pace, accelerated its rhythm with each new dose of caffeine.

Mark kept his word – as promised, he did everything he could and some six hours later, tired but satisfied, he came out of the operating theatre to notify Christine of a positive outcome. However, it was still too early to celebrate. The next few days, and then weeks, would be vital.

*****

As time passed, Philip got better and better. After the surgery, the doctors decided to keep him in the induced coma to give his body a chance to recover and regain some strength.

At first, time dragged slowly – minutes, hours, days, but even when the days began to silently fly by, one after another, Christine could not stop thinking about what had happened to her; over and over again in her memory returning to Sherwood Forest, to Nottingham, to Locksley village.

Hard as she tried, she couldn't get it out of her head. Wherever she went, she saw him. She saw him in a café, in a shop and in the hospital parking. Every time she saw a tall, dark-haired man with a striking profile, or a man distantly resembling him, she was startled; her heart stopped and then began to pound in her chest as she gasped for air.

Mark was worried about her, but Christine refused to accept any help from him. She laughed in his face when seeing her condition, he offered to prescribe her antidepressants.

He didn't give up on the thought of winning her forgiveness, but Christine did not respond to his attempts to make amends, and declined all of his invitations. From time to time, they met in the hospital, and discussed the state of Mark's father but that was the extent of their communication.

Gradually things began to get back on track. Her life returned to its measured rut – home, work, meeting with clients and lawyers, lunches with colleagues, hearings, arguments in the court, documents, letters, and meetings again... like one long, endless day; her evenings were spent in the hospital sitting by Phillip's bed. Although he was still in the induced coma, Christine spoke to him every day. She told him of the latest news, of the work in the company, of what was happening in the world.

She overloaded herself with work. She did not do this for pleasure or in pursuit of financial gain, but for the sake of distracting herself from her thoughts about Guy of Gisborne. While her mind was busy, her heart still ached. With time, Christine simply got used to that dull, moaning pain in her chest and learned to ignore it, yet, while within the passing daylight she managed relatively well, the nights were torturous. She often woke up in the middle of the night with tears in her eyes and his name on her lips, and fell back to sleep tightly clutching a pillow, not knowing whether she would ever be able to leave it all behind and continue with life as if nothing had happened.

Minutes turned into hours, hours turned into days, the days became weeks and weeks became months. Unable to cope with the oppressive feelings, Christine wore herself out. The sleepless nights and excessive workload affected her health. On the morning of the twenty-fifth of December she awoke in Kingston Hospital.

Leaving early from a Christmas party hosted by Mark the night before, she had lost control of her car. Her Mini flew off the road and crashed into a tree. After twelve hours in an unconscious state, she woke up in a hospital bed, in an intensive care unit.

While she was unconscious, she had returned to him. Christine saw him again but this dream seemed more vivid, more real than any she had seen before – it felt as if this time she really was back in Nottingham.

She could clearly hear loud music and the voices of people dancing around her. She could smell the food and sour wine, the very same that the Sheriff offered to his guests on his birthday. And then she saw him. In the distance, across the room, he was sitting at the table and did not seem to notice her at first, but then their eyes met. Spellbound, he rose from his seat and walked through the crowd towards her. Moving to the beat of the music, Christine danced away, beckoning him to follow her.

Guy caught up with her in the hall and seized her, taking her into his arms, crushing her in a tight embrace. He called her name and ran his hand through her soft hair, as if nothing had happened, as if they had never parted. She had smiled softly at him, and touched his bristly cheek. He was there, in front of her, flesh and blood, but there was something strange about him. The gaze of his blue eyes was clouded and empty. His face looked tired and his body felt exhausted.

He called her name again. His deep soft voice resonated in her heart. He moved his face closer to her. His lips were very close. Melting in his arms, Christine closed her eyes in anticipation. How long had she waited for this moment – to be back with him, to be back in his arms.

When she opened her eyes again, she was blinded by the bright light of the hospital ward. Mark sat on a chair next to her, her hand was tightly clasped between his palms.

"Welcome back," he smiled softly. "For a moment there I thought we'd lost you."

*****

After the New Year, Philip's condition significantly improved. He was taken out of the induced coma and was soon able to live and breathe on his own. Eventually, his room was rid of all the machines and devices that for the past six months had supported his life. Christine was glad to see him, once again, cheerful and confidently getting better day-by-day.

After the winter came spring and with the spring, came Easter. Later in April, in Philip's room, in his and Mark's company, Christine celebrated her thirtieth birthday.

*****

Two years after Christine's return from her trip to medieval England her life had resumed its same measured rhythm and routine.

Her heart was not healed and had not stopped hurting. However, with time, she learned to live with the constant, aching pain. Yet the dream that she had seen at Christmas, after her accident, still haunted her.

Philip had fully recovered and, with each passing day, he got stronger and stronger. For the past few months, he had been visiting the office, trying to get accustomed to the current affairs of the firm.

It was a Saturday, an August evening, no different from any other. Finished with filing and archiving the documents for the trials completed in the last month, Christine was getting ready to leave the office, when on the way out she collided with Philip and Mark, who as she walked by, came out of the meeting room. Dressed very smartly and too business-like for a Saturday evening, Philip was wearing a suit and tie. In his hands, he held a leather folder for papers.

"Philip! What are you doing here?" she could not help but wonder. "I didn't expect to see you here today, especially at this late hour!"

"We had a board meeting," he rolled his eyes and waved his head in the direction of the door. "It seems, while I was sick, they have forgotten how to run a business!"

"I am sure that you'll be able to sort it out," she answered with a soft smile. "You always knew how to keep the firm in proper order."

"I wish I had your confidence!" he said, frowning. "They think I'm too old and cannot manage the affairs!"

"They want to close the firm?" Christine's eyes widened. "But they can't!"

"They are, you see, saying this firm needs someone young, fresh blood!" he said. "But let's not talk about that, my dear. Good that I have met you here, I think with all this work and my illness, we have forgotten about our little tradition of Sunday lunches," he smiled changing the subject. "How about we meet tomorrow?"

"Yes, of course!" Christine replied happily, realising how much she really missed his company.

"Perfect!" he answered with a soft smile in his eyes. "Mark will drive me to your place tomorrow then, about lunch time."

In a warm fatherly gesture, Philip wrapped his big arm around her shoulder, and together with his son, they headed towards the exit.

*****

The next day at about twelve, Mark brought his father to Christine's, and having promised to pick him up around six, retired, leaving her and Philip to fully enjoy each other's company.

"It's only now I've realised just how much I missed our Sunday meetings and conversations, my dear," said Philip after lunch, lounging in a large deck chair in her back garden.

Christine poured herself a glass of wine, took a glass of fresh lemonade for Philip, and sank into a chair beside him.

"Yes, you are right," she said in a low voice, "with all this running around and chasing God knows what, we forget the simple pleasures and values of life."

For a while, they sat in silence, watching as the wind chased grey rainy clouds through the sky and ruffled the greens of the trees. They listened as little birds chirping happily flitted from one branch to another.

They didn't have much time to enjoy the warmth of the Sunday afternoon. Soon the blue sky above their heads was covered by dark clouds, the wind rose, and the first droplets of rain began to fall from the sky.

While Christine was stowing away the chairs, Philip walked into the hall and came back with the same black leather folder he had been carrying yesterday.

"So, this is not a courtesy or a social visit, after all," she said with a cunning smile.

"Nothing escapes you, my girl," he smiled back.

He took her hand in his and patted the back of her palm, then guided her to the couch and sat her next to him.

"What is it?" Christine asked, looking at the folder. "Their proposal? Want to discuss it?"

"No, not really," he said, handing the folder to her. "I was planning to give it to you as a gift for your engagement. But since the wedding is out of the picture, I think there is no better time."

"Philip, I'm intrigued! What is it?" she asked, genuinely curious.

"Open it," he smiled briefly in return.

She hastily undid the metal clasps on the folder, opened it and ran her eyes over a piece of paper that was lying on the top and then lifted her bewildered eyes back to Philip.

"Philip, what is this?"

"Read it aloud, if you please," he smiled.

"Minutes of the Extraordinary meeting of the Board of Partners of "Laferi and Partners"..." she began.

Having listed the names of those present at the meeting, she moved to the agenda.

"... The purpose of this meeting is to approve the change of name of the partnership and redistribution of interests..." she looked up at him again. "Philip, do you mean to leave the firm?!"

"Keep reading, please," he said, all too briefly.

"By a unanimous decision of the board of partners, it has been decided..." she continued, turning to the next page and then suddenly stopped.

"It has been decided..." Philip echoed after her.

"To rename the Partnership to "Hawk, Laferi and Partners" and to add a new member – Christine Hawk... approved that Philip Laferi is transferring his controlling share, and the new partner is entering the partnership with a controlling interest of fifty percent..." she looked at him blankly. "Philip, I don't understand..."

"You have worked so hard for this firm for so many years and have done so much. This is my way of saying thank you," he said.

"Thank you? Oh my, this is a very nice "thank you" gesture, indeed, and I appreciate the notion, of course," she was taken aback, "but you want to give me half of the company. The firm is your baby!"

"I'm old, Christine, and I can't work like before. The firm needs new blood! And then, I will in any case still have my twenty-five percent," he winked at her cheerfully.

"I don't know what to say, Philip," she said, still a little baffled.

"Don't answer anything now. Think about it. I have already made my decision. All the signatures are there. Now, it is up to you."

Christine got up from the sofa and put the folder on the table. She walked to the window and stood there for a while, watching as the raindrops quickly ran down the glass, creating random patterns on its surface. Philip's offer was too good to refuse, but at the same time, she couldn't take away half of the company that he had built over the last thirty years.

"By the way, you never told me what happened to you during that time," suddenly changing the subject, he spoke again after a brief pause.

"Mmm," she tried to pretend that she didn't understand what he was referring to. Philip arched a brow. "It doesn't matter," she smiled. "In any case, you would never believe me. I myself, sometimes begin to think about it as if it was some sort of a strange dream."

"Sounds fascinating!" Philip smiled. "You know, I'm always in for a good story."

He patted the sofa cushion, inviting her to sit next to him.

Not saying another word, Christine obeyed. She sat next to him and, after taking a deep breath, began her story. As soon as she started talking, she realised how important and necessary it was for her to get it off her chest; how much she needed to release the feelings that for the past two years had been suppressed inside her. She told him everything, withholding no details.

Philip listened attentively, closely following the thread of her story. Several times a light smile appeared on his face.

"You probably think that I've gone completely mad," Christine smiled, finishing her story. "Or that, I got so upset that I ate some magic mushrooms, and spent all that time hallucinating," she laughed but, although she tried to speak lightly, there was sadness in her voice. "But I still, down to the smallest detail, remember everything that happened."

She got up and walked into the kitchen. She put the kettle on the stove and waited, silently listening as the water began to boil. For some time, Philip was silent too. Christine brewed some fresh tea and went back into the room.

"Although, to tell you the truth, I myself began to doubt if it actually happened to me or if I just made it all up," she handed him a cup of tea. Philip caught her eye.

"Did you love him?" he asked bluntly.

"I still do," she said softly, her voice shaking. She sat down on the sofa next to him and then, suddenly, her face became very sad. "Philip, I think I'm going mad... I see him everywhere, I hear his voice."

"Oh, my dear," he hugged her tight.

"Why does it hurt so much? I thought that it would get better with time, but I can't stop thinking about him," her eyes glistened with looming tears. "I cannot do it anymore, I can't. Philip, I do not want to be strong. I am so tired... If you only knew... Every night I see him in my dreams and every night my heart is torn apart."

"There, there, my dear."

He tried to reassure her, but now in his arms, she was no longer the same Christine that he was accustomed to seeing over the past ten years. Right now beside him, on the couch, sat the girl, who, at the age of eighteen, had lost the only dear person to her and could not cope with her loss.

"It will get better, you'll see," he said, lifting her face to his.

"How?! I know I will never see him again," she took a deep breath and exhaled slowly. "I need to calm down," she said, to herself.

She left Philip alone in the room, and went back to the kitchen to make coffee.

Philip walked to the window. He was quiet. While they had been speaking, the rain had stopped banging over the roof and windows. The sky began to clear; the sun was coming out again. He looked at the summer sky and his face broke into a wide smile.

"Christine! Come here, quick!" he called loudly.

"Coming..." a voice came from the kitchen.

He didn't want to wait until she came out and he hurried to fetch her.

"Come, you have to see this!" he grabbed her arm and pulled her after him. A wide grin decorated his face.

"Where are you taking me?" Christine laughed, barely having time to pick up the cup of coffee from the table.

"Look!" he said, guiding her to the window.

Christine gasped loudly, her fingers opened. The silence that reigned in the room was broken by the sound of shattering ceramic

– the cup of coffee she was holding fell from her hand and with a loud clatter smashed into small pieces. In the blue skies stood the bright arc of a rainbow, and underneath it, in a mirror reflection, slowly began to appear its sister. At first, it was very dim, barely noticeable, but with each passing moment, it was getting brighter and brighter, pulsing, coming to life.

Not daring to move, she was still standing at the window, unable to tear her eyes away from the bright light that divided the sky.

"Christine," Philip said quietly, "I think it's time for you to go."

As if waking from a dream, Christine turned to Philip. She smiled, hope shining in her eyes.

"I'm sure he's waiting for you on the other side," said Philip. He hugged her and kissed her goodbye. "Go. Go!" he whispered.

A lone tear slid down his wrinkled cheek, when behind the closed door, he heard the roar of the engine and the squealing of tires. Christine was driving away from him forever.

"Be happy, my girl, God bless," he whispered softly as he was left to stand alone in the middle of her living room.

*****

Pushing the gas pedal hard into the floor, she drove her Mini into Richmond Park.

Christine knew the route by heart. Within the two years that had passed since her return, she had often visited the meadow.

At first, while Philip was sick, she was spending most of her free time in the hospital. But since that fateful accident on Christmas Eve, something had changed, and again and again, she was drawn to this place. She came here several times and wandered around. Her heart ached, tormented by a passionate desire to see him again. When it became warmer and when the weather allowed, she spent every free weekend here, but the passage never opened. There were rains and thunderstorms, there were rainbows, but since that ill-fated day when the Sheriff returned to Nottingham, she had not seen the double rainbow again. Today everything had changed!

Having driven off the road and left the car among the bushes, she ran into the clearing. The bright light shone and flowed, filling the whole space around. Her feelings overwhelmed her. Uncontrolled by her, her eyes became wet with the build-up of tears.

Through the tall grass, she ran to the tree. Christine walked around it from the other side and stopped. She stood on the threshold of the shining space. Doubt began to creep into her soul. The desire to see her love again was replaced by fear. Much could have happened in these two years.

"What if," ruthlessly hammered in her head. *"What if he has forgotten me or worse, did not survive."*

In a wild rhythm, her heart thumped in her chest. Christine lifted her eyes up to the light. It shone, its radiance was brighter than she had ever seen before. The bright golden light was still pouring out of the huge trunk, enveloping it, beckoning her in. She looked at the light. Its soft, swirling motion had a soothing and somewhat hypnotic effect, driving away anxiety, inspiring hope, as if it asked her to cast aside all the doubts and fears, trust it and to succumb to its power.

Christine cast a quick glance back, silently saying goodbye to her old life. She didn't know what awaited her ahead and what destiny had in store for her, but she knew it was all for the best. A broad smile adorned her face.

She took a deep breath and stepped into the light.

*** END OF BOOK ONE ***